This is

chick-Lit

F
THIS

$14.95

DATE

This is Chick-Lit

Edited by
Lauren Baratz-Logsted

BENBELLA

BENBELLA BOOKS, INC.
Dallas, Texas

"Two Literary Chicks" copyright © 2005 by Jennifer Coburn
"The Infidelity Diet" copyright © 2005 by Harley Jane Kozak
"Confessions of a Three-Eyed Freak" copyright © 2005 by Ariella Papa
"The Commitment Phobe" copyright © 2005 by Cara Lockwood
"Mama Knows Best" copyright © 2005 by Kayla Perrin
"Nice Jewish Boy" copyright © 2005 by Karen Siplin
"Dead Men Don't Eat Quiche" copyright © 2005 by Deanna Carlyle
"Shell Game" copyright © 2005 by Lauren Baratz-Logsted
"Café con Leche Crush" copyright © 2005 by Heather Swain
"The Database" copyright © 2005 by Caren Lissner
"Dead Friends and Other Dating Dilemmas" copyright © 2005 by Julie Kenner
"Trash Talk" copyright © 2005 by Karin Gillespie
"Meeting Cute" copyright © 2005 by Andrea Schicke Hirsch
"Every Girl's Dream" copyright © 2005 by Gena Showalter
"Secret Agent Chick" copyright © 2005 by Raelynn Hillhouse
"How to Be a Millionaire" copyright © 2005 by Stephanie Lehmann
"Takeoffs and Landings" copyright © 2005 by Johanna Edwards
"The Ring" copyright © 2005 by Rachel Pine
Additional materials copyright © 2005 by Lauren Baratz-Logsted

BenBella Books, Inc.
6440 N. Central Expressway, Suite 617
Dallas, TX 75206
www.benbellabooks.com
Send feedback to feedback@benbellabooks.com

Printed in the United States of America
10 9 8 7 6 5 4 3 2 1

Library of Congress Cataloging-in-Publication Data

This is Chick-lit / edited by Lauren Baratz-Logsted.
    p. cm.
    A collection of 18 stories, mostly American authors.
    ISBN 1-933771-01-1
    1. Short stories, American. 2. Chick lit. I. Baratz-Logsted, Lauren.

    PS648.C415T47 2006
    813'.0108—dc22

                                                                  2006012227

Proofreading by Stacia Seaman and Yara Abuata
Cover design by Laura Watkins
Cover Illustration by Allison Bard
Text design and composition by John Reinhardt Book Design
Printed by Victor Graphics, Inc.

Distributed by Independent Publishers Group
To order call (800) 888-4741 • www.ipgbook.com

For media inquiries and special sales contact Yara Abuata at yara@benbellabooks.com

For my brother, Seth Baratz, who is obviously not a chick but who has been very supportive of my career

~With Love

Contents

Introduction

I read for many reasons, but the primary reason is to be entertained. Chick-lit is entertainment. A wide range of stories designed to draw readers—particularly women—in and, for just a little while, transport them to a new world with new friends, new relationships and new struggles to overcome. Although often with a modern twist, chick-lit represents classic stories and classic entertainment, which is why chick-lit (albeit without the label recently bestowed by marketing types) has been around for centuries.

This collection was born out of anger.

Back in April 2005, an item appeared on Publishers Lunch, the online newsletter read widely in the publishing industry, announcing a forthcoming collection of stories titled *This Is Not Chick Lit*, bearing the subtitle "Original Stories by America's Best Women Writers."

Not surprisingly, I, and many others of my ilk—i.e., writers of chick-lit—were upset.

I've been in the book business for nearly a quarter of a century, having started out as an independent bookseller in 1983 and working variously as a *Publishers Weekly* reviewer, a freelance editor, a sort-of librarian and now a novelist. In all that time, I cannot remember a single instance of a genre being as widely reviled, while at the same time being as wildly popular, as chick-lit. Doris Lessing, Beryl Bainbridge, the late Susan Sontag—all have come out at one point or another against what they perceive as the derisory and somehow inferior genre.

Of course, Lits facing off against Chicks is nothing new. Indeed, the first instance I can find of ostensible Lit bashing ostensible Chick is from Charlotte Brontë, writing to George Henry Lewes on January 12, 1848, on the topic of Miss Jane Austen:

> Why do you like Miss Austen so very much? I am puzzled on that point. What induced you to say that you would rather have written *Pride and Prejudice* or *Tom Jones*, than any of the *Waverley* novels?
>
> I had not seen *Pride and Prejudice* till I had read that sentence of yours, and then I got the book. And what did I find? An accurate daguerrotyped portrait of a commonplace face; a carefully fenced, highly cultivated garden, with neat borders and delicate flowers; but no glance of a bright vivid physiognomy, no open country, no fresh air, no blue hill, no bonny beck. I should hardly like to live with her ladies and gentlemen, in their elegant but confined houses. These observations will probably irritate you. But I shall run the risk.
>
> Now I can understand admiration of George Sand...she has a grasp of mind which, if I cannot fully comprehend, I can very deeply respect: she is sagacious and profound; Miss Austen is only shrewd and observant.

One can almost picture the creator of Rochester and her very own Jane gnashing her teeth, muttering all the while, "What do they all see in her? Why, there aren't even any *moors* in her books!"

It is, as of this writing, 157 years since Ms. Brontë sent her letter, and it would appear that not much has changed.

2

For a long time, I was in denial about being an author of chick-lit. When I first sold my debut novel, *The Thin Pink Line*, a satire about a fake pregnancy, to Red Dress Ink back in 2002, I didn't even know—silly girl!—that Red Dress Ink was *the* chick-lit publisher. All I knew was that at long last I'd sold one of my books. And I was happy. But as time went on, I found myself confined to the Pink Ghetto, the chick-lit label that had attached itself to my work like a designer-label barnacle, and it began to rankle. Who wants to be pigeonholed?

And then came the announcement of *This Is Not Chick Lit*. Who ever heard of such a thing in publishing, a book defining itself by what it was not? What next: *These Are Not Mysteries*? *This Is Not Science Fiction*? *This Is Not a Literary Coming-of-Age Story*?

In the midst of my anger, I tore off a guest essay for Ron Hogan's very democratic Web site, www.beatrice.com, by the end of which I'd thrown down the gauntlet. I dreamed, I wrote, "of putting together a response collection...."

On June 4, at 9:30 A.M., I met with Glenn Yeffeth, publisher of BenBella Books, at Book Expo America in New York. I'd previously worked with Glenn, providing an essay for a collection of fiction and nonfiction on Jane Austen's *Pride and Prejudice*, but we'd never met face-to-face before. I told him about my dream and Glenn, no fan of any form of literary snobbery, was very keen on it. He agreed that if I could assemble a group of seventeen authors willing to contribute, in addition to myself, we were good to go.

As we spoke, I realized something: even though the project had sprung from something negative and been forged in anger, I didn't want our collection to be negative, or angry, at all. On the contrary, I wanted the collection to be a positive thing, an affirmative statement of what chick-lit *is*.

Finding seventeen other writers who were willing to contribute was not difficult. There were many I knew that I wanted to include right away and, once word of the project leaked out, I began hearing from authors I'd never had any contact with before, all asking if they could somehow be a part of it.

Once I had my seventeen authors in place, again wanting to be positive, I set them a particular task: since one of the criticisms leveled at chick-lit, by people who have obviously either read none of the books or only sampled a few, is that it's all Manolos and Cosmos, cookie-cutter books about women juggling relationships and careers in the new millennium—not that there's anything wrong with those books!—I wanted these stories to have chick-friendly plots but also be invested with theme.

The group easily rose to the occasion, and the following is a roundup of the stories you'll find within these pages. Please be advised: none of the stories solve the problem of what to do about Iraq or deliver a prescription for curing cancer. But then, how much of fiction, either genre or literary, ever does? The stories do, however, have an awful lot to do with friendship and laughter, love and death—i.e., the stuff of life.

Four of the stories deal loosely with the topic of dating, but each one is as different from the others as Agatha Christie from Sue Grafton or Jane Smiley from Zadie Smith. In Kayla Perrin's "Mama Knows Best," the title rings truer than Robert Young ever could have imagined; in Karen Siplin's cross-cultural "Nice Jewish Boy," the only black woman at a bris meets the only eligible man for her...sort of; in Johanna Edwards' "Takeoffs and Landings," the heroine learns that there are better and worse things than having to squeeze a plus-sized body into a skinny airplane seat; and in Rachel Pine's scathingly funny "The Ring," a too-cool heroine gets her comeuppance.

Since kids, whether we have them or not, make up part of the consciousness of any woman, two of the stories deal with that issue: Heather Swain's "*Café con Leche* Crush," wherein a woman mired in postpartum stress attempts to drown her sorrows at the local coffeehouse, and Stephanie Lehmann's "How to Be a Millionaire," about a mother's contemplation of a return to the workforce.

No collection of chick-lit would be complete without a handful of women trying to negotiate life through the use of desperate measures, and here we have three: Harley Jane Kozak's "The Infidelity Diet," which combines mystery with infidelity and weight loss; Cara Lockwood's "The Commitment Phobe," in which the heroine artfully makes use of an ex-boyfriend; and Karin Gillespie's "Trash Talk," which prescribes a new purpose for Dumpster diving.

And no collection of chick-lit would be complete without its fair share of cautionary tales, either—stories that poke fun at the folly of being fallible human beings. Ariella Papa's satirical and metafictional "Confessions of a Three-Eyed Freak" is about the perils of focusing on one body part to the exclusion of all else; Caren Lissner's "The Database" is a futuristic story about the computerized search for love; Julie Kenner's "Dead Friends and Other Dating Dilemmas" is about being careful who you allow to control your love life; Gena Showalter's "Every Girl's Dream" is about a woman who has to complete her ten-item to-do list by the age of thirty...*or die*; and my own "Shell Game" is a magical-realist story of what happens when women lose their identity within a relationship.

If there's one story that should be a poster child for the collection, it's Jennifer Coburn's "Two Literary Chicks," about two writing friends—one Lit, one Chick—who meet up again after a time apart.

There are two writers collected here whose stories represent their first works published in a book: Deanna Carlyle, who delivers a trans-atlantic tale of mystery in a French restaurant in "Dead Men Don't Eat Quiche," and Andrea Schicke Hirsch, who provides a cautionary tale about dealing with a new beau's wretched child in "Meeting Cute." I know you'll be hearing more from both writers in the future.

We even have a special guest star: international bestseller Raelynn Hillhouse, creator of the Cold War thriller *Rift Zone*. As fortune would have it, on the same day one of the original contributors to the collection had to bail out due to being overextended, I received an e-mail from Raelynn in which she'd written a parody of a pompous writer that was one of the funniest things I'd ever read. Half joking, I asked her, "Gee, can you write me another three thousand words like this, because...?" She picked up the challenge and less than twenty-four hours later I received a copy of "Secret Agent Chick," a rollicking spoof of spy stories.

It was nice to have someone who writes in a completely different genre reach across the aisle to join us in our endeavor. Speaking of which....

Not long after my initial meeting with Glenn, I wrote four guest essays at www.literarychicks.com, the second of which was a piece called "Reaching Across the Aisle" that contained, among other things, the following:

In American politics today we see the perils of not cooperating. When Republicans and Democrats stay firmly entrenched on their individual sides of the aisle, little gets accomplished and unpleasantness ensues. It's not that it's not important to hold on to one's ideals, but so much more can be achieved when people seek out their similarities, the middle ground, rather than staunchly adhering to the my-way-or-the-highway approach.

And in publishing it's no different.

It used to be that there were two major camps in publishing, Literary and Commercial. And within the area of women writers, that distinction has lately devolved into the following: Chicks and Lits. The former resents the greater review attention bestowed on the latter; the latter resents the greater sales of [the former's] hot market. But what if, instead of wasting our time throwing stones at one another, we were to pool our reader resources toward the end of greater benefit for all?

At the end of the essay, I provided an annotated list of literary writers I felt sure fans of my own work would love. And, as an extension of the original "Reaching Across the Aisle" essay, I've asked each of the contributors to provide the name, title and a short description of a literary writer she feels confident her own fans would love. So, after the stories, you'll find an appendix listing just which Lits each Chick chose.

I also asked each writer to provide a short statement to be included at the top of her story about what chick-lit means to her, either positive or negative. It is my hope that this experience will be a complete one for readers of these pages, one in which they will find out a little bit about what we think, what we write and whose work we admire.

Despite all the controversy, which will no doubt rage on, I remain convinced there are basically only two kinds of books in the world: good/well-written stories and bad/poorly written stories. The rest, as someone far greater than me once said, is just sound and fury, signifying nothing.

I've worked on a lot of projects in the past year. As of this writing, which happens to be December 7, 2005, I've written two books and most of a third. And yet, very little I've done professionally in the last year fills me with as much pride as standing before you now, with my colleagues and my friends, and saying to you, positively:

This is Chick-Lit.

6

Jennifer Coburn

As a feminist, I find the attack on chick-lit more than a bit disheartening. Is this where we are—one group of women writers mocking another, deeming its work irrelevant? Are women really criticizing each other about what they read?! An author recently commented that the term chick-lit sounds as if the writing is about, for and by women, nothing more. Nothing more?! Why isn't that enough?! I love chick-lit and am proud to be associated with this genre. People who don't appreciate it should stop moaning about the relevance of chick-lit and simply spend their time reading what they like.

Two Literary Chicks

Marley was the first to see Jo as they walked toward each other on Seventh Avenue. She didn't recognize Jo as her old classmate at first. It was the skimpy outfit that caught Marley's eye. She wondered why adult women felt the need to seek attention by dressing provocatively. Jo sported a charcoal gray pinstripe wool suit with a micro-miniskirt that looked like something out of *Playboy*'s "Girls of the Boardroom." Admittedly, the woman's legs could support such exhibitionism, but the reckless flaunting of sexuality bothered Marley. And those shoes! How did women balance themselves on such wobbly spikes—or manage to figure out which direction all those straps were supposed to go? Who had time for such nonsense, Marley thought self-righteously, unaware that she was now clutching the envelope containing her 600-page manuscript.

Jo was also assessing Marley before either of them recognized the other from their days together at NYU. She wondered how a woman could appear so effortlessly chic. Marley wore plain black pants and a matching button-up jacket reminiscent of Mao Tse-tung. Capping her unmade-up face and black rectangular specs was a strawberry blond wash-and-wear shag. It looked as though she made it from shower to door in less than fifteen minutes and yet she looked stunning. She had such style and confidence. Jo found it discouraging. Here she spent so much time and effort—not to mention the pain of stilettos and Wonderbras—on her appearance and someone else pulled it off better without even trying.

Jo wasn't the type to be jealous of another woman's good looks until that evening she saw Madame Mao approaching. Then she realized that it wasn't envy she felt. It was sheer antipathy for the woman she now recognized as the self-proclaimed smarty-pants from college.

It had been six years since Marley and Jo had met in a ten-person creative writing seminar that met thrice weekly to exchange comments on each others' work. Suffice it to say, Marley and Jo rarely had praise for one another's writing. Marley didn't have a single comment about Jo's short stories for the first six weeks of class. The truth was that she resented having to read what she and her friends privately referred to as "bubblegum." It was a waste of her time, she thought. It took time away from her own work and taught her absolutely nothing about the craft of writing. Many times, she would skip reading Jo's stories altogether. One day, the teacher asked what Marley thought of Jo's new piece. "You've been rather quiet today," she noted. "Do you have anything to offer?" Marley shook her head that she didn't. "I'm sure you must have *some* reaction to her work." Marley resisted the urge to roll her eyes. Her *work*. If anyone was playing at the keyboard it was Jo. Marley continued to nod her head. When the teacher finally forced her to comment, Marley said Jo's writing was "irrelevant."

Jo was equally unimpressed with Marley. She found her stories to be self-important pseudo-literary drivel that rambled on endlessly about nothing. She didn't put it quite as bluntly in class. More like, "Twelve pages describing a set of curtains seems a bit excessive." She really wanted to shout, "Who cares *this* much about drapery?!" Marley told Jo she simply didn't understand the significance of the curtain as a metaphor for the thin veil that separates one's inner life from the outer world. "Oh please," Jo said, growing more defiant. "What about telling the reader a story? Where was the conflict? How 'bout a plot?"

"You just don't get it," Marley returned with a shrug. She couldn't care less what any of them thought, especially Jo and her type.

Marley longed for her youthful confidence these days. Her manuscript about a young woman's turbulent childhood with a tyrannical, alcoholic father had been rejected by four publishers. Each editor took the time to tell Marley that she wrote beautifully and would love to see her "next effort." All four said Marley had a knack for painting gripping, painful images. Her writing was fluid and melodic. Her manuscript reminded them of Janet Fitch's bestselling masterpiece *White Oleander.* But something was missing. There was something that kept the reader at arm's length. If Marley reworked the entire manuscript in such a way that allowed the reader to really connect with the protagonist on an intimate level, two editors would be willing to take another look. Neither was specifically asking her to do so, though. They both dismissed Marley's 600-page memoir saying they were sure it would "find the right home" somewhere. Marley felt like an ugly mutt that had just been passed over for a golden retriever at the animal shelter.

Jo's eyes darted for an opportunity to cross the street, but the busy stream of white car lights clogging Seventh Avenue forced her to remain on the sidewalk. There was no way to avoid Marley Jamieson. In about ten seconds, their eyes would meet and they would have no other choice but to stop, act like they were delighted to see one another and pretend they cared about what was going on in each other's lives. They might even believe it for a moment. In a glimmer of optimism, Jo might suggest they have lunch, then immediately regret it when Marley offered a lame excuse. Jo promised herself that she would maintain a cool demeanor, not letting Marley see how much she still got to her after so many years. Life had been good to Jo. There was no reason for her to feel anything but confident.

"Marley?" Jo perked. "Is that you?!" Immediately she chided herself for sounding like the captain of the cheerleading team, which she actually was in high school. Marley knit her brows, trying to place where she knew this raven-haired knockout. Was she a receptionist at one of the magazines she wrote for?

Jo screamed silently. *Is she really going to pretend not to know me?!* Jo declared war. "They say the memory is the first to go," she said sweetly. "It's Jo Evans from NYU. We took creative writing together, remember?"

"Oh, right, of course," Marley replied. "Right, how are you?" Marley had heard about her classmate's successful debut novel in the alumni newsletter. Loathe as she was to admit, she'd heard all about it from her writers' group, a gaggle of seven ultra-snooty women who appreciated the literary significance of a belabored description of curtains. Even they said that Jo's book was "pretty well done...for chick-lit." Marley knew Jo's book must have been terrific if this crew had read it...and deemed it decent, but she'd dismissed its appearance on the bestseller list as a result of people being so damned stupid. No one appreciated quality literature anymore. Chick-lit was like the goddamned pretty girl who shows up in eleventh grade and becomes instantly popular when substantial people had been snubbed for years. People were so damned superficial and the fact that Jo Evans could have a bestseller was proof of that. Marley silently vowed that she would pretend she had never heard of her silly little book. If Jo brought it up—which she undoubtedly would (you only wear skirts like that if you're dying for attention)—Marley would simply act as if news of such trivialities hadn't reached her.

"So great!" Jo replied. *Go ahead, ask me!*

"*So great*, huh?" Marley said in a tone that was clearly mocking Jo's simple choice of words. She wondered why she always had to be such a bitch to women like Jo. Why couldn't she just let Jo tell her she was "so great" and let it be? Why did she need to take swipes at someone just because she was enjoying a little success? Marley could see that she had hurt Jo. Her body language was that of a cat gearing up for a fight, but her face gave her away. Her eyes widened and her lips pursed, wounded. Marley apologized. "I've had a rough day," she confessed. Backtracking, she revised. "Editors can be so trying with all of their revisions." She gestured to the envelope holding her manuscript.

"Oh, I know," responded Jo. *Ask me! Ask me!* Jo wondered why she needed validation from this virtual stranger. Who needed her anyway? But Jo already knew her answer. She was a bottomless pit of need. She needed to be noticed, to be admired, not just by some, but by all. When her book appeared at number nine on the *New York Times* bestseller list, Jo wondered what the other eight books had that hers didn't.

"So you're writing?" Jo asked. She wondered how much longer this small talk had to go on.

Marley wanted out, too. She would happily saunter off just as soon as she convinced Jo that she was carrying the next literary masterpiece in her tattered envelope—and that she had never heard of *Brooklyn Heights*, the chick-lit adaptation of the Emily Brontë classic. Who gave a shit about Cliff and Cathy in their brownstone overlooking the Manhattan skyline? Maybe 600,000 dipshit women, but not Marley.

Jo continued. "Have you had anything published?" *Ask me already! Why does she assume she's the only one writing professionally?!*

"I've been working on this for six years," Marley said. "You know how long it takes to write something if you want it to be quality work."

"I guess if you're struggling with it," Jo shot back, not realizing what a true jab her comment was to Marley. Both were more than ready to end their obligatory chat. It had been a full two minutes that they stood on the boundary of the West Village feigning interest in each other's lives only to advance their own standing. Each wished she didn't care what the other thought of her. And yet each of them did.

Trying to even the score, Marley defended her marathon drafting of a novel that hadn't a single nibble from the publishing industry. "This is not chick-lit," she smarted.

Jo had grown so weary of this refrain. So many of the self-proclaimed literati dismissed chick-lit as if it were completely inconsequential. Both economically and socially, chick-lit was a force to be reckoned with, and yet the smarty-pants posse treated it as though it were gum at the bottom of the shoe of the book world. Jo recently read that chick-lit books generated $72 million in sales a year. That's a lot of books sold. Jo felt proud to be part of the genre because anything that popular was clearly resonating with women, giving them a fun story, a few insights and laughs—an escape from this otherwise heavy world. *This is not chick-lit,*

Jo silently repeated Marley's comment. *What exactly was that supposed to mean? What type of person defines her work by what it's not, rather than what it is?*

As much as Jo wanted to end this bitchy little reunion, she wasn't going to leave until she set Marley straight. "What exactly does *that* mean?" She had entirely missed the fact that since Marley had made reference to her book not being chick-lit, she must have heard about *Brooklyn Heights* and its success.

Marley could see that she had offended Jo again. She seemed to be on automatic bitch mode these days, though that was not her intention. She hadn't meant to upset her agent, though on second thought, her suggestion that he was incompetent might have been worded a bit strongly. And her boyfriend—well, ex-boyfriend as of six hours ago—said he couldn't take her "toxic energy" anymore. (What could you expect from a guy born and raised in California?) Marley knew she was a little frustrated these days, but she just felt she was being direct with people. "I'm sorry," she offered Jo. "That didn't come out right. It's just that when I think of chick-lit, it just seems like books by, for and about women, nothing more."

"Nothing *more*?" Jo repeated. "What more does it need to be considered important in your eyes, Marley? I mean, really, do you have such a low opinion of women that books by, for and about us somehow fall short of being worthwhile?"

Jo could see that her comment had hit Marley hard. Marley stumbled through a few meager attempts to explain herself, but it was clear: Jo had won this battle. Marley was ready to stomp off when a taxi drove by and whistled at the two women. His front tire sank into a pothole that could have passed for a small lake. Filled with dark water from the morning shower, it emptied into a giant splash that covered Marley from her hair to her utilitarian flats. Marley felt a familiar rage. She wanted to kill that stupid taxi driver. But her anger quickly dissipated when she saw Jo's look of concern. "Are you okay?" Jo asked genuinely. Marley shrugged. "I guess the cabbie's a fan of chick-lit." Jo laughed.

"I live a few blocks from here," Jo said. "Why don't you come to my place and get dried off? We're about the same size. I'll lend you some dry clothes."

Marley was tired. Tired of being angry. Tired of fighting. Tired of pretending she was okay with the idea of taking the bus home, soaking wet in filthy water. "Okay," she said, softer than Jo had ever heard her former classmate speak.

The two walked silently for the next few minutes until they reached a quiet enclave of brownstones that no longer looked like New York. Cherry Lane was lit with actual gas lamps. Large windows allowed peeks into cozy homes with natural brick walls, fireplaces and original art. It was the sort of place one might imagine salons or women's suffrage meetings taking place at the turn of the last century. "This is your place?" Marley asked, quickly hoping that her shock wasn't offensive to Jo. To err on the side of caution, she followed up immediately. "It's absolutely gorgeous."

Jo gave a little shrug as she walked to the bathroom to grab a towel for Marley. "It was my parents' place before they moved to Florida," she shouted from the other room as she gathered clothes for her friend to change into. "Rent control since the seventies." Jo appeared in the living room where Marley waited.

Marley changed. From Jo's bedroom she shouted to her, "I like how you've framed your book cover."

"Would you believe I changed my comforter to match it?" Jo shouted back.

Emerging from Jo's bedroom, Marley felt kind of cute in the baby blue Juicy Couture workout suit. "Is it me?" she asked, spinning to model.

"Looks better on you than me," Jo replied. "I hate it when that happens." Handing her friend a plastic shopping bag to take home her clothes, Jo tossed a copy of *Brooklyn Heights* on the top of the black heap. "Give it a try. You might enjoy something by, for and about women. I wrote it," Jo said.

That night Jo was tidying her apartment, thinking about how much more pleasant Marley was after having been christened by puddle water. *Taxis should splash people more often.* On her coffee table, she spotted an unfamiliar-looking envelope with Marley's name on it. Her manuscript. She wondered if it would it be obtrusive to open it and take a look. Jo posed a question her mother always asked her when facing a moral dilemma: "What are you hoping for?" If she was hoping that Marley's book would be a dreadful reincarnation of the curtain story, she would leave it be. If she was honestly rooting for a good read, she'd open it.

As Jo devoured every page of her friend's manuscript, she couldn't help blubbering at the tragedy of it all. This father character was so difficult to please, so demanding and so hard on his daughter. Any reader could see that this little girl was growing up to feel utterly inadequate. It was such a moving epic, but something was missing. By midnight, when Jo reached the middle of the manuscript, she figured it out. The narrator's voice was the problem. It was so detached. The reader had to work too hard to get to know her because the style was so completely removed and expository. It was like listening to a doctor telling you about his patient's fatal illness. The words perfectly explained what was happening, but there was a protective distance from the emotional component of it all.

Jo wondered if she could ever offer this feedback to Marley. Would she even take seriously the criticism from a mere "chick-lit" writer? Besides, what good would it do? Marley already had an editor who had offered her comments. Hers were probably nothing new or particularly useful. *Closet Webs* would likely go straight to the number eight spot on the bestseller list without Jo's unsolicited feedback.

Meanwhile, in the East Village Marley was still in her friend's Juicy loaner, curled up with *Brooklyn Heights*. "What the hell," she had surrendered as she unpacked her plastic bag. Two hours later, she was wiping away a tear from her eye. She was not crying in sorrow as Jo was, but rather laughing so hard that her eyes were watering. *How very funny Jo is*, Marley thought. *How very funny life is.* She wondered how long it had been since she'd laughed like this—or laughed aloud at all. Months? Years? Jo's book not only made Marley laugh, but also made her think about the nature of romantic relationships, female friendship and crazy relatives. What a revelation it was to discover that there is value in pure fun.

Marley wondered if she would ever muster the generosity to tell Jo how much she enjoyed her book and how quickly it read. She polished it off in just four hours, which made her feel rather smart on a day otherwise filled with rejection.

The next evening Marley picked up the phone and dialed Jo's house. "Hi, Jo? It's Marley. Do you have a minute?"

"Sure, what's up?"

"Oh, well, I wanted to thank you for lending me the sweat suit and see when would be a good time for me to return it. It's very comfy, by the way. Where did you get it?"

"No problem. You can keep it if you like. I've got a million. Listen, I've got to tell you, I started your manuscript last night and it is absolutely wonderful. Heartbreaking, really. It makes me want to really start digging deeper in my own stuff, you know, instead of always going for the laugh?"

"You read it?!" Marley gasped, remembering that four rejection notes were enclosed in the envelope along with the manuscript. Not to mention the note from her agent saying it was time to stop being so pigheaded and start making adjustments that would make her book marketable. "So then you know?"

Jo hadn't seen the notes buried behind the last page. "Know what? Are you telling me that you're the little girl in the story? I haven't gotten to the end yet, but I kind of figured it was you. Even though we don't know each other well, the character had a, well, *you* type of feel to her."

That wasn't a good sign, Marley thought. The little girl grows up to be a bitter, lonely woman who becomes addicted to prescription drugs and attempts suicide.

Marley inhaled deeply. "Jo, when you finish the book—if you finish, that is—you'll see a pile of rejection letters from various publishers."

"So what?" Jo laughed. "You wanna know how many rejections *Brooklyn Heights* got before it got published? They'll be eating their hearts out when this hits the bestseller list."

"Jo, mine's not going to hit the bestseller list."

"Don't say that! Have a little confidence." She laughed at her ability to dispense advice she desperately needed to follow.

"It's not going to be published," she admitted.

"Oh," Jo said to fill the silence. "I thought you said...." She drifted. Marley didn't explain. She didn't have to.

An uncomfortable silence lingered.

"Maybe when you finish it, you could give me your thoughts on how to tighten it up a bit," Marley suggested. "I mean, 600 pages is rather long."

"It's not the length," Jo hedged. "It's just that I never really feel like the narrator lets you in. I mean, I'm hearing about this terribly painful childhood, but it seems so, I don't know, far away. But I should shut up until I finish it."

"I loved yours," Marley said. "It was hilarious."

"You didn't find it to be 'irrelevant'?" Jo asked. Marley didn't remember her comment from six years ago, so she missed the reference.

"Not everything needs to be relevant to matter," Marley returned. "I have to tell you, though. It was a lot more substantial than I thought it was going to be."

"Really?" Jo said, her single word begging for more.

"I was totally unprepared for that emotional punch at the end. Very touching."

"Seriously?"

"Oh, come on, Jo!" Marley said. "You must have heard this before. You're on the goddamned bestseller list. *Cosmopolitan* called your book its 'fearless, fabulous pick of 2006'!"

"You read *Cosmo*?"

"It was on your book cover," Marley explained. "So, do you want to maybe catch lunch some time? Or are you too busy?"

"No, I'd love to. Sounds great. Your side of the Village or mine?"

"How 'bout somewhere in the middle? Astor Place?" Marley asked.

"Astor Place it is."

JENNIFER COBURN is a chick-lit writer living in San Diego with her husband, William, and their daughter, Katie. She is the author of *The Wife of Reilly, Reinventing Mona* and *Tales From the Crib*. Coburn's debut novel has been optioned for film by Freedom Productions and Gold Circle Films. Her fourth novel, a sequel to *Tales, The Queen Gene*, will be released in February 2007. She has written for national and regional newspapers and magazines, and especially enjoys writing about mothering.

Harley Jane Kozak

Chick-lit, for me, is a twenty-first-century marketing term that describes a genre that's been around for eons. It's a story primarily by and about and for women, Everywoman, with Everyday concerns, which is to say relationships, family, work, children, fashion and, especially, romance. There's good chick-lit and bad, lightweight and profound, highbrow, lowbrow, funny, poignant. . . . It's a term I find more flippant than offensive—but then, I'm not easily offended.

The Infidelity Diet

It was during a five-mile run with the dogs that I realized my husband was having an affair.

I was seven years into the marriage and two and a quarter miles into the run when various details clicked into place, like magnets thrown against the refrigerator. There was the diamond stud earring I'd found wedged in the passenger seat of Christopher's BMW an hour earlier, which brought to mind other small, unsolved mysteries: whispered phone conversations abruptly cut off when I entered the room. A pack of Trojans in the bottom drawer in the guest bath, buried amid ancient

17

Band-Aids and an expired bottle of calamine lotion. New cuff links, monogrammed. A trace of perfume. There were the late nights at the office, nights I called him and got no answer.

And there was Fé.

Thinking about Fé disturbed me enough that the dogs took notice. Spot and Plain had raced down to the creek to hurl themselves into its muddy depths before racing back, wet and smelly, to check on me. Their ears went up when they saw I'd slowed to a walk, nearing the end of the trail, like I'd been hit by a cramp, like I couldn't get any air. I pulled the plug on my iPod, on Waylon Jennings singing, "You Picked A Fine Time to Leave Me, Lucille," and let the headset cord dangle. I wasn't ready for country and western commiseration; that's a later stage of grief. I wasn't ready for grief at all. I was still working up to rage.

Fé. Black hair. Cognac eyes. Parade-float smile. Sophistication. Charm: a flattering interest that engaged you in conversation, preempting uncharitable thoughts. She was my husband's client, had been his client longer than I'd been his wife, which conferred certain rights. She came for dinner at our house and served us dinner at hers—well, presided over the dinner her maid served—and knew the birthdays of our children, as well as what play I was directing at school. She'd even attended once, closing night of *Henry V.* Sitting with—aha!—Christopher. Who hadn't shown up at the high school for one of my directorial efforts since our courtship days. Christopher, whose response to *Twelfth Night,* the most accessible of the comedies, had been, "What language are they speaking?"

Fé had a husband of her own, Albert, but he was a colorless man who eschewed sunlight, spending his life indoors polishing his portfolio. Vacations were casino-oriented: Monaco, Las Vegas, Macao, so Albert could make money as Fé spent it. It was easy to imagine that Fé would need someone else's husband to round out her life. My husband.

Foul devil. Black magician. Lines from *Richard III,* my current production, popped into my head. Did they describe Fé, though? Or Christopher?

"Take him." I said it aloud, on the trail. There was no one in sight. "Take him!" I yelled, which made the dogs stop and look back at me. "Take him," I gasped, working back up to a run. Take his dry-cleaning, his size 16-36 dress shirts and his 34 briefs and v-neck and crewneck T-shirts and 100% cotton casual socks. Track down the replacement bristles for his electric toothbrush and memorize every one of his three hundred sixty-eight food preferences, aversions and allergies. Run with his dogs. Service his car. Clean his house, every day except Tuesdays. I did not have perfect skin, or a diamond stud in my belly button that showed to advantage when I wore a bikini—not that I'd worn bikinis since 1999—but I had a talent for managing the life of a high-maintenance man while remaining a low-maintenance woman, which is what I'd thought Christopher required. Now it occurred to me I knew nothing at all about what Christopher required.

Fé was not low-maintenance, although she had the gift of appearing so, of making it all—life, I'm talking about—look simple. No doubt she was a good sport, as long as there was a four-star-hotel stay in sight and a personal masseuse at the end of the day. How long she could keep it all up on Christopher's salary was another question.

During mile four of the run I focused on logistics. I mentally packed the children's suitcases and got us as far as my sister Emmie's in St. Louis. We'd stay in motels along the way, wherever we found a well-timed vacancy sign. The kids would be happy, as long as there were swimming pools. I'd be an emotional wreck, but big deal. People survived worse. Christopher would suffer more, not knowing where we were, not calling the shots.

I would not phone home. I would calmly drive him mad.

My next move was clear. By the time I'd fed the dogs and showered, I was ready to approach this as I approached all projects, from picking a preschool to stuffing a turkey: I took a survey.

Emmie was unequivocal: "You have to confront him."

This came as a surprise, given our heritage. My sister and I came from a long line of tight-lipped, 'til-death-us-do-part women. "What's the worst that can happen?" she said, her voice distorted on the speakerphone. "Divorce? If Mom and Grandma had been more confrontational with the men they married, they might've beat cancer. Or not gotten it in the first place." I thought about that, about splitting up as a kind of preemptive chemotherapy. Divorce: the new antioxidant.

"Just have it out with him," Emmie said. "The sooner the better. To-night."

An hour later Ludmilla, my colorist, disagreed. "First, you must get your ducks in a row. Once he knows you suspect him," she said, painting my roots with her pastry brush, "poof! He hides his assets and you and the children have nothing. He will move to Bel Air and you will get an apartment in the Valley." She did a crisp fold of the foil and nodded at my miserable, astonished face in the mirror.

At least Ludmilla's loyalties were with me, even though it had been Christopher who'd found her, at the debut of my first gray hair. The Nice 'N Easy fumes in our bathroom made him ill, and she came highly recommended by his accountant. "I will get you the name of a divorce lawyer from Zina, my Tuesday five o'clock," she said. "Zina just left her second husband. Whatever you do, stay in the house. Make him leave. And do not economize. You must document your living expenses for the judge. Everything. Fresh flowers, children's birthday parties, car washes. Whatever you need to maintain your life, write it down. Then add twenty percent. You know, like a tip."

My friend Tracy, whose sons were my daughters' ages, had been through this with her first husband. "There's one upside," she said, watching with me from the sidelines of soccer practice that afternoon. "What no one tells you is that you can lose ten to fifteen pounds those first weeks, when you discover the infidelity. Eventually you'll gain it back, especially if you turn to booze during the divorce stage, but it can really jump-start a diet."

Tracy, like Emmie and Ludmilla, did not question the basic assumption that Christopher was cheating. Unfaithful husbands, it seemed, were as common as laundry.

I watched her son Ian kick a soccer ball right through my daughter Juliet's legs, scoring. Something hit me in my solar plexus.

Juliet and Cordelia. They adored Christopher, worshipped him with a slavish, preadolescent devotion. I imagined them carrying backpacks stuffed with clothes, books and Polly Pockets, marching down the sidewalk to Christopher's convertible, climbing into the booster seats crammed in the back. Waving goodbye to me. Grimly. Me waving back. Crying. Wednesdays. Every other weekend. Alternate holidays.

Christmas without my children? I'd rather join the Marines. For that matter, I couldn't make it to St. Louis, not even to drive my husband mad, if it meant leaving the dogs behind.

We all have our bottom lines. These were mine.

Plan B was simple: ignore the affair. Take the high road, turn a blind eye, do what classy women have done since time immemorial. Did Jackie Kennedy throw fits? Not to our knowledge. She smiled serenely and survived infidelity at the highest levels of government and we, the people, admired her.

I lay in bed, waiting for sleep, and thought about how thin Jackie was. Was Tracy right? Had it been the infidelity diet, all those years? Jackie was always a little sparrow of a woman—Rose Kennedy, too, come to think of it, and *her* husband, Joe, was a notorious philanderer. My God, Tracy was on to something.

The problem with Plan B was that I was no Jackie Kennedy. I wasn't even Hillary Clinton. They could conduct affairs of state while their husbands conducted affairs; I couldn't even supervise second-grade homework at full capacity. "Who cares about the *Nina*, the *Pinta* and the *Santa Maria*?" I'd wanted to scream at Juliet. "Your father is screwing Fé!" I'd had to go bite on a kitchen towel.

And sleep deprivation would not improve things.

I had no defense against insomnia; I'd never had it before. After twenty minutes in the dark, trying to recall if it was part one or part two of *Henry IV* that gave us *O sleep...how have I frighted thee, that thou no more wilt weigh my eyelids down and steep my senses in forgetfulness?* I got out of bed to look it up, which led to a half hour of working on *Richard III*, looking for scenes to cut. Then I turned on the TV. I pretended to be Christopher, flipping channels with the remote, zoned out in his leather recliner. He was working late tonight. Most nights, these days. Two or three in the morning was not unusual for him, when up against a deadline.

Or a warm body.

Late-night TV was pretty interesting. I had no idea. There was some graphically sexual stuff, which was a little too topical for me, under the circumstances. I settled on a criminal justice show with an FBI polygraph expert explaining how to tell if a suspect is lying.

21

"If the eyes go off in an upward direction," he said, "they're thinking about how an innocent person would answer. A truly innocent person doesn't have to stop and think. Similarly, a guilty person will repeat the question, in order to buy time to make up their answer. As in, 'What do you mean, did I kill Bob?' when asked, 'Did you kill Bob?'"

I took notes. Then I fell asleep, waking at 4:00 A.M. with pen in hand. The TV was off. I stumbled to the bedroom and crawled into bed alongside the lump that was Christopher. He did not roll over and hug me to him. This might have meant nothing, since he was asleep, but why had he not wakened me when he'd come in?

Because he was having an affair and didn't want me to smell her on him.

I got out of bed and went to the closet and grabbed the uppermost shirt from the mountain of pale shirts awaiting their trip to the cleaners. I sniffed. It smelled like Christopher, a combination of deodorant, shaving cream, hair product, soap and perspiration. Of course. He'd have been careful to remove his shirt before embracing Fé. I kept sniffing. I grew lightheaded from sniffing, overwhelmed by nostalgia, by the scent of my husband, the scent dearer to me than any except for Juliet and Cordelia. He was the air I had breathed for the last decade of my life. The best decade of my life.

God help me, I loved the bastard.

I crawled back into bed and attached myself to his sleeping back, like a monkey. Somewhere in the night, he turned and drew me to him.

The next day I came up with Plan C. This would take courage, as it involved Full Disclosure. Cards on the table. Like one of those testimonials from the women's magazines my mother used to clip recipes from: "How *His* Infidelity Can Make *Your* Marriage Stronger." It would be updated from the '50s into a New Age format, requiring us to open chakras and lay bare old resentments. Draw up accountability contracts. I'd have to own my part in it, what I'd let our marriage devolve into, that it was vulnerable to attack from Fé. Like not insisting on Date Night. Like letting the girls climb into our bed whenever they had nightmares, and stay there till morning. We'd go to counseling. Do therapy homework. In the end, we'd have better sex. That would be nice, sex that fell outside the range of the familiar. Sex that didn't include one or both of us falling asleep halfway to orgasm.

I drove the girls to the bus stop and was back home dressing for school when Christopher came in from walking the dogs. I heard him downstairs and felt that Now or Never sensation in my chest and knew I couldn't spend another obsessive day or sleepless night, knew that I was going to speak up.

When he came upstairs, I was sitting on the bed. He started talking about the Feeney dogs next door, how they were always in heat. How did he know that? I wondered.

"How do you know that?" I asked.

"What?

"How do you know when a bitch is in heat?" I asked. "Does she bat her eyelashes?"

He began to explain canine mating rituals, taking off his hiking boots and tossing them, sending little clumps of dirt flying onto the pale yellow carpet. When he paused, I heard myself say in a wooden voice, "Are you having an affair with Fé?"

The word "Fé" coincided with him pulling his sweatshirt over his head, so that it was impossible to check out whether his eyes went off in an upward direction, the way they were supposed to do if he was lying. When his head was free again, he looked at me calmly and said, "What?"

The TV FBI polygraph expert might call this stalling, but it could also have been that the sweatshirt hood had covered his ears.

I asked again. "Are you sleeping with Fé?"

He frowned. "No. Don't be silly."

And went into the bathroom, and into the shower.

Leaving me sitting. Stunned. A wife should know when her husband is lying, but in fact, I didn't know. I only knew that I wanted to believe him, which is not at all the same thing.

It's not even close.

Plan D was suggested independently by Emmie, Ludmilla and Tracy. Plan D was to have an affair.

"With a European, someone who knows how these things are done,"

Ludmilla said, calling with the number of a divorce attorney, just as she'd promised.

"Don't get me wrong, I like Christopher," Emmie said, "but realistically, it's not like he's even going to notice, unless you leave love letters lying around. So go for it."

"Get your needs met," Tracy said. "That's the phrase to use. You're not cheating on your husband, you're getting your needs met. Jargon is everything."

But Plan D had a few problems, the first of which was that I was out of practice. Probably I hadn't emitted pheromones, or whatever those bodily secretions are, for ten years. I wasn't even sure where they were stored, assuming sleep deprivation hadn't killed them. The second problem was that I did not know absolutely that Christopher was sleeping with Fé. And I needed more than circumstantial evidence. *Othello* had been my thesis project. I knew about the dangers of jumping to conclusions.

"If you're looking for a confession," Tracy said, "forget it. Some guys have a chivalry thing going on, where they won't rat out their co-adulterer. They think they're taking the high road by not coming clean."

That sounded like Christopher. Unless he left me for Fé. Then he'd come clean. "We never meant to hurt you," he'd say, a master of the cliché. "It just happened."

If he left me, he left me. I could handle crisis. What I couldn't handle, apparently—what interfered with my eating and sleeping and waking and work and play—was uncertainty. So if I'd never get an admission of guilt, and circumstantial evidence wasn't enough, what did that leave?

Proof. I needed proof.

Private investigators, judging by the Yellow Pages, are as rampant in Los Angeles as pool cleaners. "Spousal surveillance" was the service I needed. But I couldn't imagine how I'd afford it on my meager little personal account, and writing a check on our joint account would be the fast lane to divorce court, if Christopher didn't strangle me first.

Happily, I'd always been a do-it-yourselfer. Also, I'd been up late watching cop shows, and reruns of old detective favorites from the '70s, and it didn't look that hard.

The tricky part was lining up a babysitter. I finally worked out a deal where Stefanie, the next-door neighbor's sixteen-year-old, would bring over her homework, once the children were asleep, for a very reasonable rate if I threw in all the junk food she could eat. Hers had been an organic-only, no-preservatives vegan household ever since her father had moved out. Plus, she had no curfew.

Tuesday night, we were on.

I was at school until nine, rehearsing the notorious Lady Anne scene, wherein Richard III woos the widow of a man he's recently murdered, nearly having sex with her atop King Henry's coffin. It's not an easy scene to pull off. I'd cast the senior class bad boy in the lead, too handsome for hunchback Richard, but with all the requisite charisma. Lady Anne, a junior, was a smart girl, smart enough to question the transitions from outrage to forgiveness to flirtation in the course of a few pages. I told her to hang on; when she was a little older, she'd understand the power of a man giving her the full force of his attention, if he had half the wit of Richard Plantagenet.

Meanwhile, I kept phoning Christopher's office. No answer. I returned home, paid off my regular sitter and got Stefanie settled in with a new bag of Pepperidge Farm cookies. I drove to Christopher's office in Santa Monica, saw that his BMW wasn't in its parking place, and that his window, visible from the street, was dark. I then drove to Hancock Park. No BMWs on Fé's street. It could, of course, be parked in Fé's four-car garage, behind the house.

I walked up the front steps and rang the doorbell.

And braced myself.

The house was well-lit. Would Fé come to the door in a dressing gown? Or Concepcion, the housekeeper? And what would I say, to either of them? How would I explain my presence at 10:30 P.M.?

The door opened. Albert stood there. He wore a plaid bathrobe and leather slippers. I had never known any man, other than my late grandfather, to wear slippers.

"Hello, Albert," I said. "Hope I didn't wake you."

"Not at all," he said. "I'm waiting for the stock market to open in Germany. Won't you come in?"

Hard to imagine my husband shtupping Albert's wife upstairs as Albert sat in his den, tweaking his investments. I could ask if Fé was home. And

25

then what? Take her aside, and ask if she were cheating on her husband with mine, and have her deny it, and then tell Christopher, who would then be angry, along with duplicitous, distracted and overworked?

"Thank you, no," I said. "I just stopped by to…invite you to a little Christmas open house we're planning. On Christmas. Eve. Christmas Eve."

"What a lovely idea. Sadly, we'll be in Aix-en-Provence."

"Oh. Sad, indeed. Well, perhaps next year."

I left hurriedly. Let Albert wonder. I wondered myself how people survived the banality of their own lives. For me, not even Christmas in Aix-en-Provence could compensate for the vision of Albert in slippers. Who could blame Fé for preferring Christopher and his Brown University sweatpants, T-shirt and bare feet?

I drove back to Christopher's office. His car was parked in its space now, his office window illuminated.

It was entirely possible that Fé was up there with him, having sex on the drafting table in his partner Jerry's office. Right where they designed the marketing strategy for her perfume company.

I went in. The security guard had me sign the visitor's register. I read it upside down, looking for Fé's name. In vain. Possibly she used an alias.

Christopher's ad agency took up half the fourth floor. The main door was ajar. I followed the low-level lighting past the reception desk to the offices and listened to the sound of a distant vacuum cleaner.

Christopher looked up from his desk, startled to see me standing in the doorway. Startled, then alarmed. "What's wrong? Are the kids all right?"

"Yes, fine. I just…."

"What is it?" He stood. "Who's with the kids?"

"Stefanie, from next door."

"Feeney?"

"Yes. Christopher, have you been here all night?"

"More or less. What's up?"

How to explain any part of it? "I miss you."

"I miss you, too." He waited, frowning.

I took a deep breath. "Wanna have sex on Jerry's drafting table?"

"What?"

"I've always wanted to."

Christopher smiled. "Dressed like that?"

26

I looked down. I was in overalls and clogs, with tie-dyed socks. A turtleneck. A heavy sweater.

He said, "Does this have something to do with the play you're directing?"

"What? No."

"Honey," he said. "I've got the Kubertschak presentation in a week and at least three more hours of work ahead of me tonight. Can I take a rain check?"

"Yeah. Fine. Sure."

Christopher walked me out to the car, his arm around me. I tried to sense Fé's presence on him, her custom-blended perfume, but all I smelled was a faint trace of pizza.

He kissed me goodbye at the car door, a kiss as chaste as one he'd give his stepmother. I'd seen him kiss the dogs, Spot and Plain, with more zeal. "Drive safely," he said. "And let's not use Stefanie from next door on a regular basis. I don't trust a family with non-neutered pets. Oh, and I need dress socks. These are shot."

"Yes," I said. "That happens."

I went home and watched TV until two in the morning. This time I bypassed the forensic shows in favor of graphic sex on cable.

"I've sunk to watching pornography," I told Tracy at soccer practice.

"Porn has its place," she said. "But most of it's crap. I prefer sex toys."

"I wouldn't even know where to buy sex toys."

"Oh, sweetheart," she said. "The Hustler Store."

The next day, having no morning classes, I drove across town.

There was parking on Sunset, directly in front of the Hustler Hollywood. I'd hoped for something more covert, but at least there was a café entrance, for people pretending they were there for the cappuccino.

Near the café, to my delight, was a book section. I started with *Sex for Dummies* by Dr. Ruth Westheimer, which was as wholesome as a cookbook, and then, for good measure, browsed through the cookbooks. I rummaged through bondage and a few self-help books by former hookers. My favorite title, for no real reason, was a coffee table tome called *Tom of Finland*.

Having thus established my literary credentials to any fellow customers—there were none, by the way—I ventured farther into the store. The clothing section looked cheap, and it seemed unwise to own a T-shirt that said "cocksucker" now that Juliet and Cordelia were reading so well. The accessories and props were plastic and jokey, and a lot of them I didn't understand anyway, things with feathers and fur attached.

I was contemplating a canister of whipped cream and a jar of body chocolate, then realized that Christopher would never ingest whipped cream that didn't require refrigeration, and that for less money I could melt a bar of Valrhona in a double boiler and wear it. He might eat that. Me, I had no appetite for anything. Eventually, I settled on a bottle of erotic massage oil that promised to evoke a sensation of total rapture, and a couple of political buttons. The salesclerks, who I expected to be hard-bodied and dressed in leather, were indistinguishable from those you'd find at Nordstrom Rack.

Two nights later I tried the erotic massage oil on Christopher, but I'd just reached his shoulder blades when the sensation of total rapture produced deep, throaty snores.

I was now experiencing episodes of melancholy alternating with anxiety. To combat this, I started doing the Stairmaster after play rehearsals, while watching the highbrow erotica Tracy was sending over from Sally's Video. ("Not porn," she said. "Erotica.") Exercise, according to *Cooking Light*, was a legitimate treatment for depression. One night, while huffing away, watching *Prospero's Books*, it occurred to me that my problem was not just the probability my husband was having an affair, but the fact that we had no sex life to speak of. When had we last done it? Six weeks ago? Eight weeks?

Did we have no sex life because he was having an affair, or was he having an affair because we had no sex life?

And if he weren't currently having an affair, would he eventually have an affair because we had no sex life?

The not knowing was killing me.

I hopped off the Stairmaster, dripping with sweat and energy, and proceeded to ransack the house, Spot and Plain following me, room by room.

I looked through drawers and closets, and desks. In the guestroom I found a Phish T-shirt that belonged to Christopher's younger brother,

Alex, and a tube of toothpaste for sensitive teeth that I recalled coming from Alex's girlfriend Amy, houseguests the previous Thanksgiving.

Did Alex and Amy use Trojans?

Didn't Amy wear diamond stud earrings?

Also in the guest bath I found the scale I'd semi-purposely misplaced a year earlier. I stepped on gingerly, and found I was eleven pounds lighter than the last time I'd weighed myself. I stared at the number, stunned. I took off my clothes and tried again. Twelve and a half pounds. The infidelity diet was working. Did that, ipso facto, indicate infidelity?

At least I wasn't delusional, thinking my clothes were hanging on me in a decidedly unsexy way. I must have been starving and I didn't even know it. Time to fork over some bucks to buy new jeans.

My eyes drifted upward, to a box of old clothes stored in the guest room closet. I climbed on a chair to grab it, and on the way down caught sight of myself in the mirror.

Naked, except for bikini panties from Costco.

I had a memory of Christopher, early on in our courtship, pulling me naked to a mirror. He'd stood behind me, hands circling my waist, making me look. Wanting me to see the beauty he saw, instead of the flaws I saw.

There were so many more flaws now.

The box I held, resting on my hipbone, was labeled "pre-pregnancy clothes." I read the words backward in the glass. Below the box, at my bikini line, I saw the scar of the C-section that had brought Cordelia into the world.

That, at least, was beauty.

The jeans fit, my bachelor girl jeans on my married woman's body.

I continued my spousal investigation, finding nothing racier than old love letters from me, stuffed in a Kenneth Cole shoebox, along with Father's Day cards from the girls.

Among Christopher's business papers was an e-mail from Fé reminding him that all correspondence after mid-December should be sent to the Aix-en-Provence address, where she and Albert would be for most of the upcoming year, overseeing the construction of a new house.

This told me something about the future of Christopher and Fé, but nothing about their past. I kept going.

His credit card receipts revealed no surprises, except for some not-insubstantial bills from Giorgio Armani. There was a reason this man looked so good. And that couldn't have been easy for him; Christopher cared about every dollar spent.

Money. Money could be proof.

It was at this point that I decided to blackmail my husband.

I typed the note on the school's computer, using a plain font and thirty percent recycled paper. I then drove it to Ludmilla's salon, where Ludmilla's assistant, Hervé, took it across the street to El Pollo Loco for the messenger to pick up and deliver to Christopher's office. The note would never be traced back to me; I, being a vegetarian, was not a habitué of El Pollo Loco.

It occurred to me that I was approaching the outer limits of sanity, and perhaps even crossing the border. That the drama of my life now equaled the drama of whatever illicit affair my husband was involved in.

And I had no exit strategy. I had left myself no breadcrumbs to show me the way back to Normalville.

When I returned from rehearsal that night, Christopher was home. The sitter was gone. The television was off.

He sat at the kitchen table, littered with program cover art for *Richard III* and my director's notes essay, half-finished. He motioned for me to sit opposite him. He said, "How was your day?"

I could not have been more startled if he'd pulled out a set of bagpipes and started playing. Then I remembered the blackmail note. He must've gotten it.

"Your day," he repeated. "How was it?"

He was looking at me. When was the last time we'd made eye contact? "We had a run-through tonight," I said, sitting. "Lady Anne can't stop upstaging herself, and Richard doesn't know his lines. And I have to cut our running time in half."

"Make them do one of those—what do you call them?"

"Speed-throughs."

He nodded. "Speed-throughs. Get their attention. Wake them up."

I nodded. He nodded. We sat, nodding, the nods getting slower, until it was like our heads were doing a slow dance across the kitchen table.

"So," he said.

"So."

I saw in his eyes an invitation. All I had to do was RSVP.

I looked down, my eyes drifting to my director's notes. *Was ever woman in this humor wooed? Was ever woman in this humor won?* Act I, scene 2. I looked up again, thinking of the next line. *I'll have her, but I will not keep her long.*

I opened my mouth to say yes, but nothing came out.

After a moment, Christopher got up and left the room.

The next morning I struggled through ninth-grade drama, unable to focus on the *Midsummer Night's Dream* monologues I'd assigned, due to stress and sleep deprivation. Afterward, I headed to the blackmail drop-off point.

The concierge desk of the Hotel Cinq was manned by Ludmilla's brother, Boris, and it was there that the envelope with the money was to be delivered. Boris had called me on my cell, saying, "The eagle has landed," showing a flair for espionage. I was worried about involving Boris in something I suspected was illegal, but Ludmilla said she and Boris had survived Russia back when it was the Soviet Union and were scared of nothing. She added that if I were to give Boris a tip, it would not offend him.

I drove to Hotel Cinq, my heart palpitating.

My blackmail note had been bland, right out of a "Letters for All Occasions" reference book: "If you don't want you're wife to know about your mistress, deliver $600 to the concierge desk of the Hotel Cinq by tomorrow night, attention 'Jonathan Doe.'"

I purposely misspelled "your" to deflect suspicion; Christopher knew what a stickler I was for "your" versus "you're."

I'd picked six hundred dollars because that's the amount of cash he could take out of the ATM over two days and could reasonably afford. I'd wanted to make it easy for him.

Now I wished I'd made it harder. I wished I hadn't done it at all. I did not want money. I didn't want knowledge. I wanted my illusions intact, my suspension of disbelief.

There were other possibilities, weren't there? The envelope could contain a note demanding evidence of the evidence. Or a counterthreat, to call the police. Or a "go to hell" dare. Would these prove innocence, or simply indicate bravado, coupled with frugality?

But why bother with a note at all, when silence sent such strong messages?

And if the envelope did contain cash, was that a de facto admission of guilt? Might there not be another scenario in which an innocent, albeit frugal, person might give six hundred bucks to a blackmailer?

No.

I was about to have knowledge of my husband's treachery, and then I would have to do something with that knowledge. Wouldn't I?

I took a right on Federal, pulled into a loading zone parking space, opened my door, and vomited into the street. Score another point for the infidelity diet. I sat, shaking, thinking about Juliet and Cordelia, and how I'd never want either one to lose her lunch over some man. Not to mention her mind.

I made it out of the loading zone and to the Hotel Cinq. The lobby was cold and hip and Ludmilla's brother bowed as he handed me the padded manila envelope and accepted my two twenty-dollar bills—what is the correct tip for an accomplice?—and I took a seat on the most uncomfortable seating module I have ever encountered.

The envelope lay in my hands, the words "Jonathan Doe" written on the outside in Christopher's handwriting.

I opened the envelope.

Inside were six hundred-dollar bills.

And a note.

And tied with a ribbon, lingerie. Champagne silk. La Perla, Beverly Hills. Worth more than a minivan trunk full of groceries from Costco.

The note said, "Get a room. Pay cash. Wear these."

The thing about innocence is, you can't prove it. Not in a court of law, not in the bedroom. There is only guilt, and reasonable doubt. You take your pick. And then you live with it. For a day at a time. Or an afternoon.

Because even with guilt, there's the possibility of redemption.

I did get a room. It cost three hundred and forty-nine dollars, and that worked out to two dollars and ninety cents a minute, plus tax, because Christopher had a one-thirty meeting. He made the minutes count. I kept the change.

The lingerie fit me. It would not have fit Fé, who had much larger breasts. It took no time at all to get the lingerie on, but an hour to remove it, as we were eventually moved *to leave the keen encounter of our wits and fall something into a slower method.* Act One, scene 2. This, of course, was something I did not say out loud. There were also questions I did not ask. Life is short, in a three-hundred-and-forty-nine-dollar room.

By the time I was naked, and we'd done everything it occurred to us to do, twice, I was overcome by a hunger so powerful that my husband ordered room service.

"You're getting too skinny," he said, hanging up the phone and rolling back to me. He put his hands on my body, tracing the outline of my ribs with his fingers.

I closed my eyes, and saw sleep, like a ship on the horizon, make its slow approach.

"Then feed me," I said.

HARLEY JANE KOZAK, a sometime actress, lives in Topanga Canyon, California, with her trial lawyer husband, two big dogs and three small children. Her debut novel, *Dating Dead Men*, won the Agatha, Anthony and Macavity awards. Its sequel, *Dating is Murder*, came out last spring, and she's now writing number three, working-titled *Dead Ex*. Her short fiction has appeared in *Ms. Magazine, Soap Opera Digest,* the *Sun* and the *Santa Monica Review*.

Ariella Papa

One of the things I really like about the direction chick-lit is taking is that it's beginning to encompass so much more. At the heart, I think it's telling stories about women that people can relate to and having fun at the same time. This story started out as traditional chick-lit and then got hijacked somewhere along the way. It was inspired by a dream, and that's the best place for a story to come from.

Confessions of a Three-Eyed Freak

I want you to understand, from the beginning, that this was never about being beautiful. I just wanted to be normal. Is that so wrong?

It all began when I decided to get my birthmark removed.

I finally had enough money to get the rather large cocoa-colored mark on my neck removed. It was shaped like Australia, at least that's what my parents told me when I was a little girl. They also called it a beauty mark and for a long time I considered it a mark of my beauty.

But since then, I've learned that my parents are liars and the first sign of that was when I got to kindergarten. I announced to the teacher that I had a beauty mark and displayed it, proudly tugging down the neck of my Charlie Chaplin T-shirt.

"Why, Ariella," said Ms. Weinberg. "Isn't that nice."

But for some reason she was not as delighted by it as my parents had been. By the time I got to second grade, one overweight, over-bitten smart aleck named Jason told me that I was the ugliest girl in all of P.S. 84.

"No, I'm not," I said defiantly. "Look."

By this time I had a Ms. Piggy T-shirt and I pulled it down so he could see my magic mark.

"That looks like cocky and I can see your titties."

"Asshole," I said. I had recently learned that word and wasn't as afraid to say it as I was the f-word.

"I think your neck is dirty," my first boyfriend said as he was awkwardly trying to unhook my bra. "You got chocolate on it."

"No," I said. "That's just my beauty mark."

"Oh," he said. Then, his mission successful, he became distracted.

I was no longer pleased with my abnormality. I tried to cover it up with makeup, turtlenecks and scarves. I rarely wore anything low cut.

In college a boy told me that the sexiest part of a woman was her clavicle. My ugly mark sat directly above my clavicle. I thought it was getting darker as I got older.

I tried everything.

Then, in the course of about a year, three of my good friends decided to get married. Each woman asked me to be her bridesmaid. And every time I joined my pal and her other bridesmaids for the mandatory stab at the ego known as dress shopping, I watched them register the way my mark looked in any number of ill-fitting but revealing dresses. Sure enough, each bride-to-be decided on a stole or a shawl or a jacket "for the church." But of course I knew it was to hide my deformity.

But then I published a book and finally I had a little bit of extra money. Looking back, I probably should have invested it or maybe I could have used it to pay some bills or spent it on part of a down payment on actually buying an apartment instead of renting. But I didn't and now I wish I had.

I found the offices of Dr. Tickle through a colleague who got a raised mole removed. The mole was near her breast and she liked to refer to it as her third nipple.

"Insurance doesn't pay, though. They wouldn't pay for you to get that removed," she said, gesturing to my stain. I thought that I detected a bit of disgust from this three-nippled woman and I did not appreciate it.

Nevertheless, I made an appointment for consultation with Dr. Tickle and hurried to her office on Park Avenue. She shared office space with three other dermatologists. They did things like tattoo makeup on, re-move varicose veins and laser-remove hair. She had a nice selection of magazines in her office. In one magazine I read about ways to know if my man was really enjoying having sex with me or if he fantasized about having sex with someone else.

I was pretty sure that my boyfriend, Mike, was satisfied with me. He didn't even mind the neck stain I had.

"I think you're beautiful," Mike had said as he was getting ready for work that morning. He bent and kissed my clavicle and I thought I felt my map of Australia throb.

Dr. Tickle consulted me for a total of three minutes. She was going to use a laser to get rid of the offensive mark.

"It's like a little zip," she said.

I noticed a splotch on her cheek below her ear and wondered why she hadn't zipped herself.

"Will it hurt?" I asked.

"You'll feel some mild discomfort. It's a lot like getting a tattoo re-moved."

"I've never had a tattoo," I said.

"Oh," she said. "I think it will take at least three sessions. Then you can decide if you want to come back. Each of the sessions will be $300."

$900 is a lot of money. For some reason I thought my busty colleague had only paid $300 total. Apparently I was wrong. But $900 is really a small price to pay for peace of mind.

"You'll want to sign up now for time with the laser. We only rent it once a month and if you cancel within less than ten business days we will charge your card."

It just so happened that we were only eight business days from when they were renting the laser. It was do or die. Or, perhaps, it was do or continue to be discolored.

"I think you'll be a perfect candidate for this," she said.

"Okay," I said and I signed up. When I signed up, I put down a deposit of $200.

There were many other women in the waiting room on the day I went for my first appointment. I tried to gauge who was there for what. They were all reading the good magazines. I was left with *Parents* magazine and read about ways to get your child to like his or her new sibling.

Would my offspring have the same mark of the devil? But it wasn't like I could afford kids. I could barely afford peace of mind.

"Ariella Papa," Dr. Tickle said, opening the door into the waiting room.

"Hi," I said. As I got up the *Parents* magazine slid out of my lap onto the floor. I went into the room behind her. Another woman was already in the room. She had glowing and hairless skin. I wanted to reach out and touch it. Was there a foundation to make my skin look like that?

"I'm Wanda," the woman said. "I am your laser nurse."

"Hello," I said. I sat down on the table. "Ariella."

"Let me see," Wanda said efficiently. I was no longer a person, but a patient.

"Okay, *café au lait* mark, I see," Wanda said. When she said that it sounded almost as nice as "beauty mark." Like coffee, but French. I liked coffee; maybe, I thought, I could learn to like this. Maybe I should have spent the money on a trip to France.

But it was all happening fast and I had already put down a deposit.

They took Polaroid pictures of my neck. Dr. Tickle muttered, "Before and after."

This meant someday there would be an after. A clear-necked after.

Dr. Tickle and Wanda fussed at the counter for a little while. Dr. Tickle was choosing which pair of giant goggles to put over her glasses.

It was between what looked like mirrored ski goggles and large green goggles that dwarfed her glasses. She chose the large green goggles and when she turned to me, she looked like an alien hunter. The earpiece of the goggle extended to just above her own birthmark. Hers looked like Massachusetts turned upside down. She was studying my neck carefully. I smiled at her, but she didn't notice.

"Okay, lie down and put these on." She handed me a pair of small copper-colored goggles that would fit right over my eyes. I lay back on the table, feeling my stomach tighten. With the goggles over my eyes I couldn't see anything. I wasn't sure I trusted the situation. Was Dr. Tickle going to remove my birthmark or was Wanda?

It didn't seem like a good idea anymore.

I was in total darkness. I didn't like it.

"You're going to feel a pinch. We'll start with a small amount and then will turn it up," Dr. Tickle said. Her voice was far away. A small amount of what? Then I heard three small beeps and felt my neck pinch and burn. My eyes filled with tears and my hands closed around my thumbs.

"You're responding very well," Dr. Tickle said. I didn't think I was. I hated it. "I think we can turn it up."

Beep. Beep. Beep.

Whatever was being turned up hurt. I didn't think I could take it.

Beep. Beep. Beep.

Can I just get up and go? I thought. *This is too much. I will live with the birthmark. I just don't want another—*

Beep. Beep. Beep.

"Let's see if we got everything," Dr. Tickle said. *Please let them have gotten everything.*

"I think we just need a little more over here," Wanda said. *Over where?*

Beep. Beep. Beep.

Oh, over there. I hadn't thought it was even that big. Even the continent of Australia wouldn't have been that big. I was going to stop them.

"Okay, uh, Adrienne, uh, Ari-Ariella," Dr. Tickle said. "You're all done."

I wished that if she was going to make my skin feel like it was burned off, she could remember my name.

"Thanks," I said. I pulled off the goggles and sat up on the table. Dr. Tickle handed me a tissue to wipe my teary eyes.

"It's already fading," Dr. Tickle said. She brought a small mirror over to me. I looked into it, lifting my chin. It had faded a little, but not much.

"It will fade even more over the next couple of weeks. Make sure you make your appointment now for next month. We already know what day we'll have the laser."

My neck was stinging and I patted it as I handed the receptionist my credit card and made my next appointment with the laser.

"I don't really see a difference," Mike said later in the evening. He was standing behind me looking at my reflection in the bathroom mirror. "It looks the same to me. I think it's a waste of money."

"I know how you feel," I said. I hate when he's right.

We went to bed. My neck was still kind of stinging. Dr. Tickle had said I should expect a slight chance of redness. It was less than one percent. She'd never mentioned stinging post zipping. I thwarted Mike's efforts at intimacy with a loud obnoxious yawn.

"Okay, baby," he said and wrapped me up in his arms. "Good night."

I didn't fall asleep for a long time, but when I did I dreamt I was sitting at a big round table and everyone I know—although perhaps it was only eight of my girlfriends—was staring at me. They were staring at my birthmark.

"You have it because you like to write," said one.

"A birthmark?" I was confused.

"No," another said laughing. Then, as you can do in dreams, I switched places with her. I became her and I could see myself. Instead of having a birth mark, I had a—

"Ugghh." I sat up in bed. I looked at the clock. 7:30. Mike didn't have to wake up for another hour and a half. I rubbed my neck. It felt crusty. Shit! I got up and went to the bathroom.

The only light in the bathroom was the Frida Kahlo nightlight, but it was much brighter than ever. Something was wrong. Instinctively, I went to flip the switch, but I realized I could see without it.

I inhaled when I saw it. My birthmark hadn't faded. Instead I had an eye. I screamed. I heard Mike race in. I was on the floor.

"Did you see a mouse?" he asked, turning on the light. He looked down at me and then rubbed his eyes with his knuckles. I wanted his face to be normal when he looked at me again, but it wasn't. He pointed at me.

"Did you, shit, did you get something? Did you get a tattoo?"

"No," I said. I was really scared. I thought I was still dreaming, but I felt the cold tiles beneath me. I started to breathe deep. Mike gave me his hand and I took it and stood up. I didn't look back into the mirror. I couldn't.

"I'll get you some water," he said and he left the bathroom.

When he came back he held the water out to me. He didn't look at me. I think he was doing the same test on me that I had been doing on myself. He thought it would just go away.

"Look at me," I said. "Look at it."

"I—" He shook his head. He didn't want to, but then he did.

"Is it still there?" I asked. Mike nodded very slowly. He looked like he was going to cry.

I turned toward the mirror with my eyes closed. I felt him put his hands on my shoulders.

Before I opened my eyes, I noticed that I could see myself looking in the mirror with my eyes closed. I could see myself and I had an eye above my clavicle. I opened my eyes, the two that I controlled. The room was brighter. My third eye blinked.

"It doesn't even match," I said, verging on hysterics. "It doesn't even match."

"It's okay," Mike said. He kissed the back of my head. "It's okay, shh!"

It was true. The third eye was nothing like my other two. It was much darker. It was as if it was lined in kohl naturally. It was almost almond-shaped, the lashes were long and the pupil was dark. On another woman it would have been beautiful. If there were two of them in the right place.

"Oh my God!"

"We'll call the doctor," he said. "We'll call the doctor first thing."

"Now," I said. "Let's call her now. Let's go to the emergency room."

"No," he said quietly. "Let's go back to bed."

I shook my head. He insisted. Maybe he still thought this was a dream. Maybe he was right. I didn't know if the dream was his or mine. I didn't know why either of us would dream this.

We went back to bed. I closed my eyes, but I still saw my ceiling. I tried hard to control my third eye, without really wanting to believe it was there. If I touched it I would be admitting defeat. I would be giving it permission to be real. But if I was dreaming I needed to get back to sleep.

"Spoon," Mike said sleepily and I turned so he could spoon me. I pulled a blanket up over my third eye.

After another hour, the alarm went off. I hit snooze. Usually Mike slept through it, but I could feel that he was already awake. He was spooning me so he couldn't see it, but the room felt too bright and so I suspected the eye was still there.

"Do you want me to look?" Mike asked.

"Yes," I whispered. But I knew what he was going to find.

I turned and he sat up in bed on his elbow and looked down at me. He let his breath out deep through his nose.

"It's there, isn't it?"

"Yes," he said. "Do you want me to call the doctor?"

"No," I said, getting up. "I will."

I still freelance for television part time, but I was off that day. It was a writing day. I was working on a book called *Up and Out*. But I didn't think I was going to get much done. I called Dr. Tickle's office. The receptionist answered. I had been so innocent the day before when I handed over my credit card and everything was a little dimmer.

"I need to speak with Dr. Tickle. I need to come in and see her."

"I'm sorry, Dr. Tickle started her vacation today and she will not be back for another two weeks."

"You're fucking kidding me!" I yelled into the phone. I reached up and wiped my third eye. It began to itch. The brightness subsided while my hand was in the way.

"I don't respond to that kind of language," the receptionist said. She hung up on me.

"Fuck!" I screamed and flung the phone across the room. Mike came in to the living room from the bathroom. There was shaving cream on half of his face. Thin white lines divided the other half where he already shaved.

"What happened?"

"I cursed at the receptionist. She said the doctor is out for two weeks."

"Convenient," he said.

"Why convenient? This is weird. I can see out of this eye, you know. I can see you better than ever."

"Do you like what you see?" He smiled and did a pirouette.

"This is no time to be cute," I said.

"Well, call back," he said.

"How do we even know that she did this? I mean, how could she?"

"I don't know," he said. "I think you should call back. See another doctor."

He was right. I'd never told the receptionist my name; maybe she wouldn't recognize my voice. I called back. He stood by me, watching me punch the numbers, sneaking glances at my neck.

"Hi," I said. I tried to sound much cheerier than I had before. "I would like to make an appointment with one of your dermatologists."

"Did you call already? Are you the one that called and cursed at me?"

"I didn't curse at you. I cursed—" I looked at Mike for help and he shrugged and looked away from my neck. "I just cursed."

"Well, I don't respond to that kind of language."

"I know, you said. I'm sorry. I just began to get a birthmark removed yesterday. Now, I have an emergency."

"I'm certain that you signed a release."

"You don't understand," I said. Above me, Mike mouthed, *Calm down.* "I have an emergency. It's not like a scar or a rash—that's what I signed the release for—this is different. I have an eye."

"An eye?"

"Yes, you know, like you see out of." I shook my head and might have whispered, "Shit."

"Look, I don't have time to be cursed at." The receptionist was getting frustrated with me. Who could blame her? I wouldn't believe me either if I hadn't seen it with my own eyes. Jesus. "And I don't have time for games."

"It's not a game. I really have an eye, a seeing eye. In my neck. I need to see a doctor. You don't want to be responsible for a lawsuit, do you?" Mike slapped his head with his hand. I knew I had gone too far.

"Are you threatening me now? Cursing wasn't enough for you?"

"Don't hang up! Just get me an appointment with someone else. This really is an emergency." I was pleading now.

"Well, I'm sorry, you are Dr. Tickle's patient. You are going to have to wait until she comes back to get your eye out." Something in her tone said that she didn't believe me.

"Is there any way you can get in touch with her?" I was trying, really trying, to be sweet to this woman.

"I can leave a message with her service. I'll let her know what your emergency is and she will decide when to get back to you."

"What am I supposed to do until then?"

"I don't know, buy some makeup." The comedienne hung up.

I looked up at Mike. I'd never noticed how big the pores were in his skin.

"Do you want me to stay home?" he asked. Mike works for a popular music video channel. Instead of playing music videos they have shows about the fifty best songs to have sex to. Mike works on those shows. He can tell me the number one song for almost everything we want to do in our lives, although I doubt there is a number one song to get another eye removed.

"No," I said. "Don't stay."

"What are you going to do?"

"What should I do?"

"Do you want to go to the emergency room?"

"Well, I'm not really in pain. And I'm not sure I want to go out like this. What if it gets out? I don't want people to see what a freak I am." Any minute I was going to lose it.

"Maybe it will go away."

"Does it look like it's getting lighter? Does it look like it's going away?"

"No," he said. "Are you going to be okay?"

"Yes," I said. But I wasn't sure.

He returned to shaving and kissed me goodbye before he left.

When he was gone I wiped the foggy mirror and stared at the third eye. It really was beautiful. I tried hard to control it. It was impossible to make it open and close. But I was watching myself look at myself in the mirror.

All of a sudden the third eye winked at me. It was playing with me. I laughed. I reached up to touch the lashes. My third eye closed in a seductive way and reopened.

Then Mike was at the door to the bathroom. "Didn't you get dressed?"

"You're home early," I said.

"Actually, I'm late. I was trying to call you. I thought you were out."

"No," I said. I was confused. "What time is it?"

"It's 8:00."

"It's 8:00 P.M.?"

"Yeah, what have you been doing all day?"

"I don't know," I said, looking around the bathroom. "I guess I've been here."

I helped Mike make dinner, but between stirring the stir-fry I kept going back into the bathroom to sneak looks at my eye. I didn't want to not be able to see it. And I didn't really care about how much clearer I could see textures and shapes. I just wanted to look at it and I wanted to watch myself looking at it.

Mike came to watch me from the bathroom door. I could barely bring myself to look at him, but I did. I turned to him, but my third eye kept looking at the mirror so I could see myself look at him. Was that how I always looked at him? It was nice. I looked at Mike with love.

"You look happy," I said.

"I am."

"Well, do you want to eat?" I thought about asking him to eat in the bathroom, but I didn't think I wanted him to know how much I wanted to look at the eye. I admit now that it was pretty weird.

We sat at the coffee table and watched TV while we ate chicken and veggie stir-fry. The dinner was really good. Mike likes watching certain sitcoms sometimes. He thinks sitcoms are dying out. He thinks they will be replaced by reality shows and countdowns. He worships the few remaining sitcoms that exist. He gets sucked in.

I excused myself to go look in the bathroom mirror after every three bites.

"Are you feeling okay?" he asked during the commercial. I saw him glance at the third eye.

"I'm fine."

"Maybe you should put a scarf on," he said.

"I'm not cold," I replied.

When we went to bed, my third eye stayed open for a while looking around my darkened room. But after a while, it closed like the other two.

In the morning I raced to the bathroom before the alarm went off. I was relieved to see it was still there. It made me special.

I heard the alarm go off in my room. Usually I would try to wake Mike up gently, but that day, I didn't want to lose my spot at the mirror.

"Mike!" I shouted from the bathroom. He didn't answer. "Mike."

My third eye closed each time I yelled, like I was speaking too loud.

So I stopped yelling and Mike overslept.

He was annoyed when he came into the bathroom. He was also in a rush. I like to look at him rumpled in the morning and sweet, but this morning I just sort of glanced at him and patted him and didn't apologize for not waking him up.

"Can I stay in here while you take a shower?"

"If you want," he said. "Are you going to try to get out of the bathroom today?"

"I don't know." I lost track of time when I looked at my third eye. He was out of the shower in what seemed like seconds.

"Ariella, I need to brush my teeth."

"Okay," I said, still studying the eye.

"I mean I need to use the mirror."

"Oh, right," I said. I grabbed a small compact from the bathroom drawer. I opened it and sat outside the bathroom looking at my third eye in the smaller mirror.

"Are you almost done?" I asked repeatedly. Now it seemed like time was going slower. How thoroughly did he need to brush his teeth?

"All yours," he said, coming out of the bathroom. I resumed my post looking at my third eye and watching myself look at it. I sensed that Mike was still nearby, but I didn't look at him.

"Don't you have to work today?"

"No," I said. It was another writing day. I don't think of writing as work. Although I knew that if I spent that day as I spent the last one, I would get off my schedule.

"When are you working again?" I don't think he believed me. I think he was starting to suspect something. I think he thought I would purposely miss work for the eye.

"I have a video edit tomorrow." I was working on some promos for a new kids' show.

"Okay," he said.

The phone rang many times throughout the day, but I couldn't get it. I mean I could have, but that would have meant leaving the bathroom. I couldn't bring myself to leave the bathroom. I had to go to my edit the next day. I was getting paid for it. But I didn't know how I was going to handle it.

The thought of not spending the day with my eye made me start to cry. My third eye, seeing my tears, squinted.

Perhaps crying is something this eye will not do, I thought. *My third eye is a triumphant happy creature.*

I stopped crying, comforted by the victorious eye.

My third eye was amazing.

"Were you in here all day?" Mike said, startling me. I didn't hear him come in, even though the bathroom is right next to the door. I took his hand and pulled him into the bathroom so my third eye could look at him in the mirror without my two other eyes having to stop looking at my third eye.

He smiled at me. I smiled back, but I wasn't sure if I was smiling at him or at my third eye.

"Can we eat in here?" I asked. He stopped smiling.

"I'm not hungry."

I stayed in the bathroom until the middle of the night when my two eyes started to look tired. I crawled into bed where Mike was already sleeping. I reached up and rubbed my third eye's lid until it closed.

I was late for my edit, of course. I had trouble brushing my teeth quickly. I liked watching my eye react to my morning beauty routine. And it hurt to put a turtleneck on. As I walked to the edit facility, I wondered if my eye was scared when it felt the cold of the outside world and couldn't see it. I rubbed my neck gently to soothe it.

I snuck to the bathroom many times throughout the session. The way the edit room was set up, my editor sat in front of me at an Avid and I sat behind him with a laptop opened. I kept my small compact on the keyboard. I tugged down the neck of my turtleneck while my editor was busy color-correcting shots with his back to me. It was a small mirror, but I made do and I was glad to see I could survive the outside world with my eye.

On the way home from my edit, I stopped and bought a small hand mirror. It was much bigger than the compact, but smaller than my bathroom cabinet mirror. This would be perfect for the situations when I had to leave the safety of the bathroom. I preferred to spend the day alone with my special eye, but I knew that it wasn't practical.

I made Mike dinner that night, because he was working late. I made stuffed shells. I kept my new hand mirror next to me on the kitchen counter. I stirred the ricotta cheese and nutmeg with one hand and held the mirror in another.

I wondered if my eye ever got hungry.

I set the table. We were going to eat at the table, not on the couch. I wanted to allay Mike's fears.

When Mike came home, I handed him a glass of wine. I could tell he was impressed that I set the table.

"*Bon appetit!*" I said as we started to eat.

"This is delicious," he said. "You made a great dinner."

"Why, thank you," I said. I thought it was safe to take a peek at my neck eye. I stashed my mirror on one of the chairs and I picked it up and twisted carefully to get a true reflection of the eye. I heard Mike sigh and it took me a second before I could make myself look at him with any of my eyes.

"Did you call the doctor?"

"She's on vacation," I said, still not really looking at him. I heard him scrape his fork along the plate. He made an annoyed noise, but I wasn't finished looking at my eye yet.

"What about one of the other doctors?"

"I can't, Mike. Dr. Tickle is my doctor."

"Well, you can't just walk around with that on your neck!"

"Why not? I feel great. I see great." I brought the hand mirror back down to the table, but I still glanced at it as stealthily as possible.

"Your eye gives me the stink eye," he said.

"I don't know what to say. Maybe because it knows that you hate it."

"So now you think it has a mind of its own?"

"I just think you should be nice to it."

"Are you losing it?"

"No, I feel very normal."

"Well, it isn't normal."

"It is," I insisted. "It's special. It's unique."

"I can't believe you are just accepting this."

"Why not?"

He shook his head and gathered up the dishes. We didn't say anything to each other for the rest of the night.

That night in bed, I felt Mike's hand creep up to my neck in his sleep. I pulled it away and held tight to his fingers.

I should have been working on my novel, but every moment not in edits trying to get the launch campaign of a show off the ground, I stared into the mirror.

The dream I'd had on the eve of the neck eye said it was supposed to help me write. Instead, my neck eye distracted me from everything.

My friend Kathleen came over one day after work. I could imagine how strange it was for someone new to see, so I tied a silk scarf around my neck. As soon as she came in, I knew she knew already. Her eyes kept glancing to my neck. I suspected Mike told her boyfriend Matt who told her.

"What's going on?" There was a little bit of a smile on her mouth. We were sitting on the couch. My hand mirror was so close by, but to look at my neck eye I had to tell her.

"I'm fine. Excuse me." I ran to the bathroom. I pulled down the scarf. My neck eye winked at me. Should it be our little secret?

Kat knew, but she hadn't seen it. Did I dare share it with her? I knew she would be upset if she knew it was there but I didn't show her. I should have been proud of it; it was beautiful.

I looked at my third eye and it met my two eyes directly. Okay, we would tell her.

I grabbed two beers from the fridge and went back into the living room, where she was seemingly immersed in a *Shape* magazine. I wasn't fooled.

"So I got my birthmark removed," I said.

"You did?" she said, relieved to be able to openly glance at my neck. She is not a good liar. I felt like we were reading off a script. "How does it look?"

"Well," I said, removing my scarf. "See for yourself."

Her two eyes widened. Her mouth formed a little "o". She was speechless, and then she covered her mouth with her hands. I couldn't tell if she was horrified or mystified or what.

"Well, what do you think?"

She shook her head. "It's beautiful."

I took a deep breath and smiled. I was free to look in my hand mirror. What a relief.

"Thank you," I said. "Other than Mike you're the first one to see it."

"You are so lucky," she said.

"Did you know?"

"Yes," she owned up. "But I never imagined it could be like that. Oh, it just winked at me."

"It does that," I said. We giggled at the sheer joy and beauty of my neck eye.

"Nice job telling Matt," I said to Mike when he got home.

"I needed to tell someone," he said. He sat on the bed and rubbed his hands over his face. I couldn't resist a quick peek in the mirror when his eyes couldn't see me.

"Why? It's my thing." My voice grew soft, calmed by the sight of my neck eye and how sad he looked.

"It's just so weird," he said.

"It's another part of me," I said. "I accept it. Why can't you?"

"I don't know," he said. He looked at me and then looked down at the eye. I watched him with both eyes as my third eye looked at him directly. "I guess it is sort of pretty."

"Yes, it is," I said.

Then he kissed me and I felt my third eye fluttering closed.

I went out to dinner with my friend Mia. We wound up at a restaurant in Chinatown. We were sitting at a big round table with strangers.

I feel comfortable with Mia and there isn't much I wouldn't tell her, but I didn't know how to break it to her. I was wearing a hoodie sweatshirt. I think I was starting to push the limits. If the eye had an eyebrow that it raised, it would have been visible over the top of my collar.

I wanted to be open about my eye. I wanted the entire table to see it. It would be perfect. Why should I deny them? If only their faces were mirrors.

"You seem distracted," Mia said. She is a therapist and thus extremely intuitive. "Is it Mike?"

"No," I said. "Well, not really. It's me."

How could I tell her that I couldn't stop looking at a part of myself? I had become obsessed. She is not my therapist, I don't have a therapist, but if she had been she might have said I was a narcissist or a bigger, scarier term that I'd never even heard of.

I slurped up one of the delicious pork dumplings. Some of the broth inside the dumpling dribbled down my chin and neck and into my eye. I rubbed my neck over my shirt.

We went to another bar on Mott Street, Double Happiness. I worried that the smoke would bother my third eye and it had already been through too much. But I hadn't seen Mia in a while and I was anxious to spend time with her.

She sat facing the door and I sat across from her facing the wall. It was dark and the music was loud. No one was paying attention to us except the waitress who brought us drinks.

Mia was talking about a boy, but I couldn't hear her very well over the music and I couldn't concentrate, because all I could think about was the moment I could show her my neck eye. I wanted to again feel the relief I felt when I showed Kathleen.

I wanted to see her think it was beautiful. I didn't want to be a freak.

We got another round and I decided to interrupt. I couldn't risk the waitress coming back in the middle of my story. I told her. I had to explain a lot to her. This woman, who had known me since I was three, didn't even remember I had a birthmark.

"Don't you remember it looked like Australia?" These were not the details I wanted to get stuck on.

"Kind of," she said, glancing down at my neck. "I never really noticed. Is it completely gone?"

"Well, yes. But I got an eye in its place." She tipped her head.

"Ariella, what do you mean an eye?" I pointed to one of the two she was already familiar with.

"Like this." I wondered if she gave her clients that look, but I don't think she would risk making them think they were as crazy as her look made me feel. "Forget it. Just forget I said anything."

"No," she said, reaching across the table. "Let me see."

Before I could stop her or adequately prepare her, she unzipped my sweatshirt. I suddenly saw her more clearly. She pulled her head back.

"You see," I said. I felt slightly triumphant. I wasn't crazy after all.

The waitress came back to see if we wanted another round and I zipped my shirt up quickly. The place was dark again. We ordered more drinks and when they arrived I asked Mia to continue her story.

"Why don't you unzip your sweatshirt a little? I didn't really get to see it." I suspect she was hypnotized by it already. It was a rare and wonderful thing. I nervously unzipped a little. I knew it was still too soon to unleash my eye on the world.

"Okay," I said. "Just don't stare at it. Tell your story. Act normal, in spite of everything."

Mia told me the rest of her saga. She was pretty good about not staring, but she did keep glancing down at my neck eye. When she finished and before I could offer my opinion she said, "Wow! I feel so much better now."

"Well, I'm glad," I said. "Sometimes you just need to talk about it."

I was prepared to offer her some other friendship cliché, but she shook her head.

"It was the eye," she said. "I felt like you or it were really listening to me. There is so much compassion in that eye."

"Thank you," I said. I saw her eyes fill with tears. "What is it? I thought you felt better."

"It's so beautiful to be looked at like that. I wish I could look at my clients like that. I wish I had a third eye of my own."

Mia spent a great deal of time convincing me that the eye was something I should be proud of. I remember one time she told me that therapists don't really advise you, they ask you questions until you come to the conclusion that was inside you all along.

I have always trusted Mia's advice, but now that she is a licensed therapist I feel that her advice or leading me to the water or whatever you want to call it is even better.

When I got home I stood at the foot of the bed looking at Mike until he woke up.

"Jesus," he said, sitting up in bed. "Why didn't you turn a light on?"

"Sorry," I said. I sat on the bed. "I didn't need it."

"How was your night?"

"It was a lot of fun. Mia's doing well."

"Good," he said. He turned over and cuddled with our stuffed monkey.

"Can I talk to you for a minute?"

"Mmm," he said, already falling back to sleep.

"Mike," I said. I knew I sounded annoyed, but it was serious.

"Okay, sure." He sat up and switched the light on. I had taken off my sweatshirt. He glanced at my eye and looked away.

"I thought you were getting used to it. The other night I thought you liked it."

"I did," he said. "I do."

I raised my two eyebrows at him, unsure how my third eye was acting.

"Okay," I said. He looked me squarely in the eye. "I'm not going to be afraid anymore. I'm going to let everyone see the eye."

"What?" Now he looked back at my two original eyes.

"Yes, I don't mind. In fact, I really like it. I'm going to wear a v-neck for once in my life. I'm going to let the eye free for Lars Lundgren's Halloween party."

"You're kidding."

"I'm serious. I'm not asking you for permission. I'm just letting you know how it is. I don't want you to be embarrassed." This was a test. Therapist Mia would not approve.

"I'm not embarrassed," he said, reaching out to me and thus passing my test with flying colors. "Do you think people are ready for it?"

"That's why I thought it would be easy to do on Halloween. You know everyone is expecting the unexpected. This is certainly unexpected."

"You know that Matt told me that all that Kathleen does now is doodle your neck. She's become obsessed with it." Kat loves to doodle. It's a lost art. She filled notebooks with doodles, she covered any paper she could get her hands on. I was flattered that my eye was the new subject of her doodles.

"So have I."

"Just be careful. You got a message from your editor today. The book is supposed to be delivered at the end of next week."

Fuck! The book. I'd forgotten all about it. I'd forgotten what it was that was giving me all this free me-time. I was only halfway done.

"I know," I lied. "I'll spend the whole day working on it tomorrow."

Instead of working on my book, I worked on my Halloween costume. I have always hated dressing up. Ever since the Tylenol scare when we lived in Queens and my parents decided that a fun thing would be for me to not be allowed to go out. Instead I went to each of the four rooms of our apartment where I found my parents pretending to be other people who would give me candy free of razor blades. Since then I haven't really cared about dressing up.

But this year would be different. It was like my eye was having a debutante party. I loved it, but was I ready to be on display?

"You look hot," Pat Connolly said in Lars Lundgren's backyard. He is a friend of Mike's, but instead of noticing my third eye, he was nodding at my cleavage. He had never seen it before. Very few people had.

"Thanks," I said. "What are you supposed to be?"

"A vampire rock star. You?"

"Um, a goth with a third eye."

"Yeah, that's cool," he said. His eyes were still directed to my below my third eye. "I bet you could wear that shirt again, you know, when it's not Halloween."

Mike, who was getting a lot of leverage out of the alien homeboy costume he got last year at Ricky's, brought me a bottle of Negra Modelo and kissed my long black wig.

"Are you cold?"

"No," I said. We were out in Lundgren's yard in Brooklyn. I saw Kathleen's boyfriend. I hoped to see Kathleen, but Matt said she stayed home.

"To doodle," he said. He and Mike shook their heads.

I weaved my way through goblins, cheerleaders and the people who like to wear those ironic costumes it takes you a long time to understand to the bathroom line. Clowns and belly dancers were grooving in the living room; they couldn't have cared less about my third eye. Maybe Halloween was the wrong time for the eye to come out. Maybe it wasn't that big a deal after all. I waited in the bathroom line. No one saw the eye. Then the bathroom door opened and a man came out. He looked directly at my eye.

"That's cool," he said. He came closer to me and bent to look at it. I got a whiff of strong cologne. *He must be foreign*, I thought. I detected an accent.

"Thank you."

"How did you do it?" He reached up to touch my throat and let his fingers fall over my eyelashes. Then he gasped when he discovered it was for real and smiled up into my original two eyes. "It's incredible."

My eye spread a joy throughout my body, but it was the kind of joy that makes you feel guilty and ashamed. This man could have been the soul mate of my third eye. Perhaps it's true that foreign men appreciate women's bodies more than American men. Somehow my eye pulled me closer to his face. I was no longer in control. Any minute I was going to put my hands on his shoulders and either push myself away or bring myself closer.

It was my shoulders that felt hands, not his hands, but Mike's. Mike introduced himself to the guy, whose name was Bartholomew. What a name!

"I see you already met my girlfriend and her eye," Mike said. He glared at me.

"Yes, it's quite extraordinary."

"Yeah," said Mike in a way that wasn't impressed with the eye, me or Bartholomew.

"Well, nice to meet you," Bartholomew said. Then he left.

"I called a car service to take us home," Mike said. "It will be here in five minutes."

When Mike turned to start saying his goodbyes, I wanted to study his face, but instead I saw his alien mask on the back of his head.

I understood then why I always hated Halloween.

Mike didn't say a word in the car as we crossed the Manhattan Bridge. I didn't either, although I had a lot to say. The man driving us was listening to a Spanish radio station that sounded like a lot of fun. All I understood was "cuarenta y cinco" which I think means "forty-five" and the disc jockey said it over and over again.

Mike didn't say a word as we got ready for bed. He threw his alien mask on the couch. The giant one-piece that made up his homeboy outfit was stashed in a corner. I washed all the makeup off my two real eyes and gently washed the eye shadow off the third eye. I twisted from side to side to get a look at my breasts in the v-neck. My third eye followed, enjoying it, too.

Mike didn't say a word when I got into bed, but my third eye could see that he was awake and looking at me. I wished he would realize how powerful it was. The silent treatment was more my tactic than his. He didn't know how to do it properly, so he turned to *harrumph*ing.

"Do you want to talk about something?" I switched on the light. I wanted him to be able to see, too.

"No."

"You said you weren't embarrassed."

"I'm not."

"As soon as we got there you were trying to cover me up."

"I just thought you were cold. It was cold."

"It was cold, but you had ulterior motives. I am proud of it. I like it."

"It was flirting with a guy in the bathroom line."

"I can't control it."

"That's the problem, don't you see? It was batting its eyelashes at some other guy." He looked at my eye and slammed the wall with his hand.

"You are getting a little too excited."

"It just rolled its eye at me."

"I can't control it!" I screamed. And then he reinstated the silent treatment.

He didn't say a word in the morning. The alarm went off and he got up. The moment he was out of the room I checked the eye in the hand mirror.

I knew I had a problem.

The first step is acceptance.

I took the cordless phone into the bathroom. I had no control over the eye and I was beginning to feel like I had no control over anything. I thought I might have to call someone for help.

The eye stared directly at me. Occasionally it narrowed, angrily.

"Don't you ever cry?" I asked it, but there was no way to know the answer. Maybe I could teach it a blinking Morse code. Maybe I should cut it out.

The phone rang. I answered. Maybe help was calling me. No such luck, it was my editor.

"Ariella, the book is due. If we want it to be published on schedule it needs to start being edited."

"I know," I said. She was right, but I couldn't bring myself to leave the bathroom. I just wanted to look at the eye. I lied, assuring her that it would be done in time.

"You were supposed to help me," I said to the eye when I got off the phone. I was trying to remind it of the dream.

The phone rang again. With all my heart I wished that it were Mike. It wasn't.

"Ariella, this is Dr. Tickle."

"Hi," I said. Suddenly I wanted to cry. "How was your trip?"

"It was wonderful. The Greek islands are wonderful this time of the year."

"How nice." My eye was looking at me spitefully, daringly. I could not control it, but it thought it could control me.

"I got a very curious message. Whoever wrote this has atrocious handwriting. It says here—" She laughed, nervously. "It says you got an eye where your birthmark was."

"I did." I heard her gasp, but she covered.

"Actually, that's a quite normal side effect, but I assume you'll want to get it removed."

"Yes," I said. The eye widened in horror. So I said more for the eye than Dr. Tickle, "How about that?"

"Well, have you gotten a second opinion?" I heard worry in her tone. She was thinking lawsuit. I toyed with that idea for a minute, but I wanted it out. I wanted to go back to being in control, to meeting my deadlines, to enjoying my boyfriend.

"No."

"Well, why don't you come in as soon as you can? How is this evening around 6:30?" I found it extremely suspicious that Dr. Tickle had no other patients, but I was desperate to rip it out.

I wanted to be normal again. Not beautiful, not special, just normal.

And that was this morning. I wrapped my neck up in a scarf and refused to look at it anymore. I had second thoughts my entire way over to Dr. Tickle's office on Park Avenue. For once there is no one in Dr. Tickle's waiting room. The magazines have all been put away. The receptionist is the only one here.

As soon as I give the receptionist (the one I cursed at?) my name, she hurries me back to the examining room. Within seconds, Dr. Tickle is at my side.

"Can I see it?" I unwrap my scarf. I see her face and understand through my third eye that she is petrified. In all nineteen years of being a certified dermatologist, she has never seen anything like this.

I don't know how I know this, I just do.

"Well?" It takes her a moment to compose herself.

"Well, I rented a laser to take it off."

"Where's Wanda?"

"Wanda?"

"The nurse that was here the last time."

"I don't need the nurse. It's like removing a mole. I can do it by my-self."

"Okay," I shrug. This is all kind of sketchy, but I'm desperate. I take my hand mirror out of my jacket pocket and look at my eye one last time. It looks afraid. If only it had behaved, it wouldn't have had to be like this.

"Now, I just want to let you know the up- and downsides of this," Dr. Tickle says.

"There's a downside?"

"Yes, you are going to have a scar." All of this was for nothing. "But I will help you remove it, free of charge."

"Thanks," I say. It's about time I got something out of this.

She starts to push me back on the table. "Is there anything else?"

"There is an eighty-eight percent chance you will live."

I sit back up on the table. Our faces almost collide. "Does that mean I might die?"

"It's very unlikely," she says. Her voice is shaking. "Very unlikely."

"Twelve percent is pretty likely."

"It's just because it's so close to the jugular."

"I'm not sure." Maybe I should get a second opinion from a lawyer.

"Honestly, what kind of life will you have if you don't?" She is, at last, firm and confident. "You have to get it removed."

"I guess you're right."

"I am," she says. "You know, I want to take a picture first."

"Take two," I say and she snaps the Polaroid twice. She gives me one of the pictures and I shake it as she once again lays me back on the table.

She covers my two eyes with the goggles I can't see through. I can still see her through my third eye. It makes her uncomfortable. I don't see her true disgust until she has my eyes covered. It's funny that she never asked me if this eye could see.

I have to do this. I can't have my eye tempting everyone. It was cool for a while, but it's gotten out of control. I suppose I could sue and live with it, but I don't want to be fodder for talk show hosts. I don't want to be a Hot Topic on *The View*. I just want to go back to how things were. Sure, I'll never wear deep v-neck sweaters that accentuate my décolletage, but I will have a boyfriend who loves me and can look at me.

Whatever happens, it's worth it. I am going to be normal, somehow.

My third eye starts to cloud and goes out of focus as Dr. Tickle lines the laser up with it. Tears. Tears fill my third eye, at last. They drip down into my bra.

"Are you ready?" Dr. Tickle says.

"Yes." I see her sigh. She isn't certain. Nobody knows. This could be it. I am not in control.

"Here we go," she says and bites her lower lip.

BEEP. BEEP. BEEP.

ARIELLA PAPA is the author of the novels *On The Verge*, *Up & Out* and *Bundle of Joy?* She is also a freelance television writer and producer. She lives in Brooklyn, New York, with her husband Mike and her dog Sophie. You can visit her online at www.ariellapapa.com.

Cara Lockwood

I tried to explain chick-lit to my dad for the first time a couple of years ago. I told him that chick-lit books are typically funny, sometimes endearing, stories about women in their twenties and thirties struggling to make sense of the world.

My dad—a man's man who played high-school football and earned the nickname "The Tank" for mowing down opposing players, and currently does not feel comfortable talking for long periods about anything but sports—said, "But why are they naming your book after the gum?"

It took a bit more explaining. Not Chic-let. But chick-lit.

"Oh, like chick flicks," he said, realization dawning.

"Yes, just like chick flicks."

"Hmpf," he said, considering. "Well, you know what? Who cares what they call it? A good book is a good book. A good movie is a good movie. End of story."

And that's how I feel about chick-lit. There are some great chick-lit books out there. And it really doesn't matter what you call them. Funny and engaging stories are always going to have a place on the bookshelf. So who cares what we call them? Let's just enjoy reading them.

The Commitment Phobe

The Problem

Kate believes her relationship with Pete will end in one of two ways: either he will marry her, or she will kill him.

It is really quite simple.

She's been patient for three years. Three whole years. That's eighteen months longer than she's been patient with anyone else, and by now almost all of her friends are beginning to think Pete is one of *those* guys, a Relationship Squatter. The kind who never intends to marry you, but who feels perfectly content to make sure you don't marry anyone else, either.

Kate is twenty-eight. She's already two years past the average age of brides in the nation. She's running out of time to find Mr. Right. Her eggs are already in decline, and she wants three kids. She can't afford to lounge around and hope Pete makes up his mind one day.

Not that Kate is keeping score, but she can't help but notice that in the time she has known Pete, five of her friends have married. Two of them have had children. Three of them bought houses in the suburbs. And, as Pete likes to point out with unnatural enthusiasm, one got divorced.

Kate has been more than patient. What is she? A leased car? Like every woman, of a certain age, with a certain boyfriend, she has come to that turning point—either this is going all the way or it isn't going anywhere at all.

"What you need is to give him an ultimatum," says her friend Liz, the only married friend of her circle who admits readily that she had to pack her husband's bags and throw them on the sidewalk before he proposed.

"That doesn't work. It always backfires," says Stacey, who lost her last boyfriend because she put too much pressure on too early. "You don't want to scare him off. Just give him a lot of obvious hints."

All of Kate's friends, married and single, have an opinion on this subject. All of them feel like they know exactly what Kate's problem is, and how to fix it.

"You have to tell men how things are. They'll never figure it out for themselves," Liz says. "They're like dogs. They respond to simple commands. And a rolled-up newspaper doesn't hurt, either."

"I thought you were supposed to use positive reinforcement," Stacey says.

"Whatever. The point is men need leashes, and that's what we're for." Liz takes another sip of her Shiraz. "Married men live longer than unmarried men. We're good for them, they just don't know it."

"Maybe you could just wait a little longer," Stacey suggests.

"Wait? Until when? Her ovaries shrivel up and her ass spreads three dress sizes?" Liz scoffs.

The Talk

Pete is sitting on the couch playing the latest version of some beta-level game his company, Netgamer, has designed, something involving lots of big guns and lots of green alien blood. Even slouching on the couch, Pete manages to retain his ruffled, boyish charm. His floppy brown hair, which never seems to be quite in place, is dangerously close to falling forward into his blue eyes. Pete is a ten-year-old stuck in a thirty-one-year-old's body. He is Tom Hanks in *Big*.

"Pete, we need to talk," Kate says in a tone that implies he ought to hit the pause on his controller.

Pete gives an exaggerated sigh, rolls his eyes to the ceiling and pauses his game.

"After all this time, you still don't understand game flow," he sighs.

"It's just a game."

Pete flops back on the couch in exaggerated frustration. "*Just* a game, Kate? God, you're killing me."

"Pete. Be serious. I want to talk."

"Should I get my cyanide capsules? Is it going to be one of those 'talks' that's really an interrogation? Am I going to lose testosterone just by listening?"

"You've got more than enough to spare."

"That goes without saying." Pete puts down his game controller and jokingly flexes his biceps. "Now what is it, dear?" He folds his hands in his lap and blinks rapidly to show he's listening.

"You know what this is about," Kate says, giving him a shove.

"Uh-oh. The old trick question. Hmmmm." Pete pretends to be thinking. "Okay, I got it. You're not fat."

"Wrong answer."

"You are fat?"

"Pete! Be serious."

"Okay. No, I do not think about other women when we have sex."

"Try again."

"Yes, I think you're as attractive as when we first met."

"Thank you, but that's not it, either."

"Tough one," Pete says.

"Be serious. This is a *relationship* talk."

"We're in a relationship?"

The Boyfriend

Pete is in love with Kate.

In fact, his friends have recently started to point out the evidence of this fact: how he involuntarily speaks in "we" without even noticing. How he's lost interest in nights at the pubs and marathon football watching with the boys. How he doesn't even notice anymore when other women are flirting with him, or when they are hinting around for his number. How his once-fanatical commitment to his company softball team has waned slightly (he missed three games last year alone). How his life has easily become divided into two categories: BK and AK—Before Kate and After Kate.

There's also the fact that Kate has effectively charmed all the relatives she's met—including his mother and older sister, Jenny, who reminds him almost every time they talk how lucky he is to have found a girl who's not only smart, funny and stunning, but one who will tolerate all of his bad habits (including video-game playing, fart jokes and his inability to take anything too seriously).

He has thought he will marry Kate—someday. It's like all those life plans he is perpetually putting off—like someday he'll parachute from an airplane or see the Egyptian pyramids. It's definitely on his list of things to do before he turns forty.

But what's the rush? He doesn't like dancing, and there's dancing at weddings. He also doesn't like on principle the idea of parting with three months of his salary for a diamond ring. It seems a bit lopsided to him. How come the guys don't get anything? He could go for a Jet Ski.

But this is why Kate says he's not very romantic.

The Advice

"You can't just tell him you want to get married," Liz cries, shocked, the next day at work. The two share a cubicle wall in the ad department of *Glam* magazine. "Have you even been reading our magazine?"

Liz holds up the pink fluorescent cover of the latest edition that screams "Make Him Hot, Hot, Hot, Hot for You!" and "Is Your Boyfriend a Commitment Phobe?"

"Of course I don't actually *read* the magazine," Kate says. She works in *ad sales*, for goodness' sakes. All she cares about is that her advertisers don't end up on pages opposite stories about genital warts. "All the stories are the same."

"I can't believe you just said that," Liz says, her voice dropping to a whisper. "You do know that you're *supposed* to read the magazine."

"I read my horoscope sometimes."

"You're impossible," Liz says, flipping open her dog-eared copy of *Glam*. "Read this," she commands, tapping the page with her perfectly manicured nail.

The strategy to making your guy commit, according to *Glam,* is:

1. Go out on dates with guy "friends" or ex-boyfriends (to show how independent you are)
2. Go on vacation without him (to show how independent you are)
3. Talk about moving to another country/state/city/apartment (to show how independent you are)
4. Make a big financial purchase (to show how independent you are)
5. Act as if you're already his fiancée (to show how independent you are—you don't even *need* his input to become engaged!)

"See? Only when he thinks you don't need him will he propose," Liz says. "So the last thing you want to do is *tell* him you want to be married. That's not very independent, is it?"

"You can't be serious," Kate says. "What is this? A bad episode of *I Love Lucy*? That kind of man-manipulation never works."

"It does so. Ask Carrie."

"She didn't."

"She did."

The Ring

Carrie, who oversees sales for the southern Midwest, and whom everyone generally dislikes because of her fascist-like campaign against instant-messaging in the office and because her boyfriend, Ben, sends enormous flower arrangements every week for no reason, is indeed engaged.

And she has not just a regular ring, but a diamond that could sink the *Titanic*.

"Oh my God," Kate squeaks, without even intending to. It's the largest diamond she's ever seen not on Jennifer Lopez.

It's, in fact, the exact cut and shape that Kate herself would've picked out (and has) on the Diamonds Are Forever Web site, where you can make your own engagement rings. In the last few months, Kate has spent more than a few hours on that site. It isn't healthy, she knows, but she can't help it.

"It's gorgeous," someone else says. There is a crowd of women around Carrie, her lack of popularity in the office temporarily offset by the size of the rock on her finger.

"Is it insured?" asks another.

And so on and so on.

Kate feels queasy. She always does when someone in the office gets engaged. Carrie is the third person this month. Already, the ad meetings have become impromptu jewelry shows. Every week, it seems, someone else is flashing a new diamond.

"All it took," Carrie says, eyes bright, "was one trip to Belize with an ex-boyfriend. We've been dating three years, but I haven't been back one week and Ben's already proposed."

The Plan

Kate does not have ex-boyfriends that she'd like to see for one minute, much less a whole weekend trip. This is typically why they're ex-boyfriends, and not current boyfriends.

And of course, when Kate didn't want to see them (ninety-nine percent of the time) she ran into them constantly—usually when she wasn't wearing any makeup after a sweaty trip to the gym, or at nine in the morning (also sans makeup) at Starbucks on a Saturday. And none of them, frankly, can make Pete jealous.

Let's review:

There's John, the pseudo-rock star, who at age thirty-two still plays air guitar in front of his bathroom mirror while singing "Pour Some

Sugar On Me." There's Tomm (two m's), the aspiring writer who once said her hair reminded him of cedar trees and then made out with her roommate. Don't look for meaning. There isn't any. There is Jason, who fears chicken. There's Danny, who refuses to eat carbs and harped on her about her weight. And finally, Tim, a Greenpeace activist who once chained himself to a tree to prevent a forest from being chopped down.

Sadly, Pete has been her sanest boyfriend to date. The others are laughable.

Liz, on the other hand, has a Rolodex filled with suitable, normal, semi-sane exes. She managed this by being superbly picky about each man's income, table manners and prowess in the bedroom before settling on the man she would eventually marry. Liz, being five-ten and gorgeous, could afford to be so picky. Kate, however, who was voluptuous or stocky, depending on your point of view, tended to attract men with issues.

"I know just the ex for you, he's perfect," Liz says.

The Pseudo-Ex

Mike Jenner is thirty-two, dark-haired, tall and a freelance writer by trade. He lives in New York, and the love of his life is a brown dog named Baxter. He agrees to pose as Kate's fictitious ex-boyfriend because he thinks it will make a good freelance story for *FHM*, where he works. He also agrees because he thinks this will prove his theory that women are, indeed, crazy.

"Is she pretty?" he asks his ex, Liz.

"She's just your type," Liz promises. His type is Girl-Next-Door, which Liz most certainly is not. Mike usually went for the Mary Anns of the world, but Liz was his one exception. Liz is definitely a Ginger. But hey, a guy has to have variety.

This, he thinks, should be interesting.

The White Lie

"You're going where?" Pete asks as he mows down a row of green aliens, the latest beta version of his newest test game.

67

"New York. There's an ad position open at *FHM*, it's a good job. Mike told me about it."

"Who's Mike?"

"We went out on a couple of dates when I used to live in New York. You remember. He's a writer."

"I thought that was Tomm."

"Nope. This is Mike. He's the one who can actually write."

Pete pauses his game and looks at Kate.

"You never told me about a Mike."

"I could've sworn I did."

"Where are you going to stay?"

"At Mike's."

The Fight

"No, you're not," Pete says.

"Yes, I am."

"You're my girlfriend, and you're not."

"It's expensive to stay in New York and Mike's offered me his couch."

"You're not going to go," Pete says.

"Don't be silly. You're just my boyfriend. It's not like we're married or anything, so what's the problem?"

Pete, who falls silent, mouth slightly agape, wonders where this breezy new commitment phobic girlfriend has come from. What happened to the Kate clamoring for commitment? The one who flipped through wedding magazines at the bookstore? It sounded like she *didn't want to be married*. It sounded like she wanted to jet off to New York and rekindle things with this Mike person, who by the way she had *never*, ever mentioned.

Something that he took as a bad sign. What was she hiding from him?

The Attraction

Given the fact that Liz does not have any boyfriends who aren't gorgeous, Kate was expecting someone with the rugged, good looks common in Liz's dating pool. What she isn't expecting, however, is for him to be smart and funny and flirty. Very dangerously flirty.

"Tell me again why a girl who looks like you do needs to pretend to have an ex-boyfriend?" Mike says, leaning in to grab her bag. Just looking at Mike, she feels a charge, the kind of thing she usually feels when she looks at pictures of Brad Pitt in magazines.

Usually, this kind of man never bothers to give her a second glance on the street. But he seems interested. More than interested: intrigued.

"I have a commitment phobic boyfriend," she says, realizing how desperate and stupid that sounds.

"Well, either he wants to marry you or he doesn't," Mike replies, matter-of-factly. "Did you ask him, point-blank, if he wants to get married?"

"I thought this would be more fun," Kate jokes.

Mike gives her a slow assessing look, starting with her shoes and running up her body in a way that implies he is not going to bother being polite.

"Oh, I can guarantee you that it will most definitely be fun," he says, giving her a slow, wolfish smile.

The Flight

Pete finds himself on Flight 299 to New York, wondering if this means that he is actually whipped, the current theory that his friend (Vince) now used to explain any strange behavior (like Pete forgoing meeting the boys for a night out watching the Chicago White Sox in favor of watching it at home on the couch, snuggling with Kate).

"Don't you think she's hiding something?" Pete asks the grandmotherly woman sitting next to him in seat 32A. He has, for the past half hour, been telling her the whole sordid story, because he is *that* bothered by it. His girlfriend. Spending the night in the apartment of one of her ex-boyfriends, whom she's conveniently forgotten to tell him about.

"In my day, you often dated a lot of boys at once," the woman offers. "That is, until you got a ring."

Right. The ring.

Pete can't help but think: Has he waited too long? Is he going to lose her to some *FHM* writer who lives in New York and left that message on their machine last night saying, "Can't wait to see you, Baxter's missed you"?

The man has a dog. It doesn't seem like a fair fight.

The Date

Mike takes her to a romantic, low-lit Italian restaurant in Little Italy. It's supposed to be part of the plan, except that Mike seems to be taking things very seriously, and Pete isn't even around. And at this point Kate doesn't think Pete is going to come. She's overplayed her hand. He's probably just sitting at home on the couch without giving her another thought.

Kate takes in Mike's chiseled features and his barely there sexy stubble. Kate knows that she ought to be attracted to Mike. He's smart. He's funny. He's got a really nice dog. And he's drop-dead gorgeous. But Kate can't help but think of Pete.

Pete standing in his boxers in front of the bathroom mirror, trying to figure out if he's got hair growing out of his ears or not. Pete cuddling up to her on the couch, letting her feed him pizza. Pete making her laugh by doing a spot-on impression of George W. Bush.

And Kate realizes then that she's completely in love with Pete. There can be no Mikes when there's a Pete.

"I'm sorry," she says, standing up. "I think I can't do this anymore."

"What?" Mike asks, bewildered. "We haven't even ordered yet."

"I know, but you see, I think I really am in love with my boyfriend, and it's not fair to him for me to sit here with you."

"What about him taking you for granted? Him not proposing?"

"I think I would just rather be with him," Kate says, getting up and putting her napkin on the table. "I'm sorry."

Mike just shakes his head. To him, this just proves that women are indeed, crazy.

The Confrontation

Pete sees them through the window of the restaurant. They are right where Liz said they would be, the exact restaurant.

They aren't holding hands, but they are leaning in over the table. Not just Mike the Ex, but his girlfriend, too. She's leaning! Pete knows what the "lean" means. People who are just friends don't lean in over the table to talk to one another. People who plan to have hot, sweaty animal sex lean like that, arms almost touching, the electricity between them evident from across the street. And she is laughing at something he is saying. She's *laughing*. That's even worse than seeing them kiss. It feels like a betrayal. She *likes* this guy. She is going to get naked with him, Pete's all but certain.

And then, something happens. Kate looks distracted. She gets up and picks up her purse and coat and heads to the door. She's leaving him! Pete feels relieved. Outside, he steps in front of her.

"Pete," she cries, genuinely shocked. What does she expect? Him to stay home while she has sex with her ex? Hardly.

"Kate—wait," cries the ex-boyfriend, who comes out of the restaurant after her. Wow, but he's tall (why didn't she mention he was this tall?). He stops and looks at Pete. "You must be the boyfriend. Nice coat, sport."

Sport? Who calls anyone "sport" aside from Pete's eighty-eight-year-old grandfather? Please. And he's definitely freakishly tall.

"Pete, what are you doing here?" Kate asks.

"What am I doing here? What are *you* doing here? I saw you. I saw you laughing at his jokes."

"That's because they're funny," the tall—and decidedly muscular—ex says. Pete is beginning to worry that he won't be able to take him, if it comes down to that. This guy probably outweighs him by thirty pounds of muscle at least. Maybe forty. Pete hasn't gone to the gym in a long while.

"I didn't ask you," Pete says, trying to test out his aggression, see if maybe the Jolly Green Giant isn't actually so tough after all.

"Calm down, sport," says the giant. Okay, so he isn't at all afraid of Pete's aggressive tactics. Good to know. Pete turns back to Kate.

"If one of you would let me talk, I was going to say I'm ready to go home." She looks at Pete, and Pete knows that things are starting to go his way.

"First, tell me if you were going to sleep with him," Pete says, pointing to the Jolly Green Giant.

71

"What? No, I wasn't going to sleep with him."

"But you looked like you were. And why didn't you tell me about him? I thought you told me about all your exes. What are you hiding?"

"Well..." Kate just shakes her head. "I don't believe you," she says, sighing. "You fell for it."

"I what?"

"You totally fell for it. Hook, line and sinker. This isn't one of my exes at all. This is Liz's ex."

The Giant waves at him. "That's me, sport."

"No one is talking to you," Pete snaps.

Kate opens her purse and takes out the magazine article and shows it to him. "See? You fell for Number One. See?"

"This is just a trick?" Pete says, reading over the magazine article, thinking, *I just spent five hundred dollars on airfare and it was all a hoax.* "You did this on *purpose*?"

Kate nods.

Pete runs his hand through his hair. "I don't believe it. I can't believe you manipulated me like that." Furthermore, he can't believe that he now has the high ground. He's gone from the commitment phobe/stalker boyfriend to the one who is wronged in about thirty seconds.

"I didn't think it would really work. I didn't think you were that simple or that shallow," Kate says.

"What about our three-year relationship led you to believe I was complex?" Pete sighs. Pete knows he should feel angry, but he's starting to feel relieved. There isn't a Jolly Green Giant in his girlfriend's past. There's no past sex, no current sex and no future sex, either. Things are starting to look up.

"Are you mad at me?" Kate asks Pete. And Pete realizes that while he should be mad, he isn't. Going to this extreme just to get a marriage proposal, well, it shows just how much she loves him. It may not be a Jet Ski, but it's still a nice gesture. He has to give her that.

"If you wanted to get married, we should've just talked about it," Pete says.

"We did talk about it," Kate points out.

True, but he just didn't think that Kate wanted it this badly.

"Look, Kate, I know you want to get married, and if you do, I do, too."
Kate's face lights up. "You do?"

"Of course I do. I knew from the moment I met you that I wanted to marry you."

The Ring

And then, Pete pulls from his coat pocket a black velvet box, and he kneels on the ground in front of the restaurant, with the Jolly Green Giant standing nearby and the valet parking guy looking on.

"Kate, I love you. Will you be my wife?"

And there, sitting in the black velvet box, is Kate's perfect engagement ring. The solitaire in platinum with adjoining baguettes that Kate put together herself on the Diamonds Are Forever Web site.

"But how did you know?"

"I saw it on your computer," Pete admits.

"You snooped through my files?"

"You left it up," Pete says. "I didn't snoop. I just sometimes pay attention."

And Kate knows then that she is completely and totally in love with Pete. And that he is completely and totally in love with her. And everything is right in the world, and she feels like singing.

Behind them, Mike sighs and turns to go home, muttering under his breath, "Women *and* men are crazy."

Kate ignores him. She throws her arms around Pete's neck, and they kiss long and deep.

The Epilogue

"So when are we getting married?" Kate asks Pete on the flight on the way home.

"We have to set a date? Why do we have to set a date?"

Kate gives Pete a playful punch in the arm. "I'm not going to want to have one of those three-year engagements."

"You mean we actually have to get married? I thought we could just be engaged forever."

Kate narrows her eyes and frowns.

"Kidding! I am just kidding."

"Not funny."

"We could go to Vegas tomorrow."

"Vegas!" Kate exclaims, appalled.

"Kidding again," Pete says, giving her a playful grin.

"You are so not funny," Kate says.

"I know you're laughing—on the inside," Pete says.

CARA LOCKWOOD is the author of *I Do (But I Don't)*, which was made into a movie for Lifetime Television, as well as *I Did (But I Wouldn't Now)*, *Dixieland Sushi*, *Pink Slip Party* and *Wuthering High*. Cara lives with her husband in Chicago, where she is currently at work on her next novel.

Kayla Perrin

To me, both as a writer and a reader, the chick-lit genre has been a welcome breath of fresh air. It is a validation of the imperfect-yet-lovable woman. The chick-lit heroine doesn't have to have it all together. She can be struggling to find her place in the world, struggling to find Mr. Right without guilt when she's over thirty, struggling with her weight or her looks or struggling in the workplace. There is a touching vulnerability to the chick-lit heroine, one that in my opinion accurately reflects the modern-day woman. Not the often-unrealistic heroine of other types of novels, the chick-lit heroine knows what she wants and is willing to put herself on the line to get it. In the stories I create, and in the ones I read, I relate to the chick-lit heroine. The chick-lit heroine is me.

Mama Knows Best

Sometimes, a bombshell shakes your world with so much force you don't know how you're supposed to react. You don't know the appropriate thing to say, or the appropriate thing to do. So you say and do nothing.

"You still there?" Donna asks me. She's my best friend and would have been my maid of honor—had my scheduled wedding taken place four months ago.

"Yeah, I'm still here." I'm in my kitchen, actually, gazing at the empty sink. It is clean—but not sparkling.

"You . . . have nothing to say?"

75

I take a deep breath. Ponder Donna's question. And finally speak. "Last night, my mother asked me if I ever polish my kitchen sink."

"Huh?"

"Polish my sink. Do you believe it?"

"Chantelle...."

"Do they make some sort of sink polish for stainless steel?"

"You're asking me? The woman who doesn't know which way is up on a broom?"

"Hmm."

"Come on, Chantelle. Tell me how you feel about—"

"Maybe I can check at Publix." Publix was one of the grocery stores in my South Florida neighborhood. "If there *is* some sort of sink polish, they ought to know about it."

"Honey, I wouldn't worry about what your mother said."

That's easy for Donna to say. She doesn't have a mother who could compete for the title of World Neat Freak.

But what Donna doesn't get here, which I'm not quite able to bring myself to say, is that I fear my mother is right. That I *can't* polish a sink. That I *can't* keep a house clean—that I couldn't even if my life depended on it. My mother isn't just talking about my domestic skills when she talks about my domestic skills. What she's really saying is: *You'll never land a man if you don't become a better homemaker.*

Maybe she's right.

Maybe that's why, as just reported to me by Donna, my former fiancé has announced his engagement to another woman—*only four months after we didn't walk down the aisle.*

"Yeah, I should really check it out at Publix. Or online. Maybe they sell stainless steel sink polish on eBay."

"Chantelle, why don't we get together?"

"Do you think that's why he dumped me?" I suddenly ask. "Do you think he looked at my sink one day and thought, 'no way in hell can I live with this woman'?"

"Okay, now I'm starting to worry about you."

"Four months, Donna. *Four months.* How does a guy get engaged to someone else in four months? Hell, it took him three years to finally pop the question to me."

"I know."

"I don't understand. What am I not getting? I'm thirty-three, have a decent job. Am I destined to be forever single?"

"Of course not."

"Yeah, like you wouldn't say that. You're my best friend."

"That's it. We're going out. I'm not going to let you mope around at home tonight over the world's biggest jerk. I only told you because... well, because you're my best friend, and I felt you had a right to know. But the last thing I wanted was to send you into depression."

"I'm not depressed." *Liar.* I was *something*—even if I am over my ex.

Because let's face it—how could you *not* be over a guy who, on the day of your wedding, admits to you that he slept with a stripper at his bachelor party?

If nothing else, his timing sucked. Couldn't he have done it *before* we'd set the date, *before* the dress was bought and paid for? Hell, he should have done it before he'd thought about proposing.

"Hello? Anybody home?"

"Sorry. What did you say?"

"I understand you're a little depressed—"

"I am *not* depressed." Okay, so I am—a little—but I'll be damned if I'm going to admit it. "I've moved on."

"You have a right to be upset."

"Quite frankly, I pity the woman Mike's hooked up with," I say. "Probably someone so desperate to get married, she's willing to put up with anything. *Unlike me*, thank you very much."

"Well, good," Donna says. "As long as you're not up—"

"Oh, Donna!" I moan long and hard, and feel like I'm going to have a meltdown. "I don't understand. How could he do this?"

"Okay, we're going to get together for dinner tonight. I'm making an executive decision here, and it's my treat. I say we gorge on steak and lobster somewhere with a beautiful view. Monty's sound good?"

"Yeah," I say absently. "Sure."

Honestly, I was over him. I was. I can't believe I'm suffering some type of emotional setback like this. It's friggin' embarrassing.

Donna's right. Getting out will probably do me good. Eating steak over a view of the water, with yachts cruising nearby.... It's exactly what I need.

And I'm up for anything that will keep me from adding dishes to my clean-but-dull sink.

Donna and I make arrangements to meet at Monty's at seven. She'll only call me back if the restaurant says there are no available reservations. And considering it's Sunday, I don't anticipate that problem.

Three hours later, just before I leave my house, I have a lightbulb moment. I wipe some olive oil over the surface of my kitchen sink. And I smile.

Finally, it shines.

"Now I get it," I say to Donna when we're at Monty's, a popular restaurant at the Miami Beach Marina. We're waiting at the bar because our table isn't ready yet, and we're both sipping Cosmos. "That's why my mother has been so...hell bent on setting me up on this blind date."

"You think she knew?" Donna asks.

"Maybe. She and Mike's mother both work in the same bank office. I'm sure their paths crossed. Mike's mother would probably tell her, even if it was just to rub salt in the wound." The one thing I hadn't regretted when Mike and I split was no longer getting Sheila Matthews as a mother-in-law.

"Ouch." Donna finishes off the Cosmo.

"The thing is," I go on, "is that the guys my mother has tried to set me up with since I've been single have been total squares. Like that last guy—the one she met when he did some business at the bank."

Donna gestures to the bartender, then asks me, "What did he do again?"

"Hell if I know. Some kind of bird-watching something or other in the Everglades. I couldn't get past the first date to figure it out."

I am momentarily distracted by the appearance of a fine-looking brother at the bar. He's alone, but I assume waiting for someone, and he slips onto the seat to my right.

I act like I didn't see him as I sip more of my Cosmo.

"So you don't want to go on this blind date—right?"

I fully face Donna, remembering the conversation at hand. "I didn't... not until you called."

"Look, if you don't want to do it, just tell your mom no." She asks the bartender for another round of Cosmos. I open my purse, but she snatches the Louis Vuitton clutch from my hands so I can't pay.

"You don't know my mother," I say. "If I tell her no, I'm gonna hurt her feelings. Besides, despite how meddling she can be, I know she loves me and wants what's best for me. And I hate to say it, but she was right about Mike." She hadn't trusted the hot-blooded Jamaican as far as she could throw him. But I'd attributed that to her desire that I find a nice Trinidadian man—a man much like my father.

"Then go out with this guy. Just drive your own car so you're not stuck there."

I smile at that. That's a strict policy of Donna's—don't let a guy pick you up for a date. That way, if he turns out to be a dud, you can excuse yourself for a bathroom break and take off.

It's sad to say, but that's the state of dating in the new millennium. Especially in Miami, where there seem to be more creeps than keepers. Donna, despite being a gorgeous and successful black woman, can't find a guy who knows how to commit. The two who *have* committed to her ended up being stalkers.

Seriously, it's slim pickings out there.

Oh, hell. Maybe I *should* have forgiven Mike.

I sigh sadly, thinking again of Donna's shocking news. And then I notice that she is no longer looking at me. She's staring beyond me, a look of horror etched on her pretty brown face.

Great. The cutie beside me must be gesturing inappropriately at her. Figures he'd be too good to be true....

"Okay," Donna says slowly. "Don't freak out."

"Me freak out? You're the one freaking out here."

"Maybe we should just leave." She throws a twenty on the bar beside our new, untouched drinks. "Yeah, let's go."

I stare at her in complete shock. "What are you talking about?"

"Nothing. Let's just—there's a back way out of here, right?"

I can't imagine what Donna's going on about, so I turn to look over my shoulder.

And then I see.

Oh God, no....

My heart slams against my rib cage, I'm so entirely stunned. The shocking news Donna told me earlier is a piece of cake compared to this.

Mike-the-freakin'-louse-who-broke-my-heart-on-our-wedding-day has just entered the bar.

With a Tyra Banks look-alike.

And now I get it. Why Mike slept with a stripper the night before our wedding. Because I'm the ugliest woman on the planet.

If the Tyra Banks standard is what he craves.

"We can go," Donna says. "Honestly, there's no need to stay here. Let's head to the strip for dinner, or back to Kendall, even."

I grab my new Cosmo off the bar and down it in one long gulp. There's no going anywhere now, because Mike has spotted me. And do you believe it—the louse has the friggin' nerve to smile?

"I wonder if that's *her*," Donna whispers. "The *stripper*!"

Now my jaw hits the bar. Could it be? "But if that's *her*, she was supposed to be a fling! They're not supposed to be engaged!"

"Oh, no," Donna mumbles. "They're coming this way."

My stomach takes a serious nosedive. How can I face Mike-the-freakin'-louse-who-broke-my-heart-on-our-wedding-day? Especially when I don't look anywhere near as good as the knockout on his arm?

Should I turn around, smile? Should I pretend I didn't see him? Should I—

"Chantelle," I hear in a familiar deep, bedroom voice. "Is that you?"

I close my eyes and cringe. Then, swallowing my fear, I paste a smile onto my face and swivel around on my chair. "Mike. What a surprise."

He nods, his stupid grin saying he's incredibly happy. That and the snug grip he has on Tyra's tiny waist.

You're supposed to be grieving after losing me, you pig!

Oh, God. I want to die.

"Hi, Mike," Donna says. There's no warmth in her voice. "Who's your...friend?"

"This is Sara."

"Without an *h*," Sara points out.

Sara. Without an *h*. Lovely.

"I called a couple times and didn't get you, and I didn't want to leave a message."

"Oh?"

Mike looks to Sara, then back to me. "I wanted to be the first to tell you—Sara and I are getting married."

My hand gropes the bar. I find Donna's drink and wrap my fingers around it like it's a buoy in Biscayne Bay.

"Probably around Christmas," Sara adds, bubbling with excitement.

"You don't waste any time, do you?" Donna asks under her breath.

To say I'm devastated is an understatement. I mean, when Donna had called to say she'd heard Mike was engaged, I'd hoped he'd found some homely woman willing to put up with his philandering ways. I did not expect supermodel material.

"Yeah, I'm pretty excited about it," Mike says.

You pathetic pig.

"And what about you?" Mike won't stop smiling. "What have you been up to?"

As if he cares.

I see a little smirk on Sara's face. Nothing too obvious, but it's smug and makes me realize that I have to do something. I'm not sure what that something is until I reach to the right and take the hand of the man who is sitting beside me—the hottie who looks a lot like Will Smith. I pull his hand onto my lap and say, "Well, I'm dating, too."

Beside me, the man's eyes widen a bit in alarm, and I try my best with my own eyes to convey that he needs to play along. "Sweetheart, this is the ex I was telling you about. Mike. The one who slept with a stripper on the night before our wedding." I take enormous satisfaction from the fact that Sara's lips pull into a tight line. Guess she isn't the infamous wedding wrecker. "Mike, this is my new beau." My mind scrambles to come up with a suitable name. "His name is . . . Tom."

Great name, Chantelle. Way to go!

"Tom?" Mike asks for clarification.

"Yes." I've chosen it. I have to stick with it. "Tom."

At least the guy hasn't pulled his hand from mine and accused me of being a psycho. In fact, a little smile dances on his lips, one that says he finds this amusing. Thank God, because that means he's game to play along.

"Tom" extends a hand to shake Mike's proffered one. "Hey, man. Good to meet you."

81

I force a chuckle and lean close to the stranger, noting that he smells good. Damn good. He slips an arm around my waist.

"Tom is amazingly good to me," I go on. "Really, really sweet. I think it's...serious." I glance at "Tom." "Don't you?"

"Oh, yeah," he agrees.

If I'm not mistaken, Mike doesn't seem as happy as he did earlier. In fact, he takes a step backward.

"Well, it looks a bit crowded here," he says. "We should probably head out. Maybe get dinner at a restaurant at Bayside."

Not only does Mike look a little unhappy, so does Sara.

"See you later," I say. My smile is pure sugar as I give a little wave, then I turn back to "Tom," gazing into his beautiful dark eyes in a sickening show of our fake affection.

"They're going," Donna tells me, and only then do I look their way. A little laugh escapes me when I see Sara pull her hand from Mike's. Then she storms ahead of him, and he disappears out the door after her.

Ooh, I'm feeling so much better.

If a little embarrassed.

I ease away from the stranger, whom I felt entirely too comfortable with. I offer him a sheepish grin. "Sorry about that. But thanks for playing along."

"No problem," he tells me.

"That was my ex," I continue. "A real class act. We should have gotten married four months ago, but obviously that didn't happen. Not that I'm upset about it, mind you. Of course, it hurt like hell at the time. Especially after being together for four years."

"Sounds like it's his loss."

"I couldn't agree more. Like I said, I'm over him. I just didn't want him gloating with that...that rake. Bet she doesn't eat more than a carrot a day."

It suddenly dawns on me that I'm rambling, and that this poor, absolute hottie stranger is sure to have had enough of me.

I feel a pang of regret. He *is* really cute. And clearly a nice guy. But if there was any chance of him asking me on a date, I've shot that all to hell.

"Thanks again," I tell him. "For helping me out of an awkward situation."

He shrugs, a humorous smile on his face. "No problem."

Donna grabs my hand. "They just called our name."

And not a moment too soon. Someone needs to save me from my-self.

"He was hot." Donna states the obvious.

"Yeah. And thanks to Mike showing up when he did, he must think I'm a psychotic bitch who's not over my ex. Damn. I'd been hoping to work up the nerve to talk to him under normal circumstances. Sheesh. No wonder I'm thirty-three and still single."

"Stop beating yourself up. You'll meet someone nice."

"Soon enough for me to give my mother the grandchildren she so de-sires?"

"Of course." Donna smiles sweetly at me.

But I don't believe her. After all, what else is a best friend supposed to say?

I steal one last look at "Tom." I wish I'd met him under different cir-cumstances, but there's nothing I can do about it now.

Oh well. You win some, you lose some.

"You knew, didn't you, Mom?" It's Wednesday, and I've had three days to mull over the reality that Mike clearly didn't love me. If I'd missed the neon-sign clue in his admission to me the morning of the wedding, I certainly couldn't miss it now.

My mother sighs softly as she faces me at her kitchen table.

"Why didn't you tell me?" I ask her.

"What was the point? I didn't want you upset."

"You thought I'd never find out?"

"Of course I knew you'd find out," she tells me. "I just hoped it would be after you'd already met someone else. Someone decent and loving who would worship you the way you deserve."

The way my daddy did with her, God rest his soul. Why were there no good men like that anymore?

"And you think Carlton is that kind of guy?"

"Sweetheart, I think you're going to adore Carlton. Trust me. I have a feeling about this one."

"I hope so, Mom." And I do. Because if Carlton is another geek with no sex appeal, I am going to cut my mother off from ever setting me up on another date.

The smell of jerk chicken fills the house, one of my favorite meals. My mother is providing dinner for me and Carlton tonight, though she promises to head to the mall after she introduces us.

For the nth time, my mother wipes her already spotless counters, then glances at the clock and grins. "Five minutes to six. He should be here soon."

"What does he do?" I may as well be half interested. I'm going to be spending an evening with this man.

The doorbell chimes before she can answer.

"Why don't you ask him yourself?"

I get up from the kitchen table, then take a deep breath before heading to the door. Please God, don't let him be a loser. Please God. . . .

I swing the door open.

And then I stand there in shock.

"Chantelle?" he asks, the deep timbre of his voice familiar. He's holding a bouquet of yellow roses.

"Carlton?" How can this be?

"What a surprise. Nice to meet you—again."

I stand back and open the door wide. Somehow, I do this casually, because inside I'm freaking out. I can't believe this coincidence, that the gorgeous guy from Monty's is the man my mother has arranged for me to meet.

"Carlton." My mother sweeps into the foyer. "How are you?" She glances at me. "I see you've met my daughter."

"Yes, I have."

He winks at me behind my mother's back, and then I erupt in a smile.

"I told you you'd like him," my mother whispers.

Once again, I glance at Carlton, see his gorgeous smile and warm eyes.

I've been given a second chance to make a first impression.

Thanks, Mom. You finally got it right.

KAYLA PERRIN lives in Southwestern Ontario. She has a B.A. in English and sociology and a B.Ed., having entertained the idea of becoming a teacher—but she always knew she wanted to be a writer. Teachers were being laid off in Toronto when Kayla graduated, so she pursued her first love of writing. She now has twenty-six published titles to her credit, including romance, mainstream and children's fiction. She is a *USA Today* bestselling author and has won several awards, including twice winning a spot on the Romance Writers of America "Top Ten Favorite Books of the Year" list, a Career Achievement Award from *Romantic Times Magazine* and an Arts Acclaim Award from the city of Brampton. Kayla's novel *Sweet Honesty* was optioned for a movie of the week. You can visit Kayla's Web site at www.kaylaperrin.com.

Karen Siplin

It's the writer's job to show people how they're behaving through the characters she creates. I believe chick-lit writers are able to do this in an entertaining way—a way that removes the reader from her everyday reality for a few hours and makes her smile.

Nice Jewish Boy

I never thought I'd find myself in the back of the Pearlsteins' car anticipating a bris for matters other than helping an old high-school friend celebrate the birth of his son. But Mrs. Pearlstein promises there will be plenty of nice Jewish boys there, and I think the more men I go out with, the easier it'll be to know when I've found the right one.

"We'll say you're an Ethiopian Jew," Mrs. Pearlstein announced right before we got into the car.

I stopped in my tracks and told Stephanie I was turning back.

"Ma, if you say that I'll kill you!" Stephanie screamed.

"I'm *kidding*," Mrs. Pearlstein said and winked at me.

I've known Mrs. Pearlstein for fifteen years. She wasn't kidding.

It isn't unusual for me to be the only black person at a bris. I'm used to it. Not only because Stephanie Pearlstein has been my best friend for fifteen years and has dragged me to every family celebration her mother ever forced her to go to, but because I was raised in a Jewish neighborhood in Coney Island. When I turned thirteen, I attended over a dozen bar mitzvahs. Joy Kim, the one Korean girl in our co-op, could always be found sitting next to me enjoying stuffed derma and gefilte fish with ten of our closest friends. We were popular with the boys in the neighborhood, though neither one of us was kissed until we left the area to attend high school.

My being the lone black person at a party, any party, is only weird for people who don't know me. They either feel they can't be themselves in my presence, or think they're feeling my pain at being the only "person of color" in the room. In truth, being the only black person at a bris is like being the only straight woman in a gay male bar. It only gets painful when people start wondering why I'm there. And then I become the center of attention. I prefer being ignored.

Actually, it's more awkward when there's one other black person in attendance because we're never sure if we should acknowledge each other or pretend we haven't noticed the other is there. There's always that freakishly odd moment when we make eye contact, nod and look away, fearful that someone will notice and either try to marry us off or set us up on an intimate coffee date before we've even exchanged first names.

We arrive an hour after the bris is scheduled to begin. All the pretty townhouses in Breezy Point Village look the same and Mr. Pearlstein is not happy. He has spent the last twenty minutes complaining about thirty-year-old girls who still need their parents to drive them to parties. Neither Stephanie nor I know how to drive.

"Stanley!" Mrs. Pearlstein shrieks. "The Glicks are our friends, too."

When Mr. Pearlstein continues to complain, Mrs. Pearlstein resorts to ignoring him and tells us how well-off Jeffrey's friends are.

"We don't want wealthy, we want nice," Stephanie says.

"I picked nice," Mrs. Pearlstein tells her. "Look at your father."

Finally, Mr. Pearlstein stops the car in front of a lone blue balloon tied to a wrought iron fence. He gets out and fixes his pants. Mrs. Pearl-stein gets out of the car as well and asks her husband to open the trunk so we can take out the gifts. Stephanie and I stay in the car to reapply our makeup.

"Are you getting out of the car or are you gonna sit in it all day like two idiots?" Mr. Pearlstein roars from outside. He shakes his head. "I swear, one is dumber than the other."

"Fuck you!" Stephanie screams back as we get out of the car and help her mother retrieve our gift-wrapped boxes for the baby.

"Stephanie!" Mrs. Pearlstein is horrified.

"He called us idiots," Stephanie points out. "Is that nice?"

Mrs. Pearlstein flashes her husband a warning glare.

Jeffrey Glick opens the door before we reach it. He's married-fat and balding. At first I thought it was cruel that Mrs. Pearlstein wanted Steph-anie to be here, but I look at Jeffrey and I understand Mrs. Pearlstein's motives. Stephanie still has her teenage good looks and Mrs. Pearlstein wants to show her daughter off.

Jeffrey Glick was Stephanie's boyfriend in high school. They dated for two years, despite attending Yale and SUNY Albany respectively. Two years is nothing to throw a stick at in Stephanie-years. For a while she'd say things like, "If we're together for three years we might as well get married." Mrs. Pearlstein was alarmed until she was sure Stephanie still planned to graduate from college. And then Mrs. Glick and Mrs. Pearl-stein became friends. Jeffrey and Stephanie broke up the summer before they started sophomore year. Jeffrey didn't want a long-distance rela-tionship and his mother thought they were too young to be so serious anyway. He met his wife at Yale a year later.

We've all kept in touch, though I don't think we would have if the In-ternet didn't exist and Jeffrey didn't still entertain sexual fantasies about Stephanie. When he e-mails me, it's usually to ask whether Stephanie's seeing anyone.

Jeffrey grabs Mrs. Pearlstein and hugs her tiny frame until she pulls away, saying, "No offense, but I'm not your size. You might break some-thing. Be careful with Stephanie. She's delicate like I am."

Jeffrey laughs jovially and shakes Mr. Pearlstein's hand. Mr. Pearlstein nods, grunts and pushes past him, into the house. Then Jeffrey looks at us and beams. He hugs Stephanie, closing his eyes and squeezing her too tight. He hugs me as well, not as tight. He smells like baby powder and strong aftershave.

"Come in, come in," he says, letting me go. "We're waiting for the mohel."

"What's your son's name?" I ask as we enter the house. He forgot to mention it in his e-mail.

"Baxter," Jeffrey tells us.

"A nice biblical name," Mrs. Pearlstein says and winks at me.

Jeffrey pretends not to hear her.

The house is lovely. The walls are off-white and decorated with framed Georgia O'Keeffe prints. The windows are huge and sparkling; the furniture is white and immaculate. I imagine it takes a hell of a lot of determination to maintain white furniture. I also try to imagine what it would be like to live here with a husband and a child—safe, content, unchallenged. Would I be satisfied? Part of me would be, I think. There'd be fewer question marks.

The living room is milling with people. Mr. and Mrs. Pearlstein greet everyone with hugs and kisses on both cheeks. Automatically feeling antisocial, Stephanie and I retreat to a corner of the room and sit down. Of course, all eyes are on us. It's a combination of me being the only black girl at the bris and Stephanie's short skirt.

"Shit," Stephanie says, legs jiggling.

I know what she means. Already I've recognized two women we used to hang out with and I can't remember their names. Like Jeffrey, they're heavy and look much older than we do. I pretend I don't see them.

"I can't believe these people are married with kids," I say. "I still feel like I'm twenty."

"Eighteen," Stephanie corrects, then adds, "They don't look happy."

Stephanie's right. They don't look happy. The women are all huddled together talking, glancing at Stephanie's short skirt. Their husbands are huddled together at the opposite side of the room, also glancing at her short skirt.

"Is this what we have to look forward to?" Stephanie asks.

I don't have an answer for her so I say, "Hungry?"

We head into the kitchen, where Mr. Pearlstein is already standing by the food table, nibbling. We grab plates and pile on chopped liver, brisket and slices of the most beautiful sable I've ever seen. Mr. Pearlstein stops eating and eyes us warily. While I've no doubt he loves his daughter unconditionally and approves of me as her best friend, he never hides his disappointment in our inability to date great men, find decent jobs and learn how to drive. Mr. Pearlstein's afraid he'll be driving us to parties well into our fifties. Sometimes I'm not so sure he's wrong.

Jeffrey's mother drifts into the kitchen to refill her drink. She puts her arms around us and kisses our cheeks. "Girls, how are we doing?"

"Fine, Mrs. Glick," we say in unison, grinning like two eight-year-olds.

"Have you moved into your own places yet?" she asks us.

"No," we say.

"You're still at home?" Mrs. Glick sounds scandalized.

"We're saving," Stephanie tells her.

Mrs. Glick clucks. "You Brooklyn babies. You never leave, do you?" She squeezes our shoulders and shakes her head. "Mardi's buying a two-bedroom condo on the Upper East Side," she adds about Jeffrey's twenty-three-year-old sister. "We told her to do it now, before prices in Manhattan go through the roof again. She wants to be close to her new job. Did Jeffrey tell you about her new job?"

Stephanie nods vaguely.

"She's working with Trump International." Mrs. Glick breathes each word slowly for maximum dramatic effect.

I'm sure my face mirrors Stephanie's blank one. "You must be proud," I say politely.

Mrs. Glick beams. "Have you seen her yet?"

We shake our heads and Mrs. Glick rolls her eyes. "Wait 'til you see her. *She got so big.*"

I think big meaning fat, but when Mardi walks down the stairs two minutes later I realize Mrs. Glick means big meaning tall and glorious. The last time I saw her, she was scrawny and pale. Mardi Glick flips her hair behind her shoulders and waves at us sweetly as she glides into the kitchen, but doesn't say hello. We watch her choose three plump strawberries and a few pieces of cantaloupe. I make eye contact with Stephanie. If we had a chance at meeting men here, we can forget about it now.

"Say hello, Mardi," Mrs. Glick commands her daughter.

"Hello," Mardi says carelessly as she sails out of the kitchen.

"She's gorgeous," Mrs. Glick swoons, watching her. "Isn't she a gorgeous girl?"

Mrs. Glick looks at us through the silence, then stares at our overloaded plates. Stephanie glances at me. We put the plates down on an empty spot on the table.

"Do you have any children yet?" Mrs. Glick asks me.

I pull back and look at Mrs. Glick with a frown. "Why would I have kids, Mrs. Glick? I'm not married."

Mrs. Glick goes crimson. "Oh. Well. I didn't know...."

"You know I'm not married. You just asked if I still live with my parents."

The look on Mrs. Pearlstein's face from the depths of the living room tells me to shut up because my voice is carrying and Mrs. Glick's grandson is about to be cut. I have no right to freak out over a simple question. Ruffled, Mrs. Glick changes the subject and explains the various foods on the table to me.

Because I was raised in a Jewish neighborhood, I'm very familiar with the Jewish menu. My mother makes the best potato latkes on Coney Island. Ironically, Stephanie was raised on baked ziti and lasagna. I'm the one who introduced her to the joys of gefilte fish and chopped liver. Maybe Mrs. Glick should be explaining the food to Stephanie instead. In order not to embarrass her further, I listen.

"Thank you, Mrs. Glick," I say when we're done. "I think I'll try the sable."

Mrs. Glick nods her approval. "I always knew you had good taste."

When Mrs. Glick leaves, Mrs. Pearlstein arrives with the panic of competition etched all over her face. She pushes some hair behind Stephanie's ears so "they can see how green your eyes are."

Stephanie rolls those green eyes for my benefit. "Mrs. Glick is ridiculous," she says.

Mrs. Pearlstein looks at me, a hint of sympathy in her eyes. "The Glicks aren't the nicest people," she admits quietly, "but let's keep in mind we're in their house. We'll talk about it later."

"Don't listen to her," Stephanie says. "Mrs. Glick, I mean. She used to give me hell about choosing Albany over Binghamton. What's the big deal? They're both SUNY. I'm glad she's not my mother. Look at Mardi. She's miserable."

Mrs. Pearlstein and I look at Mardi. She's standing across the room, laughing hysterically at something someone just said.

"Yeah." I nod. "She certainly *looks* miserable."

Mrs. Pearlstein puts one arm around my shoulders and her other arm around Stephanie's waist. She squeezes tight. "You're beautiful girls."

"Women," Stephanie corrects.

Mrs. Pearlstein lets go of us. "Of course," she says as she leaves. "Women."

Stephanie sighs. "Mardi's got her whole life ahead of her. My father had to drive us here."

"And Mrs. Glick thinks I'm unmarried with children," I add. I turn back to find my plate of food. It's gone.

"Nice spread." A young man who can't be more than sixteen is standing next to me. He has shaggy brown hair, an adorable pug nose, baby smooth skin and eyes so dark they seem unreal. He's wearing jeans a size too big and an oversized shirt with the words Morehouse College across the front. "Ever been to one of these before?"

"Yes," I tell him, plopping three new slices of sable on another plate. "Many."

"Me, too." He smiles and I see the gold tooth with the letter *K* engraved into it.

Oh dear, I think.

"We're gonna dance," he says, moving closer to me.

"To what?" I ask.

He blushes fiercely and adds, "If they put on some music."

I soften and grin and say, "Okay," because there's no harm in agreeing to dance with a kid at a bris without music.

"Kenneth." A woman slips her arm through my child admirer's and smiles at me coldly. "Is that all you're going to eat? Why don't you try the brisket?" she says without taking her eyes off me.

Kenneth blushes again.

"I'm Jennifer," she tells me. "Jeffrey's aunt."

"Nice to meet you," I say.

"This is my son Kenneth," she says.

"Nice to meet you, Kenneth," I say, feeling increasingly uneasy because his mother is glowering at me. "Do you, uh, go to Morehouse?"

Kenneth and his mother both look at his shirt, then back at me.

"Kenneth is fifteen," his mother informs me in an accusatory tone. "He hasn't even started applying to colleges yet."

"Oh."

Kenneth looks at me. "I plan to apply to Morehouse, though."

I glance at his mother. Her grip on Kenneth's arm tightens. And then it dawns on me. She thinks *I'm* coming on to her son. I sigh heavily, feeling slightly embarrassed and annoyed. I put my plate down, still hungry, but unable to bring myself to eat. "Try the sable," I say. "I hear it's terrific."

I turn back to Stephanie just as a strangled sound leaves her mouth. I look at her, alarmed, ready to dislodge some chopped liver stuck in her throat. But Stephanie isn't choking on chopped liver. She's staring at Mardi and the man Mardi's talking to. I recognize the guy immediately.

Joel Silverman. The most popular boy in high school and Stephanie's one unrequited love. What's he doing here? He moved to Hong Kong three years ago.

"Well," I say because I don't know what else to say.

"I hear ya," Stephanie says. "I always knew he wasn't very bright. Who the hell would fly from Hong Kong to New Jersey for a bris?"

There's a mixture of animosity and regret in Stephanie's voice, which I understand. Joel also went to SUNY Albany. After Jeffrey broke up with her, Joel asked Stephanie out and they dated on and off for a few years. Still popular, not to mention the most beautiful boy in school, Joel wouldn't commit to dating Stephanie exclusively, firmly planting a seed of insecurity in Stephanie forever. She's never forgiven him for it.

When Mardi and Joel notice us, Stephanie takes my hand and holds it like she needs moral support. I guess she does. Joel smiles. Mardi doesn't.

"*Pearlstein and Smith*?!" Joel bellows like a frat boy.

I wince and he strides over. We kiss cheeks and shake hands and stand in a semicircle, quiet and awkward.

"So," says Stephanie.

"I saw you when you came in," says Joel. "A sight for sore eyes."

"Oh boy," I say.

"How are you?" Joel asks, inching too close to Stephanie.

"Great!" She tries to sound enthusiastic. It's always smart to make married ex-boyfriends think your life has been nothing but fantastic since the relationship ended. But I know my best friend's voice is too high-pitched, which means she's uncomfortable. She flashes me a look that says, *Help me out here.*

"How have *you* been?" I step in.

"Same shit, different day," Joel answers.

"Only in Hong Kong," Stephanie says in the same high-pitched voice.

"And now you're married," I point out.

Joel nods. "Four years," he offers proudly. "You see my wife? Sylvia. I think you know her." He points out one of the women I noticed when we arrived.

"Yes," Stephanie says stiffly. "We know her."

From across the room, Sylvia half-waves.

"When'd you hook up with Sylvia?" I ask, surprised Jeffrey never mentioned Joel married one of our high school classmates.

"She went to Yale with Jeff," Joel explains, a huge smile plastered on his face. Not as huge as Stephanie's, though. "We used to hang out."

"Oh," Stephanie and I say.

I give Stephanie a *hang in there* look as Joel touches her arm and gently steers her away from me, leaving me standing in the middle of the kitchen alone. The least he could have done was disguise the desertion with an offer to get me a drink. I watch them walk over to the kitchen sink, conveniently out of Sylvia's view. Stephanie looks helpless, but I stay where I am and let her fight this one out on her own.

When I turn away, Kenneth's mother is still standing by the food table. She's staring at me, wearing the appearance of a woman who has been challenged. I know mothers are protective of their sons, but I usually have to sleep with them before I merit this kind of look.

She smiles. "I hear you went to school with Jeffrey."

"I did."

"I got into Yale, but I decided to go to Dartmouth instead."

"Not Yale," I clarify, though I'm sure she already knows this. "High school."

Kenneth's mother nods, eyebrows raised. "Are you invited to a lot of these things?"

"I wouldn't say a lot," I tell her. "Enough."

She nods. "I bet you're glad you don't have to do this kind of thing. It's nerve-wracking, waiting for the man who is about to cut your son to walk through the door. How many boys do you have?"

"Boys...?" I flush. "I don't have any boys. I'm not married."

"I know. I just thought...." Her voice trails off and she smiles. Unlike Mrs. Glick, Kenneth's mother isn't sorry she "mistook" me for a single mom. She very much meant to. And while being asked how many children I have by people who know I've never been married is nothing new, it still infuriates me that this woman has decided to use an annoying stereotype as a weapon to try to hurt me. I look at Stephanie. She's pushing up against the kitchen sink, trying to put some distance between herself and Joel. I head over there and hear Joel say, "I've missed you."

"Me?" Stephanie squeaks.

"Yeah, you. I don't think I ever got over you, you know."

Uh-oh.

"Hey, you two," I say. "How's it going?"

Joel turns around and smiles at me. "Excuse me for a minute," he says. He squeezes my shoulder before he walks away. Stephanie continues to lean against the sink, deep in thought.

"What?" I say.

Stephanie looks me square in the eyes. "He asked me out."

"What do you mean he asked you out? He's married."

"Exactly."

I watch her for a minute. I suspected he was trying something, but I didn't think he'd really have the nerve.

"He said, 'I live in Hong Kong. What's the big deal if we see other sometimes?'"

"Jerk," I say.

"What did I do to make him think I'd do that?" she asks.

We stare at each other.

"You didn't do anything," I say.

"He never would have asked Mardi to have an affair with him," she says, miserably. "And I know for a fact Mardi was having sex at fifteen."

"Really?"

Stephanie nods. "She lost it to a blind date."

"Oh, shit."

"It's sobering to know all the men in the room think they can fuck me without consequences. I lost my virginity when I was nineteen."

I lost my virginity six months after Stephanie. In our quest to find the right man, Stephanie and I have encountered many boys who don't have a problem fucking us, but would never take us home to their mothers. Losing your virginity at nineteen becomes enormously significant when you're us.

That's why we get along so well, I think. People see us and automatically assume the wrong things. They look at me and assume I have children, even after I've told them I'm single and still live at home with my parents. They look at Stephanie and assume she'd sleep with a married man just because she's single and wears short skirts.

A hush blankets the house when the mohel arrives. He's tall and distinguished in a suit. He carries an old-fashioned doctor's bag, and his eyes go over everyone carefully. He only nods at the men. Jeffrey introduces him to Mrs. Glick and they speak for a moment. I notice the mohel checking out a table of glasses filled to the brim with wine. Mrs. Glick looks horrified as he reaches for a glass and downs it in one swallow.

Mr. Pearlstein walks over with a grin on his face. "I think the mohel had a little too much kiddush wine before he even got here," he says in a voice loud enough to be heard across the room.

I give the mohel a closer once-over. His face is definitely flushed.

"Is the mohel supposed to drink before he slices?" Stephanie asks.

I feel queasy and Mr. Pearlstein shakes his head.

"Poor little guy," Mr. Pearlstein laments, meaning Baxter.

A group of old-timers look at me, put their fingers over their lips and say, "*Shh*," even though I wasn't the one talking. It's easy for me to be loud at these things without saying a word.

Jeffrey leads the mohel up the stairs to the baby in the master bedroom. Mrs. Glick follows them halfway, then comes back down to announce she's too nervous to witness the ceremony. For some reason, she chooses to stand next to me instead of Mardi. I can't imagine I'm more comforting than her own daughter.

"We don't do the actual cutting in front of everyone," she explains and I nod. She puts her hand on my shoulder. I stiffen. "Only the immediate family."

I nod again, stepping away from her. She moves with me, her hand absently rubbing my back.

"Did you think the mohel appeared to be"—she leans closer to me—"*tipsy?*"

Mrs. Glick is vulnerable and nervous and my heart goes out to her all of a sudden. It must be hell to know the mohel about to cut your grandson is drunk. I shake my head and give her a soothing smile. "No, I think you probably imagined that. Baxter's going to be all right."

Mrs. Glick's other hand flutters up to touch the gold heart around her neck. She still looks concerned, but no longer scared. And then the baby lets out a blood-curdling wail. Mrs. Glick and I cringe. Her nails claw my skin and I stifle a yelp. Everyone else stares at the floor. Then Jeffrey is at the top of the stairs, calling out to his mother to come up and see the baby, telling the rest of us that it's over and everything went well.

"Mazel tov," someone says, holding up a glass. We all do the same and a chorus of mazel tovs and the sound of clinking glasses fill the room. Mrs. Glick leaves my side to console her grandson, but not before she turns back to me to say, "Thank you, honey. Sometimes we just need a little extra comfort."

I stare after Mrs. Glick, baffled.

"I guess I need to ask for a rain check for that dance."

I turn around to see Kenneth, the fifteen-year-old in the Morehouse College shirt, standing next to me. He's carrying a plate and a glass of red wine. His smile is slightly embarrassed, but sincere.

"Hello," I say.

"Here." He holds out the tempting plate like a peace offering. "I've been watching you. You've been trying to eat since you got here without any luck."

"Thank you, Kenneth." I take the plate.

Kenneth steps closer and I fight the urge to step back. The way a girl rejects a boy when he's fifteen usually sets the course for how he'll reject women when he's a man. I decide to be gentle.

"I chose a little bit of everything," he says and we look at the plate in my hand. "My mother's catering company handled the food, so I can attest that it's excellent stuff. I'm sorry about her."

It isn't a good sign when a boy has to apologize for his mother, but I think it also must be painful. I pick up the fork on the plate and try the gefilte fish. "It's really good," I tell him, meaning it. "Gefilte fish is one of my favorite things."

"Is it?" He looks surprised, and then he blushes again.

"Sable is another," I admit, cutting into a thin slice of the smoked fish. I think I know what everything else is on the plate, but I ask him anyway. Kenneth describes all the various foods he's chosen for me, and after I've tried everything he takes the plate and hands me the glass of wine to wash it all down.

They say the way to a man's heart is through his stomach. Nice Jewish boys know it's also the way to a woman's. Kenneth takes my fork and eats from the plate and it's almost as if we're old friends. I watch him and wonder what he'll be like when he's a man—twenty-one, even. When he's out of high school, on his own.

"This was very kind of you," I say and smile when he blushes for the third time in my presence. "Thanks for making me feel special."

"I think you're pretty," he says. "And you look like someone who should be treated like she's special."

Now I blush. "Thanks," I say again.

So there were boys at the bris, as Mrs. Pearlstein promised, but the boys at the bris were boys we've already dated. Or boys still in high school. The boys we've already dated are married. And there was something about the way the unmarried boys smiled at us that alerted me neither Stephanie nor I had a shot at anything respectable or serious.

"Any prospects?" Mrs. Pearlstein asks on our way home.

"No, nothing," Stephanie says.

Mrs. Pearlstein tsks. "Next time," she says. "Pretty girls. What boy in his right mind wouldn't want either one of you?"

Stephanie tells Mrs. Pearlstein to turn on the radio and we spend the rest of the ride home listening to Disco Saturday on Stephanie's favorite radio station. We decide Jeffrey invited us to the bris as an excuse to get us to see how well he turned out. The ultimate revenge. But the food was good and it's always an ego booster to see the people from your past aren't aging as well as you are. And then I think of little Kenneth and the appetizing plate and wine he brought me after the cutting was over and I think the day wasn't a total bust. I went to the bris to meet a nice Jewish boy, and I did.

KAREN SIPLIN was born in Brooklyn, New York, and received her Bachelor of Arts degree in film production from CUNY's Hunter College. Her first novel, *His Insignificant Other*, was published in Serbia in June 2004. Her second novel, *Such a Girl*, was a Main Selection of Black Expressions Book Club in 2005. She has worked as a telephone operator at the Four Seasons Hotel in New York City and as a celebrity personal assistant. Visit her at www.karensiplin. com.

Deanna Carlyle

Maybe it's a generational thing, but I've always had a positive association with the word "chick." For me a chick is a modern woman with a fresh mental outlook—whatever her age. When I use the word "chick" to talk about myself, I own it, and no one can sully or demean its meaning for me. That's liberation. That's what happens when you don't believe in the myths that patriarchal culture assigns to women and their cultural production. Vive la libération. Vive la chick!

Dead Men Don't Eat Quiche

When my mother announced that she and my dad were planning to visit me in Paris for their second honeymoon, I did not exactly jump for *joie*. Nor did I do *le danse Snoopy* when she mentioned they'd be staying for two weeks. My mother, you see, is the bestselling author of *Machiavelli in Heels*. Maybe you've seen her on TV or heard her on her AM talk radio show, berating women like me to shuck their wimpitude and to wangle their way to the top. Yep, that's my mom.

I have to admit I've missed her in a "Stockholm Syndrome" sort of way. When I left California I figured I wouldn't see my parents again for at least another five years, especially as they're strapped for cash. Ever since my mother's second book made like the *Titanic* and tanked, she's been straining to stage her comeback and regain her position as the family breadwinner. And as for my dad, well, he hasn't worked since the Carter administration.

Yet for their thirtieth wedding anniversary, they intended to break open the piggy bank and celebrate *à la mode*. "You only live in this incarnation once," my mom reminded me when she called to announce their visit. "Besides, I miss my Becky."

"I go by Becca now, Mom."

"To me you'll always be Becky. That's the name we gave you and that's the name we—"

"So when are you arriving again?"

And so it was decided. My parents would visit me in a month. Almost enough time for me to clean my attic room and get a job.

My folks arrived at Charles de Gaulle airport on a Thursday evening with a cartful of scuffed designer luggage and an armful of hugs for their only child. I was surprised to hear they'd flown first class. I could tell from my dad's crinkled brow that he'd been against the idea. This was confirmed as we were waiting for the RER train to Paris when he pulled me aside.

"Can you talk to your mother?" he said from behind his camera. He'd switched on his new digital gadget and was filming the burnt-out cars beside the RER station. "She wants us to eat at a place called *Le Phoque d'Or*. It's $300 a head!"

"Dad, when was the last time you two did something romantic?"

He lowered the camera. "All right, but can you at least get her to agree to the youth hostel?"

"A youth hostel? Dad, you're sixty-one years old."

"Or we could stay with you...?"

"Come to think of it, there's a hostel in the Marais that's actually quite nice. Did you bring your own sheets?"

"No, Mom, I do not have a boyfriend."

It was three hours into my parents' visit and already I was feeling the strain. We were crammed into a hatchback Renault taxicab, careening around the Place de la Bastille toward our restaurant on the Left Bank. We'd just endured an ultraminimal interpretation of *La Traviata* at the Opéra Bastille, which from our vantage in the back row of the top balcony had looked more like a flea circus than a tragic love story.

"So, ever since that fellow died," my mom went on, "that playwright—what was his name?"

"Lionel."

"Ever since Lionel died, you haven't been out with a man even once?"

She was referring to my late, not-so-great boyfriend. Long story, but basically he was murdered six months ago and I was the prime suspect. I nearly ended up in the French equivalent of Guantánamo. But I managed to figure out who poisoned my ex in time.

"No, Mom."

"Not even one date?"

No way was I going to tell my parents about my long-distance sex-on-the-run arrangement with a commitment phobic cop.

"It's understandable," my father said, adjusting his clip-on tie. "You're still grieving."

I wished I could agree with him. The truth is I was over my late ex even before he died.

"Maybe that's it," I said, admiring the Bastille column overhead, with its greenish shaft and gilded statue of *Liberté*.

"Oh, sure, grief can go on for years," my dad went on. "When Magdala died, Bob grieved for five years."

"Dad, Bob is an iguana. How can you tell if he's sad?"

"Iguanas happen to be very expressive reptiles. You just have to know how to read them."

As he spoke our taxi swerved onto the Avenue Henri IV, heading toward the Seine and squishing me tighter between my parents. We could easily have walked across the river from the Opéra Bastille, but mother's four-inch heels wouldn't have survived the journey. My father, on the other hand, was wearing black leather tennis shoes with his summer suit, the jacket flap of which he kept adjusting. Clearly he was uncomfortable. He hadn't worn a suit since 1977 when he quit General Electric and made a show of slicing up his ties.

"You're in for a treat, Becky," my mom announced, and Dad swiveled his camera lens at us. "*Le Phoque d'Or* is considered the finest restaurant in the world. It was also the first place in the world to use forks. Before that, Europeans ate with their hands from a hole in the middle of the table. Can you imagine?"

I flashed on a memory of my late boyfriend eating his McDonald's hamburger with a plastic knife and fork. "No."

"I'll be sure to include that fork bit in the script," Dad said from behind his camera. I bet he would. His idea *du jour* was to edit and sell this videologue of his and mom's second honeymoon to the TV networks. He thought our family was that fascinating. As it turned out, we were.

We pulled up in front of the *Phoque d'Or* a minute later and wedged ourselves out of the taxi, then made our way up the rickety elevator to the building's top floor. When we entered the restaurant, my breath caught in my throat. The bay windows commanded a view of the Seine and the eastern tip of the Île de la Cité, backlit by pink and purple streaks above the spires of Notre Dame. My father rushed to the windows to get it all on video. My mother, meanwhile, had just endured a shock to her otherwise hearty system. She stood glaring at the *maître d'hôtel* over the frames of her bifocals.

"What do you mean, no reservation?" she said in a voice that could only be described as loud and American.

The *maître d'hôtel*, a nattily dressed older man in a gray toupee, glanced again at his reservation sheet.

"I am afraid zere has been a leetle misunderstanding," he said with an imperious sniff. "We show no reservation for a Monsieur and Madame Bukowski and zeir—how do you say?—daughter."

"This is impossible," my mother boomed. "We made that reservation over a month ago."

"In any case, ze restaurant is closed to ze public. Tonight we have a private party."

"Rob, show them our duck number."

My mother was referring to a special service offered by the *Phoque d'Or*, which raises its own ducks. If you order in advance, you get a postcard with the serial number of your duck stamped on the card.

My father duly produced our duck number, but the *maître d'hôtel* merely frowned. "Ah, zat explains ze problem. Zis reservation was made before ze computer virus, ze 'Simonsez,' I zink it was called. We lost all our documents."

"This is unacceptable." My mother pointed at the elegantly dressed crowd sitting at the linen-bedecked tables. "Our dollars are as good as these people's euros."

"Now just settle down, Eileen," my dad said. "I'm sure this nice *may-der dee* here can fit us in some other night." He turned to the *maître d'hôtel* with an apologetic smile. "*Nest-paws*?"

The man consulted his calendar. "We have a table for three available... in two months."

"Two months?" My mom's voice rose an octave. She proceeded to berate the poor man, who managed both to cringe and to peer down his nose at her at the same time. My father was inching toward the entrance, tugging at my mom's handbag, while I stood with my eyes closed, praying the black marble tiles would open up and swallow me whole.

My prayers were answered in a much pleasanter way, for just as my mom was threatening to sue the restaurant owner, a deep French voice behind me said in perfect English, "Excuse the interruption, but you are more than welcome to join our party."

By now I'd opened my eyes. A ruggedly good-looking man of about thirty stood before me. He had a natural tan (not one of those up-to-your-eyeballs fake ones), thick wavy brown hair and eyes so gray they seemed to glow. I instantly forgot all about my sex-on-the-run arrangement with my long-distance commitment phobe. I was in love.

"We are just finishing with the first course," the gray-eyed man went on, "but we have three seats free at my table. My brother and his family missed their flight from America."

My mother's jaw had stopped moving mid-threat. It hung open, showing her mangled stick of Dentyne gum. My father was no less impressed. He was discreetly filming our gracious host from waist level. I could understand their amazement. This was the first time in all three of our lives that a Frenchman had gone out of his way to be polite.

"I am Adrian Dumelle," our host announced as he escorted me and my parents to his table, which commanded a stunning view of the Seine and the Notre Dame, silhouetted against a magenta sky.

"And this is Seymour Rabaud." He gestured toward a bald man in his early thirties who had politely stood up at our arrival. "An old school friend."

Seymour inclined his well-oiled head and tugged at a thick brown goatee. He wore a black turtleneck even though it was summer and what appeared to be a permanent smirk.

"And this is Fabienne Levesque." Our host indicated a golden-skinned woman wearing a micro-mini skirt, a beaded yellow satin top and a sour frown. "My cousin."

Fabienne merely nodded as she slid a dismissive look at my outfit, which I have to admit was a bit offbeat. I was wearing my best friend Nina's fashion-school creation, which made breathing optional. Think semi-sheer, full-body girdle with straps. *Look on the bright side*, I thought as I squeezed onto a creaky Louis XV chair, *at least I won't overeat*.

"And last but not least, Brigitte." Our host gestured toward a lanky, nut-brown woman in a leopard print dress whose small breasts where crammed up to her collarbones by her push-up bra. "How should I refer to you, Brigitte?" our host asked teasingly. "My favorite mistake? My soon-to-be ex-wife?"

Brigitte stared directly at our host. "*Va te faire foutre.*"

Translation: Go bleep yourself.

"What did she say?" my mother whispered in my ear.

"Pleased to meet you," I whispered back.

As my parents and I settled in at our table, a few men at the other tables glanced my way, smiling suggestively. I wondered if they were checking me out, or if they were more interested in Fabienne and Brigitte. In either case, I enjoyed the attention.

Our host—who insisted I call him Adrian—did his best to put me and my folks at ease. Unlike some French people, so he told us, he was a friend of America. He loved our popular culture and our language and the great open spaces of the Southwest. As he spoke he kept pouring me wine from his family's vineyard in St.-Émilion, introducing each dollop with a little story about the lime-soil fields around his ancestral *château*. It was all so charmingly French.

"We have a special connection to America in my family," Adrian said as the second course plates were being set before us. "I went to school there. My brother and cousins as well."

By now his pale eyes and long black lashes had begun to mesmerize me. I blushed as the *maître d'hôtel* arrived to explain the dishes that made up the second course. My French is passable, but I have to admit I could only make out three words of what the *maître d'hôtel* said: *vin*, *quiche* and *peut-être*.

I'd just sliced off a bit of what looked like fish when my mother leaned close and whispered, "Incredible. According to the woman next to me, these people are blue blood."

"What?"

"The man you've been talking to is a viscount!"

I nearly choked on my *peut-être* fish.

"Are you sure?"

"Of course. Find out if he's still single."

"Mom!"

"Shh. He's looking." My mom turned her attention back to her plate, leaving me to fend for myself with Adrian, the viscount.

Much as I hated my mother's crass opportunism, I had to admit that the fact our host was not only charming and sexy but also a viscount stimulated the area of my brain marked "Love Zone: enter at own risk."

Not that I dared show it. For the rest of the second course I made polite conversation with Adrian about the food (which turned out to be frogs' legs) and the wine (this particular bottle came from his cousin's vineyard in Bordeaux) and cultural differences (not all French are rude; not all Americans are nice).

After my third glass of Bordeaux, I found myself actually able to speak French again. But then I made a faux pas. Adrian had asked if I liked the oil painting hanging on the wall beside our table.

"Personally, I've seen better in my high school art class," I said studying the ugly dabs of dirty color. "But I like the shape of the frame."

"It's a Monet," quipped Brigitte, the dour ex-wife.

Everyone at our table laughed while I turned bright pink. Adrian, however, seemed to be on my side.

"I quite agree," he said to me once the snickers had died down. "As Flaubert once said, 'One must not always think that feeling is everything. Art is nothing without form.'"

My parents, on the other hand, were a social success. My father regaled the tan, satin-topped cousin Fabienne with his tales of visiting Paris as a young GI on leave from Germany and how he learned the expressions "*ma petite chatte*" (my little pussy) and "*voulez-vous coucher avec moi ce soir?*" (you want to sleep with me tonight?) This was news to Mom, who glowered at him, but after another glass of Bordeaux she forgave him. Then my mother took center stage and pitched her book, which would come out in French soon under the title *Machiavelli en Corset*. And of course, my dad got the whole charming scene on video, and when my mother insisted he turn off the camera, he set it beside his plate and covered it with his napkin. But I could see the red light was still on.

Meanwhile, my feelings for Adrian were rapidly veering from mild desire toward something approaching a romantic swoon. His eyes told me he felt the same way, and so after my fourth glass of wine I made a private decision to embrace my good luck. I wanted this man, damn it, and I was going to try to win him. Why shouldn't I have a chance at love with a good catch? I had a right to happiness as much as anyone else. It was nature's way. And the American way: life, liberty and the pursuit of happiness. It was in our constitution, for goodness' sake.

I touched Adrian's arm...and he glanced at my breasts, and I had to restrain myself from indulging in fantasies of a life divided between Paris and St.-Émilion as the Vicomtesse Dumelle, wife to this perfect man in our charming *château*, complete with 2.5 bilingual children and nightly romantic strolls through our vineyard, followed by a gourmet meal and even more gourmet sex. This meal was just a foretaste, and I was loving every bite.

I would have stayed at the table for the next course, but I was concerned I might have *épinards aux lardons* between my teeth. Plus I wanted to check my makeup and outfit to make sure I looked good for Adrian. So I excused myself and headed toward the ladies' room.

As I weaved my way to the side hallway, I caught a few calculating looks from the men and cold stares from the women. The latter must have seen me flirting with the most eligible bachelor in the room. Well, that was life, ladies, I thought as I entered the marble expanse of the restroom. We were put on this earth to find our way and to meet our mate.

It was natural selection, that's all; nothing personal that he preferred me to them. Tomorrow their chance would come, just as today my chance had, and I was damn well going to take it!

I was leaning over the bathroom sink, digging spinach from between my two back molars, when Adrian pushed open the ladies' room door. We locked gazes in the mirror, and a second later he pulled me into the first stall, the French kind that are enclosed and private and in this case entirely in white marble and cherry wood.

"Where would you like to be kissed?" He breathed the words into my ear, sending a jolt of pleasure straight to my groin. "Here?" He gently tapped my lip. "Or here?" His fingertip trailed down my cheek to my throat. "Or perhaps...here?" He circled one of my nipples, and I inhaled sharply.

"I'll take option number two."

This seemed the safest choice. We were both fairly ripped from the wine, but I was still keenly aware of my job as female of the species to put the natural brakes on that imp Eros to insure a proper courtship.

Adrian obliged me and for the next few minutes I luxuriated in my fantasies of enjoying these same kisses in our chateau in St.-Émilion while our 2.5 children slept snug in bed, and our vineyard cooled in the misty night breeze. I was just warming to the idea of the count uncorking a bottle of our private reserve Bordeaux, when I felt his hand snake under my dress and tug at my "string," as the French refer to thongs.

I grabbed his hand and redirected it to my breast.

"Let's not ruin this perfect moment."

"There are no perfect moments."

"This one feels pretty perfect to me."

He shook his head. "It's like Flaubert once said, 'Reality does not conform to the ideal, but confirms it.'"

Him and his Flaubert quotes! "What would Flaubert say about this?" I grabbed his arms and kissed him.

"He would say, 'Are you wet for me?'"

"And I would say not yet, you impatient man."

I was wet, actually. Though I would never admit it. I had to be a little bit coy....

"May I ask a different favor of you then?" He was panting slightly.

"Depends."

"May I have your"—his cheeks flushed—"how do you say, your underwires? As a souvenir of this beautiful evening when we first met?"

"You mean my underwear? Or my bra?"

"Underwear. Like, pantiettes."

"You mean panties?"

He nodded his agreement.

"Not a good idea. This dress is made of semi-sheer fabric. Without these panties, I'll reveal all."

"*Je t'en prie*, as a memento of our first night." His voice spread over me as smooth as dark chocolate, but I sensed from its edge he might be losing his temper. Or was my imagination playing tricks on me?

"Sorry," I said teasingly, "but if you're good, someday I'll give more than my panties."

This time his voice grew steely. "Lift up your dress."

"No means *non*." I'd tried to say it as a joke, but Adrian wasn't laughing. To my shock, he lunged at me, then slammed me against the stall, shoved up my dress and tore off my undies. I stared at him in disbelief, the back of my head aching and my heart thumping so hard you could have heard it in the Marais.

"Why the hell did you do that?"

My voice was shaking, and I could feel adrenaline rushing through my veins. I became aware that I was panting, partly from leftover arousal, but mostly from hurt rage. If he so much as touched me again, I was prepared to gouge at his eyes.

"As Flaubert once said, 'That man has missed something who has never left a brothel at sunrise feeling like throwing himself into the river out of pure disgust.'"

"Huh?"

"But then I suppose you wouldn't understand."

With this he pushed out of the stall, leaving me behind quite panty-less and even more clueless. Was he some sort of pervert or misogynist? Or both? I slammed my fist against the stall. Damn my rotten luck. Once again I'd earned my title as the reigning Miss Maniac Magnet.

My face burning and chin held high, I made my way back to our table clutching my purse in front of my hips and praying no one would notice the dark shadow between my legs. In the main room several couples were dancing to live music. Adrian was no longer at our table, thank God. I glanced around before taking my seat and spotted him behind an ice sculpture with a group of men—showing them my thong.

And then I understood. He'd engaged in some sort of bet or competition with his friends.

The humiliation! Blinking back tears, I sat with my parents and stared at my dessert, unable to understand what anyone at our table was saying. The walls seemed to be closing in on me, and I wanted nothing more than to leave, but no way would I let a vicious viscount ruin my parents' anniversary. So I said nothing about the incident all through dessert and coffee, during which our host thankfully kept his distance. All around me the sound of French laughter grew louder, as if mocking me, as if everyone present had guessed at my stupid fantasies about the viscount, and the even stupider reality.

After dessert my parents asked about our missing host. I told them I'd given him my phone number, and we would see what came of it.

"This is so exciting, Becca," my mom said. "You never know, maybe someday we'll meet Princess Caroline and Prince Albert at your wedding."

I gave her a weak smile. My mother is a royalty buff. She's up on the latest blue-blood pregnancies, affairs and tragedies. And for the past ten minutes she'd been chatting with the guests at our table as if she and they were on a first-name basis with Europe's aristocracy. "Did you hear that Letitia is pregnant again? Where will Charles and Camilla vacation this year? Isn't it a shame about poor Stephanie?"

My father was also clearly warming to France and to the French. He'd moved on from stories of sexual conquest as a young GI to high-adventure tales of iguana rescue missions, and everyone at our table was drunk enough, or their English was bad enough, that they laughed in all the right places.

Except me. I drained my glass of dessert wine and asked the hovering *maître d'hôtel* for another. From my parents' fond looks, I could tell they were proud of me for making my way in Paris. This could have been a warm moment for us, but I knew it was based on pure illusion.

And then just as Dad had reached the high point in his tale of rescuing Bob the iguana from a Hell's Angels den, a woman rushed up to our table, identified herself as the Marquise Leroy and pointed at my father's camera.

"You!" she cried in the shrillest French I'd heard in years. The soprano in *La Traviata* had nothing on this lady. "Yes, you, paparazzo! Turn off that camera."

The guests in our corner of the banquet room began to murmur. "Paparazzi? Where? Who let them in?"

"It's people like you who killed Diana!" The marquise grabbed the camera, her bangles clanging, and a melee ensued, during which my dad clung to his camera and the guests mobbed around him trying to take it, while my mother shouted something about suing the lot of them if they so much as mussed my father's hairpiece.

Shell-shocked, I withdrew to the window, clutching my glass of Sauterne. This evening had been a total disaster. It was as if the second Franco-American war had broken out. I supposed it was up to me to visualize trans-Atlantic peace. I did a few yoga breaths through alternating nostrils and concentrated on the view of Notre Dame, the flying buttresses above me and the tranquil Seine below. And when that didn't work, I inhaled my glass of Sauterne.

The melee meanwhile had died down, and by all accounts it was time for us to leave. I'd say so. We'd overstayed our welcome ten anti-American insults ago.

I'd drunk too much wine, though, and if I didn't get back to the ladies' room in a hurry, I'd make my sheer dress even sheerer. So while my mother donned her summer coat and my father straightened his hairpiece, I glanced around the restaurant for Adrian, who was nowhere to be seen. Good. The coast was clear.

But when I reached the ladies' room a minute later, he was waiting for me.

With a famous *Phoque d'Or* fork sticking out of his throat.

"Not the imbecile, you imbecile, the *embassy*," my mother was shouting into her cell phone. "Get me the embassy!"

It was ten minutes after I'd discovered Adrian forked to death in the

Ded Men Don't Eat Quiche

ladies' room. The four main murder suspects—including me—were being herded into the *maître d'hôtel's* office to wait for the police to arrive. The *maître d'hôtel* was beyond upset about the murder and his restaurant's ruined reputation, not to mention the ruined fork. He'd confiscated my father's camera to give to the police, because as I'd so helpfully pointed out, the digital footage showed all the people who'd gone to and from the bathroom area over the past half hour.

"Don't worry," I called to my parents as the office door swung shut between us, "I'll think of something." I had after all solved a murder case before.

The *maître d'hôtel's* office was a curious mix of ancient and modern. A clear glass desk dominated the room over a faded Persian carpet, and the minimalist paintings dotting the walls jarred with the hand-painted Louis XV chairs. It was onto one of these chairs that I lowered myself, still holding my handbag in front of my hips. I glanced about at my fellow suspects, who to my surprise turned out to be my former tablemates as well—namely, Adrian's satin-topped cousin Fabienne, who sat rubbing her bare arms as if she had a chill, and beside her, Adrian's old school pal Seymour, who nervously ran his fingers over his bald head. Next to Seymour lounged Adrian's leopard-print soon-to-be ex-wife Brigitte, studiously clicking at her cell phone's number pad.

We'd all been recently filmed going to and from the restrooms, in addition to the poor viscount himself, of course. I say "poor" because while he may have been a major-league creep, he shouldn't have had to fork over his life for that fault.

Stumped, I sat back and racked my brain for a plan, and I'd just hit on the idea of telling the cops about the viscount's panty hunt when suddenly Fabienne sprang to her feet and glared at Brigitte. "You think you can get away with this?" Her satin top shimmered as she drew a deep breath. "Everyone knows about that prenup and how much you'd inherit."

Brigitte adjusted her push-up bra and leveled a steady gaze at Fabienne. "This from a woman who kisses and kills for a living."

"My first husband was seventy-three years old!" Fabienne stamped her foot on the Persian carpet, sending up a poof of dust. If her micro-mini skirt rode any higher it would have been a tube top. "You accuse me, you...you...you vulture?"

Brigitte kept her pitiless gaze fixed on Fabienne. "Adrian dumped you. It hurt. Get over it."

"I am over it. Are you?"

"*Mesdames*, please," Seymour called from where he'd taken up residence behind the glass desk. "Can we have a moment of silence? Adrian just died."

"As if you care." Fabienne swung her chandelier earrings in Seymour's direction. "He told me about your threats."

"I don't know what you're talking about."

"It's called pillow talk," Brigitte interjected. "Adrian never could keep a secret."

"I don't care what you call it. He was my best friend. I won't have you two dragging his name through the mud like this."

Fabienne laughed. "The man was a sieve." She slinked over to Seymour and leaned over the desk, her earrings swinging as she exposed her generous décolleté. "He told me all about your financial straits. You think no one else knows you owed him money? Let me guess. He was blackmailing you, *non?*"

"That's not true."

"We'll see what the police think," Fabienne said. "They can access bank accounts. It'd be terrible if the press found out you're broke, wouldn't it? There goes your chances with the girls, Romeo."

Seymour lowered his eyebrows in a Neanderthal-like glare. "You breathe a word of this, and you'll be sorry."

"Is that a threat?" Fabienne asked. "Oooh, my pistol and I are scared."

Seymour was about to reply when the office door swung open and Inspector Pimpineau walked in. I recognized him at once from when he'd investigated my late boyfriend's murder, and from the way his eyes widened, I could tell he recognized me, too.

"Mademoiselle Bukowski, what are you doing here?"

"Trying to enjoy an evening out with my folks?"

Everyone in the room turned to me, suspicion gleaming in their eyes.

"I don't even know these people!" I added. "I'm just a guest at this restaurant."

"Sorry, mademoiselle," Inspector Pimpineau said, "but the wait staff saw you go into the bathroom at a time when this was turned off." He hefted Dad's digital camera. "Moreover, your fork is missing from its place setting. We'll be checking for fingerprints, of course."

"Someone else could have picked up my fork." I said in a small voice, suddenly aware of the depth of the deep *merde* I was in.

Pimpineau gave me an apologetic shrug. He took hold of my elbow and started murmuring French legalese as he carted me from the office. I was being arrested, whereas the other suspects were only being voluntarily questioned. How unfair was that?

My walk of shame from the office to the elevator was only twenty feet, but it felt like a mile.

"Becky," my mom called as I passed by. For the first time since she'd arrived in Paris, she gave me a soft look. "We'll think of something. Do they have pro bono lawyers in this country?"

My father had out his spare camera and was filming my arrest. He switched to the zoom lens and called out, "At least they're against the death penalty over here. That's something, right?"

All I could do was nod and clamp my teeth over my lower lip. On our way through the foyer, Inspector Pimpineau stopped at the podium by the restaurant's entrance and asked the *maître d'hôtel* to write down a phone number for where my parents could reach me. The good man did as he was asked, writing in a careful hand and making slow, single strokes for the number one. "I should never have let you in," he said as he handed the note to my pale, blinking parents. "I will surely lose my position."

The elevator door slid open a minute later and I was escorted inside. I watched, listless, as a guest who was leaving at the same time punched the first-floor button. The elevator button lit up and suddenly I felt as if my brain had lit up as well. *Of course,* I thought, *the number one! The number one!* I turned to Inspector Pimpineau.

"I know who did it!"

Epilogue

It's been a week since my parents' disastrous thirtieth anniversary at the *Phoque d'Or*, and I've enjoyed every second of my freedom, by which I mean not only freedom from my parents, who left Paris the day after the murder, but freedom from the long arm of the French law.

I let the police work out all the little details, but the main proof pointing to Adrian's killer was my discovery. You see, when I saw the *maître d'hôtel* writing an American-style number one with a single stroke, I realized he must be in disguise. French people write their number one with two strokes, one curved upward, one straight down, and yet the *maître d'hôtel*, from the sound of his perfect French, was most definitely a Frenchman.

From these facts I inferred that he must be Adrian's brother, the one who'd been schooled in the U.S. and had supposedly missed his flight home. As it turned out, this brother was to inherit *beaucoup* money pots. He'd arranged a second identity, dressed as an older man and claimed to have been sent by an exclusive employment agency. The real *maître d'hôtel*, meanwhile, had been befriended and drugged and was sleeping off the day in his apartment. A perfect plan. But what the killer hadn't counted on was me and my folks barging in on his private party.

As for my parents, I got a postcard from them in Rome. My father wrote: "I lost my spare video camera at the Colosseum, but I suspect your mother hid it." And my mother wrote: "Those Romans sure understood power. I have a new idea for a book, *Empress to Impress*, how modern women can emulate Alexander the Great."

All I can say about my parents is it takes two to tangle. At least they're still together, which is a lot more than I've achieved in the relationship department.

On the plus side, I've just finished an on-spec review of *Le Phoque d'Or*. I'm waiting to see what the editor of *Franglais* thinks of it. I can just see it now: me in St.-Tropez reviewing a five-star hotel, with my long-distance lover permanently close.

But first things first. Let's not get carried away with overheated fantasies. My long-distance commitment phobe is passing through Paris this weekend and has invited me to dinner. That's something I can count on. That's reality, and reality is hot enough.

Novelist and screenwriter **DEANNA CARLYLE**, a.k.a. the Euro Chick, is co-founder of the International Women's Fiction Festival held each year in Matera, Italy, and originator of the popular online list serv *Chick-lit: Women's Fiction Markets and Tips*. To network with 1000+ chick-lit writers and to get a full list of chick-lit book releases each month, visit Deanna's site at www.deannacarlyle.com.

Lauren Baratz-Logsted

No author of chick-lit that I know of ever set out to be the literary equivalent of the Antichrist. Like authors of all stripes everywhere, we put on our pants one leg at a time and we endeavor to write stories that will entertain the reader and sometimes make the reader think.

Shell Game

1. A Woman with Aspirations about a Gourd

Okay. Fine.

I'll admit it (all the while hoping this'll be the strangest admission I'll ever have to make in my life):

Ever since I was a young girl, I dreamed of one day becoming a pumpkin wife.

A pumpkin wife? you say.

Yes, a pumpkin wife, I say. You know, one of those wives like in "Peter, Peter, Pumpkin-Eater"? I wanted to be the wife Peter put in a shell, one of those wives that were kept there very well.

Which is no small aspiration to have, not when you're a stockbroker with one of the biggest firms on Wall Street, the kind of estrogen-laden stockbroker-on-wheels who makes the Testosterone Club hiss-whisper as you soar on by, "Oh God! Sheila Stone! She's got bigger balls than Chuck Norris."

Which is not to say this *isn't* all somehow my mother's fault. After all, I've been blaming Dear Old Mom for everything that's gone wrong with my life in the last thirty-six years. Why stop now? I've preferred to bestow all credit for anything good on Dear Old Dad, who expired of a heart attack not long after he got his first glimpse of me, a completely unrelated event.

"I think people had it better in the good old days," my mom would say during our weekly lunch at her house in Westport. "Look at the problems the poor blacks have now, getting beaten to death by policemen. You don't think they had it better before?"

When, I'd think to myself as I bit down on a carrot stick with the kind of vengeance that would have made Bugs Bunny proud, *when did they have it better? When they were beaten as slaves? When they were hosed down in the streets? When was it better before?* Sure, it wasn't an ideal world we were living in, and atrocities still happened every day, but a world in which everyone had a legal right to vote and the possibility of working in any field was still a damn sight better version than any world—at least any United States world—that had gone before.

"And all these groups that want to be liberated," my mother would go on, adding another ladleful of creamed soup to the bowl I was already not eating, "they keep thinking that things are going to be so much better once they're liberated. The blacks, you women," she'd add as if she wasn't one of us, flashing a diamond ring the size of a potato to prove that maybe she wasn't, "tell me what has all of this liberation gotten you? You fought for freedom so you'd have the right to work as dogs? You fought for freedom so you could have a career *and* raise kids *and* take care of a household? For this people burned their bras? I mean, I don't understand it. *My* generation had it better than you girls have it today. And *I Love Lucy* had it better than anybody."

Well, a person couldn't argue with that. I'd take a bite of dessert figuring, with a full mouth, I wouldn't even be tempted to try.

"Tell me the truth, damn it," my mom would say, slamming her heavy silver fork down emphatically, as if I'd just been giving her one argument after the other, "didn't people have it better in the good old days?"

I'd wipe my mouth, through with standing it. "Whose good old days?"

This clearly exasperated her. "Anyone's good old days! Anyone's days that aren't today's." Now she was confused herself. "At least I *think* that's what I want to say."

"When," I'd ask deliberately, "were things so much better? When Jewish people were getting turned into lampshades during World War II? When there was no electricity and no indoor plumbing? When Austen and the Brontës were around, and a woman had three options—count them, three: being married, being a governess or being a prostitute? How about when people lived in caves...?"

"Oh, well," she'd say, rising, ostensibly to take away the dishes but in reality to just cut me off, "if you're going to get so *technical* about it...."

Of course, the most annoying thing of all was that a small, niggling part of my brain *did* think my mother had a point there. Oh, not about blacks or any other would-be liberated group. But women? What woman who had grown up on *I Love Lucy* didn't think Lucy had it better? Lucy didn't need any liberating; Alice Kramden might, with that depressing apartment and a husband who wouldn't even let her put a poster on the wall, for chrissakes, but Lucy sure didn't. There she was, in glorious black and white, not working for a living, buying new hats whenever she wanted to. Lucy had a man to take care of her and she was obviously having the time of her life.

I, on the other hand, was a career woman trying to have a romantic life in the '90s. In case no one has pointed this out to you before, dating is not all it's cracked up to be.

I should know.

2. Some of Sheila's Duds

Sometimes, it seemed as though I had dated them all.

There were many guys who were relieved I was as high-powered as they were, relieved at the possibility of having someone to come home to at night who would be able to relate to whatever they had gone through in the world of corporate America that day, someone who, being as or more busy than they were, might not even be there yet.

I can remember one postcoitally glowing Saturday night with my co-worker Blake when neither of us had to be back at work until Tuesday, the Stock Exchange being closed on Monday for one of those annoyingly ubiquitous holidays and thus giving us enough time off from work that we felt as though we could actually do something relaxing for twenty minutes. I had my head on Blake's naked shoulder and was thinking of chocolate.

Blake, for his part, had gotten so relaxed he was actually making hypothetical remarks about the future. This was major progress since Blake was the kind of man who was so at home in his thousand-dollar suits that, like cigarette trails for someone strung out on LSD, even stark naked, you could still see the glowing wake of his suspenders.

"Of course," he said, "if we *were* to ever kick this puppy up a notch— you know what I mean, the 'marriage' thing" (Blake spoke frequently in half-quotes) "we'd have to equip ourselves with an entire support staff." He abruptly removed his arm from around my shoulders, causing my head to drop on my pillow with a soft yet clearly discernible thud, and began ticking off what we'd need on his fingers. "First off, we'd need a wife."

"A wife?" I interrupted, erroneously assuming this was the job he'd been trying me out for.

"Of course. Someone to take care of all the little things for us, someone to supervise the rest of our support staff. Then we'd need a cook— goes without saying—even if we don't use her much and she's just on call twenty-four hours a day. A maid, *natch*, someone to keep the place clean just in case we ever have time to entertain and so the mess doesn't get too annoying for us. Personal trainers, a guy for me and a girl for you, so neither of us has to expend any unnecessary energy on jealousy." He'd obviously thought about all the angles. "Personal shoppers, so that—oh!" and here he interrupted himself. "Kids! We've never said anything about kids! What do you think? The 'adoption' thing? The 'surrogate mother' thing?"

What I thought was that this was it for Blake. Even if it wasn't, it was definitely it for me. And it wasn't even as though I was all hellfire sure myself I wanted to "do" the "baby" thing at all; it was merely that Blake had finally succeeded in finding my last nerve and jumping on it like it was some kind of trendy trampoline. Like Goldilocks in the house of those "Bear people," as Blake might say, I was off to find something more suited to my tastes. I also promised myself, with God as my witness, Scarlett, I'd never make the mistake of having sex with someone who was also in investments over a long holiday weekend again. Things just got too weird whenever I tried that.

Then there was Tad, Tad who was only marginally younger than me—nine months—but acted as though he was doing an older woman a great big favor every time he whipped out his equipment. Not that he didn't look perfectly happy to be having sex; men are always happy to be having sex at any time, I've found, during the first six months of a relationship anyway. In fact, while nothing can be a completely reliable barometer of future long-term happiness in a relationship—probably because there isn't such a thing—I think it's pretty safe to say if a man shows reticence about shtupping you in those halcyon days of the first six months, it's a good bet long-term bliss will not follow and this is not the relationship that will sail you smoothly into old age.

But back to Tad and his equipment. It was great equipment; it was just too bad he looked so self-satisfied whenever he got the chance to use it.

Of course, Tad's attitude toward his own penis wasn't the most annoying thing about him. When you're a high-powered executive—and I was—you make sure you have sex regularly, just like you make sure you go to the dentist twice a year. However, you don't have a lot of spare time to devote to analyzing the ins and outs of the mating game, any more than you have time to really think about the drill. Once that cavity's filled, baby, I'm outta there.

No, the really annoying problem with Tad was he had yet to decide what he wanted to be when he grew up—which, given the fact he hadn't been a minor for as long as he'd been a minor, was a major problem—and, from the way he just sat back and enjoyed it every time I picked up the check, which was every time, I could see his ultimate career ambition was to be married to somebody like me so he wouldn't have to be anything when he grew up or even grow up at all.

Not cut out to be anybody's Sugar Mama, after I was through fishing I quickly cut bait. It's tough to stay excited for long about a man who can sit back and drink White Russians all night without batting an eye when you pick up the tab.

3. Brent Breaks the Camel's Back

Finally, there was Brent, who was an overachiever at underachieving; Brent, whose parents, when the O.J. Simpson scandal had broken, had tried to prevail upon their son to change his own first name to something potentially less controversial; Brent, who had grown up in the most exclusive neighborhood of the most exciting city in the world and whose ultimate goal in life, he told me three months into our relationship, was to find the perfect wave to ride.

"But you've never even been out of the tri-state area," I protested.

Which was true. When Brent was a child, his parents had been so scared of the possibility of kidnapping they'd barely even taken him out of the city. By the time he'd grown to adulthood—his body at least—the habit was ingrown and he had a tendency not to travel in much wider than a twenty-block radius of the Carnegie Deli on West 57th Street. Luckily, he had the metabolism of a surfer, even if he'd never see any tsunamis that weren't televised, and thus the full-pound pastrami sandwiches he ate on a regular basis weren't adding any girth. As I watched him sitting there in his torn jeans, leather jacket and sunglasses—reluctantly inching up on forty, he was going through his second biker phase already—I ate only the broth from my matzo ball soup and fervently wished my metabolism could say the same.

"I can change," Brent said, elbowing the ketchup aside and placing two nonrefundable one-way tickets to Hawaii on the no-frills deli table. This was not as daringly romantic a gesture as it might sound. Brent had a trust fund that made the pin money that Ted used to give Jane seem miserly. He could therefore, were he to change his mind about Hawaii (read: chicken out), throw those two tickets into the trash with the same mindlessness most people check off the one-dollar campaign-fund-donation box on their IRS return.

"Only in theory," I said in response to his claim to changeability, knowing full well endless time on a Hawaiian beach with Brent was not my cup of nirvana.

"What do you have against me?" Brent pouted.

What did I have against Brent? Well, for starters, there was his attitude toward working for a living; or not working, I should say. True, silver-spoon-in-mouth people like Brent don't necessarily *have* to work if they don't want to, but it is nice when they do. Look at Ted Kennedy.

But Brent didn't want to look at Ted Kennedy. And as much as Brent's parents tried to get their only son interested in the idea of doing something useful with his life—although I doubt they would have shared my definition of Ted Kennedy's liberal-leaning life as being "useful"—they couldn't get him to budge. In fact, it's my belief everything Brent ever did was somehow a part of his mission to remain a bad boy in his parents' eyes, a fairly sad comment to make when the boy in question is looking at forty.

When Brent and I first met, he had initially been over-the-moon enthusiastic about my stockbroker status. Considering how incongruous this was, given his carefully crafted underachiever persona, this was something of a surprise. He introduced me to his parents, and I could literally see the relief suffuse their eyes at the thought their son had finally taken up with a woman who *did something*, even if that something was nothing more noble than helping people who already had plenty of money—people not unlike themselves—make even more money. But as I grew to know Brent, I slowly began to twig to what was going on behind those trust-fund eyes of his.

Sometimes I watched Brent over the flickering candlelight of a dinner at his parents' home and I would swear I could actually see him, from spite, accepting a position doing something very worthwhile . . . once his parents' bodies were both stone cold. Until that time, however, he had me with which to torment them. If they were thinking I was going to drag him up, they were thinking wrong, for Brent had other things in mind. Having finally presented them with a woman who was bona fide viable daughter-in-law material, it was his plan to bring her down to underachiever status as the final blow. The Hawaii plan, I saw, was merely the ultimate vehicle for doing so. Brent was determined to remain an underachiever, at least for as long as his parents both should live.

And now he wanted to drag me down with him.

It seems reasonable at this juncture for you to begin wondering what I was doing with Brent in the first place. Simple. Whenever Brent wasn't doing his damnedest to be Jack Kerouac, an immobile Jack Kerouac, he was the best-read man I'd ever slept with, one who could talk Smiley as well as Shakespeare—and sometimes both at once—with the best of them. I, for my part, was a closet reader of fiction, a bold admission for a stockbroker to make, even if there is no one around to hear it but you.

Plus, the sex was great.

Do you sense a repetitive theme here? Is it possible to make the argument that one of the primary reasons women stay in doomed relationships is because they're shallow enough to be satisfied with great sex?

Hardly.

I'd stayed in many doomed relationships where I wasn't having great sex at all. I simply prefer not to go into them at length here. Rather, I favor the idea of having them pass in a blur. Barry the biter. Sam, who made a sucking sound through his teeth, like a plastic whistle from the Cracker Jacks box, every time he sucked on my breasts, which was often. Harry with halitosis. Not that I claim to be perfect myself. On the contrary, I'm sure if you asked my rejects what they have to say about me, they'd probably give you an earful, starting with, "Too fond of having the crease between her shoulder and neck kissed." But this is my story, not theirs. The only person who gets to complain about dissatisfaction here is Sheila.

Bottom line on Brent: I said no to Hawaii.

Carrying the Goldilocks analogy to its illogical conclusion, then, I had tried three of the main genres of men currently on offer—the overachiever who thinks every man/woman should be for him/herself; the underachiever who wants the woman to achieve so he doesn't have to; the underachiever who doesn't want anyone else to achieve either so he doesn't have to feel so bad—and was still hungry. Why, after what I'd been through, I don't know. After all, do I need to point out here that Blake, Tad and Brent were not the only three men I ever dated in my life? Do I need to point out they are merely the prototypes of the kinds of eggs I was breaking on a regular basis in my trivial and vain pursuit to make an omelet?

I thought not.

And every time I came home from another failed date, there was my mother's annoying voice in my head. "What's the big deal about freedom? What's so great about it? In *my* day, women had it so much better...."

4. Mom Catches a Fish for Sheila

You can imagine, then, how surprised I was when Dear Old Mom turned out to be the least enthusiastic recipient of the news I was finally getting married. To a doctor. Who didn't want me to work anymore.

"Oh, well," she said, almost vaguely, "if that's really what you want to do with your life, I suppose you know best. After all, you're the one with all the options...."

I had met Peter (yes, I know) at, of all places, the birthday party my mother had thrown for herself in honor of her own sixty-fifth. Leave it to my mother, among inviting a total of sixty-five of her nearest and dearest to mark the occasion, to also include her favorite ear, nose and throat man.

I first made the acquaintance of Dr. Peter Piper (yes, I know again) over the top of a shrimp tree.

"Good shrimp," he'd observed, putting a half dozen more on his paper plate. Not the smoothest opening gambit, I'll grant you, but when you consider my other immediate conversational opportunities included my deaf great-aunt and my cousin who I detested, I dove for the shrimp man.

"Yup," I'd concurred, proving myself to be an equally adept raconteur, all the while hoping he didn't notice the trail of cocktail sauce seeping out of the corner of my mouth from where I'd popped one in with the hopes of illustrating my point, "you've gotta love a good little shrimp."

Well, I consoled myself as I dabbed at the evidence of my slovenliness, at least you couldn't really argue with the veracity of my statement.

He didn't even try.

Instead, using his own paper napkin, he reached out his hand and oh so delicately wiped at a red spot on my face that I'd missed. "I'm Peter Piper," he said afterward, holding out his hand, "Dr. Peter Piper. I'm the honoree's ear, nose and throat man."

"Sheila Stone," I said, somewhat taken aback, but taking his smooth and notably ring-less hand nonetheless. "I'm the honoree's unmarried daughter, the one she's been trying to marry off for, oh," and here I made a big show of consulting my Rolex, "for about the last thirty-six years." Well, I thought, even if it was an awkward way to do it, we might as well get these things out of the way right up front, like advancing age and marital status being emphatically *not*. If I could have found a way to sneak into that single sentence the fact that I still had all of my own teeth, loved the color green and had always wanted to see Africa but had never found the time, I can assure you I would have done so.

You might be hard-pressed to imagine it, but, believe it or not, it got a whole lot better from there.

I gave him cocktail-party advice on some stocks he was considering and he told me what the best strategies were to avoid getting really hard hit during allergy season. All the while that he was cautioning me about the dangers of excessive dairy products, not to mention the yeast in beer, I observed his face, taking in the pleasing conjunction of features: the wavy dark hair, the amiably intelligent green eyes, the perfect nose that probably hadn't known an allergy in its life and the kissable lips. Then, for the full-length shot, I took in the slightly above-average height and the swimmer's body. Overall, the effect was oddly not perfection, but it was certainly not the sort of specimen I'd ever been known to kick out of bed for eating chips. Oh, and he was also about my age.

Then, after stocks and noses, we discussed the situation in Europe, the dregs of the Clinton/Lewinsky/Starr sideshow and what should really be done about Dr. Jack Kevorkian, both of us agreeing: nothing. We also discussed Nepal as a concept, how difficult it is for high-powered people to find time for the *right* relationships—meaning not just *any* relationships—and whether or not either one of us thought about having children. It should be pointed out, perhaps, that none of what we discussed was necessarily discussed in the order in which it appears on the pages here.

Then we ate slices of my mother's birthday cake—which was chocolate with strawberry filling and vanilla butter-cream frosting, in case anyone needs to know—with me deliberately though regretfully eschewing the frosting, normally my favorite, now I'd been made aware of the dire effects it might have on my breathing passages. Finally, we each wiped our own mouths, tossed our paper napkins aside, exchanged phone numbers with promises to keep in touch and called it a night.

Three months later, we were still dating.

We ate, we danced, we talked, we had sex, we even talked afterward: everything was as perfect as I thought it could ever get. And the conversations! We talked about things that mattered and things that didn't; about how neither of us had any intention of lining George Stephanopoulos' pockets with our money now he'd decided to capitalize on the misfortunes of the man who'd given him the best opportunity he could have ever hoped for, an opportunity he couldn't have *bought*, by writing a tell-all account in exchange for a lot of cold hard cash; about how we agreed that, in college, we'd both known dozens of women who would have behaved *exactly* as Monica had, given the slimmest opportunity (well, except for saving the dress; no one either of us had ever known would have ever done *that*) and that anyone who claimed they didn't know any women like that were probably the same kind of people who would try to tell you they'd smoked but never inhaled.

Okay. So maybe we talked more about things that didn't matter than about things that did. But so what? He picked up the tab on an insistently regular basis and didn't treat me as though I was just a fellow professional who just happened to have some conveniently placed body parts, and I thought I was falling in love. So sue me.

So, maybe we didn't talk about things that mattered all the time, but sometimes. . . .

"Sheila, did you ever think about settling down?"

The blues sax was wailing. My man's arms were around me as we danced, my head on his shoulder, and the bar was just the right size by New York law for there to be some good old-fashioned atmospheric smoke in it. It would have been just like Bogey and Bacall were it not for the fact he didn't look a thing like Bogey, I knew somewhere in my heart of hearts he was more a pragmatist than a romantic and, no, I confess, I didn't look like Bacall, either.

Inside, I was thinking, *What??? Is he maybe about to ask me what I think he's about to ask me?* Outside, maintaining the calm hauteur I hoped would allow me not to blow my big chance, probably the biggest chance I would ever get, I said, vaguely, "Hmm?" as if awakened from a dream. Delicate yawn. "Settle down?" Minor catlike neck stretch, seductive yet still suitable for conservative dance floor. "Mm," nuzzle back onto his shoulder, "I guess I've thought about it from time to time."

Who the hell was I trying to kid here?

Well, him actually. And, believe it or not, I was doing a pretty damned good job of it from all appearances.

"But have you ever thought about settling down with me specifically?"

At the risk of sounding annoyingly eager, if only to myself, inside I thought, *Boy, have I!* Outside, I gave another demure, "Hmm?" Catwoman yawn redux. "I guess so."

"And what do you think, Sheila?" Here he used his hand to gently tilt my chin upward, so I was now forced to look at his head, which was silhouetted against the multicolored halo glow of the dance floor lights. "Do you think you could bring yourself to marry someone like me?"

No longer able to contain myself anymore, I flung myself at his neck. "Yes!" I practically shouted, demureness a thing of the temporary past.

The way I figured it, we could hammer out the finer details later.

5. Later, Over Pie

Later came about fifteen minutes after, when, on the way back to my place—Peter had come in for the weekend from Connecticut—we stopped at a little all-night coffee shop to talk wedding.

"Get the chocolate cream pie," he said. "They always make the greatest chocolate cream pie here." Even though he lived in Connecticut and worked there three days a week in private practice, two days a week he consulted at a city hospital. Somehow, with only two days a week there—and those being work days—he'd managed to sniff out the best places to have anything you could imagine, while I, on the other hand, having lived and worked there full-time for years, couldn't even find a place that didn't try to sell me stale bagels.

"But my waistline," I began, "the wedding...."

He dismissed women's innate fear of gaining weight *before* the wedding with a practiced flick of the wrist. "Fugeddaboudit," he said, doing an odd Italian gangster imitation that fell somewhere between Robert De Niro and Joe Pesci. "You look great. And besides, women worry too much about everything they eat all the time. If you just make sure to eat all the right things, then why not treat yourself to some of the good things, too? So long as you don't gain weight, what's the big deal?"

I neglected to point out that, since most women I knew had dieted the proper functioning of their own metabolism right out of existence, were I—as an example of one of those women I knew—to eat all the right things *plus* the extras, there would be a very big deal, and that big deal would be me. The reason I neglected to point this out was that, even though I didn't have a ring on my finger yet—it would come two weeks later, in a Tiffany box and with a price tag I didn't even dare imagine—I was now engaged. Instead of pointing out then I was reluctant to test unconditional love against an upwardly mobile arrow on a bathroom scale, I ordered the chocolate cream pie and even enjoyed the damn thing.

"What do you picture married life with me being like?" Peter said, seductively, stirring his coffee.

"I don't know," I shrugged, my mouth half full of chocolate cream. "What do you picture?"

Peter took one of my hands, the one that wasn't wielding the fork that was ravenously digging into the pie, in both of his. He looked into my eyes. I hoped he couldn't see how much I was enjoying the cream aspect of the pie. For the last three months I'd avoided dairy products as if they were Brussels sprouts on his original allergy say-so back at my mother's birthday party. Now here he had actually been the one to recommend the pie. Had he forgotten how bad dairy products were supposed to be for me? Was he perhaps softening me up for some kind of kill?

But no. There he was, still holding my hand, still looking into my eyes, and what he had to say was:

"I picture us living happily ever after in Connecticut."

I raised my eyebrows. "Connecticut?" There had been a very good reason why I had chosen to be the kind of stockbroker that did not commute in from the suburbs on Metro North, and that very good reason could be summed up in a single word: Mother.

If I lived in Connecticut, I would be closer to that single word.

But when Peter started talking about it being a better place for a family to live, and I assumed he was obliquely getting at the idea of us having kids one day, I found I had to agree with him. True, Giuliani had somehow miraculously managed to transform Times Square into Disney World—well, almost—but Connecticut was still a better place to raise kids. Thinking that, I decided to agree to an idea that would put me within the same state lines as my mother for the first time in over a decade. Maybe I could move to Connecticut with Peter but keep my apartment in New York. Then, if I didn't tell her, and if I was never unlucky enough to run into her at Stew Leonard's, she'd be none the wiser.

"Connecticut's acceptable," I finally said, having at last reasoned the whole thing out. "Just so long as we get me enough head scarves and dark glasses for when I need to do the grocery shopping, I should be fine." Seeing the puzzled look on his face, I added, "I'm kidding. Seriously, Connecticut will be great. You'll still have your practice there and here, and I can get used to commuting five days a week. Hell, we can come in on the train together on the days you're in the city. It'll be fun."

"Wait a second. You're planning on still working after we're married?"

"Well, of course. Didn't you expect...?"

He looked hurt. "Frankly, no. I mean, I know you're good at your job and everything, superb even. But whenever you talk about it, you never really sound enthusiastic, not like some of the career women you meet. I just assumed what you did for a living was something you were just doing until...until...until...."

I patted the top of his hand to forestall his obvious feelings of awkward embarrassment. "Until you came along?" I mercifully finished his sentence for him, although in my version I presented it in the form of a question. Thank you, Alex Trebek.

"Well," he said, pausing long and having the grace to look mortified at his own caveman beliefs, "yes."

It was no fun to watch someone I was still in the first glows of love with twist in the wind. I decided to let him off the hook easy this time. "Well," I admitted, "maybe this time you assumed right."

"Really?"

"Sure, it'll be great. I'll give up my job. It'll be fun. I'll get to finally find out how the matron half lives. Besides, I can always go back to work if I find being a stay-at-home wife isn't my cup of Clorox."

But he hardly seemed to notice that last caveat. Instead, he had one final surprise for me.

"And I want to plan the wedding for us."

"You do?" I was surprised. Wedding planning was hardly men's work—and it now seemed obvious, at least to me, that our future relationship was going to be divided into men's and women's work. It certainly wasn't the work of a busy doctor. Still....

"Everything?" I asked, thinking he couldn't possibly mean it.

"*Everything*," he emphasized. "The place, the food, the honeymoon, your dress: everything."

I licked some whipped cream off the back of my spoon and thought about everything I'd be giving up if I went along with this. After all, doesn't every girl dream of one day planning her own wedding right down to the smallest detail, of having the power to be Queen for a Day? I thought of all of the important little aesthetic decisions Peter would be making: baked potatoes or oven-roasted; short train, long train or no train; Cancun or Cozumel. Then I thought about the reality of the situation that lurked behind Little Girl Sheila's rose-colored vision of wedding planning: the endless fights with my mother about idiotically trivial things like how to cook a goddamned tuber, for crying out loud, and what the optimum length of material was for a ridiculously high-priced one-time-only dress.

I caved.

"If you really want to plan everything for us, that sounds heavenly to me."

6. Just What Kind of Man Is Peter Piper?

And, for the most part, ceding control *was* wonderful.

I mean, it was great having him in the fitting room with me at the bridal salon while I tried on dress after dress, tirelessly debating the merits of this and that style with the salon attendant, reviewing all of the veil options before settling on a wreath of fresh dark roses twined with baby's breath instead. I felt like someone out of an old movie, or maybe even a new one, someone like Marilyn Monroe, or Julia Roberts in *Pretty Woman*, someone who was involved with a man who was so in love with her and all the potential she represented he was even willing to go *shopping* with her in order to ensure her becoming the totally perfect package she could be.

And, as for the caterers, he didn't even bother with any kind of potato. He asked if they could do a risotto with the salmon instead, suggested they cut the butter they normally used for it with white wine, offered to pay more, placated the chef when he balked and somehow managed to wind up friends with everybody.

Was there a downside to Peter, was there anything wrong with him?

Of course there was. There's not a man alive there's not something wrong with.

Did it bother me when he came to stay with me over the weekends and, after hunting for something in the kitchen, he managed to leave every cabinet and drawer, save one, open?

"What," I asked, "did someone suddenly sound the air-raid warning and you had to evacuate in a hurry? Do you have something against the cabinet under the sink, that that's the only one you should ignore?"

"Huh?" had been his classic response, completely oblivious.

Did it bother me when, replacing the toilet paper on those weekends in my home—*in my home*, let me emphasize—he did it with the end of the paper going absolutely the wrong way, with the end coming at you from over the top instead of from behind, which is the way every sane person hangs toilet paper?

A lot.

Finally, did it bother me that his nurses and patients, albeit fondly, called him Dr. Peter?

Emphatically, yes.

But who was I to feel like I had a right to complain?

After all, I was finally going to get what I'd wanted. I was going to be *I Love Lucy*. I was going to be Mrs. Peter Piper, Pumpkin Wife.

"Well," my mother said, when I told her we were getting married, "he is good with ears, noses and throats," making me doubly glad of my decision *not* to tell her I was moving back to Connecticut.

"Omigod!" my girlfriends had all gushed when I told them how much Peter seemed to like being in charge of planning things like our honeymoon.

Okay, I confess. With my obsessively busy life as a stockbroker, I didn't have time for girl*friends*—heavy emphasis on the hard s—nor did girls in general seem to want to spend much time with me. I had exactly one girlfriend, sans s; her name was Hilda and, yes, the truest part of the lone sentence in the last paragraph was that Hilda liked to gush. It's a mystery how we ever wound up being such good friends.

"Omigod!" Hilda again. "Men never like to plan things like that! It's like it's against their gene pool or something!"

Hilda also had a strange grasp on how things like biology worked.

"Omigod, I know!" I gushed back, becoming infected by her as I did whenever I was thinking about actually being happy about something.

She leaned across the little round table in the just slightly larger bar, eyes brighter than if she had a cocaine habit. "Do you know where he's going to take you?"

"I don't know for sure," I said, leaning forward to mirror her position. There was a hint of salivation in the air, on both our parts. "All I know is that it's in the Caribbean."

"Oooh! How romantic!"

I was grinning so hard at this point my teeth felt as though they were going to fly out of my head. "I know!!!"

7. Honeymoon in Haiti

Of course, when, after the beautiful wedding ceremony, all completely planned by Peter, the Caribbean island turned out to be Haiti, I was mildly shocked. I know this is going to make me sound like a geographical moron or something but, somehow, ever since he'd said the Caribbean, I had been envisioning Bermuda. So, you can see where, if I had been envisioning Bermuda, but then opened my eyes to find Haiti, I might be a little nonplussed. After all, I don't know about you, but I find it tough to feel safe in any country where, whenever I pass by a mirror, I think to myself that, yeah, if I lived here, I'd probably hate me, too. Still, so long as we remained within the all-expenses-paid resort we were staying at, which only felt a smidgen like a military compound, I felt completely safe. And I was getting to do a lot of what I had come on my honeymoon primarily to do: Each night, under the multicolored lanterns of the outdoor dance floor and with the cruise ship-style Caribbean combo accompanying us, I was in heaven, I was in heaven, and there was nowhere else that I would rather be, than with Peter's arms around me, dancing cheek to cheek.

Overall, I have to admit my honeymoon was one of the most marvelous times of my life. True, I got sick on the inferior food at the resort on a fairly regular basis. If this was the best the island had to offer paying guests, you had to wonder what the islanders themselves subsisted on, and then you found you didn't have to wonder anymore about why many diseases were more common here than back home and the life expectancy was shorter. (Of course, that may have had some connection with there having been a history of murderous dictators in the region as well.) Still, despite my sociological/anthropological observations, I managed to squeeze in an amazingly good time. I capitalized on the occasion's potential in terms of doing silly things, like using it as an excuse to wear colorful sarongs *apres* swimming every day, slung low and tied cavalierly across my hips, and drink piña coladas and mai tais, also every day, not because I'd ever liked the taste of either but, rather, simply because I could.

And then there was the sex.

The sex I like to think of as island sex.

In Haiti, for the first time, Peter treated my body like it was a giant piña colada Popsicle, and I mean that in the nicest and least nauseating way possible, licking me all over. He had the most amazing tongue—not dry, not gooey, but an *amazing* tongue. When it finally made its way up between my thighs, settling on the cleft between my legs, I looked down on the top of his head and thought with awe, *Where have* you *been all my life?* I promise you: you would have done anything for him as well.

Some of my girlfriends—well, actually just girls I'd come across in my life, with me not having any full-fledged girlfriends but Hilda and her not being married—had told me positive horror stories about their own honeymoons. These were women who had lived with their men for years before tying the knot: just long enough to know if divergent views on what direction the toilet paper should come at a person from represented a sufficient stumbling block to peaceful cohabitation but far too long to think the idea of sex every day sounded like anything more than work. I'd even heard one co-worker—who'd waited so long to marry the man she lived with that, instead of thumbing *Brides* before the big event, she found herself thumbing *New Woman* and *Cosmo* for articles with titles like "Can Your Might-as-Well-Be-Married Relationship Be Saved?" and "Resuscitating Your Sex Life When You're in it for the Long Haul"—pass the remark to another co-worker in the bathroom upon returning from her honeymoon that, "God! If I'd known Mike was going to actually want to have sex with me on Maui, I never would have agreed to get married!" In light of that, you can see why all of the *oohs* and *ahs* I was able to spontaneously feel every night and every morning made me feel relieved and glad Peter and I had married after such a relatively short period of dating.

In fact, the only discordant note came one night when, after dancing, after we'd returned to our room and after I'd taken a shower, I emerged from the bathroom, towel-drying my hair, and caught Peter perched on the edge of the bed watching CNN.

"Oooh!" I squealed, very much in Hilda mode, making myself comfortable at his feet, with my legs turned to the side. "Headline News! I've felt so out of touch the past few days. And I just love Lynne Russell! What's going on? Is the Dow up? Are we at war with anyone? Did Elsa Klensch show Calvin Klein's spring line yet?"

With an expert flick of the wrist, Peter terminated CNN.

"Hey! What'd you do that for?" I protested.

"Because I don't want you filling your pretty little head with everything that's going on in the world," he replied, a response that, in another life, would have troubled me greatly.

But I wasn't in another life; I was in this life. I was on vacation—hell, I was on my Haitian honeymoon—and the man I loved was sliding down the side of the bed, touching his lips to mine, undoing the tie at the front of my terrycloth robe and gently yet urgently forcing me to the floor. Who gave a flying fuck about Lynne Russell anymore?

Anyway, I was sure all Peter meant was he didn't want me filling my pretty little head with the outside world *while we were on our honeymoon.*

Hah.

Of course, I *would* pick up a parasite on my own honeymoon, either from the water or from the water that was used to make the ice cubes in our tropical drinks, or from the tinned coconut milk, completely unfamiliar to my Diet Pepsi system, that was used in the Bird of Paradise Resort Specials I drank with such relish during the first two days. Whatever it was, I was sick one way or the other every fifteen minutes for the next four days after our plane touched down at Kennedy. This resulted in my losing those last ten pounds in the most unwelcome way possible, and making an appointment with the gastroenterologist after the continual heaving and diarrhea left me dangerously dehydrated and weak, an appointment at which he got to stick a sadistically long and curved object up my butt while I got to ask him why anyone in their right minds would pick such a thing as a specialty at medical school.

By the time I had recovered from my honeymoon, my life was well on its way to becoming no longer my own.

8. The Pumpkin Wife

Would you believe me if I told you his house, as I first saw it upon our return from Haiti, was Halloween orange and the chimney that came out of the top, being an oddly brass twisted affair, was tarnished and as a result, well, green? I won't try to claim it was round, but its walls certainly weren't squared off in any conventional sense either.

It may be hard to fathom that I'd somehow managed to wed Peter without having first even once seen the Connecticut house where he lived, but there you have it.

"We could paint it?" I asked more than told, tentative, as he rolled our luggage up the walk.

138

"Why?" he countered, completely puzzled. "It's perfect just the way it is."

"I'll take care of the checkbook from now on," Peter said.

"Fine."

Who cared about writing checks? I had my new environment to get used to.

"Wear this dress to the Smiths' on Friday," Peter said.

"Fine."

It was a relief not to have to go shopping for something new, a relief not to have to worry if something new I bought, that looked so right in the store, might somehow be wrong.

"I've made arrangements to have the groceries delivered from now on," Peter said.

"Fine."

Ah. There was that tongue again. I really had no desire to go out for anything anymore.

But there *does* come that day, in every woman's life, when she has to go out no matter how borderline agoraphobic she's become: I had my period, Peter had never thought to put Tampax on the grocery list—his specialties were ears, noses and throats, after all—and there was none in that oddly shaped house. In a circular on the counter I saw CVS was having a half-price sale. Well, what sane woman can really resist half-price Tampax at CVS?

I was waiting in line to pay for my single-item purchase when I heard a familiar voice.

"Sheila? *Baby!* What are you doing here?"

It was my mother, of course.

How do you explain to your mother that, after marrying, you'd moved back to the state in which she'd always resided, and yet you'd never bothered to apprise her of that fact?

"Mom, I've been in Connecticut since Peter and I got back from our honeymoon. I guess maybe I should have mentioned it earlier."

"*Mentioned it earlier*? You never mentioned it at all!"

"Well, I'm mentioning it now."

"That's only because you have to."

True. But I didn't say that.

"I guess I've just been so busy," was what I did say.

"With what?"

"With being a wife."

Raised eyebrow. "Oh?"

"Well, it is what I am now."

"Tell me," she said, "what is it about being a wife that has you so busy?"

So I told her...about Peter taking care of the checkbook...and my wardrobe...and the groceries...and how *safe* my life had become. After all, wasn't that what she'd always wanted for me, all those times she'd bemoaned my living in the city, bemoaned my single status, bemoaned—no nicer way to put it—*me*?

"My God, honey, this isn't what I had in mind at all. Safe? Sure, I wanted you to be safe. But a prisoner? A prisoner who doesn't know what's going on in the world and who only leaves home for a Tampax special? Why, even *I*, when I was married to your father—God rest his soul—kept up with what was going on outside of the house. I was always up on current events."

"You were?"

"Of course. Your father wanted someone he could talk to about things while he had his double Scotch on the rocks—two ice cubes with absolutely no water—every night when he came home from work. He wanted someone to talk to, he told me to read the newspapers, I did, and so I was always aware of what was going on in the world."

Well, that was one way of staying connected....

Still, I still thought it might somehow all work out.

I gazed down fondly at that familiar head between my legs.

"I'll take care of the investments," Peter said.

That was when I froze.

Take care of the investments??? my mind screamed.

Then I remembered what my mother had said on the day of the Great

Tampax Excursion. And I remembered three little words from my stock-broker days, words that had even helped carry me through the aftermath of the crash of '87:

Fuck. That. Shit.

What does a girl do, even a really big girl like me, when she finds herself in over her head?

She calls in the cavalry.

She calls in *her mother*.

"You live in *that* house?"

We were standing on the curb outside of the—might as well admit it, because it's true—*giant pumpkin*. I'd called my mother an hour earlier and given her directions, had met her outside, and that's where we were: standing out on the curb, staring at that giant thing my husband had put me in. *Really*.

It was nighttime, Peter had left for one of the few things he did without me—the Ear, Nose and Throat bowling team, which was taking a weekend-long trip to the regional championships in Orono—and every light in the house was lit.

If it wasn't for my mother's natural inclination to talk-talk-talk, she might have been rendered speechless.

"You live *there*? My God," she awe-whispered, "I always wondered what kind of person lived *there*."

"Your daughter?" I asked-answered.

"No," she said, and you could hear a steel door somewhere slam shut. "*Not. My. Daughter.*"

"What do we do?" I asked.

She couldn't stop staring. Well, can you blame her? Would *you* be able to stop staring at that thing?

"We could set it on fire, turn it into a jack-o'-lantern," I suggested.

"It looks like it already is one, baby," she said.

"I could just leave," I suggested.

"No, you can't," she said.

"I can't?"

"No, because you're under a spell."

Oh. Right.

"Well, then," I finally said, "what do *you* suggest?"

Several hours later, we were sitting in her kitchen, taking the first of the pies out of the oven.

"Do you think he'll like it?" she asked.

"Do you think I care?" I countered.

We clinked forks and then dipped to sample at the same time, starting the long slow process of eating the house that Peter had built for me.

"Tell me," my mother said, "how do you say that again?"

"*Fuck. That. Shit.*"

LAUREN BARATZ-LOGSTED lives in Danbury, Connecticut, with her wonderful husband Greg Logsted and their gorgeous daughter Jackie. Lauren is the author of the published novels *The Thin Pink Line*, *Crossing the Line*, *A Little Change of Face* and *How Nancy Drew Saved My Life*, all dark comedies; *Vertigo*, a literary novel set in the Victorian era with erotic and suspense undertones; and the forthcoming Young Adult novel *Angel's Choice*. Lauren also has an essay in BenBella's Jane Austen-themed anthology *Flirting with Pride & Prejudice*.

Heather Swain

Labels in literature exist so publishers can market books. Anyone who believes in her own label too stridently is a victim of that marketing. Chick-lit has expanded so far beyond its original genre definition that the only thing all books with that label have in common is that they're written by a woman, about a woman, for a woman. So, if you want to call my work chick-lit, fine by me. From Jane Austen to Colette, to the other fine writers in this collection, I believe I'm in excellent company.

Café con Leche Crush

I have escaped. The rubber soles of my very sensible snow boots crunch across fresh snow dusted over a layer of ice on the quiet sidewalks of my neighborhood. Big wet snowflakes cascade lazily from the black night sky, careening under the streetlights to land in my eyelashes. When it snows like this in Brooklyn, the usually bustling streets become deserted and feel like a stage—hushed and ready for a performance. Well, watch this, world, because I'm out!

I haven't been outside for days and days and the cold air makes me giddy. Cars moving slowly down the streets make me giddy. The few other intrepid souls outside, some with dogs, make me giddy, too. I want to scoop up handfuls of snow and pack it into tight wet balls, then hurl them at all signs of life while jumping up and down like a lunatic yelling, "Hey! We're all outside! Hurray!" Of course, I'm so entirely bundled up in my long underwear, turtleneck, two pairs of socks, sweats, coat, scarf, hat and gloves that I could no more bend over to make a snowball than I could do a cartwheel and land in a split. Plus, merely the thought of bending over makes the incision just below my bikini line ache and itch.

Before I left our apartment, Jasper leaned against the doorframe and asked, "You sure you want to go out?" I could see the consternation etched in new, tired lines across his forehead.

"Yes, of course," I said too harshly so I took a breath and tried to soften. "I just need a little break. Some fresh air."

"Be careful, Hannah," he warned in his newly adopted Mr. Safety tone. "Don't slip," he called after me. "You could open up your stitches."

I know that he was imagining me sprawled over a snowdrift, blood gushing from my gut, turning the pristine snow bright red, and me being too stubborn to ask anyone for help. "No, no, I'm fine. Really. I can manage," he thinks I'd say as I clawed my way home on elbows and knees, dragging my entrails behind me. That's how Jasper's mind works, especially now that he's a father.

I've made it to the end of my block. The farthest I've been away from home by myself for the better part of a year. Since Zeb and Riley were born, I keep coming upon the realization that I no longer have two other people riding along inside of me like little astronauts in my womb. This freedom makes me feel potentially reckless. I could jaywalk. I could cross against the light. I could even jog backward down the middle of the street with my eyes closed if I really wanted to and I wouldn't be putting anyone but myself in jeopardy.

Instead of doing any of those things, I only have to turn right to get to my planned destination, Esteban's Bodega, but suddenly at the end of my block, I panic. Bells and whistles go off in my head. Some kind of innate maternal alarm screeches its warning, "Alert! You've gone too far! Go back!" I picture teeny tiny versions of myself in paratrooper gear rushing through my brain, diving headfirst into my arteries, swimming their way to my major muscle groups so they can turn me around and send me marching back to my babies.

As I force myself to turn the corner, the paranoia starts. What if our apartment building catches on fire while I'm gone? What if one of the boys chokes on his own saliva? What if they're abducted by someone posing as a Greenpeace worker and sold to a childless couple from Dubuque? It's too early to leave them. They're only two weeks old. How selfish am I to walk away from them, so helpless, so dependent on me? And for what? A lousy cup of *café con leche* from my favorite bodega five blocks away. I'm despicable. Not fit for motherhood. Social Services will probably show up at my door, not to take my boys away, but just to slap me around a little until I come to my senses.

Except that the *café con leche* isn't lousy. In fact, it's delicious and I've been craving it since I was three months pregnant. But, from the moment the purple plus sign showed up on the pregnancy pee stick, I didn't allow caffeine to touch my lips. Or sushi or rare steaks or deli meats or booze. I didn't lie on my back or take hot baths. I never rode a horse or went sledding or participated in any risky behavior whatsoever, because I believed that pregnancy was the hard part.

It took me over a year to get pregnant and then I was plagued by every annoying but never entirely alarming issue. Debilitating morning sickness? Check. Spotting in the first trimester? Check. Hypertension? Check. Gestational diabetes? Check. Back pain? Check. Early contractions? Check. And at the end, three weeks of mind-numbing bed rest. I bore it all, figuring if I could just get through the pregnancy then everything else would be easy and come naturally. My babies would be born in a swirl of love and latch onto my nipples like little hamsters to their water bottles. I'd glow with maternal grace and spontaneously sing lullabies while coaxing stubborn gas bubbles to burst with my warm, confident hands. I never worried about motherhood until Zeb couldn't figure out how to nurse.

Each time he takes my breast, his little tongue pushes my nipple from his mouth. He tries and tries to get a drink until we're both hysterical with frustration. All the while, Riley, apparently oblivious to the whole fiasco on the other side of my body, suckles away, growing fatter and happier every moment. Looking back, if I had known how hard the first two postpartum weeks would be, I'd have been sledding on a horse while gorging myself on sushi and sucking down Irish coffees the whole time I was pregnant.

My building is no longer in sight now. I sense freedom and something inside of me screams, "Run! Run away! As fast as you can and don't come back!" I could. I could hop a train, grab a cab, go to LaGuardia and book a flight to Venezuela or Uzbekistan or Mozambique. I could simply disappear into the falling snow.

I did my part. Carried the boys to term. Sweated and cursed through twenty-six hours of slow excruciating labor only to be told by a surly midwife (who implied my lack of progress was personal failure on my part) that I was being kicked out of the birthing center. I didn't dilate far enough so they moved me to the labor-and-delivery floor, as if I were about to birth two pizzas.

When I complained that the beautiful, natural, coming-into-the-world party we'd planned for our boys was quickly being transformed into a drugged-up, medical student fantasy, Jasper said, "Come on, Hannah. It doesn't matter. Let's just get them here."

"It'll be a while," said the new nurse as she slipped an IV into my arm.

"Mind if I get a sandwich, then?" Jasper asked me, wan and exhausted from his endless hours of fruitless encouragement.

"Sure," I said, defeated. Go on. Move about freely. Enjoy yourself. Flirt with interns. Steal drugs from the pharmacy closet. Eat whatever you want. I'll be over here, paralyzed from the waist down, hooked up to a monitor, sucking on ice chips. But you go ahead. And that's when Zeb crashed. His little heartbeat plummeted like a sparrow dead in flight. The room erupted into a maelstrom of nurses, doctors and residents.

Jasper had already hightailed it off the maternity floor so no one could find him as they rushed me into the O.R. I was alone while they strapped my arms down in a T and put an oxygen mask over my face. The last thing I saw was the nurse furiously scrubbing my giant belly before two others strung a blue sheet up in front of my eyes. Luckily the epidural had kicked in enough that the doctor could slice right through my middle and yank the babies out, like little plucked chickens, all before Jasper had time to bite into his BLT.

Now, I'm standing outside of Esteban's Bodega, gazing at the warm yellow light emanating from the plate glass windows. Not much has changed since I waddled by here a few weeks ago, heavy with the bulk of three bodies stuffed into one. The same dirty red-and-white striped awning still hangs crookedly above the entrance. A cardboard cutout of a babe in short shorts and a cowboy hat still holds out a Miller Lite. Handwritten signs for "Egg and Cheese + Coffee $1.99" and "Marlboro Lights $4.98" and "Absolutely No Credit" remain in the windows.

Inside I can see Esme, Esteban's gorgeous niece, at the cash register and the regular guys milling about or hunkering down on stools, sipping cups of coffee, arguing over politics and bullshitting each other about women. The conversations are animated, half in English and half in Spanish, full of friendly jabs and thinly disguised insults.

I open the door slowly and am hit by a wall of warm, rich coffee-scented air. I am timid as I enter and at first hang back. I pretend to study the newspapers stacked by the door and for a moment I am interested in the headlines. The world could've been taken over by sea urchin-shaped aliens and Jasper and I wouldn't have known it unless one of them showed up at our door. Then I hear Esme's voice.

"Ohhh!" she squeals. "Look, look. It's Hannah." Then she uses my nickname, coined after old Mr. Gonzales misheard me the first time I introduced myself. "It's our *Gringa!*" The men on the stools turn to look as Esme rushes from behind the counter to grab my wrist and pull me forward. "We all wondered if the babies came because you haven't been here for so long. Didn't we?" She turns to ask the others, who mumble and nod noncommittally, but smile and wave kindly at me, as if maybe I was missed.

The warmth of their reception could easily make me bawl. Not that it's especially hard to make me cry these days with hormones raging like tropical storms through my sleep-deprived body and muddled mind. Still, I'm truly touched that anyone cares I've been gone or that I've returned. Despite my persistent presence in the bodega over the past five years, I've always felt like an interloper, tolerated then forgotten as soon as I walked out the door. Now I think, *Perhaps I do have a place here.* I screw up my courage and I look for Esteban.

He leans across the counter on his elbows. He is a gorgeous man.

Tall and erect with broad shoulders and long limbs. He moves with the speed and grace of a soccer prodigy, nimbly juggling three or four tasks all at once. "You're back," he says coolly, evenly, with a hint of a grin playing on his lips, then sweeps a dark silky swatch of hair out of his eyes with one smooth rake of his fingers. The only clue to his age (near fifty, I suppose) are the lines etched around his eyes and down his cheeks that give him the rugged beauty of cliffs battered by the sea.

The heat of the small space fills my body and I prickle with sweat. "Yes," I say as I shed my winter layers—gloves, hat, scarf. I shove them all into my pockets and unzip my heavy coat. "I'm back."

Esme grabs my hands and spins me side to side. "*Mami*, you look gorgeous!" she says. "Doesn't she?" she asks the men.

I'm suddenly self-conscious to have this much attention on my battered body. I'm a big frumpy mess in sour-smelling sweats. My breasts are swollen to the point of hilarity, as if some horny thirteen-year-old boy drew them on his notebook. My belly is distended so that I still look five months pregnant. My hair's a mess, my nails are ragged, and my skin is as sallow as an anemic albino. And my ass, don't get me started on the state of my ass. Suffice it to say, gravity has not been kind over the past nine months.

Despite all this, the men in the bodega smile and nod and give me the okay sign and thumbs up. I blush, oddly grateful for their approval. Something Jasper certainly hasn't given me lately. Mostly he seems confused by me now. His touches have become reserved, uncertain and practical: a hand on my elbow to help me stand, an arm around my shoulder to comfort me when I'm frustrated with nursing Zeb. Gone are caresses and hugs and stolen kisses, as if I'm too fragile or not deserving of such attention.

Esme lets go of me and says, "Having a baby makes a woman so...." She juggles her hands in front of her body. "What's the word in English?"

"Voluptuous," says Esteban. I glance up at him. He nods to me and winks.

I know virtually nothing about Esteban outside of the bodega. I don't know where he's from originally but the strongly accented English he speaks tells me that he probably ended up in Brooklyn rather than started out here. I've never heard mention of anyone in his family other than Esme and there are no pictures of a woman and children taped to the side of the cash register. But I like that I don't know anything because that way the bodega remains an illusory place where I can be the kind of saucy, irascible woman I'd never attempt to be elsewhere in my life.

"So, you ready for the real thing, *Gringa*?" He holds up his coffee press and flexes his arm muscles, sending gales of laughter through the room.

I'm drowning already. Not coherent enough to make a sentence without the words *breast pump* and *umbilical cord* and *hemorrhoid*, let alone some witty, flirtatious retort. All I can do is stammer and blush and nod my head like a mute.

As always, Esme saves me. "Get up, lazy ass." She shoos Carlos, the youngest of the regulars, off a stool. "Make room for the new mother. She had twins, you know. Two boys." Then she turns back to me. "God bless them," she says and squeezes my arm.

Carlos snags his small cup of *café cubano* and hops off the stool that he presents to me with a flourish. "Twins?" he asks and shakes his head. "Esteban, give her two *cafés*!" Then he leans over the counter between Albert the mailman and old Mr. Gonzales and adds, "With plenty of milk."

The men chuckle as Esme swats at them. "Pigs," she says playfully.

Esteban ignores the commotion. "You know, *Gringa*, *café con leche* is really only for breakfast."

No, I think, *this can't happen*. I can't have trudged all the way in the snow, ignoring the twinges of pain in my gut every time my feet slipped on a patch of ice only to be told that I can't have a *café con leche*. My face must betray my deep dismay, because while I'm working out a way to beg and plead for an exception, Esteban says, "But for you, breakfast is anytime."

I smile, I beam, I glow. I probably even gurgle like Riley does each time I pull my breasts out and offer him my nipple. "Thank you, Esteban," I say. "*Gracias*. You don't know how much I've missed...." I falter, then swell with bliss. "All of this!" I say and wave my hand around.

He nods, then sets to work on a fresh pot of coffee just for me. Esteban makes his *café con leche* from thick, dark, strong coffee. The kind that fills your head with a dizzying aroma of mountains and earth and burlap sacks on the backs of pack animals. First he grinds the beans as water comes to boil in a kettle behind him. Then he gently pours the water over the grounds and carefully pushes down the plunger on his old coffee press. Next, he mixes together equal amounts of whole milk and thick condensed milk plus a pinch of cinnamon into a small saucepan.

"So," he asks, without looking up from the alchemy he's performing with grounds and water and milk and heat. "How are they?"

I want to ask, *Who*? Because for a fraction of a second, as I watch him prepare the coffee, I forget that I have two little babes at home. "Oh, the twins?" I ask stupidly, because for that tiny snag of time, I was transported back to when I came in here nearly every morning for my *café con leche* fix and held a space that was mine alone. "They're fine," I say in what must amount to the most massive understatement in the universe.

I don't mention that Jasper and I are buried in the chaos of diapers, wipes, burp cloths and tiny stained clothes. Nor do I mention the nursing situation with Zeb. I simply smile and say again, "They're just fine, thanks for asking."

"Good, good," says Esteban then looks up as we wait for the coffee and milk to cook.

"They say that a woman reaches her sexual peak after she's had her first child," Albert says from the stool at the end of the counter. Everyone leans forward just slightly. "And it gets better after each one."

"Is that right, Señor Gonzales?" Esteban asks. "You should know. How many children did your wife have?"

"Nine," says Mr. Gonzales and he wiggles his eyebrows lasciviously.

Anywhere else in the world, this kind of talk would infuriate me. I'd protest, huff and likely stomp off after a well-placed comeback on behalf of all women. Only here it's different because in the past I've participated, too. I've razzed these guys about dates and sex and marriage and made my own snide comments to Esme about penis size and multiple orgasms. I've proven myself a willing accomplice to the sometimes-adolescent humor of this crowd. Not only that, but I've enjoyed it.

As the heady fragrance of the coffee fills the moist warm air, I begin to perk up and get my game back. "So, since I had two babies at once...?" I leave the question hanging. It takes a second for it to sink in.

"Ay, ay, ay." Mr. Gonzales slaps the countertop then elbows Carlos in the ribs. "Her husband will never get a rest!"

"Ah, forget it," says Carlos. "After my wife had our son, she hardly looked at me again."

"That's because you're ugly," says Esteban, and everyone laughs.

I smile contentedly as I watch Esteban whisk hot, sweet milk and strong, dark coffee together in a ceramic pitcher. The conversation goes on around me, but I tune it out. For the first time in weeks, I'm truly at ease because I'm not anticipating Zeb's unhappy cry.

Jasper and I have done everything good, conscientious parents are supposed to do when a baby can't figure out how to nurse. We've talked to doctors, gone online, even hired a lactation consultant who gave us tongue-and-cheek exercises for Zeb's itty bitty mouth. I pump, we supplement with a bottle, then we try the breast again and again. Everyone says it'll just take time and that Zeb will eventually get the hang of nursing, but I'm not so sure.

When I become completely defeated by the situation, reduced to a quivering, crying mess, Jasper looks at me with his dark brooding eyes and says, "Just stop, Hannah. Don't try anymore. You're making us all miserable."

"What am I supposed to do?" I implore.

"Just bottle-feed him, for God's sake. I'll take Zeb. You take Riley."

Jasper doesn't get it, though. To only give Riley the comfort of my perfect mother's milk straight from the source means I've chosen him over Zeb and I can't do that. Nor can I stop Riley from nursing. So I'm stuck and every few hours, anxiety mounts in our house until at least two of us, if not more, are crying. That's why I had to leave tonight. I had to remind myself that there is a happy, relaxed, slightly bawdy version of myself. That I'm not just the beleaguered, brusque baby wrangler I've recently become.

Esteban transfers the frothy mix from the pitcher into a clean white mug. He carefully spoons milk foam on top of the steaming drink before dusting it with cinnamon. Then he sets the mug on a small plate, adds a fat slice of buttered toast to the edge and sets it down in front of me. I close my eyes and wrap my hands around the mug, letting the warmth seep into my fingers and palms. I lean over the cup as the steam caresses my skin. I'm no longer in wintry Brooklyn. The coffee has transported me to the tropical climate of some beach town below the equator.

I bring the mug to my lips for that long-awaited sip of *café con leche*. It's even thicker and sweeter than I remembered, almost like warm caramel. Then the slightly bitter twinge of coffee cuts through the milk and the cinnamon dances on my tongue, waking up my taste buds from their long dormant caffeine exile. Esteban watches me, his fingers poised before me on the edge of the counter. He smiles at my childlike joy as I tear the bread in two and dunk it in the coffee. With the next sip, my mind explodes.

I am with Esteban. Rolling across the tangled sheets of an unmade bed. My hair is long and wild. My body lithe beneath him. I hear the ocean roiling outside. Waves beat against an empty beach while seagulls shriek from far away. I am on top of him, my hair hanging down on his chest. I am whole again. Unencumbered by stitches. Unexpected by anyone else but this man who wants only to give me pleasure. *"Voluptuous,"* he whispers in my ear and I submit, willingly, happily, hungrily.

I see his smile, the way his eyes crinkle at the edges, and how the furrows in his cheeks deepen into laugh lines as we move. I see the same face watching me as I hold the cup to my mouth and explore the edges with my tongue for any missed drops. He holds up the pitcher and raises his eyebrows. I push the empty mug to him and he refills it then watches me again as I gulp the contents, my mind racing through scenario after scenario of me alone with Esteban on some deserted beach. When the coffee is gone, I sit back and sigh with pure pleasure.

"Happy?" he asks.

"Yes," I say and think, *I never want to leave.* Never want to go back home to the squalling, demanding life I've become mired in. I know I'm still important there. The sole source of my sons' nutrition and all that. But let's be honest. Women used to die in childbirth all the time and their babies made it. If I never returned home, Jasper could have the satisfaction of taking over the feeding. Knowing him, he'd spontaneously lactate and nurse the boys himself. Zeb would probably latch right on. Or they'd grow up on formula like all the baby boomers whose mothers were led to believe breastfeeding was for unwashed heathens in southern continents. When it comes right down to it, I'm no longer indispensable, Jasper has made that clear. This realization comes to me as both a relief and as a wash of sadness. If I can't even feed my sons, am I of any real use beyond another pair of hands to clean up after them?

And what about Jasper and me? Our lives have become so fraught with frustration over the nursing situation that we hardly speak, let alone joke or touch. Will I ever make him laugh again? Or make his eyes light up with desire when I step out of the shower? Or hold his head on my lap to stroke his hair after he's had a terrible day? Now we simply pass each other in the apartment, trudging like zombies, each with a howling baby bouncing on our weary shoulders.

I know Jasper is trying his best to help. He has become my partner, my aide, my night nurse, my manservant. Everything but my lover. I gaze up at Esteban again. If he were my lover, I bet we'd never have this problem. If he were my husband, he would've never left my side while I was strapped down and cut open. If he were the father of my children, he'd never suggest that I stop trying to feed Zeb because Esteban understands the magnitude and beauty of nourishing someone else.

Caffeine and sugar hit my system with a jolt. I feel like I've been hooked up to a generator and for the first time in months I am buzzing. I watch Esteban wash and dry cups. I take in his sinewy forearms, the slope of his shoulders, the broadness of his back. When he turns around again, I lean across the counter, cup my chin in my palm and grin.

He smiles back at me. "What, *Gringa*? What are you smiling about?"

"Nothing," I tease. "The coffee was just so good. Exactly what I needed. There's no one else who does it like you."

Esteban snaps the dishtowel between his hands and stands up straight. "I am the best."

I've never gone beyond a mild flirt with Esteban. I don't carry him around in my mind and I've never before entertained the *what if* and *if only* thoughts of a crush. But tonight I'm ready to cross a line. "I bet you're good at a lot of things," I say and just as I'm about to elaborate on all the other ways he could make me happy, the bell above the door tinkles.

Another regular, a cabdriver named Henry, hurries in. He raises his gloved hand and says, "*Café cubano, por favor.*" Esteban sets to work, leaving me alone with my libidinous *café con leche* thoughts and my aborted attempt at seduction.

The conversation around me has turned to politics. Esteban is engrossed in defending a Puerto Rican candidate for mayor. The men erupt into Spanish and Esme rolls her eyes at me.

"They must miss you, *mija*," she says and I know immediately that she means my boys. With their invocation, my breasts begin to tingle. I feel my milk let down. Anticipation and dread come over me.

Esteban waves off some diatribe by Albert as he hands Henry a small cup of *café cubano* with a lump of sugar on the side.

"Eh, too much for me," Carlos laughs as he pulls on his gloves and waves goodbye. Mr. Gonzales fumbles in his wallet for dollar bills. The door opens and closes. Men come and go and I think, *They are all someone's son.*

I miss my boys, then. Their small ruddy faces and nearly blank blue eyes. Their tiny hands opening and closing like morning glories in the sun. The way they smell like buttermilk and how they fit so perfectly into the crook of my arm.

Mr. Gonzales struggles up from his seat. "Congratulations on your sons," he says to me with a gentle pat on the back. "Each one is a blessing."

"You'll bring them with you next time, won't you?" Esme asks.

I pause and consider this question. I've never come here with Jasper or any of my friends for that matter. The bodega has been a place just for me. I'm not sure that I want to share this part of my life. I look at Esteban, my *café con leche* crush.

He smiles and nods. "Yes," he says. "Bring them by. I'll make them steamed milk with a little bit of honey and cinnamon. All my kids loved it when they were little."

Ah! So Esteban has children? *Of course he does*, I think, and nearly slap my forehead. Immediately, the flimsy walls of my illusory bodega start to crumble. I see clearly that we all have our lives outside of here. Carlos and the wife he continually complains about in a way that emphasizes how much he loves her. Mr. Gonzales' stories of always bailing at least one child or grandchild out of trouble. Albert and the frustrations of his job. This is the place that we all come to forget those lives for a while because here we are recipients. We rejuvenate ourselves on Esteban's coffee before we head back in the world to face our problems and embrace our happiness.

"Yes," I say, grateful to have this place for myself and for the possibility of sharing it with my family. "I'll do that. I'll bring my boys with me some time." I gather my things and lay five dollars on the counter. Esteban pushes the money back to me.

"Buy diapers," he says with a laugh and turns away.

I open the door and am greeted by the sting of cold air. I hurry home, careful not to trip and fall.

When I get back to our building, I pause on the sidewalk and listen. Nothing. I step in the foyer and listen again. Quiet. I mount the stairs, my ear carefully trained for Zeb's misery, but the halls are silent. Is this good or bad? The whole way home I had imagined that both boys would have erupted into tiny twin volcanoes of vomit, snot and shit. I pictured Jasper running from one screeching baby to the other, hushing, shushing, soothing and pleading for them to calm down. I almost laughed to think of Jasper getting his ass kicked by two six-pound brutes. So what's this silence mean? Have they left me for a better mother? Perished from starvation while I was gone? Or does Jasper simply have things under control?

I unlock the door and slip in the apartment as quietly as I can. I tiptoe through the hallway and peak around the corner of the living room. It's empty and my heart races. Maybe something horrible truly has happened. I hurry through the hall toward the bathroom. The kitchen. The twins' room. All empty. I rush to our bedroom and throw open the door.

There they are. My boys. All three of them passed out on top of the covers. Jasper is in the middle with Zeb and Riley on either side, curled like tiny seashells under his arms. They are so peaceful sleeping together like this and I realize that I am resentful, jealous and feel left out. Then it hits me. I'm mad at Jasper. It's been building since we started trying to get pregnant. With every failed attempt my anger mounted. I became more infuriated every time he didn't understand my anxiety during the pregnancy, during each pain of labor that he could do nothing about, as he left my side in the hospital when I needed him most, and now for not fixing this problem with Zeb. He's been the dumping ground for all of my unexpected aggravation and disappointment of becoming a parent. But seeing him here with our sons, I understand how unfair and displaced my fury with Jasper has been. I know none of the problems have been his fault. What else am I supposed to do, though? Blame the boys?

I turn my gaze to Riley. His little rosebud lips work in and out as if he's nursing in his dreams. His cheeks are full and ruddy, my fat happy little man. I look at Zeb. He nestles his face into Jasper's armpit and sighs. My poor, sweet little bird. I could never blame either of them for an ounce of trouble.

So who does that leave? Myself? Haven't I been through enough already? Perhaps I should blame God, but I don't believe in a vengeful God out to spite me. The truth is there is no blame. No malice, spite or ill will on anyone's part. I simply have to accept that motherhood will always be full of sacrifice, potential heartache and endless mistakes but will forever be worth all the difficulties. And perhaps this awareness is my first real act of parenting.

I am cold and lonely standing by myself so I tiptoe around the bed and slide in next to Zeb. He stirs and waggles his tiny head toward me as if he's caught a whiff of my milk. Automatically, I lift my shirt and unclasp the hooks of my nursing bra. Jasper's eyes flutter open and I hesitate. We stare at one another and I'm afraid that he'll scowl and tell me to stop. Instead, he smiles drowsily at me. I recognize this smile. It is a smile from before. Before all the domestic detritus of parenting cluttered our lives. In his groggy state Jasper actually looks happy, relaxed and in love. This is the Jasper that I've known for ten years, the one that I've been missing.

Carefully, he rolls Zeb toward me. I am calm and I offer my bare breast, gently touching my nipple to Zeb's mouth, hoping that tonight my milk will be just a little bit sweeter. As he snuggles up against me I know that this is the moment I've been waiting for. All of us cuddled together happily on the bed. This is the family that I imagined all along. I know it won't always be this way, though. There will be more hard times ahead, Jasper and I will continue to disagree, but for now, I am satisfied as Zeb opens his lips and we try again.

HEATHER SWAIN is the author of two novels, *Eliot's Banana* and *Luscious Lemon*, and the editor of *Before: Short Stories About Pregnancy*. Her fiction and nonfiction have appeared in literary journals, Web sites and magazines. She lives in Brooklyn, New York, with her husband, two children and dog.

Caren Lissner

Women have so many choices nowadays, but the tough part is making the ones that work for the next sixty years. "Chick-lit," whether an individual book falls into the entertainment or literary category, helps us laugh and think about all the risks, responsibilities and ramifications of our choices. I see chick-lit as not necessarily defined by being literary or just pleasure reading (it can be both, or either), but as a genre that adult women can empathize with and learn from, and a great addition to modern writing. It also got many of us (including me) into publishing, an industry that's nearly impossible to break into no matter what you write.

The Database

It was naturally expected that any woman who was still single at twenty-one would sign into the Database—but Laura had resisted for four years.

Even in the face of intense pressure from parents and friends, even in the face of pending legislation, even in the face of late-night comedy routines mocking people like her, Laura just couldn't sign in.

It wasn't necessarily the technology that riled her. The Database had come a long way since its invention back in 2008, when it was Database 1.0. Now, seven years later, it was up to 7.0 and much more precise.

The National Singles Database (NSD) had quickly become something everyone had to use. Most people logged into the NSD as soon as they turned twenty-one, although there was some talk of letting younger folks join. Individual states were considering age limits to block the potential change, ostensibly to protect children, but everyone knew the move was secretly funded by the women's lobby, who didn't want to compete with eighteen-year-old girls.

Things had changed quickly with the NSD. The original Database had only asked a hundred personal questions, but now it was up to a whopping 1,250, and there was talk of NSD 8.0 including 1,500.

Laura always felt a little sick when friends pressed her to log in to meet a man. She clung to old-fashioned notions of finding love through fate, even though her best friend Zoey told her countless times, "Sometimes fate needs a little help." Laura told Zoey she should be the NSD's spokesperson.

Laura lived in a brownstone in Philly whose bay windows looked out on Walnut Street. The corner of her bedroom by the windows, where she set up her home office, had two exposed brick walls. It was hard to tape or nail her graphic art projects into the bricks above her computer, so she bought special hooks that could be forced into the mortar.

On her far wall was a bookshelf full of old-fashioned romances, like *Milkrun* and *The Trials of Tiffany Trott*, where characters met men in bars. It sounded heavenly.

Laura sometimes asked Zoey and her other non-single friends to fix her up. But even that became contrived, because all her friends had joined the National Friends Database (NFD) to expand their social group. Sometimes people logged into the National Friends Database because they wanted to acquire a Black Friend or a Gay Friend. However, there was increasing moral opposition, and not just the cries of perceived tokenism from the far left; people were alarmed at the rise of "pooling," or making a new friend for the summer just because that person's profile said they had a pool. This trespass was becoming more rampant now that winter was ending, and for the last week *Prime Time Live Friday* had been announcing a special report on "pooling." People were starting to leave the pool question blank.

Take that, NFD, Laura thought. *It's none of your damn business.*

So what made Laura finally decide to give in on February 1, 2015?

The morning started with her crafting signs for a client on Restaurant Row. The design firm for which she was a consultant worked with both local businesses and national chains. Laura loved toying with shapes and symbols. Even as a child, she'd played with blocks while other kids played with blogs. But this particular assignment bored her, and she yearned for something—some*one*—to think about during the downtime.

She imagined coming home, stretching out on the red futon beside her hardworking honey, tickling his flat stomach and swapping stories of corporate iniquity. "They expect me to be Mr. Fix-It," he'd groan, and she'd lay her head on his chest and assure him she understood. Then they'd head out to dinner, past South Street's usual band of hipsters, spinsters and Dumpsters.

The day that Laura finally logged onto the NSD was a Thursday. She was twenty-five, and it was twenty-five degrees out. In a high corner of her bedroom, the flat-screen TV blared a commercial: "Tonight on *Prime Time Thursday*: are they developing a Baby version of the NSD? Find out why parents may be setting their kids up...for disappointment."

Laura sat in her gray chair and swiveled backward to face the bay windows. Across the street was a tall metallic stack of hip studio apartments, a new building called the Ion. When it got dark, the fluorescent pink lighting in the word "Ion" ricocheted off the metallic poles and arcs. In summer, a small fountain shot up and turned pink in the lighting.

Laura watched people enter and leave the Ion for a while. Then she turned back toward her desk. She talked softly to her cat, Kitty, for a few minutes. Kitty snoozed and purred, her orange fur lifting and falling with each breath. Laura tapped the spacebar and Kitty vanished from the screen. She remembered the days when people had real pets instead of screensaver ones.

Question #226 in the NSD was, *Are you allergic to organic animals?*

The icon for the NSD—a pair of slender hands holding each other on top of a keyboard—was still on her computer from back when she had bought it. Maybe the fact that she hadn't erased it was a sign of her inevitable compliance.

Suddenly, a gaping loneliness yawned open in her soul. Why had she been stupid for all these years? There were millions of men on the NSD, and she'd rejected them out of sheer stubbornness.

Laura had to admit that part of her problem was that she had never been good at writing e-mail. She was always putting her foot in her keyboard, and writing wasn't a talent of hers. Everyone was good at different things. She was best at in-person communication, with its visual cues and nuances. But there was no more time for excuses. Everyone she knew had met their match via the NSD. Time to plunge in.

Initially, the system fed Laura the standard introductory questions: age, height, education. But as the queries became more detailed, she remembered why she hated the NSD.

How many times have you smoked marijuana? How do you feel about cooking? Cloning? Spooning? Do you agree with the federal ban on Halloween? At what temperature do you set your thermostat?

Laura pushed boldly on by reminding herself of the two clear advantages of the NSD. One, it eliminated doubts, stamped out the notion that there might be someone better out there. What if you married the girl next door, but your perfect match was really in California? The Database backed up your relationship by science, theoretically extending its potential longevity and durability.

And two, there were NSD Centers across the country that could verify important parts of your profile. For a fee, the NSD Health Center certified you as 100 percent disease-free. A different center verified that you looked like your pictures, within 3 percent certainty. The certifications would appear as icons in your profile.

Years ago, there had been too much divorce, cheating and the spread of disease. The NSD increased the integrity of the coupling process— and both parties got the security they needed. If love was the most important thing in the world, why leave so much to chance?

Do you drink eight glasses of water per day? Do you do impressions? Who is your favorite White Stripe?

Beads of sweat formed on Laura's forehead. She assured herself that the end result would save time.

How often do you speak to your parents? Do you have an e-cat? Do you plan to watch the next televised execution? Do you think America is really ready for a dwarf president?

She tilted her chair back. Spots of moonlight drizzled over her body.

Do you eat sugar cereal? Did you vote for Barack Obama? If there was a mouse in your place of residence, how would you get rid of it?

Laura turned back to the street. On the second floor of the Ion, a young guy tapped at his computer in his window. Laura saw him there often. He had a pale swoop of light brown hair that straggled across his forehead. He was always alone in the window. It seemed like she'd have better luck walking across the street and ringing the guy's bell, even in the dark of night. Why be subtle anymore? The NSD made one thing clear—you wanted to find a mate. In the old days, there was a stigma, but that was plain silly. Everyone wanted someone—it just depended how much public humiliation you were willing to endure in the pursuit.

It was time to own up to your loneliness!

Laura watched as the guy in the Ion building wrestled off his T-shirt and reached forward to turn off his light. Laura still had hours before *she* could turn in. She sighed and returned to her monitor. Only one thousand, one hundred and ninety-two more questions to go.

Do you burn scented candles? Do you eat early-bird specials? How often do you ride roller coasters? Do you ride the ones that go upside down?

Her eyes were dry as gauze. It was time for a pep talk, or at least a pep soliloquy. *It can't be that hard,* she told herself, *to answer only one thousand, one hundred and eighty-eight more questions.*

Besides, she had plenty of time left to meet someone if this didn't work out. She could have a baby for another thirty years, as long as she shopped at Egg Locker or Boy, Girl and Beyond.

By five in the morning, she was done. She knew that twelve hours later, she'd have a list in her e-mail box of the fifty most compatible men in the country. The system purposely took twelve hours in order to guard against "revenge mating," or immediately signing back on and pretending to be single because of a fight with one's lover. Too many people had been impulse-used.

At her consulting job in the morning, Laura's supervisor, Holden Jones, kept asking her inane questions. She just wanted to run home and wait for the NSD results.

As Laura watched Jones walk away, she thought about something. Jones had met his wife through the NSD, like most people. But what if he had been alive in the 1960s instead of today? Would Jones have married someone from his hometown instead? And would that person have been less right for him than his present wife? Would Jones have spent all his time wondering if there was someone better out there?

NSD question #811 was: *Do you believe in miracles?*

Well, sure. Miraculous things happened all the time—but they weren't *really* miracles, were they? Birth wasn't a miracle, just something that beat the odds. People came out of comas, but that just meant the body had repaired itself when it was unlikely. Even if you didn't understand a miracle, it had a scientific explanation. Maybe it was time Laura acknowledged that about love, too. It was just a process of trial and error—not magic.

Question #812: *Do you believe in rock and roll?*

Question #813: *Do you believe in God?*

Question #814: *Do you believe in romance?*

How can anyone answer yes to the last one, Laura thought, *and still do this?*

When 5:00 P.M. rolled around, Laura sprinted to the bus stop, pressing her skirt to her knees to keep it from flaring up. She admired the adorable blue/red SEPTA logo that looked like the yin/yang of mass transit. Laura dropped a couple of Reagan half-dollars into the change slot and didn't sit down.

She was like any other girl rushing home to wait for her man, she thought. Even if it was just going to be a guy on a computer-generated list.

The NSD e-mail was waiting in her box by the time she arrived home. It looked fairly innocent, for something that could change her life. She gulped.

The list held fifty names from all over the country. The only thing it failed to give out was each man's location, as the NSD didn't want people rejecting potential soul mates because of residencyism.

Laura glanced down the list, taking stock of names, photos, compatibility rates. On top it said: *NSD LIST FOR LAURA R. NANFO, FEMALE SEEKING MALE, NSD # 325464AAF.*

Laura read the top ten in reverse order.

Number 3: Ron. Twenty-five years old, 89.0 percent match, 5'11", 190 lbs. Intro sentence: "I like good times, good beer, bad TV and bad pizza. But is there such a thing?"

Ron wore a scowl on his face. He looked like he wanted women to think he was tough. Not really Laura's type.

Number 2: Tim. 93.2 percent match. Owned horses, jogged each morning, claimed he liked to cook. Probably lived out West. But he seemed, for all of his interests, to lack personality and warmth.

Maybe I'm not right for this, Laura thought. *Maybe I can't fall in love with someone from a description.*

She clicked the name of guy Number 1.

Something twisted in her stomach and crept into her mouth. She didn't know whether to vomit or cheer.

Daniel was twenty-six. His compatibility percentage was an impressive 97.4.

They shared several interests—e-cats, French cuisine, art, the music of the '00s. They had differences, but interesting ones. Daniel liked baseball but despised soccer. Daniel enjoyed plays but hated musicals. She found herself teasing him in her mind: *What's wrong with a little music in a stage show? So Lerner and Loewe are inferior to Dave Matthews?*

Daniel seemed like the type to engage in such battles. He wore a teasing smile. He looked a little like Ben Affleck before he went bald. But then she was really surprised: Daniel was a graphic designer.

In some other part of the country, Laura's male counterpart was spending his days hunched over a Macintosh 2015GGGXL, pounding fonts and colors into winning creations.

Why had she gone on meaningless dates when Daniel was right there?

It took more than an hour for Laura to read the rest of Daniel's responses. No wonder this worked out for so many people—after 1,250 questions, you had a good idea whether to reject someone or take a shot.

Question #1228: *Do you think it's okay to tell ethnic jokes?*
____ *Always*
_x_ *Sometimes*
____ *Never*
____ *If only family members are present*

Question #1232: *What is your preferred birth control method?*
____ *Abstinence*
____ *Withdrawal*
____ *Male condom*
____ *Female condom*
____ *Ten-minute-after pill*
_x_ *Up to my partner*

Question #1237: *If you were to go to a museum this weekend, which kind would you choose?*
____ *Art*
____ *Industry*
____ *Sports*
____ *Wax*
____ *Hard to choose just one*
_x_ *Up to my partner*

This man at times expressed creativity and independence, yet also knew when to compromise—without being a doormat. Laura still wasn't good at e-mail, but maybe she'd be aided by the inspiration that came with true love.

Dear Daniel,

("Dan" was too large a trespass this soon.)

Dear Daniel,
   Congrats—you're number one on my NSD list! Great news, huh? I see we share some of the same interests, and the ones I don't have only interest me more. So...what can I tell you?

166

And then, she told him.

She said she was independent, but still wanted a life partner to share travails and triumphs. She said she thought Andy Warhol got too much credit, but she loved the stark industrial beauty of "Knives." She said she liked when people used parentheses in their e-mails, but not smileys.

Her heart beat faster. *Maybe I'm actually okay at this,* she thought. *I was just a late bloomer.*

She titled the e-mail *#1 ON MY NSD LIST* and blasted it into cyberspace.

Then she leaned back, spent.

All evening, she waited for Daniel's response. She got a call from Alyssa, an acquaintance of hers who had heard Laura's exciting news from Zoey. Alyssa was Zoey's Black Friend.

"Good going!" Alyssa yelled over the phone. "Let me know what Dan says!" Alyssa then gave her own update. She was heavily into a serious relationship with Number 9 from her NSD list. Number 6 had turned out to be a pothead, and Number 5 was gay but had checked the wrong box. Number 3 at first had seemed to have the most potential, because he loved hockey as much as Alyssa did. But it turned out he hated the Flyers. How could anyone hate the Flyers? Alyssa had been furious— the NSD should ask which teams a person liked, not just which sports. Hopefully NSD 8.0 would be an improvement.

In any case, it turned out that guy Number 9 wasn't into sports at all. But he loved Alyssa's passion for things, including the Flyers. That, in the end, was what mattered.

Laura didn't get an e-mail back from Daniel on Friday or Saturday. She distracted herself by watching *Saturday Night Live,* even though everyone said it was better ten years ago.

On Sunday night, Laura whispered good night to Kitty, downloaded a gray e-mouse for her to bat around, and went to sleep.

Monday morning, Laura still hadn't heard from Daniel. As she dressed for work, she nervously checked her e-mail. *Maybe he's on vacation. Maybe he has a few e-mail accounts.*

She wondered if she was better off not knowing what she was missing. Was this what technology was about—making you feel like you had all these choices, that you could never be satisfied?

Work was dull that day. There was no one to share her sob stories at night. Except Kitty. She should treat Kitty better, she thought. She hadn't even given Kitty a real name.

That evening, she brought home a carton of pork lo mein and flicked on her computer. Surprisingly, there was an e-mail in her box from Daniel. She shoved Chinese noodles in her mouth as she read it.

Its subject head said:

RE: #1 ON MY NSD LIST

Laura's heart skipped a beat.

Subj: RE: #1 ON MY NSD LIST
From: dstratton@lnr.com
To: lauran25@aol10.com

Dear correspondent,
Thank you for contacting Daniel Stratton at LNR Visuals. Daniel is out of the office and will get back to you on February 12 when he returns. Thank you for writing to LNR Visuals.

LNR Visuals—that was a top design company in New York! Daniel had to be really talented.

But now she had to wait another ten days. This was torture!

She couldn't believe she'd waited this long in the first place. So many years of loneliness wasted. But perhaps fate had meant for her to take this long.

New York was close enough for an easy relationship, too. Some people logged into the NSD and got saddled with Alaskans.

Laura typed "Daniel Stratton" and "LNR Visuals" into Google and found some of his designs. They told almost too much, made her heart ache more.

Over the next few days, Laura glanced at other people's profiles on her NSD list, but none of the men were as good a match as Daniel. Wasn't the NSD about not settling?

It should be law to join up at twenty-one, she decided; then someone stubborn like her wouldn't be in this situation. There were laws governing drinking and smoking at a certain age, so why not a law forcing you to log on?

On February 12, Laura checked her e-mail every half hour. She did the same on February 13. Where had Daniel been on vacation, anyway? Paris? London? They could talk about his trip when they met up halfway in Woodbridge, New Jersey, and clinked mugs of double coconut chip cookie dough cappuccino.

On February 14, she finally heard back.

RE: #1 ON MY NSD LIST

Dear Laura—

Well, I am flattered that I got the pole position on your list. It's the little things, right? But I have to give you an apology. Actually, more of a confession. I hate the NSD. At least, hated it for many years. I know this makes me a Luddite or something, I'm very old-fashioned. Anyway, what do you know, a year and a half ago, I gave in to pressure and logged on. And that's how I met my wife. We just got back from our honeymoon. Guess I was a late bloomer, huh? I should have changed my marital status on there or gotten off, but I suppose my hatred of this thing kept me putting it off, and…well, there are so many things that happen when you're planning a wedding. I'm going to update it now before the NSD police come looking for me (ha ha; I was gonna put a smiley there but I hate them too). I guess I can't complain anymore about the NSD, because at least it brought me to Lauren!! I'm glad you enjoyed my profile; wish you best of luck—I know it's rough out there. DAN

She'd lost him before she'd even had him.

Everything whirled around her—the track lighting, Kitty's orange fur, colorful designs on the wall. She balled her fists and howled. How could she be crying over a guy she'd never met?

But that was what NSD had given her: instant e-heartbreak.

Then she thought of something else. What if this woman Daniel had married was *less* compatible with him than Laura? Laura and Daniel were 97.9 percent compatible. That was a lot. They should meet up anyway, to be sure.

Geez, now she was contemplating adultery. All because of numbers. So was love scientific, or random? Or a little of both? Or was it just too complex to analyze?

She should have gotten on the NSD years ago. But if she'd been on at twenty-one, Daniel himself wouldn't have been on yet, and she might have ended up with someone she was less compatible with than him. So fate *did* play a role—it just worked out for Lauren and not Laura.

No wonder I hate this thing.

Laura edged away from her computer. She looked out her window. The across-the-street guy was at his computer, but this time there was someone behind him, her slender fingers kneading his shoulders as he typed. Laura didn't want to meet him anymore anyway. Why meet another guy when she already had found the *best*?

Laura pressed her eyelids. If everyone spent every waking moment looking for the person of their dreams, they had to be open-minded about how they did it. But following each avenue to its extreme could drive one crazy as well. It still seemed worth it, she figured, if not to decrease the odds of being alone, then at least to cut the risk of kicking yourself later. After that you had to pick someone, trust your feelings and stick with them.

She asked herself Zoey's question again—*What if fate needed a little help?*

She figured she'd give her list another look. But instead, she merely watched the screen fade until Kitty came back on, then noticed how much Kitty enjoyed just playing with that little gray mouse.

CAREN LISSNER's humorous first novel, *Carrie Pilby*, was published in 2003. Her lighthearted essays have appeared in the *New York Times*, *Philadelphia Inquirer* and *Weatherwise* magazine. She lives in Hoboken, New Jersey, where she serves as the editor of the Hudson Reporter newspaper chain. She graduated from the University of Pennsylvania in 1993. She can be reached at www.carenlissner.com.

Julie Kenner

I read for many reasons, but the primary reason is to be entertained. Chick-lit is entertainment. A wide range of stories designed to draw readers—particularly women—in and, for just a little while, transport them to a new world with new friends, new relationships and new struggles to overcome. Although often with a modern twist, chick-lit represents classic stories and classic entertainment, which is why chick-lit (albeit without the label recently bestowed by marketing types) has been around for centuries.

Dead Friends and Other Dating Dilemmas

"Nude?" I repeat, ignoring the traffic outside the Toyota's window as I stare at this man I've known—and crushed on—since I was five years old. "Were *you* nude, too?" I hope I sound interested in a great story and not in the mental image of Evan in the buff. A mighty nice image, too, enhanced by the fact that I had, in fact, once seen him wearing nothing but a tan. The view had been brief, accidental and underscored by much mortification on the part of my then fifteen-year-old self, but I'd held the mental picture close to my heart ever since.

A trademark Evan Walker grin eases across his face, the force of it un-leashing the butterflies that had been napping in my stomach. It's been a year since I've seen that smile in person, and I'd forgotten just how nice those butterflies could feel. "What do *you* think, Syd? Did I let it all hang out?"

He's teasing me, and I play it cool. I lean back in my seat and kick my feet up on the dashboard. "I don't know. Just how daring are you?" It's a game we've played since we were little, Evan, Emily and me. Evan with his braver big-brother attitude, and Emily with her little-sisterly certainty that she could show up her older brother. And me, just hoping to impress my best friend's brother without my best friend catching on and, inevitably, teasing me.

From the backseat, Emily snorts. "Daring? Evan's about as daring as a carrot." I ignore her. We've been in the rental car for almost an hour now, and she's been silent the entire trip, which is good, considering I already know the opinion she's voiced so many times to me: Evan is off-limits; I have a perfectly fine boyfriend back in Los Angeles (and I do). I need to keep my libido under control for the weekend, and then things can go back to normal.

Honestly, though, I'm not all that happy with the status quo, and I'm tired of Emily's nagging about my love life. That probably makes me a bitch—especially when you consider the circumstances—but like Ce-line Dion says, the heart will go on. Besides, I'm jetlagged, and that makes me cranky.

I sigh, and focus pointedly on Evan, ignoring my best friend in the back. "Come on. Quit being coy. Did you join in the nude revelry or not?"

He laughs, and damned if that low, sexy rumble doesn't make me go all soft inside. "No, Syd, I didn't get naked. Instead, I got the hell out of there."

Now I join in the laugh, because I can see the whole thing. Evan chat-ting with friends and clients as they stroll down Melrose. Circumvent-ing the red velvet rope to enter Impulse, the trendy new club reported to have the best chocolate martinis in Los Angeles, then stopping short when he sees what he can't possibly be seeing: that every single person in the place is completely nude.

"I mean, talk about a shock," Evan says, amusement still lacing his voice. "I'm all for charity events, but my tolerance of philanthropic behavior ends about where my clothes begin."

"Yeah? I thought you Hollywood types jumped all over stuff like that. I bet there were so many cameras flashing in front of that restaurant that Paris Hilton's tush got tanned."

From the backseat, Emily snorts, and I hold my breath, waiting for her to say something.

"I think she's already got the all-over tan going," Evan says, and for a second I'm confused. Then I remember that we're talking about Paris.

"Right." I fight the urge to glance into the backseat. "But you're avoiding the bigger issue." I say the latter with some bravado, as if to prove to Emily that I can banter with her brother even knowing she's eavesdropping.

He glances over at me, and I'm struck by the magnificent portrait he makes. Scruffy beard, bright eyes, and the Texas Hill Country rolling by behind him. Suddenly, I'm analyzing his kissability quotient, and that's an area into which my thoughts have no business drifting. Certainly not now, on this trip. For that matter, not ever. I made a promise, didn't I?

"What bigger issue is that?" he asks, still caught up in our banter and not aware that my mind has moved on to his lips and other off-limits body parts.

"The fact that you're a Hollywood PR hound now," I say, keeping my cool.

"Is that what I am?"

"Aren't you?"

He pretends to think about that, then slams his hand on the steering wheel. "Dammit, you're right. I *should* have stripped naked and danced on a few tabletops. All in the interests of my clients, of course."

"Of course," I agree, laughing. "After all, that's what big-shot Hollywood agents do."

When I think back, it's clear I always knew that Evan would fit right in on the West Coast. He may have been born and raised in Fredericksburg, Texas, same as me, but Evan Walker had been meant for a milder climate and faster lifestyle.

I think that's one of the things I've always loved about him. Evan is exotic. He's the epitome of everything I've always wanted to be—sophisticated, witty and daring. He moved to Los Angeles right out of high school, telling me and Emily he couldn't pack his bags fast enough. Now he's an assistant agent at one of those huge agencies that you read about in the entertainment section of your local paper. Me, I only sucked up the nerve to make the move to L.A. after finishing college. And even then, I had to have my best friend in tow as a live-in security blanket. Now I'm an IT manager for one of the major banks in downtown Los Angeles. Honestly, the excitement never ends.

I stifle a sigh. I'd moved to Los Angeles after college purportedly for a new life and adventure with my best friend, who was going to win an Emmy by the time she was twenty-seven. My real reason had more to do with said friend's brother. But some plans never come to fruition, no matter how delicious they might be in theory. Suffice it to say that there are no little gold statues honoring Emily. And Evan and I are not an item, despite opportunity and intent.

"Is that why you've been avoiding me?" he asks. "Because you think I've gone too Hollywood or something?"

"I'm not avoiding you," I say. "Don't be stupid."

"Rejection makes me stupid. Considering all the lunch and dinner dates you've turned down, I'm thinking my IQ's diminished to somewhere around fifteen."

Without thinking, I glance into the backseat and see Emily rolling her eyes. "If he thinks you're going to feel guilty for doing exactly what you two agreed, then his IQ really has taken a nosedive. God, can you believe that once upon a time you actually fell for this loser?"

I turn away quickly, my cheeks flaming.

"What?" Evan asks. I just shake my head. Evan's not the least bit tuned in to his sister's rants. That privilege belongs solely to me. As, apparently, does toeing the line and enforcing the agreement he and I made last year.

"Listen, Evan...." I say, drawing out his name in the hopes that I won't have to say the actual words.

My ploy works. He lifts the fingers of his steering hand just long enough to signal me. "I know. I know. You weren't avoiding me. We agreed to ignore our attraction. To not see each other any more. Yadda yadda yadda, blah blah blah."

174

He faces me. "But what if we should never have agreed in the first place?" Very gently, he brushes a fingertip across my cheek. I turn to look out the window and fight—hard—to hold back tears.

We've reached the city limits, and I fake an intense interest in the familiar scenery so that I can avoid admitting that I'd been wondering that very thing.

"At any rate," he says after pulling his finger back, "I'm glad you came with me today. Surprised as hell, but glad."

"You know I wouldn't miss this."

One quick nod as he turns off of Main Street and weaves his way toward the Wildfire Bed & Breakfast. "I knew you'd come for her. For the memorial. But I didn't know you'd agree to take the same flight as me or share a car with me."

I can only shrug.

"What happened to us?"

In response, I point to the B&B, the ballroom of which will be filled tomorrow with food and wine, memories and tears. "How can you even ask that?"

A muscle twitches in his cheek. A tiny movement, but to me, it's as intense as a slap. "*She* died," he finally says as he puts the car in park and kills the engine. "Not us. *Her.*"

"It's not that simple," I say.

"Maybe it should be," he says, then gets out and slams the door so hard the entire car shakes.

I flick my gaze to the backseat, wondering if Emily is paying attention. She is. Her eyes, fixed and hard, stare me down, and I feel the bitter cold of her anger settle into my bones.

I open my door, desperate for the warmth of the sun, and I stand there on the warm gravel parking lot, just soaking it in, wishing it could make even the slightest dent against the chill that has set my insides to trembling.

One year ago tomorrow, we buried my best friend. Evan's sister. The Walkers' only daughter.

We'd been in town—Evan, Emily and me—visiting our families. The rain had come, a typical Texas thunderstorm. Slick roads. A drunk driver veering into oncoming traffic. The crunch of metal, and the snapping of bone.

It was all over in a heartbeat. The doctors say she didn't suffer at all. I know better. She suffered, all right. And she suffers still.

My best friend Emily Walker is dead. She's been dead for a year.

She isn't, however, dead to me.

"You were flirting." Emily's voice fills the room, her tone accusatory.

"You're not only dead, you're insane," I say, looking around and wondering where she's going to appear. "I was arguing."

She doesn't materialize, and I find myself scowling at nothing. She's been doing this to me for a year now. Haunting, I mean. I was the last person to realize she was dead. They'd told me about the accident, of course. About how the drunk driver had cut her off. About how she'd lost control of the car and spun off the road into a ditch. Lucky, they'd said, that no one else had been killed. "Else?" I remember saying. And that's when I realized that Emily—who'd been sitting on my bed all that time, sulky and crying—was really and truly dead.

The situation had, as you might imagine, messed a bit with my head. It's one thing for your best friend to die in a car accident. It's another thing altogether to have her continue to be your best friend.

At first, I'd thought I was going crazy. Once the reality of the situation got through my head, I wished I were crazy.

Don't get me wrong; I love Emily. Always have and always will. But, well, she's *dead*. And if you think the fact that I've always had a smaller waist was a point of severe jealousy in our living relationship, you haven't seen the kind of envy that can be generated when one half of a best friend unit is no longer able to wear Seven jeans at all...never mind how tiny (nonexistent?) her waist might now be.

"Arguing," I say again, firmly, and to the empty air. "Not exactly *Cosmo*'s number one tip for getting the guy to notice you."

"Maybe not," she says, "but it could be foreplay." This time, the air shimmers, and suddenly there she is. To me, she looks solid, but I've learned better. I'm the only one privileged enough to see her, and I say that with a certain bit of ironic brio.

"You're pathetic," I say. "Pathetic and paranoid."

"Fine," she says. "You weren't flirting. But that doesn't mean you didn't want to." She smoothes her skirt and sits on the edge of the bed.

You'd think I'd be used to this by now, but I'm not, and I watch, fascinated, as she sort of meshes with the mattress. Not really sitting on it, but not really in it, either.

"Hello?" she says in a typically Emily voice. "Aren't you even going to answer me?"

"No," I say, moving to unpack my suitcase. "You think you know everything, then fine. Just talk with yourself." I half hold my breath, because that is so not the kind of thing I would ever have said to Emily when she was alive. But I'm feeling almost giddily brave. I'm not sure if it's being around Evan again, or just being here for Emily's memorial. I mean, there's nothing like coming home to honor a dead girl to make you remember that the girl really is dead.

I concentrate on unpacking, but sneak her one or two looks while I do. She's still sitting there, but she's eyeing me curiously, her expression both hollow and sad. When I can't take it anymore, I turn to her. "What?" I demand.

"You two agreed to end it," she says. "And you swore to me that you meant it. Right here in this room, you swore to me."

"Sometimes things change."

The air in the room turns icy, and I brace myself for a whip of wind as her fury rises. But there's nothing. Just a well-deep sadness in her eyes.

"Not for me," she says, as she starts to fade from me. And then, only her voice is left. "For me, things will never change again."

"Sydney Colfax! My goodness, let me have a look at you!" The enthusiastic voice washes over me, the familiar Texas twang making AnnMarie sound sweet and female. Not at all the insipid bitch I know her to be.

"Hello, Annie," I say, because I know she hates it. "I didn't expect to see you until tomorrow."

"I work here part time now," she says. "I just came in to see if Mary wants me here early tomorrow. You know, to help set up the room."

We're in the ballroom, a huge room with oak floors and oil paintings plastered up on the walls. The B&B rents this room out for meetings. Tomorrow, it will be filled with friends and family, people who've come to honor Emily's memory. Right now, though, it is empty, all except the enlarged yearbook pictures of Emily, mounted on foam core and leaning scattershot against the walls, waiting to be organized and displayed.

I walk to the closest one—Emily's senior picture. She's smiling at me, a smile that hasn't faded in my memory as I'm sure it has in her friends' thoughts, and maybe even in her family's. She looks beautiful as always. Ready to go conquer the world. Or at least the University of Texas.

"Life's really unfair sometimes, isn't it?" AnnMarie asks, peering over my shoulder at the photograph.

I don't answer, but I start to walk the length of the wall, my eyes taking in the details of each photograph, a silent tribute to my best friend. Emily as cheerleeder. Emily as student body president. Emily winning Best Actress in the UIL competition. Emily on the debate team, and going all the way to State.

I was at her side through all of it, winning my own little victories. Never once, though, did I think my A+ papers and quietly received scholarships and grants in any way compared to the glory that was Emily. Vibrant, alive Emily. Even now, I don't really understand. Why take her life, when my more mundane one would hardly even be missed at all?

I shake off the melancholy and turn away from the photographs. "Yeah," I say to AnnMarie. "Sometimes, life just sucks."

"So how are *you* doing?" she asks.

I examine her face, expecting to see only a mask of good manners, and am surprised to find genuine concern.

"I'm doing good," I say. I nod a little, because it's true. I am doing good. And every day is getting better. "Yeah, I'm doing real good."

"I'm so glad to hear that. Wild horses couldn't have made me say this last year, but I was worried about you. After she died, I mean."

"About me?"

"You were always so...well, you know. Her little follower. Everywhere there was Emily, there was Sydney, too. Word around the school was she pretty much demanded you be there. Emily snapped, and you jumped."

"If you're suggesting—"

"That she was a bitch?" she offers, her thick accent and shark-white smile making the insult seem sweetly conversational. "Not at all. I don't speak ill of the dead. I'm just glad to know you're not lost without her."

I want to tell her just who the bitch is in the room, but I don't. For that matter, I can't even work myself up into a good old-fashioned righteous indignation. Because she's right. At least about me. I'd always relied on Emily. In a lot of ways, I still do.

"So I guess you and Evan are an item now, huh?"

"I...no. No, we're not."

"Oh." Her face screws up in a picture of confusion. "My bad. I just assumed. I mean, before. You know, when Emily was alive, I could see why it wouldn't work. I mean, she'd be so...." She trails off, waving a hand. "I just mean that I saw you guys arrive together. And I know you had a huge crush on him back when we were kids. And last year I heard—"

"What?" I say, almost too sharply. "You heard what?"

One shoulder lifts in a tiny shrug. "Nothing really. I just heard that you and Evan might be getting serious."

"You heard wrong," I say sharply. "I have a boyfriend in Los Angeles." Even as I say the words, though, I feel ridiculous. Technically, I do have a boyfriend, but the words still feel like a lie. Because I don't love Terrance. I wish I did, and oh, how I've tried, but I've been in love with Evan Walker since I was in kindergarten. I've spent the last year lying to everyone, including Evan and myself. All to make a dead girl happy.

I wonder whom that makes more pathetic: me, living my life to please a dead friend, or the dead friend, trying to control my life.

Wildfire has always been my favorite bed & breakfast in Fredericksburg, a town that overflows with historic homes and quaint lodgings. This particular establishment, besides having large, comfy rooms and excellent food, has a koi pond surrounded by a native plant garden, all overseen by various bits of statuary ranging from gnomes to the Virgin Mary. In other words, a place for equal opportunity meditation, all accomplished under the backdrop of gurgling water and the soft chatter of squirrels in the peach and oak trees.

I'm sitting on the bench, engaged in a bit of meditation, when Evan strolls up. He sits next to me, silent, then bumps me with his hip, a silent entreaty to shove over. I do, forcing myself not to smile at the welcome familiarity of it all.

We sit in silence for a while, the setting summer sun cutting through the trees, making the garden glow with deep orange streaks of light. It's a nice moment, and one I don't want to end. Even more, though, I want the future. And I've asked him to come here so that I can grab hold of it.

"Thanks for coming," I say.

"It's a little *déjà vu*," he says. "I almost didn't come."

"But?"

"But I couldn't stay away," he says. "Just like I can't stay mad at you."

I inspect my fingernails so that I can avoid looking him in the eye. But I'm smiling, and I think he knows it.

"Last time we were here, things didn't go all that great between us," he says, taking my hand and twining his fingers with mine.

"I know. It was hard for me. Seeing you, I mean. With Emily suddenly gone." Everything I'm saying is absolutely true, but I know he understands something different than my truth. He thinks he was a reminder. A harsh reflection of the loss we'd both suffered. In truth, he was the manifestation of a promise I made to Emily to stay away from Evan. A promise she's reminded me of day after day, staying my hand when I want to accept his dinner invitations, telling me I did the right thing when I cry at night, wondering what might have been.

I'd agreed because I'd thought her death was my fault. Not completely, but enough that the weight of it bore down on me, quashing my own desires and filling me with a need to repent. And, in part, with a need to punish. Both myself and Evan. Because if it was my fault, it was his fault too.

She'd seen us that night. Locked here in an embrace, his mouth hot on mine, his hands cupping my breasts. She'd run, a typical Emily reaction. Drive far, drive fast and think about what's bothering you.

She never made it home. More, she'd never really had the chance to cool down.

After the funeral, Evan and I had come back to this bench, and I'd told him it was over. Over before it had even really begun. I told him it was for the best. That I needed space.

I didn't tell him I'd made a promise to his dead sister. Without that promise, things would have been different. I would have cleaved to him. Cried with him, and worn myself out in grief.

I have to wonder now if that would have stymied our relationship. If maybe, in some twist of fate, Emily's promise has given us the time apart to grieve separately that will now allow us to come together without her ghost between us.

Because somehow, we *will* come together.

Somehow, I'm going to make Emily Walker leave me alone.

First, though, I'm going to forget about her, and concentrate only on the man sitting next to me.

I wake up in Evan's bed, feeling more fabulous than I can ever remember feeling. Sexy and alive, bruised and taken. No, strike that. I feel *claimed*. And, honestly, I like it.

The door to the room opens, revealing the dusky gray of dawn. Evan steps in, holding a gingham-lined basket of muffins. An utterly domestic scene, and I honestly think I might just have to jump him again right then, it's so damn sexy.

"Hey you," he says. "Regrets?"

"Just that we didn't do this before." I mean it, too, although I still have a few reservations. Emily's wrath, for one. But my best friend has made herself scarce, and that tingling in my veins that I've lived with for the last year—that sensation that lets me know she's near—is gone.

I broke my promise and, in doing so, I let her go. I probably let her down, too, and for that I'm sorry. But I had to. More, I wanted to.

I kick my legs out and reach for my underwear and jeans. I'm dressed in no time, Evan watching me with bemused eyes. "Bad choice of muffins?"

I grab one, then give him a kiss on the nose. "There's something I have to do," I say. "Someone I need to say goodbye to."

He nods, squeezes my hand. "Do you want me to come with you?" But the question is for form only. He knows I have to do this alone, and he hands me the keys to the rental car.

I lift myself up on my tiptoes and kiss his cheek. "I'll see you soon," I say, then sashay out the door, blowing him a kiss along the way and feeling—for the first time in a year—that things will be all right.

Until I left for college I'd lived in Fredericksburg my entire life. But that doesn't mean I'm familiar with every square inch of the place. And I sure don't have the route to the cemetery memorized. Which is why I'm now cruising—lost—down the wrong county road. I squint into the rising sun, trying to see the road despite the glare, and that's when I realize where I am. I'm on the little two-lane county road that Emily had been traveling when she died. My heart picks up its tempo, and I can hear my pulse in my ears as I notice the landmarks. The rock outcropping. The battered billboard. The deep ditch.

Emily died here. Right here.

I'd been looking for her grave. And, in a way, I found it.

I shake my head, suddenly chilled, and lean sideways, grappling for the glove box and the tourist map that Evan stuck there yesterday. I want out of here. I want to know the fastest route back to the B&B, and screw the cemetery. I'll pay my respects this afternoon like everyone else.

I flip open the glove box and my fingers sort through the bits of paper. Maps and the rental car agreement. I take my eyes off the road just long enough to make sure I'm grabbing the right map, but that's a split second too long.

When I look back, there she is. *Emily.* Standing in the middle of the road, right in front of my car.

I slam on the brakes, jerking the steering wheel to the left, even as my mind screams for me to do nothing. To just keep driving. *She's an apparition! You can't hit her! You're going to lose control!*

As if in a dream, I see the car start to spin, the tail whipping around to connect with the apparition, which seems to melt into the morning mist. I slam my foot on the brake—the wrong thing to do—and try to turn into the spin. But it's all over. I've lost control. The car skids, hits the ditch and rolls. I hear the explosion of the airbag deploying, and for a split second, I'm upside down, my own screams echoing in the car.

And then everything is black.

I wake up, and she's there. Emily. Right beside me in the passenger seat. Which, I realize through the screaming pain in my head, is especially unusual since the car is upside down, and she's sitting there—inverted—without even wearing a seatbelt.

I feel something sticky and look down. Some sort of pipe has pierced the side of the car, and pierced me, too. The stickiness is my blood, and it's all over my hands.

Once again, everything goes black.

This time, when I come to, I'm ready. I turn my head only a fraction of an inch, but even that is enough to make me grit my teeth against the pain. "Why?" I say to her.

Her eyes are wide and moist, but she doesn't cry. Do the dead not cry, I wonder? And then I think that I'll know the answer soon enough.

"Why?" I repeat.

"You promised me," she says, her voice barely a whisper.

"That isn't fair," I said. "You shouldn't have made me. I love him."

"No." The word is flat, harsh and holds a world of anguish. "You were mine. *My* best friend. It was about us. Not about you and him, with me just the tagalong sister."

"Emily," I say, my voice thick with understanding. Or maybe it's not my voice. Maybe it's all in my head. "Is that what you were afraid of?"

Her face contorts with unshed tears. "You were going to forget about me. Not at first. At first, you'd both think about me every day. But slowly, slowly, you'd begin to realize that whole weeks were going by. And it would just be you two. No Emily. Why should there be? She's dead, after all."

"I love you," I say. "I'd never forget you. But the living have to go on. So do the dead, you know."

"I know," she whispers. "Now we can go on together."

I've known it since I felt the blood, warm and sticky on my hand. Now, though, reality settles in. I'm dying. All alone on this road, and dying.

"I don't want to go," I say.

"I didn't want to either."

"This isn't right." My head is swimming, and the blackness threatens to take me again. "You did this. You interfered. I wasn't supposed to die."

"I don't want to be alone," she says, and now I hear the cheerleader. The drama queen. My teenage pal who always got what she wanted exactly when she wanted it.

"You can't always have what you want," I say, and there is desperation in my voice. I can hear it, smell it. I'm begging now, and I don't care. "Please. Please, help me."

She's silent, and the black closes around me. I fight my way back through the muck, spewing out words, fighting the only way I can to stay alive. "AnnMarie thinks you're a bitch, but you're not. I know you." I suck in air, my words coming out choppy but coherent. "You're my best friend, and I love you. Don't let me die here. Not now. Not like this."

The black grabs at me, clingy and thick, sucking me down like mud. As I start to drown in it, I see her face. She loves me, too. It's all there in her eyes. The love, and the remorse. For a moment, I am filled with hope.

Then I see the slow, sad shake of her head. "How can I possibly help?" she asks. "I'm not even really here."

I'm dead, I think, as the black sucks me under. And as tears stream down my face, I think I know the answer: yes, the dead do cry.

Light.

Everywhere. Bright, white light.

Heaven?

"Are you good enough for heaven?"

I recognize the voice, and I open my eyes. Evan smiles down at me.

"I said that out loud?" My voice sounds croaky, but it's a voice. And this is a hospital room. And I'm not dead. "How?" I ask, grabbing his hand and holding tight.

"I found you," he says, apparently understanding my question. "You were in the same ditch they found her in."

"But why did you come looking at all?"

Color tints his cheeks, and he looks at our intertwined hands instead of my face.

"Evan?"

"Just a feeling."

But it was more than a feeling, I'm certain of it. "Emily," I say. "She told you."

He looks up sharply, makes a scoffing noise. But I see the truth in his eyes. "Just one of those things, babe. You hear stories like this all the time. People get a feeling. They go. They rescue the damsel in distress."

"Did she say anything?"

"Syd...." From his voice, it's clear he wants to drop the subject, but I'm not letting it go.

"Just tell me. Please. It's important."

His shoulders lift, then fall in resignation. "She said she's not a bitch. And that we both should remember that."

I laugh then, laugh and pull him close. Because I was right, and I'm alive, and I'm free.

And, somewhere, I know that Emily is free now, too.

Nationally bestselling author **JULIE KENNER'S** first book hit the stores in February of 2000, and she's been on the go ever since, with over twenty books to her credit. Her books have won numerous awards and have hit bestseller lists as varied as *USA Today*, Waldenbooks, Barnes & Noble and *Locus* magazine. She writes a range of stories, from sexy and quirky romances to chick-lit suspense (*The Givenchy Code*) to paranormal mommy lit (*Carpe Demon* and *California Demon*). Visit Julie on the Web at www.juliekenner.com.

Karin Gillespie

I have loved chick-lit since before chick-lit was even a genre. In the seventies, I remember reading Sheila Levine Is Dead and Living in New York *by Gail Parent and it spoke to me in a way no book had before. Then in the eighties there was the hysterically funny novel* The Boyfriend School *by Sarah Bird. The nineties brought in* Bridget Jones's Diary *by Helen Fielding, and a genre was born. I couldn't be more delighted. These books truly speak to a woman's experiences. If the novel is done well, we recognize ourselves within its pages.*

Trash Talk

You could be arrested for this. I wasn't familiar with Peeping Tom laws but knew at the very least I was trespassing. If a policeman came crashing into the brush to find me crouched on a small hill, binoculars in hand, I planned to claim I was a bird-watcher.

"Looking for the yellow-winged finch, Officer," I'd say, blinking innocently, not certain if there was even a bird by that name. "This is private property? So sorry. I had no idea."

I'd probably get away with it, too. I was five-foot-two and bore a strong resemblance to Reese Witherspoon. Big blue eyes and a sleek blond pageboy could be valuable currencies in this world.

"All right, miss," the policeman would say, a smile in his voice. "Please move along."

If, however, a police*woman* were to confront me, she'd probably see right through my flimsy excuse.

"If you're a bird-watcher, I'm the Queen of Siam," she'd say, hands on hips. "What are you *really* up to, sister?"

In which case I'd appeal to her female sensibilities.

"I can explain. My ex-boyfriend Brice started dating another woman three weeks after he broke up with me. I'm spying on her so I can try to figure out what *she* has that I don't."

Was there a woman on God's green earth who wouldn't understand such a compulsion? Besides, it wasn't like I was hurting anyone. I was simply gathering information.

Unfortunately, I hadn't learned anything particularly revealing in the few minutes I'd been on surveillance. So far all I'd seen was the back of Lynda's brick ranch house.

"Lawn is overrun with crabgrass," I'd written in my palm-size notebook, as if this were a severe indictment of her character. "Doesn't coil garden hose."

The house had a bay window in the back, and I could peer inside her kitchen. There was an enormous bunch of bananas on the counter—more than the typical single person would generally have on hand.

"Possible potassium deficiency?" I'd jotted on the page. Or perhaps she was a smoothie fan. Everything about her seemed fraught with mysterious meaning.

I picked up the binoculars and scanned the kitchen again, making sure I hadn't missed anything. All I could see were bare countertops and a beige refrigerator with an outside icemaker.

Wait! There was a package in the corner that I hadn't seen before. I squinted. Was that a box of saltines?

My heart rose to my throat. *Saltines?* It was the middle of July—nowhere near chili season. There was only one possible reason a woman would have saltines on her kitchen counter in the heat of the summer. She was suffering from severe morning sickness because she was pregnant with Brice's child!

Wasn't it enough that Brice had replaced me only days before the heat of my body had cooled from his zebra-printed bedsheets? Now he had the insensitivity to start a family while I was still in the shock phase of Kubler-Ross' stages of grief. Suddenly, I understood how Jennifer Lopez must have felt when Jennifer Garner got pregnant. But unlike J.Lo, I didn't have Marc Anthony as a consolation prize.

There was only one thing to do. I *had* to steal Lynda's trash. If she *were* pregnant I might find more evidence: a positive EPT test, a piece of paper where she'd calculated her due date, an incriminating bottle of folic acid tablets.

I strolled nonchalantly through her backyard, and spotted her trashcan in the carport on the side of the house.

Taking a furtive look about, and praying I wasn't attracting the attention of nosy neighbors, I opened the lid, grabbed the Hefty bag and slung it over my shoulder. Then I scampered down the street to an alley where I'd concealed my car.

I was so excited about my bounty, I immediately pulled into a Wal-Mart parking lot to inspect my find.

Opening the bag, I drew back from the stench. Ewww! It brimmed with used kitty litter. I tossed it out of my car, and squealed out of the shopping center.

As I drove, I mused over my findings. If Lynda were pregnant, would she have handled kitty litter? Maybe she'd used gloves and was extremely careful. Or maybe she'd called Brice and *he'd* changed the kitty litter for her, saying, "We don't want to risk the health of our unborn child, darling!"

I wish I could tell you that this latest incident had been my wake-up call, that some small sane part of myself had said, "You've stolen used kitty litter. You've gone too far." But no, I was already plotting my next heist.

When I told my best friend Carla that my boyfriend Brice had broken up with me, she let out a war whoop and screamed, "Thank you, Jesus!" My parents wanted to take me out to the Prime Rib Palace to celebrate. My older sister Dana sent me a dozen white roses with a card that read, "Free at last!"

Before Brice and I broke up, I often defended my relationship with him. "He can be so wonderful to me. You never see that side of Brice," I'd claim, but a tiny, wise part of myself knew he wasn't good for me.

In fact, if you were to ask what was the worst thing Brice had ever done, I'd have dozens of sordid incidents to choose from, including the night he took me to Hooter's for my twenty-fifth birthday, but by far his most heinous crime was the night he told me I was too short.

We'd just finished making love and I was floating in a rosy cloud, thinking we'd finally turned some kind of corner in our relationship. My feelings were validated when he stared into my eyes and said, "I love you so much, Patty. Everything would be perfect between us if only...." He cast his gaze to the mirror above his bed. "Never mind."

"What it is, honey?" I'd asked, brushing back a stray hair strand from his face. Brice had long, loose curls, shaped like fusilli pasta.

"No. I can't tell you," he said.

"Please do!"

A pained look entered his eyes. "Everything would be perfect if on-ly...you were five inches taller."

It took me a while to find my voice. "How long have you felt this way?"

"Since the day we met."

A healthier woman would have flung back the covers, gotten dressed and screeched, "See ya later, asshole."

But all I could do was blubber.

"Brice! There's nothing I can do about my height!"

"I knew I shouldn't have told you," he said, with exasperation.

After that day, I always tottered around in ridiculously high shoes, knowing full well I'd never measure up to Brice's expectations.

Near the end of our rocky relationship, a bit of sanity finally breezed through my life. It was as if my neurotic, mixed-up self had been temporarily replaced by Dr. Phil.

"This isn't working out, Brice," said the cool, collected imposter who now inhabited my body. "You're constantly criticizing me. It's obvious I will never meet your impossible expectations, therefore I think we should break up."

I'd expected Brice to shrug and say, "Fine, baby. If you feel that way, I'm out of here."

Instead he fell to the ground, hugging my calves, crying. "Please, please, Patty. Don't leave me. Give me another chance."

He was on his knees! I'd never seen him in that position before. It briefly confounded me and I agreed to take him back. One week later *he* broke it off with me.

"Why?" I demanded.

"I need more," he mumbled.

"What do you need? I can give it to you," I begged.

"No," he said, shaking his head sadly. "I've decided you're simply too ordinary for me, and there's nothing you can do to change that."

It wasn't enough to break my heart. He'd dismissed me with an unflattering adjective. I was an ordinary midget, unworthy of his love.

A few weeks later I was at the grocery store puzzling over headache remedies. Ever since Brice had broken up with me, I'd had a persistent throbbing above my right temple. As I bent down to get the extra-strength Excedrin on the bottom shelf, I heard Brice's voice say, "Patty."

In the split second it took for me to turn my head around, I'd envisioned an entire reconciliation scene.

"Patty, I can't live without you. Please forgive me!" Brice would say, perhaps clutching a bottle of sleeping pills for dramatic effect.

But when I turned, there was a skinny brunette standing next to him. With her hand in Brice's jean pocket. Definitely not part of my fantasy.

"Hi, Patty," said Brice. "I hope you're doing okay. I wanted to introduce you to my new girlfriend, Lynda Cannon. Lynda, this is my old girlfriend, Patty."

Lynda and I both stiffened. If we'd been cats, our fur would have stood on end.

I surveyed Lynda, conducting a private little beauty pageant in my head. Which one of us would win the swim competition? Who would walk away with the scepter and crown?

In the end, I decided it was a draw. She was two inches taller than me, but I had bigger breasts.

I could tell she'd reached a similar conclusion. Instead of a smug smile and a hair toss—a sure sign that a woman thinks she's a superior specimen—uncertainty shone in her eyes as she mumbled, "Nice to meet you."

"Likewise," I said, taking one last look, hoping I'd missed an unsightly mole or an unflattering bulge.

Brice watched us closely, obviously enjoying the brief encounter, perhaps hoping we might claw and tear at each other's clothes.

As soon as I got home, I went to the phone book and found out where Lynda Cannon lived. That's how I ended up stealing her kitty litter.

"This is Dottie Fields from the marketing department of Kimberley-Clark. You have been selected to win a year's supply of one of our fine products. You have a choice between Depends Undergarments, Kotex Tampons or Huggies Diapers," I said to Lynda, holding a handkerchief over the phone to disguise my voice.

"I didn't enter any contest," said Lynda.

"You've been randomly chosen. Which of our three products would you like?"

"The tampons, I guess, but—"

Ha! Not pregnant.

"They'll be shipped to your home next week," I said, hanging up.

I kicked up my heels for a victory jig, but my glee was short-lived. Lynda might not be pregnant, but she was still sleeping with my ex-boyfriend.

Who is Lynda Cannon and why does Brice prefer her to me? That's what I was thinking as I pawed through another bag of her trash. I was regularly stealing her garbage now (except on Thursdays, the day she changed her kitty litter). I was officially a hardened career criminal, a serial trash thief. My pulse didn't even quicken anymore when I did the dirty deed.

"I think every man has a picture of the ideal woman in his head," Brice had said once during one of our pillow-talk sessions.

"Really?" I said, trying to sound casual even though alarm sirens were shrieking in my head. "What is your ideal woman like?"

Am I even close? I wanted to scream.

"She's too hard to describe," he said. "I'll just know it when I meet her."

"*When* you meet her?" I'd said, desperation in my voice. "What about me? Am I someone to amuse you, until *she* comes along?"

"She's hypothetical!" Brice said. "God, Patty!" And then, in one of his rare magnanimous moments, he drew me into his arms and whispered into my ear, "You're probably as close as I'll ever get."

But now he'd met Lynda, the woman whose orange peels and coffee grounds I was now digging through.

I'd been stealing Lynda's trash for over two weeks, and had learned all kinds of things about her during that time. She ate yogurt with fruit on the bottom and cashews. She read *Self* magazine, used Great Lash Mascara and subscribed to a basic cable package with no premium channels. Her guilty pleasure was assorted Hershey miniature chocolate bars, and she drank Kendall Jackson Chardonnay, going through a bottle about every four days. What did it all mean?

I hadn't, however, found any evidence of why Brice was with her now instead of me. I didn't know what I was looking for, precisely—perhaps a highbrow literary magazine, an empty bottle of an exotic perfume or the packaging from a pair of silk stockings. So far she seemed unexceptional.

My Dumpster-diving wasn't all for naught. Over the last couple of weeks I had learned that Lynda was smitten with Brice. Her grocery receipt revealed that she'd bought Peruvian coffee and Cherry Garcia ice cream, Brice's favorite indulgences. There were also several empty bags from Victoria's Secret, indicating she'd gone on a lingerie shopping spree, and a receipt from a key shop, which probably meant she'd made Brice a key to her house. Most upsetting to me, though, was the discarded tube of diaphragm cream. The jumbo size! Obviously they were going at it like rabbits.

I picked up the last bag I'd stolen from Lynda's trashcan and dumped its content on some newspapers spread out on my patio. As I sifted through the rubbish, I noticed numerous spots of pink amongst the boxes of Lean Cuisine and Fancy Feast cans.

"I hope that's not what I think it is," I whispered as I dropped to my knees. I fished a bit of pink from the debris, and rubbed its soft texture between my fingers. Rose petals—just as I had feared. Her trash was full of them.

Several weeks after Brice and I had first started dating, he'd stolen into my house while I was at work and prepared a special dinner of

Steak Diane and new potatoes. An uncorked bottle of Bordeaux had been set out on the counter to breathe.

After a candlelit dinner, he led me into the bedroom. A red shawl was draped over the lamp, and hundreds of pale pink rose petals were spread over the white coverlet on my bed.

He really does love me! I'd thought and from then on, every time he treated me poorly, I'd summon the memory of that night, convincing myself that the "real" Brice was the tender, rose-petal-spreading Brice.

But suddenly his gesture seemed cheap and calculated, like a move he'd stolen out of a book of seduction tricks instead of something that came from his heart. It was as if I'd fallen in love with a person I'd created in my imagination, someone who was very different from the man I had actually dated.

I continued to steal Lynda's trash for a couple of more weeks, but my heart wasn't in it. One day I simply stopped altogether.

Two months later, I was sitting in my living room reading a magazine when I heard rustlings outside my back door.

Is someone trying to break in? There'd been reports of robberies in the neighborhood lately. My Honda Accord was in the shop getting new brakes and perhaps the thief hadn't seen a car in the drive and thought no one was at home.

I tiptoed to the back door and pulled back a tiny section of curtain from the window. I had to fight from screaming when I saw a person dressed entirely in black, standing a few feet from my house. The intruder had his back to me and wore a long, brown ponytail. Just as I was about to call the police, I spied a bottle of Spray 'n Wash and a tub of Country Crock margarine near the interloper's feet, and suddenly I knew I wasn't in any danger.

I pushed open the door. "What are you doing?"

The figure startled and slowly turned around. She had an empty box of Double Stuf Oreos in her hand.

I stared into her frightened eyes and my first thought was: *What an amateur.* You don't go through someone's trash right there on the premises. You're supposed to take it with you.

"I'm sorry," Lynda stammered. "I can explain. All he does is talk about you! You're his ideal woman, and he keeps saying he made a terrible mistake letting you get away. So I just wanted to understand....I know this seems crazy but—"

I took a step toward her. "Let me get this straight. Brice claims *I'm* his ideal woman?"

She nodded and gulped back a sob. "He broke up with me a couple of days ago. He said that my breasts were too small and that I was...mundane."

I glanced at my trash spread around her feet. There was nothing special there. Just a bunch of debris.

She planted her teeth in her lower lip, and looked so scared I felt sorry for her. "What are you going to do?"

"Clean up," I said, picking up an empty carton of half-and-half and tossing it back into the trashcan.

She knelt down to help me pick up the rest of my rubbish and when we were through, she rose to her feet and swiped at her nose with her sleeve. "Brice said he was going to call you. Do you think the two of you will get back together?"

I rocked back and forth in my tennis shoes, considering the question. When I was with Brice I was an ordinary mortal; now that we are apart, I'm the ideal woman. What was the motivation to go back?

"I don't think so," I said.

I studied her mottled cheeks and swollen eyes. She'd obviously been doing a lot of crying in the last few days.

"I'm curious. Did you find what you were looking for?"

"No," she said, hanging her head and staring hard at a bottle of Downy Fabric Softener on the top of the trash heap as if it were a clue to a puzzle she desperately wanted to solve.

"Neither did I," I said.

She looked confused but I hoped one day it would become clear to her what I was trying to tell her. We were far more alike than she would ever suspect.

"As for Brice," I said as I took a step back toward my back door, "I wouldn't worry about him. He just talks a lot of trash."

KARIN GILLESPIE is the author of the Bottom Dollar Girl series. Her latest release is *Dollar Daze* (Simon and Schuster, August 2006). Karin maintains a Web site and a popular publishing industry blog called Southern Comfort at www.karingillespie.com. She is also the founder of the Girlfriends' Cyber Circuit, a virtual tour for women novelists.

Andrea Schicke Hirsch

Chick-Lit is any work of fiction that relates a compelling human story with wit, insight, intelligence and heart. Sometimes, even a male writer can pull it off.

Meeting Cute

an and I met cute on the 8:07 Sunday morning train out of Grand Central.

Well, I wasn't exactly cute at the time. I was waspishly cranky and hungover and pissed because I had to write a review of the terrible show I'd seen the night before. The last thing I wanted was company and I audibly groaned when I realized the person throwing a beat-up rucksack onto the overhead luggage rack above my head was preparing to join me. From the looks of his bag, he was probably some acne-ridden college kid with a bag full of dirty laundry on his way home to Mama.

"Excuse me...." said a surprisingly deep voice.

Without looking up, I resigned myself to putting my steno pad away and closed my eyes. I certainly wasn't going to get any work done with some strange guy breathing down my neck. Feeling the heat coming off him, I noticed he smelled enticingly of soap and freshly laundered cotton, which made me acutely conscious of the fact that my hair reeked of stale cigarettes.

"What were you working on?" That mellow baritone—so maybe he was older than I thought. Still, I wasn't going to bite. I crossed my arms and slouched down. He didn't get the hint.

"You're a writer, right?" he persisted.

"No, just making a list of errands," I mumbled.

"Oh, now I know you're lying," he said with a throaty chuckle.

"How could you know anything about me?" I winced. I had asked a question, implying the desire for a response.

"It's not so much that I know *you*. I'm very well-acquainted with that *look*."

"What look?" I said, letting my voice drip with irritation.

"Blank piece of paper, poised pen, eyes wide—vacant, yet desperate —as they stare into space: the obvious look of a writer searching for an opening line."

I finally opened my eyes and faced my neighbor. "How would you know? Are you a writer?" My words, intended to be peppery hot, ended in a feeble wisp of smoke. I was looking full into large eyes the color of the sea, elusively shifting shades of green and blue: cool and deep.

I felt my cheeks flare red. This was no beery frat boy. He had a long angular face and his blond hair—in need of a cut—was shot through with silvery threads. And the mouth that was trying to engage me in pleasant conversation was wide, with a deliciously full lower lip that was now curved up into a maddening smile.

"A photographer actually, I freelance mostly, for travel magazines. But when I have to, I write copy for brochures and the occasional article." He reached out his right hand—his beautiful, strong right hand— which I took in my own. "My name is Ian Thompson."

Swooningly aware of the enveloping warmth of his hand on mine, I could only offer a lame, "That sounds like interesting work," as I made a surreptitious glance at his other hand. No ring.

"It's fantastic," he agreed enthusiastically. "I'm just on my way home from a cruise on the Rhine."

That's when the vision of our future life together flashed before me. We were circumnavigating the globe: strolling through a sun-drenched Tuscan vineyard; standing arm-in-arm on a Thai beach at sunset; hiking across the Alaskan tundra, the ground blanketed with wildflowers as far as the eye could see. He would take the pictures and I would write the words (I am after all a journalist, albeit for a pathetic suburban rag that has no business calling itself a newspaper) as we chronicled our travels together.

"I'm Karen Applegate, girl reporter," I said. "Pleased to meet you."

When the train reached Westport (where his car was parked) we both got off and he gave me a ride to Cannondale (where my car was parked) and we had brunch (well, breakfast, really). Then I had to go home and write that damn review, but we made plans to meet for dinner later. When dinner was over we decided to go for a walk on the beach. At the end of our stroll, we decided (as the next day was a holiday) to meet the next morning at Devil's Den for a hike.

And finally he kissed me—only one kiss: soft, deep and perfect.

As I drove to the nature preserve the next morning, my head was full of romantic scenarios. I knew I was getting ahead of myself. A train ride, two meals and a walk on the beach were hardly a relationship. But I dared to hope. This man was intelligent, charming and interesting, and the prospect of being with him opened the promise of new vistas to me, a girl so mired in the minutiae of hometown life that covering a traffic accident on Route 7 felt like a big story.

When I spotted Ian's battered Toyota in the parking lot I pulled in beside it, my heart pounding with anticipation. When he recognized me, he flashed a brilliant smile so patently full of pleasure at seeing me that I blushed beet red.

As we simultaneously emerged from our cars, however, all fantasies of spending the day walking hand-in-hand beneath the dark leaves of sinuous mountain laurel branches vanished from my brain like a burst bubble. Instead of rushing to embrace me, Ian paused and looked over his shoulder to watch his passenger climb out of the car.

His passenger?

"Karen, I'd like you to meet my daughter, Pippa."

And there she stood. A child of about six, so exquisitely beautiful that it was alarming. She was small, fine-boned and graceful. Her glossy dark hair fell in soft tendrils, fanning down to her slender shoulders. But it was her eyes that were most arresting: huge, the same fathomless green-blue as her father's, fringed with thick dark lashes. I now found myself caught in their laser-like intensity as she stared at me, her regard frank, assessing—and not kind.

I knew this was bound to happen someday. You can't skid into your thirties still single and not expect to date recycled men. Hell, I certainly hadn't gotten this far through life emotionally unfettered myself. (But that's another tale—more like a compendium of short stories and novellas.) And men with pasts leave behind a trail of debts, mistakes, broken promises, jilted girlfriends, enemies, ex-wives and often—though I've never become entangled in the situation before—children. And while you can fix and forget a lot of history as time goes by, the fact of children is irresolvable, especially as they are likely to outlive you.

"What a wonderful surprise!" I exclaimed, pitch artificially high and full of manufactured enthusiasm. I knew at once that I sounded like a demented nursery school teacher. "It's so nice to meet you...Pippa? That's such a lovely, unusual name."

"It's short for Phillipa," the child explained, her voice rich with boredom. Obviously I wasn't the only moron she had encountered who thought her name was odd.

"Oh, well, that's pretty, too," I said. "My name is—"

"I know, I know," Pippa said wearily. "It's Karen, and you're my father's new *friend*."

From the acridly sarcastic inflection she gave the word, I briefly wondered how many of Ian's "friends" Pippa had endured meeting.

"Let's get this walk thing over with," Pippa continued resignedly, "so we can go get some lunch." (Right then I decided to leave my backpack in the car—there would be no opportunity for a wine and cheese picnic today. I hadn't thought to pack a juice box and Goldfish.) "And there better not be a lot of bugs," she warned, making it clear that if mosquitoes plagued her on this fine September morning, it was going to be my fault.

"It would have been nice if you had prepared me," I muttered between clenched teeth to Ian, who was marching along beside me. Pippa had run ahead of us along the trail, despite our admonishments to slow up, fearing that she might trip over a root or stone lying hidden beneath the fallen leaves.

Sure that Pippa was out of sight for the moment, Ian dared to take my hand. Ah, hand-in-hand at last; too bad mine was sweaty. When he spoke, his voice was warm and conciliatory: "I know that it wasn't fair to spring her on you like that, but I just hadn't found the right moment to tell you. And I didn't want you to overthink it and freak out. But I need you to understand that Pippa is part of the package, a non-negotiable come-with. We've been through a really bad year. The divorce was especially hard on her—though I guess that's true of most families. But I think we're through the worst of it—her therapist is very optimistic about her progress—and I really want her to know that she always holds center stage in my heart, no matter what direction my life takes. And I think, right now, my current heading is straight for you."

We had reached the top of the hill. He stopped, turned toward me and took my other hand, and beneath the sun-dappled trees, we kissed, full and long, both of us left hungry for more at the end. We gazed at each other, the stillness of the dense woods around us only disturbed by the call of a jay, the rustling scamper of a squirrel and the papery whisper of wind through the leaves.

Simultaneously we cried, "Where's Pippa?"

For twenty agonizing minutes we plunged along the trails, breaking the tranquility of the morning with our frantic calls. Sweating and panting, we reached the pond, where I had so hoped she might have lingered, throwing sticks into the water the way my nieces love to. She wasn't there. (Unless—and I know the thought crossed both our minds—she had fallen in and drowned. But no, that couldn't have happened, the water was too glassy, serenely reflecting a bowl of blue sky.)

We continued on. Occasionally we passed other hikers, and, dismayingly, no one had seen her. And then we reached a point where trails intersected and we were paralyzed with indecision. One precipitous path traveled across the huge stone outcropping that loomed overhead, the other appeared to lead into swampy lowlands. If Pippa had headed down there, surely she was being eaten alive by mosquitoes.

"What could have happened to her?" Ian exclaimed.

The tears in his eyes moved me.

"She must be able to hear us," I said, "and she must be scared to be out here all by herself. I can't understand why she doesn't answer us."

"Here's what I think we should do," Ian said, mustering decisiveness out of his anxiety, "I'll keep looking, and you go back to the car and go get some help."

"You want me to get the police?"

"I don't know what else to do."

"Ian, it's eleven o'clock in the morning and seventy degrees. She's only been missing for a half hour, tops. She's not in any danger of suffering from starvation, dehydration or exposure. It's a beautiful day, the park is full of people...."

"That's what I'm afraid of!" His eyes were wild and he grasped my shoulders, giving me a little shake. "What if someone grabbed her, hurt her and threw her down a ravine off the trail?"

"Ian, I understand what you're afraid of," I said, trying to calm him down, "but..." What I was going to say was, "...surely we would have heard her scream...." But I think that might have further fanned the flames of his fear. So what I did say was, "but I don't think we should panic, I think we should keep looking for her for a little while longer."

"But which way!" he cried despairingly, his arms flailing in front of him, gesturing to the choices that lay ahead of us. Then he burst into full-out sobs, burying his face in his hands.

Now what was I supposed to do?

"Surprise!!!"

Out from behind a boulder not ten feet up the rocky trail above us, popped Pippa, her face glowing with impish delight. "Oh, Daddy, that was so funny!" she squealed. "But, God, it took you forever to catch up to me."

I could have killed her and thrown her down a ravine with my own two hands. Immediately I chastised myself for unkind thoughts; after all, she was only a little girl.

Within seconds following our reunion, her mirth dissipated and Pipa began whining about how hungry she was and how her little feet ached, so we decided to call it quits on the hike.

I was appalled. Ian had not only failed to reprimand his daughter for her cruel and potentially dangerous prank (it wasn't impossible that she could have drowned in the pond or fallen and broken her neck). He had responded to Pippa's fiendish glee at his distress with a watery smile on his still-green-with-worry face. He even actually murmured a feeble, "That was a good one, honey."

Over lunch in a crowded diner, I was subjected to a grueling interrogation.

"My mother is prettier than you, she has naturally blond hair. That red color of yours doesn't look real. Daddy, I don't like this hot dog. Order me a grilled cheese sandwich." Her gustatory command issued, she turned her attention back at me. "So, how come you're not married? Why don't you have any children? Don't you like children?"

"Of course I like children," I replied, defensively. "Some children anyway. My nieces...I love my nieces."

Pippa sat up with interest. "You have nieces. How many? How old are they?"

"Well, Abby is four and Annie is seven. We have these great slumber parties. We spend all night eating pizza, watching movies, playing games...."

"I want to go to a slumber party. Can I come?"

"Well, we don't have one scheduled at the moment, but you'll be on the invitation list next time we do."

"Oh, please, please, can we have one tonight?"

"Nope. School night." I popped a French fry into my mouth. It was soggy.

From the other side of me on the red vinyl banquette came a humid breeze against my neck that sent a tremor of pleasure down my spine. "It would be a great experience for her," Ian murmured low in my ear, "and it would give you a chance to get to know each other better."

Wasn't this all happening too quickly? I mean, as great as things had been going the last couple of days, were Ian and I really moving so assuredly into a place where his little girl needed to get to know me? It was heartening that he seemed to think so.

"Well, maybe we could pencil one in for Friday night," I said reluctantly.

The supplies were laid in: popcorn, cookies, some contraband soda; the pizza was only a speed-dial and a half-hour delivery away.

By three thirty Abby and Annie were making camp with their Barbie sleeping bags. Luckily, they lent me their retired Dora the Explorer bag for Pippa.

Promptly at four, the doorbell rang. Pippa greeted me with a scraggly smile revealing that the Tooth Fairy had made a visit since the last time I had seen her. "Hi," she cried, as she pushed past me, leaving Ian on the threshold, holding Pippa's pink suitcase, those ocean-view eyes locked on mine.

In the living room, I could hear the girls getting to know one another, Abby's croaky little alto voice declaring, "Pippa? That's a funny name."

"No, it's not," countered Pippa, low with menace.

"Are you named after Pippi Longstocking?" Annie asked politely, ever the peacemaker.

"Who's Pippi Longstocking?" said Pippa, scornfully, making it clear that, if she didn't already know, it wasn't worth knowing.

"Can I sleep over, too?" Ian asked plaintively.

"This is strictly an all-girl event," I said, placing a hand on the firm expanse of his chest and pushing him gently away. "Out goes Y-O-U," I said before shutting the door firmly behind him.

Abby emitted a long wail of anguish before she trotted over to me. "Pippa says that she gets my new Barbie sleeping bag."

"It's okay, Aunt Karen, I'll sleep in the Dora sleeping bag. I don't care," said Annie. She was such a good-natured, generous kid.

"No!" insisted Pippa, with a stamp of her foot. "Me and Annie are the big girls, so we should both sleep in the Barbie sleeping bags. We can read; Dora the Explorer is for babies who can't read."

"But, Aunt Karen, Mommy bought that Barbie bag for me because I *am* a big girl now." She added in a confiding tone, "I don't wear Pull-Ups to bed anymore."

"You still wear Pull-Ups?" Pippa jeered.

"Not anymore," Abby retorted.

"Oh, for heaven's sake, I'll tell you what. The three of you can sleep in my bed together, and I'll sleep in the Dora sleeping bag, how about that?" I believe with that utterance, I had lost my mind. And then I said, "Okay, enough. Let the games begin."

I'm still trying to reconstruct what exactly happened next; I can tell you it wasn't a sleepover as no one actually slept and it was over before I knew it. The party started off all right. After an initial skirmish between Abby and Pippa over the same game piece, we began with a game of Monopoly Junior.

The trouble was set off when I got a phone call, which, thinking it was important, I took behind my closed bedroom door. I had been working on an investigative story on the Department of Public Works concerning a suspicious discrepancy between the funds allocated for winter road maintenance and the amount of sand and salt actually delivered to the warehouse. I believed I finally had an informant. Not so. My potential stoolie (the idiot) was actually calling to ask me out.

As I was extricating myself from the conversation, I realized I smelled smoke. I flung down the phone and raced into the living room/kitchenette of my tiny condo. With horror, I saw flames leaping on the stovetop just as the girls began to scream.

"Look out!" I shouted, pushing the three children away from the fire with a sweep of my arms. Unfortunately, as I swept the girls out of harm's way, I also caught the pot handle with my hand, sending a flood of cocoa cascading over the stove and down the cabinets to pool dangerously near the edge of my beloved oriental carpet. I couldn't stop for damage control, though, until I plucked up the still-blazing potholder and gingerly tossed it into the sink, where I doused it with water, ending imminent danger.

The resulting thick plume of smoke set off the smoke detector's piercing alarm.

The girls stopped screaming and watched with stricken faces as, to stop the deafening noise and to forestall a neighbor from calling the fire department, I hastily beat the detector off the ceiling with a broom handle. In the crushing silence that ensued, I said, "What the hell happened?"

"You should say 'heck,'" Abby reproached.

"What happened?"

"Annie decided to make cocoa," Pippa announced.

"It was your idea, Pippa," Annie protested indignantly.

"You're the one who turned on the wrong burner," said Pippa. "And Abby was the one who put the potholder on the stove. I didn't do anything."

"Aunt Karen, you're the one who spilled the cocoa and broke the smoke detector," Abby pointed out.

The sticky brown lake on the floor was spreading even more perilously close to my beautiful rug.

"We'll discuss it later. You three go into the other room and watch a movie while I clean up this mess. Then we will talk."

When I checked on the girls a little later on, I couldn't help being impressed by the amount of damage they had managed to wreak in such a short time. I guess they decided they weren't in the mood for a video. Every article of clothing that was not draped over a child was tumbled across the floor in wrinkled heaps. Empty hangers dangled forlornly in the closet; drawers bared of their contents yawned open. My makeup tray looked like a mad artist had come through, daubing and spilling indiscriminately in a flurry of manic creativity.

The look on my face must have frightened the girls; their alarmed expressions were clownishly emphasized by the garish cosmetics smeared on their faces. Crimson lipstick turned their soft mouths into comical O's. Their startled eyes were wide, ringed in black like raccoons. I might have laughed if I hadn't seen that my favorite white cashmere scarf, which Pippa was wearing as a stole, was thickly soiled with mascara.

I made myself breathe before I spoke. "Take everything off," I exhaled. "I will then run a bath. The three of you will wash off every smudge of makeup, then you will put on your pajamas, and then we will have that little talk."

"Pippa wanted to play dress-up," Abby explained calmly.

Do I need to describe the next mess, the sodden towels, the spilled talc, the pictures drawn on the mirror with soap?

My arm was submerged up to the elbow pulling wads of toilet paper out of the clogged john when Abby began screaming. The sound was followed instantaneously by a shout from Annie and an ungodly howl of rage from Pippa.

The three children were caught in an eerie tableau as I ran into the living room. Annie was standing, fists clenched and scowling, over Pippa, who had somehow been flung to the floor.

But it was Abby, poor little Abby, who held my attention. She sat on the sofa, crying in earnest while holding up her hand, her plump little pinky bent to a sickeningly unnatural angle.

"Annie hit me!" Pippa shrilled in outrage from the floor.

"She was hurting Abby," Annie angrily yelled.

"Abby was saying mean things about my family," shouted Pippa.

"My finger hurts. I want Mommy," sobbed Abby.

I know when to call for backup.

I made Pippa stay in the bedroom while we waited.

Danny and Meredith were at my door in a flash, giving me looks that expressed what they couldn't say in front of their kids. Words weren't necessary, as I couldn't have felt more terrible.

While her parents were deciding who was going to take Abby to the emergency room, Annie pulled me aside. "Aunt Karen, I'm sorry about the mess and everything."

"Don't worry about it now, honey," I said.

"Abby wasn't saying anything mean to Pippa. She was just asking her a question about why her parents weren't together. She was just curious, she wasn't teasing. And Pippa all of a sudden grabbed Abby's hand and started bending her pinky back. I told Pippa to stop, but she wouldn't let go, that's why I hit her."

"You're a good girl to defend your sister like that," I said, hugging her.

"Come on, Annie, it's time to go," my brother announced, holding his younger daughter, who was calmer but still crying in little hiccups, in his arms.

"Danny, I don't know what to say...." I started to cry myself. I felt awful.

"I'll call you tomorrow," said Danny and they left.

I found Pippa, lying on her tummy on my bed, serenely watching television.

"I called your father, he'll be here to pick you up in a little while."

She looked up at me, those gorgeous eyes wide with surprise. "But what about the sleepover?"

I was genuinely shocked. Her face was bland and innocent.

"Pippa, we think you broke Abby's finger. Her father is taking her to the hospital."

"I can still play with Annie."

"No, Pippa. Annie went home with her mother." I was more than a little worried about this kid's emotional disconnect. Didn't she get that she had done something really bad?

Pippa clambered to a sitting position, her face reddening as her eyes filled with tears. "But you promised a sleepover."

"Pippa, Abby was seriously hurt. The party is over." Finally, I had to ask, "She's littler than you, Pippa, why did you hurt her?"

"She was saying stupid things. She made me mad. I wanted her to shut up. She deserved it," Pippa said, bluntly matter-of-fact. "I would do it again."

Then, calmly, she turned her attention back to the television screen.

That kid scared me.

By Sunday morning I was still wretched. Meredith had called briefly the day before to inform me that Abby's finger was in a splint and the doctor thought it would heal fine in a few weeks. But still no word from Danny, which actually might be a good thing, because my brother has a wicked temper and was probably giving himself a couple of days to cool down so that he could forgive me. So when the doorbell rang around eleven o'clock my heart soared, thinking it might be Danny with words of absolution.

I opened the door to find Ian, not my brother, facing me, hands in his pockets, his expression somber.

It was the first time we had been alone together since that dreamy day we met on the train. I was relieved. He must be here to apologize, beg for my forgiveness, pledge to make amends to my brother and his family, promise me that he would get Pippa more intensive therapy. Surely we could work things out.

"We need to talk about the other night," he said.

"I know. Come on in. I'll make a pot of coffee."

Sitting at my small café table, steaming mugs in front of us, there was an awkward moment of silence before Ian said, "I think we need to discuss what we can do to fix the present situation. Pippa is very upset."

"Oh, I'm sure she is," I said, checking the urge I had to place my hand consolingly on his. It must be hard coping with such a difficult kid.

"You know, I don't really understand why she lashed out like she did. I'll admit she's had some problems in the past, but she hasn't exhibited behavior like that in a long time. Her therapist says that she only becomes violent and destructive when she's feeling threatened."

"I can't think of what made her feel that way while she was here."

"I do. Your nieces never made Pippa feel welcomed. In fact, she told me that they were either ganging up on her or shutting her out the whole evening. It made her feel cast off, rejected. And those feelings caused her anger to surface."

"Ian, I'm sorry if Pippa felt like the odd man out. The girls are close—they're sisters after all—but no way were they excluding Pippa or teasing her. My nieces are friendly kids."

"Sure, and slamming Pippa to the ground was such a warm gesture of friendship. She still has a bruise on her thigh. I think your niece should write Pippa a letter of apology."

I shook my head in disbelief. This was the most surreal conversation I had ever had. "Pardon me?" I said. "Let me get this straight. Your six-year-old daughter intentionally broke—*broke*—a younger child's finger. Snapped it like a twig. Her sister socked your daughter to get her off—and you think Annie is the one who should be apologizing? That is just plain crazy."

"Oh, right, of course. Your little darlings bear no responsibility for what happened. It's so easy to blame everything on Pippa." Ian pushed back from the table, his gaze cooling to a hard confrontational glare.

"Hey, those girls have been here hundreds of times without incident. Your kid comes along, next thing I know my brother's not speaking to me and I'm filing insurance claims. Ian, I'm sorry. But surely you can see that Pippa is a . . . troubled child." I was trying to keep calm, but I was beginning to see that Pippa wasn't the only one suffering from a disconnect from reality.

"Pippa is fine," Ian said emphatically, rising. "There is nothing wrong with Pippa. Your nieces picked on her. Pippa stood up for herself and I am proud of her for doing it."

And then Ian was gone and my globetrotting dreams with him.

Briefly I wondered how many more broken fingers lay in Ian's future, then felt relief—I wouldn't have to know.

ANDREA SCHICKE HIRSCH has been a bookseller, freelance editor and copywriter, teacher and paralegal. She studied theatre and English at Fordham University and has a master's degree in education from the University of Bridgeport. A Connecticut native, she lives in Wilton, Connecticut, with her family.

Gena Showalter

Chick-lit, to me, is entertainment at its best. As I read, I can laugh, cry and commiserate. I can see characters grow and learn. I can simply enjoy.

Every Girl's Dream

I, Lisa Bishop, had one year to fulfill all my hopes and dreams. Otherwise, I had to kill myself.

My best friend at the time, Stacey Lou Duprie, and I made a pact at my sixteenth birthday party. If we failed to accomplish every item on our "All My Dreams" list by my thirtieth birthday we had to rid the world of our existence.

Two days before, I had turned twenty-nine.

I sat at my kitchen table. Warm, early morning sunlight streamed through the burgundy and gold curtains, but the heat didn't touch me. I felt cold and sick, as if I'd just found a roach in my blueberry muffin—and I'd already eaten half of it.

The list my life depended on lay in front of me, crumpled but readable, almost as glaring as a flashing neon sign.

I read:

All My Dreams

1. Own a Mustang GT convertible
2. Have a perfect body
3. Spend two weeks in Paris
4. Own a kick-ass wardrobe
5. Kiss Bobby Denton (with tongue)
6. Become a Dallas Cowboys cheerleader
7. Lose virginity
8. Stop traffic with sexy looks
9. Find Mr. Right (a hot, hunky babe)
10. Adopt a puppy no one wants

Why, oh why, couldn't I have wished for something simple like world peace? But *noooo*. At sixteen, I'd wanted boys, beauty and popularity. Okay, so a small part of me still wanted those things. Just not enough to die for them.

So far, I had only accomplished one requirement on the list. Number seven. Thanks to Craig Bardello, I'd lost my virginity at Motel Six after senior prom. Not a very memorable experience, but hey, it still counted.

Numbers one and ten were doable. I could pick up a cheap Mustang at a scrap yard and flip through the newspaper to find an unwanted puppy. The others, well....

I glanced down at my she-has-such-a-pretty-face body. If I shed twenty-five pounds, I'd have a decent figure—but only if I lost the weight in my stomach and thighs and not in my breasts. Was that even possible? Every diet I'd ever attempted—and God knew I'd tried plenty—my boobs went down two cup sizes while my waist and thighs remained the same.

As for the rest of the list. . . .

I tapped my square-tipped nails on the edge of the tattered yellow paper. Two weeks in Paris. I'd never even crossed the Oklahoma state line.

And don't get me started on number nine. With my relationship track record, what Mr. Right would actually want me? I'd had several boy-friends in less than a year, and *I* hadn't dumped a single one. They'd got-ten rid of me faster than a shoe covered in steaming manure.

Gross, Lisa. Just gross.

Something had to be seriously wrong with me, but I didn't know what.

I couldn't take the time to analyze my (now nonexistent) love life, however. My very existence hung in the balance! With a sigh, I sent my gaze back to the list, picking up where I'd left off.

A kick-ass wardrobe. That sounded easy enough. But was it? For a woman on a budget, a new wardrobe was beyond frivolous. For a wom-an on a budget who had absolutely no fashion sense, a new wardrobe was also ridiculous.

O-kay. Moving on. Kiss Bobby Denton. With tongue, no less. Bobby was my childhood crush. For years, I'd dreamed about him, about the two of us making out in a darkened theater, the back of his car, the prin-cipal's office. The locker room. (I hadn't been picky). It had never hap-pened, of course. Preppy, popular Bobby had preferred preppy, popular girls. Nerd that I was (cough, cough: am), I didn't, had never and would never fit that image.

So, I had two options when it came to Bobby. Find him, grab him by the hair and force my tongue down his throat. Or smile sweetly, ap-proach him gently, then ask to borrow his mouth.

Wait. I didn't even know if Bobby was still alive. And if he was, with my luck, he was married to a supermodel and had two hundred kids. Or, even better, he was holed up in his bachelor pad, complete with leather upholstery, art deco and waterbed, waiting for his *boyfriend* to come home.

Great. Just great.

Maybe there was a fake Bobby Denton. A man with the same name who hadn't actually attended high school with me and hadn't seen my ass when I accidentally tucked my skirt into my underwear junior year. I made a mental note to look in the phone book.

Next. . . .

Become a Dallas Cowboys cheerleader. I remembered making that particular wish because I'd failed to make the high-school cheerleading squad. If an amateur team hadn't wanted a young, chubby cheerleader, why would a professional team want an old, extra-chubby one?

There had to be a loophole there, I mused, but couldn't think of one at the moment.

Moving on once more. Last on my list to accomplish: stop traffic with my sexy looks. How in the hell was I supposed to manage that with my mousy brown hair and plain, undistinguishable facial features? Maybe I could strip down to nothing but a smile, thereby allowing people to stop and laugh. *That* would stop traffic for sure.

No, I couldn't. Wouldn't. That would destroy my already low self-esteem.

Okay, something had to be done. I needed a game plan. Actually, I needed Stacey Lou Duprie, the master planner. The girl who had gotten me into this mess in the first place.

Determined to track her down, I spent the next two days searching for her home phone number until I finally met with success. Not an easy task, let me tell you, even with today's technology. Plus, most of my waking hours were spent at my business, Clean Town. I owned a house-cleaning service that, thankfully, paid (most of) my bills.

Anyway, Stacey had moved away our junior year of high school. We'd kept in touch for a while, but had soon drifted apart. I'd wondered about her over the years, of course, but had never tried to contact her. Let's face it. Stacey Lou knew my deepest, darkest childhood secrets, so I preferred to leave my past and her, well, in the past.

I waited another day to call her, gathering my courage. It was Saturday, so surely—hopefully—Stacey was home. Gathering my courage, I picked up my cordless phone and dialed the number.

Three rings later, a gruff male voice greeted me. "Hello."

"Uh, hi." My palms began to sweat, and I wiped them on my jeans. "I'm calling for Stacey Lou."

"Just a second. Stace," I heard the man call. "It's for you."

I sat at my kitchen counter and shifted uncomfortably in my seat. Stacey's husband? I wondered. If so, Stacey had already found Mr. Right. I couldn't help but scowl over that because now I was behind by one, and I didn't even have a single prospect.

"Hello."

The voice was soft and lyrical and so familiar I felt a lump form in my throat. "Hi, Stacey Lou." I coughed. "This is Lisa Bishop." I paused as the lump dropped into my stomach. "Remember me?"

"Oh my God. LeeLee?" Stacey laughed, and the sound emerged with genuine warmth. "Little LeeLee Bishop? How are you?"

Relief coursed through my veins. Stacey remembered me. "I'm good, thanks. And you?"

"Really, really good. Never better. I can't believe this. God, how long's it been?"

"Eleven years."

"Wow. Eleven years. That's a long time. What have you been up to?"

I heard the smile in her voice, and my own lips lifted. "Working, mostly."

"What do you do?"

"I'm an entrepreneur," I said, because that certainly sounded better than *I clean shit out of strange houses.*

"That's great."

"What about you?"

Stacey paused. "I stay at home, watch my son."

"Son?"

"Yeah, you know, a little hoodlum that runs around causing trouble?"

"I got that part." I just couldn't picture the sassy, always-on-the-go Stacey Lou Duprie as a mother. "How old is he? What's his name? Come on, tell me everything."

"He's six. His name is Jonathan. He's the light of my life. I wanted another child, but, well...." She coughed, as if embarrassed. "I got married about nine years ago. My husband, Richard Vaughn, owns Vaughn Electronics."

"That's great," I said, repeating Stacey's earlier words.

"What about you? Married? Any little ones running around?"

"No. I never married. And no kids, either."

"Oh."

Yeah. Oh. That summed it up nicely. For years, I had longed for a family of my own. But I refused to have children without a loving, devoted husband by my side. I didn't want a kid of mine lying awake at night, wondering why her father didn't love her enough to stick around. No, thank you. Not me. I knew too well how that felt.

But I didn't tell Stacey any of that. We were strangers now.

An uncomfortable silence grew between us. I decided to jump to the heart of the matter before Stacey bid me goodbye. I squared my shoulders and stared out the window that led into my backyard. It was small, lushly green, with a sweet-smelling magnolia tree that shaded most of the front half. "I found our list, Stacey Lou."

"What list?"

I frowned. My entire life now centered around that damn list, and Stacey didn't even remember it. "The list we made at my sixteenth birthday party." I strove to keep my tone pleasant, but didn't quite manage it. "The list about our hopes and dreams. The list we vowed to kill ourselves over."

"Oh, that." Stacey chuckled. "I'd forgotten all about it. I don't think I even have my copy anymore. What made you think of it, anyway?"

"My twenty-ninth birthday."

"Oh."

Again, oh. Stacey had never lacked for words before. "We have one year left to fulfill our dreams," I reminded her, "before we have to jump off the bridge."

Stacey laughed again. Actually laughed! "You're not serious about that, I hope. I mean, we made the silly thing over twelve years ago."

Yes, I had taken that into consideration. I really had. And I'd planned to toss the damn list in the trash and forget about it. But something had held me back. Over and over, I'd wondered: Why not? Why not do everything humanly possible to make my childhood fantasies come true?

So I said, "I have to do this, Stacey Lou. I want to fulfill every wish, every desire I harbored as a teenager." Maybe then I could be happy. Truly happy. God, the prospect almost seemed too good to be true.

"We're almost thirty, LeeLee." A censuring note entered her voice.

"Those things don't matter anymore."

"Maybe not."

"To kill yourself over them?" Stacey scoffed. "Come on. That's ridiculous."

"I agree, but it's part of the vow we made." Would I actually kill myself if I failed? Probably not. Thinking about ending my life, however, gave me a nice incentive to try harder. "Look, there's a year left till I hit the big three-oh. It's worth a shot. Whaddya say?"

"This is stupid, LeeLee. We were just kids when we made that list."

"I know that, but tell me, Stacey Lou, have you fulfilled every requirement? Have you lived all your dreams?"

My former friend paused. "Well, no."

I sucked in a deep breath and forged ahead. "Then we can help each other. Together, we can become the women we once wanted to be."

"LeeLee...." Stacey sighed. "No. I'm sorry. I can't help you. Not now."

My hopes plummeted completely. "It's all right. I understand. It was a long shot, anyway. Well, I'm sorry I bothered you."

"You didn't bother me. Please don't ever think that." There was another long pause. "It's just that I'm happy with the life I have now. I have a husband, a child and, yes, even a mortgage. But I'm satisfied. Content. I don't want to be a Dallas Cowboys cheerleader."

She remembered that, at least. "Don't worry about it, Stacey Lou. I'll figure out a solution on my own. It was nice talking to you. I've, well, I've missed you." Another lump formed in my throat, but for an entirely different reason. I swallowed this one back, too. "I hope all your dreams come true." With that, I very gently placed the phone back on the kitchen table.

Three weeks later, I stood on the scale in my small, cramped bathroom. One pound! I'd gained one crappy pound. And how many had I lost? Zilch. Zip. Zero.

Nada.

Needless to say, things were not going well.

For twenty-one days, forty-two minutes and eighteen seconds, I'd dined on nothing but lettuce, water and bread. Lettuce, for God's sake.

I scowled down at the scale. "I'll pulverize you with a hammer if you don't show me a better number."

The numbers never even wavered.

My movements jerky, I tugged on a bathrobe and marched into my equally small and cramped bedroom. *I need a new plan*, I thought darkly, slipping out of my robe and into an old, faded pair of jeans and a hot pink sweater that hung to the middle of my thighs. Maybe I should have been working on one item at a time instead of trying to do them all at once.

So far, my attempts to stop traffic had gotten me nothing more than a few (sympathetic) waves and a lot of chuckles. And saving for a Mustang convertible seemed impossible when I spent every spare cent on clothing.

Oh yeah, did I forget to tell you? I'd purchased a new wardrobe, for all the good it did me. According to my next-door neighbor's teenage daughter, pink was the new "wicked" color. Armed with this knowledge, I'd gone on a shopping spree and bought anything and everything pink, from rose-tinted blazers to mauve-colored skirts. Unfortunately, every time I wore these new "wicked" clothes, I felt like I'd morphed into a schoolgirl ballerina.

To top it all off, I had failed to locate Bobby Denton. Grrrr. No, things were definitely not going well.

A knock sounded at my front door.

I never had visitors on Sunday. Curious, I padded barefoot across the soft, gray carpet. I opened the door. A tall, thin woman with boyishly short blond hair regarded me expectantly. She had perfectly arched brows, a narrow nose, and high, almost gaunt, cheekbones. Her best feature was her large blue eyes.

"LeeLee?" the woman said, a hesitant edge to her voice.

I recognized that voice instantly. Holy mother of God! "Is that you, Stacey Lou?"

The woman smiled, revealing perfect white teeth. "Yes."

I gave her another once-over. "Look at you. You're as pretty as ever, but you've changed. Taller, maybe? Thinner. Definitely more refined." There were dark circles under her eyes, and her cheeks were more hollow.

Stacy chuckled. "You've changed, too. I remember how you used to hunch your shoulders and duck your head to keep anyone from looking at you. Now, well, you're radiant."

Wow. I gulped back tears. No one, and I do mean no one, had ever called me radiant before. I knew she was simply being nice, but I said, "Thank you." Then, before I could talk myself out of it, I wrapped my arms around Stacey and hugged her for all I was worth. "I've missed you."

Stacey returned the gesture, though her grip lacked strength. "I haven't been able to get you off my mind since you called."

"Good." I pulled back, eyeing my former friend with curiosity. "I have to admit, I'm glad to see you, but I'm also curious about your visit."

Stacey shifted from one high-heeled foot to the other. "Can I come in?"

"Of course, of course." I stepped aside. "I'm sorry. I didn't mean to be rude by making you stand on the porch."

"That's all right." Stacey walked passed me, then stopped, waiting for me to take the lead.

"Come on. Let's go to the living room." I sailed ahead, picking up scattered clothing and trash along the way. So I was a slob. Big deal. I cleaned for a living and didn't want to bring my work home. Until now, it hadn't embarrassed me.

Stacey pushed aside a load of unfolded laundry, then sat at the couch with her hands folded demurely in her lap. Her brown slacks blended with the beige and white stripes of the upholstery.

"Can I get you anything to drink?" I asked, ever the solicitous host.

"No, no. I'm fine, thank you."

Pleasantries taken care of, I settled on the rocking chair across from Stacey. "Now, about this visit," I prompted. My nosy nature simply demanded an answer.

Stacey sent me a shaky smile. "You were right, you know?"

Hey, now that was another first. "You're admitting I'm right?" I pushed to my feet and strode to the window, looking out.

"What are you doing?"

"Checking to see if pigs are flying."

Stacey chuckled. "Very funny."

Back at my seat, I said, "Just what, might I ask, am I right about?"

"We have to try."

Hope soared inside me. "You mean it? Really?"

Stacey nodded. "Dreams are important. A woman shouldn't die without first living every single dream she's ever had."

Now it was my turn to smile. "This is such a change, and I never expected it. Well, I hoped, but—" I shrugged, still grinning. "What made you change your mind?"

"I lied."

I blinked. "Come again?"

Stacey gulped and looked away. "I'm not happily married."

"Oh."

My former friend gave a shaky little laugh that lacked humor. "My husband left me a few months ago. I thought he'd come back, but—" She paused. "He has a new girlfriend."

"Oh, no. I'm so sorry." Poor thing. I ached for her. "Who answered your phone when I called?"

"My dad. He stays with me on weekends. Helps me take care of John." Stacey cleared her throat. "Can I see a copy of the list, please?"

"Sure." Once again, I stood. "Let me get it." In my room, I swiped it off my dresser, then rushed back to Stacy, hand outstretched. "Here you go."

Stacey looked it over and smiled another genuine smile. "How silly we were. Perfect bodies, perfect clothes and a perfect car."

"Isn't that every young girl's dream?"

"I suppose so. Paris was my idea, if I remember correctly."

"Yeah." I chuckled, recalling the day we'd made the list. Stacey threw a tantrum worthy of a toddler to get Paris added. I, of course, wanted Hollywood, home of the stars, and had fought to get my way. In the end, Stacy prevailed. "Don't be offended when I don't thank you for that one."

"Look who's talking, Miss Become-A-Dallas-Cowboys-Cheerleader."

"Don't worry. I'd like to kick my own ass for insisting on that. I haven't forgotten how you tried to talk me out of it."

"We were quite a pair, weren't we?"

I nodded. "I miss us." And it was the truth, I realized. I missed the innocent children we'd once been. I missed the friendship we'd once shared. Most of all, I just missed Stacey. I'd never found another friend like her.

"I miss us, too. I've never found another friend quite like you," she said, echoing my thoughts.

"I'll take that as a compliment."

"That's how it was meant."

There was a long pause. "Are you sure you want to do this, Stacey Lou? I mean, I don't want to push you."

"Yes, you do." But Stacey grinned to counter the sting of her words. "And I'm glad for it. I didn't realize how much I *needed* to do this until I spoke with my dad. He reminded me how short life actually is and how we need to live every moment to the fullest."

"Wise man."

"Yes, he is. After my mom died, he—"

"Oh, Stacey. I'm sorry. I didn't know." I pictured Brenda Duprie, full of life and energy and love, now gone, and my heart cracked.

"It's okay." Stacy clutched one of my shirts in her hand, twisting and knotting it. "She died right after I moved. She had heart problems. Dad always said she lived her life with no regrets. And that's what I want to do. Now, tell me, what have you accomplished so far?"

I bit my bottom lip. "Actually, I've, uh, done nothing."

One blond brow arched. "Well, why not?"

"I've tried, don't get me wrong. I just haven't gotten results."

"Well, I'm here now." Stacey leaned forward, and took my hand in hers. "Together, we can do this. I know we can."

I nodded. "Together, we can do anything."

"So, what do you want to do first?"

Over the next year, I lost the twenty-five pounds I'd wanted (thank you, yoga). Stacey never gained the fifteen pounds she needed, but I didn't hold it against her (much). We never bought that Mustang GT, but we did test drive a red-hot Mustang at a car dealership. Our joyride lasted several hours before we were pulled over for speeding.

We loved every minute of it, I promise you.

Stacey introduced me to her son, and I grew to love him as my own.

He liked to call me "Aunt LeeLee," and that made my heart squeeze in my chest every time he said it.

Did I ever track down Bobby Denton and slip him the tongue? You damn well better believe it. Like me, he still lived in Oklahoma and was single. Did you note that? He *was* single. I've since claimed him as my man. The kiss we shared really rocked both our worlds. He showed up on my doorstep a week later (unable to forget me, thank you very much), determined to help me with the rest of my list.

I let him.

The three of us (Bobby, Stacey and me) hosted a garage sale and a lingerie party to raise money for the next item on the list: Paris, baby. Unfortunately, we didn't make enough money. And so we decided to go to Paris, Texas, instead, since our list didn't specify Paris, France. Ah, aren't loopholes fabulous?

Before we left for our trip, though, I learned Stacey suffered from terminal heart problems, just like her mother, and she didn't have much longer to live. I tried to call off our trip, but Stacey was adamant that we go.

"This is the most fun I've ever had," she said.

A part of me knew and accepted that Stacey wanted to experience all of her dreams before she took her last breath, but it was no longer a game. This was it for her. As much as it pained me to think of losing her—and it did; God, it did—I wanted to make her last days special.

While we were in Texas, I came up with a plan to help us become Dallas Cowboys cheerleaders. I purchased two cheerleading uniforms and drove us to a Dallas rodeo, and the two of us cheered on the cowboys. Another loophole. Bobby was so turned on by that, that he pulled me into his arms the minute we entered our hotel room. Let's just say we got deliciously nasty and leave it at that.

And yes, on the way home we adopted a puppy no one wanted.

That left only one last dream to fulfill. Stacey and I had to stop traffic with our sexy bodies. But Stacey no longer possessed the strength. By this time, she was so sick she could barely get out of bed. I desperately wanted her to have this moment, though, so Bobby helped her into the car and drove us to Main Street. She laughed and weakly clapped as I flashed traffic and caused a six-car pileup.

With that, we completed the list. We had lived all of our dreams. I was happier than I'd ever been, but also sadder. Stacey meant the world to me, and I was going to lose her. Sooner rather than later.

As if she had been holding on for the list—and me—she experienced severe chest pain the day after the six-car pileup. Bobby and I rushed her to the hospital. She'd reached the end, and we all knew it. I could hardly hold back my tears. I'd come to love this woman like a sister, and I didn't know what my life would be without her. Didn't *want* to know.

As I stood next to her bed, she looked up at me and said, "We did it, didn't we? We lived our dreams." Her voice emerged soft, barely a whisper.

The tears I hadn't wanted to shed in front of her spilled free. I clutched Stacey's frail hand and forced myself to smile. "We sure did. We lived every girl's dream."

She smiled, closed her eyes and never woke up.

With Stacey's death, my heart broke in a way I'd never thought possible. She had been sunshine and roses, so fun, so . . . vital. At the funeral, I spent time with her family. We talked about her, laughed about her antics, reminisced about her life. I hugged her son, and he sobbed on my shoulder. I knew I would never lose touch with him. Stacey would have wanted me to remain a part of his life, and I planned to be there for him.

Afterward, Bobby took me home. He sat on the couch and pulled me into his arms. Our new dog jumped into my lap. "We'll get through this," he said. "We will."

I knew he was right, but it still hurt. I glanced toward the ceiling, toward heaven, where I knew Stacey was looking down at me. *I was wrong, Stacey Lou. We didn't just live every girl's dream. We lived* our *dream. And that's enough.*

GENA SHOWALTER is the prolific author of sexy paranormal romances, fun contemporaries, an alien huntress series and young adult novels. For more information about Gena and her books, you can visit her Web site at www.genashowalter.com, her blog at www.genashowalter.blogspot.com and her MySpace page at www.myspace.com/genashowalter.

Raelynn Hillhouse

*The now-infamous "bitch-slap heard 'round the blogosphere"
struck me as a call to arms in the literary capital-"C" Culture wars. (Confession #1: I love girl fights.) Choosing sides
wasn't so easy for me. (Confession #2: I'm part of the trench-
coat set; I write spy thrillers about heroines who wouldn't be
caught dead in pink.) But I knew which side of the wars
I was supposed to be on—after all, I'd taken courses at
Iowa and done the gig at Squaw Valley,
even studied character with Charlie
Baxter. But I've always had these
feelings.... (Confession
#3: I like girls—girls
who just wanna have
fun.) So what's a girl to do when she feels playful, snarky,
funny, self-deprecating, woeful and witty, but she just can't get
away from the cloak and daggers? Force Bridget Jones into a
trench coat and watch her squirm.*

Secret Agent Chick

ROCHESTER (GREECE), NEW YORK, SEPTEMBER 9TH

I pretended to read the electric meters as I watched my remaining family
gather around the casket. Tears streamed down my aunt Martha's face,
or at least I thought I saw tears, but the truth is I didn't want to be the
only one with makeup running. I pulled out a pencil, scribbled a number on my clipboard and moved on to the next house, while I kept an
eye on things. You see, that's what I do—I keep an eye on things. And
that's why I can't be seen at my own grandpa's funeral. Because I'm the
kind of girl who likes her martinis shaken, not stirred. I say my last
name first. I'm an operative, a spook, a spy.

225

I'm Flint. Caitlin Flint. Secret agent chick.

Actually it was the martini thing that lured me into this, along with my mom pushing me to follow in her footsteps and be a spy just like her. I could've gotten married, you know, I had offers, but instead I'm standing on this bush, noticing the FedEx truck circling through the neighborhood for the fourth time.

As I approached a meter on the side of a small brick house, I looked back toward the funeral party, not daring more than a fleeting glimpse. By now Aunt Martha's tears had carved channels into her makeup and I wanted nothing more than to have her hold me close like she did when I was a little girl, but I couldn't even let them know I was still alive. I was a spook haunting the graveyard, reading meters while I stole glances at my loved ones' coffins. Today it was Grandpa Woodfil; a year ago it had been my fiancé Rocky's homecoming from Iraq, a flag-draped casket and a military honor guard.

I whipped out a compact to check if anyone was tailing me, and it was at that moment that I realized blue eyes made red from crying look really mysterious. I mean Mata Hari mysterious, and Mata Hari was the sexiest female spy ever, the one who set the bar we all aspire to. Anyway, I thought it would look even hotter if my mascara had run just a little bit more, so I used my fingernail to pull down some thin lines and in doing so I nearly compromised my situational awareness because I suddenly noticed that the FedEx truck had pulled over and had parked at the side of the cemetery—directly across the street from me. A maple tree that had already lost most of its leaves was the only thing that shielded me from view as I studied the vehicle. It was the same one that had been cruising the area for the past fifteen minutes, but something seemed different.

The driver was now white. (They taught me to notice things like that in spy school.)

A blast of adrenaline hit my body and my muscles tightened. I was marked. I had led an enemy home to my loved ones, the very thing I had tried to prevent by staging my own passing. My family had long ago accepted my own death and moved on. Now, because I hadn't, I had put them in danger.

I melted to the ground. Like a sniper creeping into position, I inched myself along on my belly through the bed of gold, red and yellow leaves. Out of the driver's line of sight, I sprinted behind the house. Trampling a flowerbed of dead marigolds, I hugged the side of a garage and then squatted behind a ragged juniper.

I'm a trained professional. Don't try this at home.

I clutched the Sig Sauer under my coveralls, but I knew a frontal assault would be too public and I wanted a chat with the driver before sending him on his way. I looked around for options, easy options.

The garage door was closed, but a doggy door was built into the side of the building, so I crawled inside and patted the wall, careful not to chip a nail. I felt a switch and flipped on a light. The garage was tidy, old-lady tidy. There wasn't much to work with, but I didn't need much. After all, I was Flint, Caitlin Flint.

I opened the door of the Buick parked inside and found an insulated mug and an ice scraper. I loved the rush of a plan falling together and I couldn't wait to tell Leah, who once had foiled a hijacking with only a bottle of champagne, a swizzle stick and a cocktail napkin. I called her cell, but only got voice mail.

I left a message.

After I checked my own messages (you never know when it's the Agency and not just your best friend), I hung up and jumped from the car with the scraper and mug. I peeled off my coveralls and freed my shoulder-length hair from the baseball cap, then brushed it with my fingers before dumping newspapers from a cardboard box and pouring stale coffee from the mug.

The valve at the base of the hot water at first didn't want to turn, but I forced it open and filled my mug, then ran toward the FedEx truck, slumping to hide my tall frame. The package shielded my face.

"Hey, so glad I caught you," I said as I banged on the passenger door. The truck's height complicated things. I would have to strike the guy high so that he didn't fall forward and cause a street scene. Spies don't like street scenes, particularly at their grandfathers' funerals.

When the driver slid open the door, I threw the scalding water into his face. With the tip of the hard plastic ice scraper positioned in my hand, I sprang into the truck and struck his chest, my body's inertia magnifying the blow. In the split second that he fell backward, I spun the scraper around and moved in to slice. I saw his kick coming at me the same instant his sunglasses flew to the floor. The sight of my dead fiancé's face made me pause for a moment, slowing my pivot. I didn't get out of his way fast enough and his foot struck my thigh hard.

"Friend! Rocky! It's Caitlin! Fox Nine!" Fox Nine was my call sign—like a nickname, but way cooler.

"Caitlin?" He squinted, his face bright red. Jumping up, he threw his arms around me—tanned arms, with unbelievably well-defined biceps. We're talking Greek sculpture.

"You're alive?" Tears flowed down my face and all I could think of was how he must really be digging my Mata Hari eyes.

"I'm sorry. It was the only way I could protect you." He blinked hard, then turned away from me and closed the door. "Death's been tougher than I imagined. A lot tougher."

Well, duh.

Rocky and I ditched the delivery truck and took my rental car to Canandaigua, taking such lightly traveled country roads to flush out any tails that we got lost and didn't arrive until almost dark. He had planned to camp for the night, but my idea of camping was a Holiday Inn so I insisted upon breaking into an empty summerhouse on the lake that I thought still belonged to my sister Renée. At least I told him I thought she owned it, but the truth is this one had a hot tub and a much better view.

While I was checking out the inside of the cabin, Rocky stripped and helped himself to the hot tub. I stepped outside to enjoy nature and snapped a cell phone picture of him from the waist up to send to Zoë. She was going to be *so* jealous. Serves her right for beating me to that hunky Russian agent last month.

When I slipped into the hot tub with him, I noticed that Rocky had placed three glasses and a bottle of vodka on the ledge behind the hot tub along with a box of matches. He filled all three. "The third one's for Grandpa Woodfil. He always did watch your back. It's a tradition that after we've come home from combat, we order a shot of vodka and let it burn for those who paid the ultimate price watching our backs on the front." He struck a match and lit the vodka in the third glass. He always did the most romantic things.

"I know. I lit one for you once," I lied. And I'd meant to, but I ended up drinking it instead. I couldn't waste a perfectly good shot of vodka. Plus, I'd needed it; he was dead, I was sad, it was wet.

We drank a shot for Grandpa, then one to each other. Rocky reached for the bottle to pour another round, but I pulled it away.

"Let's get things straight," I said. "I'm still angry with you. Tonight is just a truce. Tomorrow we're at war." I could smell his musky scent and knew what my truce talk was really about—heat. Nothing gets a Marine hotter than talk of battle, and I wanted him steaming.

Coyotes yipped in the distance and an owl screeched. We watched the moonlight shimmer on the lake below, sitting in silence for at least thirty seconds before I spoke again. "I always kept you in the loop. Why in the hell did you fake your own death without at least pinging me? You know there are more honorable ways to call off an engagement."

"I didn't want to call it off, but I couldn't play by my own rules anymore. I got assigned to a new secret unit. Things were too dangerous."

"Things are always bad in this business. That's no excuse. You know I took the risk of coming to your funeral?" I looked away so he couldn't see my face—and to add intrigue. Think Mata Hari.

"I know. It tore me up when I saw you slinking around the shadows," he said.

He was so adorable. I wanted to take him then and there, but I still hadn't found out enough. So I said, "Why did you come today?"

"It was the only way I could find you. Spies are not easy to track down. I need you."

"You need me? You fake your own death, go to ground for a year, stalk me at my grandfather's funeral, and all you can say is you need me?" Actually, it kind of worked for me. "You're going to have to come clean."

"I can't."

"You must have wanted to get away from me real bad to stage your own death."

"The only thing I wanted more than to be with you was to know you weren't in danger because of me. My job is to hunt down and kill terrorists. They could come after those I love and I wouldn't do anything to jeopardize you."

He had a point, but I wasn't going to let him have it. I said, "I live in the crosshairs."

"And that's why I love you," Rocky said as he put his arm around me. The spy chick thing was working. Spy chicks are hot.

The blue flame flickered, then died out just like in the movies. It was so cool, so romantic.

I jumped his bones.

QYZYLQUM DESERT, KAZAKHSTAN, TWO WEEKS LATER

My mom was one of those first-generation feminists who thought she could save the world—and did. She could carry on endlessly about how she was behind some U.N. general secretary's plane crash in Africa, how she walked through twenty feet of snow in Siberia to get secrets out of Russia, yadda, yadda, yadda. As long as the history was ancient, my mom had it covered—or undercover. As she put it, she provided the president with quiet, simple and deniable options. Mom had drummed it into my head that I, too, had to have a successful career before starting a family, and so now Mommy's good little girl was lying on her belly on a sand dune in a desert with a name she couldn't pronounce, tasting dust, sweating and smelling of camel crap. I wasn't having a good day and if I could've gotten cell reception there, I would've called the CIA and quit on the spot. Mom and national security be damned.

I was here along with another CIA agent because something had gone badly wrong with another mission. I didn't know what, exactly. I was only given details on a need-to-know basis and the Agency and my mom both always seemed to agree on one thing—that I needed to know very little.

Whatever.

What I did know about why I was here, lying there in the sand becoming one with the desert filth, was that some joint operation with a secret military unit had gone south, and spy girlfriends kept text-messaging me rumors that it was due to a mole in the Agency—and somehow all of this was related to my assignment to eliminate two mysterious prisoners who the Agency clearly didn't want talking to their captors. So I lay there with my loaded sniper rifle with no clue as to the names or faces of the two prisoners I was supposed to neutralize. I decided to call them PITT and CLOONEY.

For the last twenty minutes, my spotter (the guy who assists the sniper hit her mark; finally, I had an assistant) and I had been watching some abandoned former Soviet airstrip from the saddle of two sand dunes. (Think of it as the desert's butt-crack, if you get the picture.) I had seen four snakes, a dozen lizards and some gerbils scurrying between the ripples of the sand, but there was no sign of the Gulfstream carrying Brad and George and this gave me far too much time to think about why Rocky stood me up in Paris last weekend. This time I was not about to buy that he brushed me off to protect me from some international evil-doers. He'd better have a damn good story whenever he surfaced again, I decided, or else this sniper's bullet was for him.

Even though we were supposed to be quiet, TOMCAT, my spotter, was talking nonstop.

"So I'm guessing the targets are Western spies working with al Qaeda and that's why the Agency wants them eliminated," TOMCAT said.

"Why not?" It didn't make sense to me, but politics never did.

I peered through the Leupold scope on the Dragunov sniper rifle. I might not be able to get cell reception, but I could still take pictures with the phone. I made TOMCAT do it. What was the sense in having an assistant if you couldn't make him do stuff? The pictures would serve as proof to my mom that this time I really was being a good girl and serving my country from where I was supposed to and not from that beach in Hawaii.

I studied a tumbleweed at the edge of the runway and calculated the wind speed. The temperature had climbed to forty-two Celsius and the humidity was so low that I knew I had to take care not to overshoot the target. The last thing I wanted to do was make myself look bad in front of TOMCAT.

"I'm eventually going to see what the targets look like, so you might as well show me a picture now," TOMCAT said, crouching at my right side.

"We've talked about this. I don't have names or faces. We're looking for the two prisoners. We're going to take out whoever comes off that plane looking like a prisoner."

I had worked with TOMCAT three times before and I'd remembered him as a quiet guy, one of the two reasons I chose him. Men should be seen and not heard, and that was the other reason I chose him—he was one who deserved to be seen. But today he needed the chatter to shed nervous energy. I could think of better ways but, unfortunately, we still had a job to do for Uncle Sam.

"Plane at eleven o'clock, turning into the wind to land," Tomcat said, kneeling in position a little behind me, to my right.

"Wind twelve to fourteen knots. Verify," I said, more because it sounded really good than because I actually knew what it meant.

It felt a little tense as we waited, and I thought I saw Tomcat check his sidearm. The sparse desert terrain ensured that no one could approach us without notice, but it never hurt to be vigilant. I reached to my right leg and made sure that my Ka-bar knife was still in its thigh holster. Sand constantly pelted me, scratching at my face, but I wasn't complaining. This desert was famous among female operatives as being the best exfoliation treatment in the world.

The small jet taxied to a stop in a sandy part of the tarmac, on the outside of the range I had expected. The additional meters would add several millimeters of inaccuracy to the shot, but that would be more than made up for: at that long distance it would drop below the speed of sound and become silent before hitting its mark. I could get off multiple shots before anyone noticed or could triangulate my position—not that I had any intention of breaking my perfect record: one shot, one kill. (Okay, so I know more than I let on. You never know when a secret agent chick will come across as too smart and scare a guy off.)

"Range me to the airframe," I said.

"Eight-two-five."

The plane sat on the runway while the engines spooled down. I fingered the shell casing I wore around my neck while I waited. It's called a hog's tooth; it sounds like a silly guy thing and it is. Only Marines who pass sniper school get it. From the way they react to it, you'd think it were a Harvard diploma. You'd be amazed at what it does to Marines when they see it hanging between my breasts. It signals that I'm part of another secret club, and secrets turn guys on.

At that moment, secrets didn't turn me on. I was thinking about anything I could other than the fact that there were two mystery men I was about to kill—or neutralize, as we say in the business. They were taking forever to lower those damn airstairs so I could get this dirty job over with. Then a man appeared in the doorway, a mil dot above my crosshairs. He was blond, average build and carried an M4 assault rifle—not worth a second glance.

"First captor in sight," I said.

A second man became visible at the front of the cabin. The doorway was too small for me to discern much other than he was tall and built. We're talking shut-up-and-take-me-now. His hands were bound in front with a plastic zip-tie: PITT.

"First target acquired."

PITT stooped, exiting with the top of his head pointed at me. Then I saw his face.

Oh my God.

Rocky.

My finger was on the trigger. Something felt right about following Rocky in my crosshairs. I wanted to kill him. It was my job to kill him. God knows I had threatened to kill him enough times, and he deserved it because of standing me up last weekend in Paris, although I had to admit maybe he really did have a legit excuse this time, actually being held captive and all. I took a long, deep breath, but it didn't clear my head. My body dripped with sweat. It was gross.

CLOONEY followed Rocky down the stairs, along with two more heavies. The shot was clear. I inhaled deeply to calm myself, then exhaled. The shot felt good, so I slowly squeezed the trigger. The recoil jerked the sight. Without a breath, I acquired the next target, and then the next.

"What are you doing? You hit the wrong target!" TOMCAT said.

"No, I didn't," I lied. "These were my real orders. You're on a need-to-know basis and you didn't need to know."

TOMCAT seemed to buy it, although obviously my boss wouldn't—and neither would my mom. Home was halfway around the world, though, so I would have plenty of time to think of something better on the plane.

I snatched up the empty shells and stripped off my sniper camouflage and ran down the sand dune to Rocky, leaving TOMCAT behind. The soft sand gave way under my feet and I slid with each step. It made me look like I was running toward him in slow-mo. I couldn't have planned it better.

"Friend! It's Fox Nine!" I shouted and waved my arms.

Rocky bounded toward me. "Caitlin! God, it's good to see you. I've gotta say, this is the most pathetic rescue I've ever seen. Where is everyone?"

"Rescue? Rocky, we need to talk."

He squeezed me tightly against him. Matted locks framed my face and I was coated in grit. I could've died, letting him see me like this, but it seemed to turn him on, so I went with it.

Mata Hari, eat me.

RAELYNN HILLHOUSE has slipped across closed borders, smuggled jewels and been recruited as a spy by two of the world's most notorious intelligence services (they failed). The *St. Louis Post-Dispatch* wrote that "she's truly like James Bond and Indiana Jones all rolled into one." Her widely acclaimed first novel, *Rift Zone*, draws from her experiences. Her next novel, *Outsourced* (Forge, May 2007), is about an operative who becomes a target in the multibillion dollar War on Terror, and the only one he can trust is his ex-fiancée—who's been hired to kill him. A former professor and Fulbright fellow, Hillhouse lives in Hawaii.

Stephanie Lehmann

These days women are expected to be ambitious yet wear six-inch heels. We're expected to be supermoms during the day and sex kittens at night. Is it fair to say the ideal woman is both Madonna and whore? It's not surprising that to be female is to feel inadequate. Chick-lit novels can be a great relief from all this. They're a dialogue between women. They provide a context where women writers create women characters that resonate for women readers. My favorite ones are truthful, intimate, revealing, funny—and question all those impossible-to-achieve expectations.

How to Be a Millionaire

I sensed it was a moment I should say something positive to my husband about our marriage. The waiter had just brought our coffees and a piece of key lime pie for us to share. It was our fifth anniversary.

I wanted Bobby to know that I did love him despite all the annoyances of daily life. And that I took comfort in the thought that we would grow old together. No matter what you might say about our marriage and its deficiencies, we'd always been close in our way. Happy to be around each other. Even though we knew each other too well to still be idealizing each other. I was about to open my mouth, but he spoke first.

"There's something I want to say." He took a sip of coffee, then placed his cup back down on the saucer. He seemed nervous, but then it was harder for him to express affection than it was for me. This was when he'd tell me how much he still loved me after all these years. "I've been thinking you should get a job."

I maintained my pleasant smile. As if to convey that of course I'd been expecting this very suggestion at this juncture of our anniversary dinner. "A job?"

"We really could use the money."

I sat back in my chair. "What would I do? I have no skills." There had to be some better way than a job for me to get money. Searching for coins on the sidewalk, perhaps? Reselling shampoo samples from Kiehls? The only thing I was good at was shopping. Hey. I could be a Mystery Shopper. Spy on unsuspecting clerks and rat them out when they were rude. I wondered how much an ambitious Mystery Shopper could make on a good day. But would I be able to sleep at night?

"It seems like the perfect time," he said. "What with Sam starting kindergarten. You have more time. We're spending more than I make. Our savings are drying up. Before we know it, we'll have college tuition to think about."

"Don't say that."

"Time marches on. Are you having some pie?"

I took a bite. It was tart. Why hadn't I pushed for the devil's food cake? I put down my fork. It wasn't that I was so against the idea of working. I knew he was right. We did need the money. And I don't mean to give the impression that I thought I was above earning a living like everyone else. Before having Sam, I'd planned on being a therapist. I'd gotten a Ph.D. in psychology, but had never been able to pass the licensing exam. It was demoralizing. I'd taken it twice and failed. Those damn multiple-choice questions! You'd think it would be easier than essay questions, but whoever wrote those tests always boiled everything down to some right or wrong answer, and it was downright insulting to the human condition. "But what would I do?"

"Maybe you want to take the licensing exam again."

"No!"

The man at the next table looked over. Did I just yell? "Fine," I said. "I'll get a job."

It's not like Sam had never been to school before. But River Park Nursery School had been just three hours in the morning. Kindergarten went all the way until three o'clock. And there was just one teacher for thirty kids. And huge sixth graders in the hallways. It had to be scary for him. So on the first day, I lingered after class began so he wouldn't feel abandoned.

There were about five of us parents standing in the back. The teacher had allowed us to do this if our child seemed anxious, but encouraged us to say a quick goodbye and slip out after ten minutes of class had gone by. Fifteen minutes had now passed. A couple of the kids were crying and quite nervous. When one mother tried to leave, her daughter literally grabbed a leg and would not let go. Sam didn't seem to notice I was still there. Which made me proud. Though I had to wonder. Didn't he feel any sadness over this benchmark in his development? I couldn't help but shed a few tears at the idea of him growing up into a big boy. I knew I should leave. But really, I had nowhere to go except home, where there was nothing to do but clean. Finally, Sam ran up to me. He was so cute in his new blue Gap T-shirt with the little collar. I leaned over. He whispered in my ear. "Mom. Would you just go?"

The following morning I dropped Sam off and forced myself to leave without crying. I took the subway to an employment agency in midtown and rode the elevator up to the sixteenth floor of the kind of highrise that might've inspired fantasies about big-city glamour when I was growing up, but now only depressed me because I could see it for what it was: a building full of people who worked at meaningless cog-in-the-wheel jobs so that a few elite others could enjoy their houses in the Hamptons. Now here I was, seeking out the opportunity to be a cog.

I pushed open the glass door. A receptionist handed me a card to fill out. I took a seat in the waiting area that looked out on about ten desks, but there was only one man at one of these desks, and he was interviewing a young woman. She wore a dark purple, flimsy but tight Forever

21–type polyester dress and white strappy sandals with five-inch heels. I wore my conservative pumps and a gray light wool pantsuit from my grad school days bought on sale at Banana Republic. I was dressed like an executive, but had no qualifications. She was dressed like a secretary, and was probably eminently employable.

The interviewer guy was probably in his late forties and wore the inevitable bad tie and cheap suit. His desk was only a few feet away, so it took no effort to eavesdrop. Miss Forever 21 had been a secretary for an investment banker at Morgan Stanley. When the banker was laid off, she was laid off with him. How could I compete with that? The interviewer's eyes were sad, and he was not unkind. I had the feeling he was on the verge of unemployment, too. "Unfortunately, I don't have anything at the moment. It's pretty bad right now."

"Okay, well, thank you." Nylons encased her rather chubby but still shapely legs. How many years had it been since I'd worn nylons?

"We'll be in touch if anything comes in," he said. "And feel free to check back in with me next month."

It was my turn. I took my place at his desk and handed him the card I'd filled out that showed I had no recent references or experience. "Well," he says, "let's see. Do you know Word?"

"Yes." I had it on my computer at home, at least.

"How's your typing?"

"Great." For filling out online shopping forms.

"How about Excel?"

What the hell was that? "No."

"PowerPoint? Quark?"

"Quark?" I said, mainly to have the chance to say that word out loud.

"What exactly are you looking for?"

"I was thinking along the lines of receptionist. Just to get my feet in the door."

Surely any intelligent person who looked presentable could be a receptionist. I had visions of myself sitting at a desk behind a small vase of flowers saying good morning to all the office workers as they arrived in the morning. I would cheerfully greet visitors as they stepped off the elevators and offer them a glass of water as they waited for their appointments. I'd also get the dirt on everyone while they took breaks and escaped their computers. It sounded fun.

"You really need to have the computer skills."

"Just to be a receptionist?"

"If you're serious, take a class somewhere."

"If I learn Quark, do you think I could get a job?"

"Maybe."

I rose. "So I'll do it. I'll take a class in Quark." But even as I said it, I was doubting my sincerity. It would take a lot of effort. A lot more effort than just saying I would.

He handed me my card and didn't say anything about checking back in a month.

I walked up Sixth Avenue and turned into a Pier 21. I pretended to be looking for new dishes or a vase or a picture frame. Shoppers had their minimal amount of power. Money to spend. Taste to please. I cased the aisles, rejected everything and walked back out feeling somewhat bolstered. Maybe I just wasn't cut out for an office job. There was always retail. Could I wrap mugs in sheets of paper and ring up sales? Wear a green baseball cap and shout out orders for lattes? Fold shelves of sweater sets all day in Ann Taylor? Would any of those jobs pay enough to afford a babysitter to pick Sam up from school? On the corner, I went to a news box and—hoping no one would notice—took out a Learning Annex catalog. Then I went to get a cup of coffee at Burger Heaven.

The restaurant was packed with the cogs. Cogs with skills. Cogs on their breaks, desperate for the small measure of gratification that could be found in a chicken salad sandwich. I sat at the counter, ordered a donut and coffee, and opened up the catalog.

Everyone knows the Learning Annex is for losers. Just looking in one of their catalogs makes you a loser. Still. They made everything sound so attainable. Most ludicrous, and right on the front page, was "How to Be a Millionaire." In a three-hour class! For just $49! It was almost worth fifty bucks just to go and see what they said. And maybe you would learn *something*. I mean, how *could* you become a millionaire after taking a Learning Annex class? I read the description. It had words like *discounted notes, income property, cash-flow strategies.* My eyes glazed over. I turned the page.

Here was a surprise. "Make over $100,000 a year part-time with vending machines." Wow. Now that sounded like something Bobby would love to do. Leave his job as a Web designer and get a vending machine route. "Insider secrets on how to make the most of vending. Which machines to stay away from. How to secure the best locations...." Who ever dreamed this was a career?

But... enough of these pie-in-the-sky dreams. The vending machine routes in Manhattan had to be completely sewn up.

I turned the page. I needed something practical. Like the "Brain Upgrade Seminar," perhaps. Or "Overcome Procrastinating Now." That reminded me of a joke I once heard. "I was going to take a class on how to stop procrastinating, but I kept putting off going." I smirked and turned the page.

Oh, yes, only losers took these classes.

Now there was something. Candle-making. I could learn to make candles and start up an online business. But what would be special about my candles? You needed a gimmick. And it would be hard to mail them so they wouldn't break. Who needed that headache? I reached the back without finding anything good. The back was the relationships section. "Massage for Couples." What kind of smarmy people would show up for that class?

Smarmy people like me?

God knew, Bobby and I could use some massage skills to rev up our sex life. Maybe this massage class wasn't a bad idea.

No. Only weird, icky people would go to a Learning Annex massage course. The normal people were taking "How to Ride a Bicycle."

"Would you like more coffee?"

The waitress was looking at the catalog with amused scorn. I closed it. "No, thanks." How embarrassing. It was like reading a *Playboy* in public. Worse.

That afternoon, after having changed out of my wool pantsuit and into jeans, I waited outside Sam's school next to a woman with a baby in a stroller. To entertain the baby while we waited for the class to come out, she sang "The Wheels on the Bus." I hated the song. I was sick of it. But the baby was so cute—especially the way it looked with such adoration at its mom. Bobby and I had pretty much agreed not to have another child. We lived in a small two-bedroom and could not possibly afford a larger apartment in the city, and neither of us wanted to move anywhere else. But now I wondered. Maybe I should just bite the bullet and start over with another baby.

Sam ran up to me and we gave each other kisses and hugs. "So," I said. "What would you like to do?"

"The toy store!"

"Now?"

"Please?"

It's true that I'd promised I would take him to Toys "R" Us as a reward for being such a good boy in school. But I didn't relish the idea of getting back on the subway and braving the crowds in Times Square. Plus it was threatening to rain. "Not today, sweetie, but soon."

"You promised."

"And I'll keep my promise. But not today."

I took him to the playground and sat on the bench while he went down the slides and ran around. Here was the problem with having another baby, and it was even worse than the songs. I found playgrounds so incredibly boring. I couldn't wait until the day I never had to sit in one again. And then there would be more diapers. And waking up in the middle of the night. How could I start over with all that?

But how could I leave it all behind?

I was actually glad when it started to rain and we had to leave. But we didn't have an umbrella, and it really started to come down. We dashed into the Rite Aid on Broadway. They had the usual cheap, boring black umbrellas. But next to them was a display of really cute ones with colorful Disney characters on the handles.

"Look, Sam. Aren't they cute? I like Sleeping Beauty."

"I like Donald Duck."

I pulled Sleeping Beauty out of the stand.

"Mom," he said. "They're for kids."

"I know," I said. "I was just looking."

He got Donald Duck. I got a boring black one.

241

When Bobby got back from work, I greeted him from the sofa, where I was watching *Access Hollywood*. Sam was in our bedroom watching something on Nickelodeon. Thank God for Nickelodeon. "I'm worthless!" I yelled before Bobby even got through the door.

"Hello!"

"I went to an employment agency today."

"I just have to get a drink."

"It was humiliating!"

"You want a glass of wine?"

"I have no marketable skills."

"Just give me a minute. We can have this conversation, but first I really need a drink."

I waited for him to get a glass of wine and a bowl of pretzels, then joined him in the kitchen.

"I can't even get a job as a receptionist. Can you believe it? I would be good at receiving people, don't you think? But they want you to have computer skills. So I looked in here." I opened up the Learning Annex catalog. "They have computer classes. There's one for Quark. And something else called PowerPoint. But it all sounds so pointless and without power, doesn't it?"

"Well...you know...." He crunched on some pretzels. "Why don't you take that licensing exam?"

"No!"

"Honey, you took all those classes. You wrote that thesis...."

"Forget it."

"You have the Ph.D. Make use of it."

"It's too late for me."

"No, it's not."

"And I couldn't stand failing that test again."

"So get a tutor. Come on. If you were seeing patients and helping them, you would feel good."

"I'd feel old. Like some old, wise person who's been through it all. And I haven't even really been through anything. I've led this sheltered existence as a wife and mother. How can I help people with real problems?"

I used to think I would make a good therapist. That was when I was in college and didn't have a clue about anything. I thought all you basically needed to do was be a good listener, have lots of empathy and help your patients learn how their unconscious impulses were directing their actions.

But no. You needed to pass a multiple-choice test.

"Maybe, unconsciously, I don't want to be a therapist, and that's why I kept failing that test." I did sometimes wonder how I could have the "arrogance" to think that I could help other people figure out how to live. Didn't I need more worldly experience? Maybe I would give someone bad advice, or laugh at the wrong moment or freeze up right when they were looking at me with all the trust in the world, needing me to say something brilliant.

"I just think," Bobby said, "you're lousy at taking tests."

"Maybe I should take a candle-making class. I could have an online business. Do it right from the living room."

"I don't see huge profits to be made," he said.

"Probably not." I flipped to the back of the catalog. "Oh, look," I said, as if I was just happening upon it. "Massage for Couples. Maybe we should take that." It was a test. If he said yes, I would do it.

He snorted. "Right."

I closed the catalog. "We could have another child."

"Really?" he said.

"Yes."

"But we have nowhere to put it."

"I was thinking about that. We could move into the smaller bedroom, and give our bedroom to the children. If it's another boy, they can have bunk beds. If it's a girl, we can build a wall down the middle, and there'd even be a window for each of them. It's perfect."

"I don't know."

"Don't you think it's kind of shallow of us to decide against having a child because of financial reasons?"

"Do you really want another child?" he asked. "Or do you just want to avoid getting a job?"

"Both," I said. "And neither."

That weekend, Sam and I took our excursion down to the Toys "R" Us. It was incredibly crowded, and I made sure to keep a close eye on him.

243

He kept wandering off to look at things, and it was kind of annoying, because he wanted to be in different sections than I did. He pulled me toward the video-game area; I wanted to check out the board games. He pulled me toward the Ninja Turtles; I wanted to see the Barbies. "Please?" I said. "Just for a minute?"

I should mention—I never played with Barbies when I was little. I did have a few of them at some point, but I had no impulse to actually do anything with them. Changing their clothes was annoying, with those plastic limbs that didn't bend. They were anything but cuddly.

But ever since I'd been going into toy stores with Sam, I'd found myself attracted to those pink boxes. I really liked seeing all the accessories in miniature. And I loved the idea of acquiring them. Not to play with. Just to display. But I didn't buy them. There was no point. We had no room to display Barbies. And it wasn't like the new ones could be considered collectables. And God knows I'd have to keep them for decades before they'd go up in value, if they ever would. And, hey. I was a grown woman! So I fought off the urge to possess CEO Barbie. And Teacher Barbie. And Police Barbie. Too bad there wasn't a Therapist Barbie. She could wear glasses and come with a teensy notepad. I could put her on the arm of the couch and discuss job options.

"Okay, Mom," Sam said. "Let's go."

"Look at Paleontologist Barbie. Isn't she cute?" She came with a miniature pink canteen.

He pulled on my hand. "Let's go to Candyland."

"Okay."

We navigated through the crammed aisles and made it to the one place in the store we could both enjoy. Candyland had bins of various chocolates and gummies that you could dig out with a shovel into little plastic bags and buy by the pound. I went for the various chocolate-covered nuts, while Sam liked the sour worms. But here was something new. Chocolate-covered potato chips. I'd never tried those. There were signs warning people not to touch the candy with their hands, but I reached in anyway and plucked one out with my fingers.

"Ma'am?" The girl behind the cash register was staring at me. "Please don't use your hands." She was frowning at me like I'd broken a law.

I gave Sam a casual smile so he could see this wasn't such a big deal.

But he looked at me with wide eyes. He was mortified. He needed me to be the grownup. And I was failing him.

Though I'd been planning to pop the chip in my mouth to sample it, I decided to take the high road and put it in my bag. We went to pay. It was awkward to wait while the same salesgirl weighed each of our bags of candy. I was definitely ready to leave that store.

We took the escalator down, passed by the stuffed animals, went through the revolving door and fell into step with the hordes of people on the street. In one hand, I clutched my bag of candy. In the other, I clutched my son's little hand. He held on tight. There were so many people. He was so small. "This way, Sam. The subway is right across the street." I said it with confidence. I wanted him to know we would not get lost. Mommy knew where she was going.

STEPHANIE LEHMANN is the author of *Thoughts While Having Sex* (Kensington, 2003), *Are You in the Mood?* (Kensington, 2004), *The Art of Undressing* (Penguin/NAL, 2005) and *You Could Do Better* (Penguin/NAL, 2006). Her plays have been produced off-off-Broadway, she is a contributor to *Salon* and she teaches classes on how to write chick-lit novels for Mediabistro.com. Originally from San Francisco, she's a graduate of the University of California at Berkeley and has a master's in English from New York University. Stephanie now lives with her husband and two children in Manhattan.

Johanna Edwards

To me, the best thing about chick-lit is that the books are so diverse. Chick-lit is all-inclusive, and everyone is offered a seat at the table. No matter what your nationality, race, income level or dress size, you're welcome here. There are books to appeal to every type of woman, and the honesty and thoughtfulness of many of these books overwhelms me.

Takeoffs and Landings

"Excuse me," the elderly man standing in line beside me asks, "but are you sure it's a good idea for someone in your condition to be flying?"

Someone in my condition? I mull his words over in my head. Wait, he doesn't mean...I feel my face go blood red. Oh my God, he thinks I'm pregnant! I stare down at my more-than-ample belly in horror. That awful mistake—that biggest big-girl fear of them all—has just happened to me.

This is not the way I intended to start my fabulous new life. This trip was supposed to make me over into Natalie Kirkland, International Travel Goddess. Instead I'm poised to become Natalie Kirkland, So Fat Everyone Thinks She's Pregnant.

"Um, I'm not," I fumble, trying to figure out a less embarrassing way to phrase this. I can't think of anything. "I'm not pregnant," I finally say, leaving off the end of the sentence, *I'm just fat.*

I silently curse myself for wearing such a baggy shirt. All my life I've been so careful when picking out plus-size clothes. I've always avoided the dresses and tops that billowed or poofed in the middle, for fear that they looked too much like maternity wear. It's never been an easy task, since most plus-size designers (is there even such a thing?) seem to think we bigger gals only want loose-fitting, muumuu-type outfits. But today I have messed up. I have broken my own golden rule and it has come back to bite me in the ass. Why, oh, why did I listen to the old adage, "Wear baggy clothing when traveling"?

"Oh, sorry," the old man chuckles, looking almost as humiliated as I feel. He sneaks another glance at my stomach. "I thought you were with child. I didn't want to have one of those 'Is there a doctor onboard the aircraft?' moments. Went through that once. It was awful."

I nod and then turn away from him, ending our conversation. I can't believe this has just happened. I wish the ground would open up and swallow me whole but, of course, it doesn't. Then just when I think the situation can't get any worse, it does.

"I'm afraid we don't have any windows or aisles available," the girl at the airport check-in counter says when I approach her kiosk a few minutes later. Her eyes scan the computer screen. "I'm going to have to put you in a middle seat."

I stare at her in disbelief. Middle seat? As in, I'm going to be squished between two people during the ten-hour flight from Atlanta to Rome? "There must be some mistake." I reach into my purse and pull out my e-ticket confirmation. "I pre-booked my seat assignment online three weeks ago. I'm supposed to be sitting in 22A."

She takes the e-ticket from my hand and gives it a cursory glance. Then she presses a few keys on the computer. "Hmm...well, it's not in the system." She consults with a colleague and then turns back to face me. "Seat 22A has already been assigned to another passenger so there's nothing I can do. You probably forgot to press enter after you filled the form in online. It happens."

"If I didn't press enter, then why did your airline e-mail me this seating confirmation?" I ask, trying to keep my tone pleasant.

"Well, it's not in the system," she repeats, unwilling to discuss the matter further. "The flight is really full this evening. I'm afraid a middle seat is your only option." She types a few more things into the computer and then hands me a boarding pass. "For future reference, no seat can be guaranteed until you check in for departure, so you might want to consider arriving at the airport earlier next time," she adds cheerily.

I am nearly three hours early, but I don't press the issue.

I stare down at my ticket. Seat 45J. Great. Not only have I gone from window to middle, I've been relegated to the back of the plane as well. Between that and the pregnancy mix-up, this is shaping up to be one of the least fun days of my life. All that's left is for the airline to lose my luggage.

I take a deep breath and try to remain calm as I make my way past the security checkpoints and over to the gate. I ought to be excited about going to Rome, but I'm overcome with dread. I should be planning my visit to the Colosseum or the Spanish Steps. I should be daydreaming about eating *bruschetta al pomodoro* and drinking red wine while I ogle Vespa-riding Italian men.

At the very least, I should be focusing on the business presentation I'll have to make in two days, which is the reason my company is sending me to Rome in the first place. But all I can think about is how I'll spend the next ten hours crammed between two complete strangers, without so much as an inch of breathing room. This wouldn't be an ideal scenario for anyone, but in my particular situation it could spell disaster. As much as I've been looking forward to my Roman holiday, I've been dreading this flight for a month now. Losing sleep over it, worrying myself sick. I am petrified, absolutely petrified, of flying.

At first glance this doesn't sound too weird. After all, lots of people are afraid of flying. The difference is, they fear the actual soaring-through-the-sky-at-thirty-thousand-feet part. For me, the phobia is much simpler.

I'm scared my size 22 body won't fit into the seat.

I'm scared the gate agent will refuse to let me board unless I purchase a second ticket. I'm scared the seatbelt won't buckle, scared my seat-mates will complain, quite loudly, that they don't want to be stuck sharing a row with "a fatso."

The last time I dared set foot on a plane was three years—and thirty pounds—ago. I got stuck on a job assignment in Tallahassee, which required taking a tiny commuter plane from Atlanta. I spent the entire trip with my ass wedged tightly into the less-than-generous seat, my body pressed against the window so as not to disturb the passenger to my right. By the time the flight was over the left armrest was practically melded to my thigh. But at least I got onboard without incident. The supremely overweight woman standing a few places in front of me in line was initially refused entry altogether.

"This airline has a policy in place for obese passengers," the gate agent had informed her in a less than discreet manner. "You'll have to buy two seats if you want to fly with us."

I'll never forget the look on that woman's face, the way her voice quivered and her hands shook as she pulled out her credit card and purchased an additional ticket. She burst into tears when the gate agent asked if she was in need of the seatbelt extender. As I watched the scene unfold my jaw dropped in horror. The seatbelt extender? I didn't know there was such a thing! Before that moment I'd never even considered the concept that the seatbelt on a plane might not fit or that an airline employee could force a big person to buy two tickets. But from that moment on I grew terrified of such things. I grew terrified of becoming that woman, of being the one told she was too fat to fly unless she bought a second seat.

I vowed not to get within ten feet of another airplane until I shed some serious weight. But the pounds came on instead of off—as they are wont to do—and before I knew it I was stuck in some sort of holding pattern, unwilling to leave Atlanta except by car. I turned down job opportunities and opted out of invitations to travel with friends. But then duty called—in the form of a coveted job assignment, the kind I couldn't say no to—and I found myself gearing up to take the plunge. After all, I couldn't pass up an all-expenses-paid trip to Rome, could I? This was the kind of thing I had dreamt about when I was back in business school. This was the kind of thing I had dreamt about when I was slaving away as a lowly intern at an advertising agency. And I had passed up so many things for so long. . . . I couldn't let a dumb thing like seat phobia run my life.

I kill time before departure by thumbing through magazines and downing bottled water. My heart is racing, my palms are sweating and my stomach is in my throat. *Maybe it won't be so bad*, I console myself. *Maybe the flight won't be as full as expected. Maybe you can move seats once you get onboard.*

A few minutes later my hopes are dashed when the gate agent announces that the flight is oversold. He begins offering vouchers for volunteers willing to give up their seats. I think it over. Maybe I should just throw in the towel, catch the next flight out tomorrow and hope for a better seat assignment then? No, I can't. I've got a business dinner to attend in Rome tomorrow night with an important advertising client. I'm twenty-eight years old; I have to be an adult about this. I agreed to come on this business trip and I can't avoid things forever. I suck in a deep breath, trying to keep my pseudo-pregnant belly at bay, and hope for the best.

I soon discover that there is one slight advantage to being seated in 45J. The people at the back of the plane get to board first. As soon as they've ushered in all the first- and business-class travelers, they call my row. I hoist my carryon bag over one shoulder and head onto the plane.

Please, oh, please don't let me be stuck next to some fat-phobic person who throws a fit when they see me, I think. *Please let me be seated by two nice, kind passengers who don't mind sharing their space with me for half a day.* I feel wracked with guilt. What right do I have to impose my big body on innocent strangers?

As I stroll down the aisle, moving past row after row of tiny, narrow seats, I try to rationalize the situation. There are worse people to be stuck next to on a plane, right? Airsick passengers. Crying babies. People who haven't seen the inside of a shower this millennium. As I make my way toward the tail section of the plane I console myself with the knowledge that perhaps I am not the ultimate nightmare seatmate. My mood starts to lift.

And then I see him, reclining comfortably in 45I. The man who called me pregnant. I know life is full of strange coincidences, but what are the odds of him being on *this* flight, and in *this* seat? He's lounging there with his eyes closed, teetering on the verge of sleep.

"Sorry to bother you," I say as I shove my bag into the overhead compartment, "but I need to squeeze by."

He opens his eyes. "Hello there!" he booms, recognition dawning on his face. "Fancy meeting you again."

"Yes, fancy that," I say, forcing a smile.

The man rises and moves into the aisle. "No sense getting too snug."

"You two know each other?" I hear someone ask. "Wow, talk about a small world." I turn around to see an incredibly handsome guy standing behind me.

"Hey, Mark!" the old man enthuses. "This is . . . what did you say your name was?"

I stare at him in confusion. What in the world is going on? "Natalie."

"Hi, Natalie, I'm Bill." He shakes my hand. "This here is Mark."

The cute guy waves.

"Nice to meet you both."

"I'm in K," Mark says as he squeezes past us and takes his seat by the window.

"Looks like we're going to be buddies for the next couple of hours," Bill says.

Well, at least they're both friendly. And, pregnant pause aside, Bill doesn't seem too concerned about sitting next to me. As soon as Mark is buckled in I make my move.

Please, God, let me fit! I pray silently as I slide into the row. *Please don't let my ass get stuck when I try to sit down!* I know it's probably not a good idea to use the word "ass" when you're talking to God, but desperate times call for desperate measures.

Biting hard on my lower lip I slowly sink down into the seat . . . and I fit. *I can't believe it! I actually fit!* And, best of all, there's a little bit of room to spare. I click the seatbelt into place. To the other passengers on the plane, nothing has happened. But, as cheesy as it sounds, I feel reborn, like a new person.

"Welcome aboard Flight 413 with nonstop service to Rome Fiumicino Airport. Total flying time today is just under ten hours...." I listen as the pilot rattles off the local time and temperature. By the time we taxi onto the runway Bill is asleep and softly snoring.

"Hey," Mark nudges me. He leans across and whispers in my ear. "I hope his snoring doesn't bother you." He gestures toward Bill. "'Cause I think he's going to be out for the whole flight. He took a couple of Xanax before we boarded." As if on cue, Bill's head tips to the side and lands on my shoulder.

Mark bites his lip to keep from laughing. "Uh, looks like he's found a new pillow. Want me to wake him up for you?"

I suppress a giggle. "Nah. As long as he doesn't start drooling, I don't mind." The truth is, I would much rather Bill sleep through the entire flight. He can't bring up the pregnancy mistake if he's off in dreamland.

"So you guys knew each other before?" Mark asks, his eyes scanning the in-flight movie card.

I shake my head. "No, we sort of met earlier, at the airport."

Mark laughs. "Yeah, same here. Bill came up and started talking to me when we were waiting to board." He lowers his voice. "Poor guy. He was so nervous about flying. He hasn't been on a plane in years. And now he's going to Italy to attend his granddaughter's funeral."

I gasp. "That's horrible!"

He nods solemnly. "I know. At first it was kind of weird when he came up and started chatting to me in the departures lounge. But then I felt awful when he told me about his granddaughter. I think he's just feeling really sad, and wanted someone to talk to."

We keep chatting as a flight attendant brings by the drink cart. I order a ginger ale and Mark gets a mineral water. I balance the drink in my hand, careful not to disturb Bill's snoring head. I don't want to move my tray table down, or I'll smack his shoulder.

"Here, you can put that on my tray," Mark offers, taking the drink from my hands.

"Thanks." I smile. I can't believe how nice this guy is! Not to mention cute.... "So does Bill's family live in Italy, then?" I ask. With his pasty pale skin and white hair, he doesn't look Italian.

"Bill's son does," Mark says. "He met and fell in love with an Italian girl and then, a few years after they got married, he moved over there. When their child got sick with leukemia Bill desperately wanted them to come back to America so they could be closer to family, but they wouldn't. It's pretty sad, actually."

Bill mumbles something in his sleep and then shifts positions, leaving my shoulder free.

"So have you traveled much in Europe?" Mark asks, as he takes a sip of his water.

"No," I admit. "I haven't been anywhere. Ever."

"Really?" He seems surprised.

"Yeah. This is the first time I've ever left the States." Just saying this makes me tingle. I can't believe I'm finally getting the chance to go abroad.

"Well, you've picked a good place to start. Rome is amazing." Mark's lips spread into a wide grin. He looks so cute when he smiles like that.

"I take it you've been there before."

"I go once every three months."

My eyes widen. "Wow, that's so cool."

"My girlfriend lives there, so I kinda have to."

Girlfriend. As in, *Back off, I'm taken.* Of course a guy like Mark has a girlfriend. I should have known. "Why do you have a girlfriend in Italy?" I ask before I can stop myself. "Talk about an extreme long-distance relationship."

He sighs. "It's complicated. Anna—that's her name—is a reporter for CNN. I'm a producer there, which is how we met. She got stationed in Italy a while back. It was supposed to be a temporary assignment, no longer than a couple of months. But then she fell in love with the culture and wound up accepting an extension. That was over a year ago. We've been doing the long-distance thing ever since."

I readjust positions in my seat. "That sounds hard."

Mark nods. "Tell me about it. I've been trying to move over there, but, well...." His voice trails off. "Gosh, I'm rambling." His cheeks flush pink. "I don't normally talk about myself so much. Especially not to total strangers. So, tell me, Natalie, what's your story? Why are you going to Rome? Business? Pleasure?"

"Business, unfortunately."

He claps his hands together. "Hey! There's nothing unfortunate about going to Rome on business. Just so long as you'll have at least one or two days off to sightsee."

I sip my ginger ale. "I will. I extended my ticket. I've got three days of business meetings, then I'm staying for five days of vacation. Trouble is, I'll be by myself, which might get kind of boring." I wonder, briefly, if he'll invite me to do something while I'm there. Perhaps grab dinner with him and Anna. But the moment passes, and he doesn't.

"No one else from your office went on the trip?"

"My boss is already in Rome. She got there two days ago. But it's not like we're friends or anything. Besides, she'll be flying back before me."

"That's too bad." Mark smiles and then turns his attention to the in-flight movie, signaling that our conversation is over.

I doze off somewhere over the Atlantic and wake up just in time for breakfast service. It turns out I've slept through dinner and two films. I wake up to find Mark snoozing peacefully beside me. Bill, of course, is still out cold.

I eat my breakfast—soggy eggs and overcooked bacon—while listening to my iPod. We're down to the last two-hour stretch when Mark finally wakes up.

"I can't believe how quickly this has gone by," he says. "Usually, the Atlanta-Rome haul is torturous, but today it's been pretty pleasant."

A few minutes later we gently nudge Bill awake. He stumbles out of his seat long enough for Mark and me to use the bathroom, then collapses into his chair again.

"I think he might have taken too many of those pills," Mark admits. "I'll help him out once we get to Rome—make sure he gets his suitcases okay and makes it into a taxi."

"That's nice of you."

Mark shrugs. "I feel bad for him."

We chat off and on for the next hour, and then Mark stands up and stretches his arms over his head. "I was thinking...do you want to sit by the window? We're going to be landing soon and I thought you might like to catch your first glimpse of Italy. It's pretty spectacular from the air."

"Oh, thanks, but I couldn't."

"No, honestly!" he says. "I don't mind."

"Really? Thanks!"

We switch seats, virtually hugging as we pass each other in the crowded row. Once we're all buckled in and secure Mark says, "I was thinking... if you're up for it, maybe we could grab dinner one night while you're in Rome? Anna's going to be working a lot so my schedule is pretty free."

I can't help but smile. "That sounds great."

"We'll plan on it, then." He looks sad.

"Everything all right?"

He swallows hard. "Sort of. The truth is, I'm kind of dreading landing. There's a big part of me that didn't want to come on this trip."

"Me too," I mumble.

"Really?" Mark seems surprised. "Why not? A business trip to Rome seems like such a great opportunity."

"It is," I admit. "I guess I was just scared." I almost mention my seat phobia but quickly stop myself.

"Same here."

"What are you afraid of?" I ask, returning my chair to its upright position.

"Things aren't going so well with me and Anna. I kind of think we... I think we might be breaking up." He bites his lower lip.

I give him a sympathetic smile.

"The plan was always for her to come home and, when she didn't, we started revising," Mark continues. "I was going to put in for a transfer or, if need be, leave CNN and look for a new job. But then Anna stopped me. She said she didn't want me to make a decision like that, not yet. After that, we decided to take a break from each other and see how we felt. I thought I knew what I wanted. But now... the closer I get to Italy, the more I feel like it's not right to be with her anymore. The more I feel like it's time to move on."

"I'm sorry," I say, placing a hand on his forearm.

"Don't be," Mark says. "Someone like Bill deserves your sympathy a lot more than I do." He pauses. "The only bad part is, I wish I'd realized this before I got on this plane. Now, if Anna and I break up, I'll be stuck in Rome for two weeks with nothing to do."

I smile. "There are worse places to be stuck."

"Yes," he says, returning my smile, "I suppose there are."

"So, I was wondering," Mark says as we stroll off the plane an hour later. "Are you still up for dinner?"

"Definitely."

"Great." He brightens. "When are you free?"

"Well, I've got business meetings for the next couple of nights, but sometime toward the end of the week would be nice." I smooth my baggy shirt down, careful to keep it from gaping.

"Here's my card," he says, reaching into his wallet and handing it to me. "I've got an international cell phone, so you can call me when you want to get in touch. But, tentatively, how does dinner on Thursday sound?"

"It sounds great." I tuck his card into my purse.

"You know something," Mark says as we head over to baggage claim, Bill in tow. "I can't tell you how glad I am that we got seated beside each other."

JOHANNA EDWARDS is an award-winning journalist and radio/ TV producer. Her first novel, *The Next Big Thing*, debuted on the national bestseller list where it remained for nearly three months. Johanna's second novel, *Your Big Break*, was also a bestseller. Johanna lives in Memphis, Tennessee, where she is currently at work on her next book.

Rachel Pine

*Who knew we'd still be in high school all these years later, with
the popular girls sitting on one side of the cafeteria as the smart
girls glare across from the other?*

*In truth, the term "chick-lit" is nothing more than a market-
ing label that the publishing industry realized could sell books.
Thousands and thousands of books, in fact, by writers who
might not have a "literary" style but were capable of cre-
ating stories that a huge, mass-market
audience would devour quickly before
purchasing another. If these
books didn't sell, they
wouldn't be published;
the equation is quite a
simple one.*

*Most of the labels that we assigned each other and were,
in turn, assigned as adolescents turned out to be meaningless.
Their only use was to divide us and give us license to dislike
others for no real reason.*

*In every John Hughes movie there's a moment when the brainy
girl takes off her glasses and we discover she's actually beautiful. The busty chick in the fuzzy pink sweater aces the math
quiz. Everyone has a blast at the prom.*

The Ring

Will we be seeing you at the week*end*?" she said as I was leaving, giving me an oh-so-Euro double-kiss. I was sure that her
accent came from somewhere within the kingdom of Queens,
but the inflection was pure Princess Diana. Excuse me, *Princess Diana.*

"I'll have to let you know," I said, inching toward the door, anxious to be on the other side of it.

I'd only met Melanie earlier in the evening, but trying to place her strange, semi-Continental speech pattern had proved to be a thoroughly distracting enterprise. Each time she spoke I'd had to concentrate carefully on finding an appropriate answer. Not to mention the effort it had taken not to laugh out loud.

This had actually been quite easy to do, given that after we'd been introduced when I first arrived she hadn't bothered to speak to me again for three hours. My date, Tim, had sprinted off to join some other attorneys from his firm in the kitchen, where they were boisterously one-upping each other, concocting flammable cocktails. I'd taken refuge in the foyer of the smallish apartment, while Melanie held court in the combination living/dining area. She was surrounded by a group made up of her former sorority sisters and the other secretaries from her office. They were hanging not just on her every word, but on her newly acquired engagement ring. I'd seen it for just a moment when I'd first come in. The diamond was exceptionally small.

Ordinarily, I wouldn't have paid too much attention to it. The whole ring thing in New York City had gotten way out of hand, what with Harry Winston, Tiffany and Jacob the Jeweler all pushing a "bigger is better" mandate that had been enthusiastically embraced by the single women who lived here. The "two months' salary" guideline now had some fine print: "including all bonuses, perks and any additional taxable income."

Melanie, obviously aware of the New York woman's innate ability to appraise a gemstone at ten paces, was doing everything she could to distract her circle from any mention of carats, clarity or the other "C's." She focused instead on the storied history behind it.

I could still hear her now as she raised her voice, all the better for the Tri-Delts and receptionists to hear. "It's been in my fiancé's family for years, you see, and I'm honoured to have the privilege of wearing it." (I could absolutely hear the *u* she'd added to the word—I'm not sure how. But it was definitely in there.)

When she'd finally deigned to speak to me, it was only because I'd corralled her as she returned from a trip to the hallway garbage chute. "Melanie, I haven't had a good look at your ring yet. I'd love to see it."

She held out her fingers to me, curled in a hand model's pose. "Oh sure, Charlotte, here you go." She slowly angled her hand left and right, in an attempt to make the ring sparkle.

I looked down at The Little Diamond That Could and tried to figure out what shape it was. It had no discernible cut, and the overly complicated filigree setting didn't do it any favors.

"It's very pretty," I said, although "dainty" and "charming" were battling it out on the tip of my tongue, eager to see which would cause her more distress.

"Oh, but isn't it?" she gushed. "It was Jonathan's mum's, and his grandmother's on his father's side before that, and it's been the traditional engagement ring given by every first-married Scott-Forbes son since the middle of the nineteenth century."

"I hope you've had it cleaned, then," I said, my tongue winning a small victory, albeit one that sailed right over her head. She gave me a puzzled look and returned to her little cabal, where the talk had turned to gowns, tiaras and the pros and cons of an all-inclusive honeymoon versus one à la carte.

"Well, I was definitely thinking ti*a*ra." She pronounced it with the "ah" sound. "Just because of Jonathan's *family* and all," she added, and heads nodded in agreement.

I was annoyed at having spent this much time here already, and growing more so every minute. Her majesty, my hostess, had obviously decided that I was too insignificant to introduce around, so I'd been speaking with the one woman at the party that I sort-of knew. She'd also been left to fend for herself, although she seemed less upset about it than I was. Jamie was a pediatrician with two kids and a penthouse on Central Park West, and she undoubtedly had little to add to their conversation. I also suspected Melanie might have been worried about a possible upstaging—Jamie was a highly sought-after asthma specialist with a recurring segment on the *Today* show. I mulled this over while Jamie went to retrieve her husband, Henry, who was out on the apartment's terrace where the "boys" had by that point congregated to drink cognac and smoke cigars.

My date, Timothy Reid, whom I'd been seeing for four months, and Jonathan Scott-Forbes, possessor of not only an heirloom engagement ring but a genuine English accent, worked at the same prestigious New

York City law firm where Henry was a partner.

"Apparently there's going to be some kind of toast," she said when she returned a few minutes later. "And Henry promised me that we'd leave right after that."

"Lucky girl. Did you see Tim outside?"

"Yeah, he said he'd be right in."

Right, I thought. *Right in. As in, whenever he remembers that he brought me.* The annoyance that I'd first felt that morning rose up again. It had begun when Tim called me while I was having a pedicure.

"Hey, Charles," he'd said, a name that he'd given me the night we'd met, and that I absolutely loved. My name is Charlotte, and that's all I'd ever let anyone call me until him. "It's a gorgeous day, don't you belong at work?" I'd asked. Tim's hours were staggering, but he was completely focused on making partner at his firm. At first I'd thought that I could never date someone who worked a 100-hour week, but as I got to know him I found his serious attitude and dedication to be complete turn-ons, just more evidence of the natural confidence that made him so appealing. And with my having to work and travel a great deal for my job as the head of marketing for a large investment bank, neither one of us was left yearning. We each understood the other's ambition and I was sure that we were right on track to become a real power couple, what with our careers in full bloom and our instinctive competitiveness.

"I'm going in for a couple of hours later on," he said. "But I needed to ask you something about tonight."

"Jonathan and Melanie's party?"

"Yeah. Jon just called me and said that Melanie wanted to make sure you weren't going to wear jeans."

"I hadn't planned on it. But really, the Evite said 'Smart slash Casual' and the party's in their apartment. Why the sudden jeans thing?"

"I don't know. Melanie likes everything a certain way, and since she doesn't know you she asked Jon to call me and ask."

"This is getting more and more obnoxious. She told everyone they needed to RSVP two weeks in advance so the caterer could know how much food to prepare, then it was a dress code on an e-mailed invitation, which is definitely a first, at least for me. Is this some kind of hugely important social event?" I was getting snotty, and I knew it, but that didn't stop me from continuing. "Because if it is, an engraved invitation would have been far more appropriate."

Surely it would have been enough to just invite Tim "and guest." But Melanie had insisted on inviting each person individually, all the better to insure the head count was correct, the guests properly attired and the various rules and regulations of the evening directly communicated to all who would be in attendance.

"She's not worried, she's just, kind of, she wants to make sure. She's got, I don't know, concerns."

"Concerns about what?"

"Well, she doesn't know you, and she didn't like my last girlfriend."

"I see. So she's already prepared to not like me. Does she know anything about me?"

"No, I only told her that I was bringing a woman named Charlotte who I'm really excited about. And then I gave her your hotmail account, not your work e-mail, so she wouldn't know anything else about you."

"I see," I giggled. "So I'm going to be the mystery woman from hotmail.com. Emphasis on *hot*."

"Maybe the emphasis was on mail," he said, and I was relieved when he started to laugh.

"Doubt it," I said looking down at my toes, eight of which now gleamed with shiny, red lacquer. "By the way, what does Melanie look like?"

"She's about five-two, light hair, a little plump for my taste."

"Plump?" I seized on the word as if it were a delicious chocolate truffle, the kind that I only allowed myself to eat twice a year.

"Just, you know, kind of round. Not fat, really, but not someone who would be in the swimsuit issue."

"Interesting," I said, very aware of my toned body, which I worked out daily with kickboxing, spinning or weight training, followed by a five-mile run.

"What?"

"Ve-ry in-ter-est-ing," I said, carefully getting up out of the pedicure chair, walking on my heels so as not to smudge and mentally reviewing my wardrobe for something a chubby girl could never, ever wear, but would certainly want to.

"Crap, Charles. Be nice. Not everyone has the same sexy, slender genes as you."

"I thought jeans were out," I said, innocently. "Besides, at 5:00 A.M., it's not genes. It's willpower."

"Why are you turning this into a contest?"

"Why is this woman so concerned with what I'm wearing?" I didn't let him answer. "Tim, my toes are finished and I need to hang up so they can do my fingers."

"I'll see you at seven then?" He sounded less enthusiastic than when he'd first called.

"Seven. I'll be there with jeans on," I said. "I mean, bells on."

"Charles, please."

"I'll be good. I promise." I hung up, angry with myself for having gone on auto-bitch so easily. It was just a party, this girl was obviously a control freak, she wasn't one of my friends—why did I care so much?

That thought ran through my head as I dressed, undressed and re-dressed over and over, trying on outfits that would have ordinarily been fine, but were instead piled up on my bedroom floor. Even though I knew it made no sense, I was hell-bent on selecting just the right clothing, something that showed that I was not to be taken lightly, ordered around or treated as someone who might not know how to dress properly. I looked at the clock on my night table. If I didn't make a decision soon, I'd be going in my underwear, which definitely wouldn't pass muster with Melanie's dress code.

Finally, I settled on a black pencil skirt, an ivory sweater with a slight shimmer knitted into it and a deep V-neck cut out of it, and my favorite boots. They were made of gorgeous black leather that fit right against the skin, ended just below the knee and had a five-inch stiletto heel. I looked at myself in the mirror, thankful for the extra two miles I'd run that morning. It was the kind of ensemble that allowed absolutely no room for error. The slightest bulge or pucker would ruin the whole effect.

An hour later, makeup and hair finished, I leafed through *Us Weekly* while waiting for Tim to arrive. When I saw that Jessica Alba had a pair of boots nearly identical to mine, I took it as a good omen. I was eager to see Tim, but was all too aware of the negative energy swirling around this party, energy I'd unfortunately helped to create. I would be glad when it was over. Tim and I would go back to his apartment, and forget about all of it. When the doorman buzzed, I gathered my coat and purse and headed for the elevator, practicing a sashaying walk.

Tim was standing in the lobby, and he flashed his fantastic smile when he saw me.

"Is this smart slash casual enough?" I asked coolly as he looked me up and down, his eyes going from my shiny auburn hair to my boots and back again. The minute I said it, I knew I shouldn't have.

"You look great, Charlotte," he said, flatly. *Charlotte. Please, call me Charles*, I pleaded wordlessly.

We got in a cab and rode the few blocks uptown to Jonathan and Melanie's apartment. I was glad for the ride because while the boots looked great, walking in them was really difficult.

"I'm sorry," I began, trying to take his hand. He pulled away.

"I don't know why you had to take everything so personally. No one was singling you out."

"Well, yeah, she was, actually. Do you think everyone got a 'no jeans reminder' phone call this morning?" I could have just agreed with him, I *did* have a bad habit of getting way more upset than the situation required, but I only plunged myself in deeper.

"I don't know. Can we just forget it and try to have a nice time tonight, Charlotte?"

"Sure, it's forgotten."

"Good," he said. "Thanks, right here is fine," he said to the driver. As we got out, he kissed me lightly on the lips and said, "Please don't worry about anything. You're gorgeous, we're going to have a nice time and later we'll hang out at my place."

We walked into the building and got into the elevator, one of those old ones where you had to pull the outside door closed yourself. There was no doorman, either, but I bit my tongue and didn't say a word. Maybe tonight would be fun, I thought as the elevator creaked up to the sixth floor.

Now, approximately five hours later, my five-inch heels felt like they were embedded in my feet, I was miserable and I was finally on my way out the door, trying to read Tim's expression. I'd begged him to take me home, and at first he'd suggested I go on my own. Eventually he'd relented and agreed to leave with me.

"But what about the weekend, Tim?" Melanie asked again as we passed through the door.

"I'll let you know, Melanie," he said, bending down and giving her a kiss on the cheek. "And congratulations. Jonathan's one lucky barrister."

"Thank you, Tim. It was great to meet you, Charlotte. I wish I could wear an outfit like yours, but I'd just look like a hippo," she laughed.

"My lovely Mrs. Hippo," Jonathan said, kissing her on the top of the head and taking her hand, interlacing his fingers with hers as she leaned into him. I had to stare straight ahead and concentrate hard to keep from rolling my eyes.

Tim and I waited for the elevator, neither saying a word. I took a step closer to him, but he only moved one step farther away. We got into the elevator and he quickly pulled the outer door shut.

"Well, Charlotte, I hope you're proud of yourself."

"What do you mean? I didn't do anything wrong. She's the one who didn't introduce me to anyone, who left me in the foyer with that pediatrician the whole time. Do you realize I've been talking about the immunization debate for the past five hours?"

"I've seen you at parties, and you know perfectly well how to introduce yourself. You can talk to anyone, and you know it. You were in a bad mood all night because you wanted to be."

He wasn't entirely wrong. "Well, do you think I wanted to talk about tiaras and package-deal honeymoons and that thousand-year-old microscopic diamond all night?" Now I used the "ah" sound in tiara.

"No, Charlotte, I don't," he said, quietly. We walked through the lobby and onto the street.

"Do you think I really wanted to sit around with her boring, useless friends and talk about nothing? Do you?" My voice was rising, trying to make him understand how incredibly rude Melanie had been.

"No, Charlotte," he continued, calmly. "I don't think you wanted to talk to her boring, useless friends all night. Although I'm curious. If you weren't introduced, and didn't meet anyone, how did you know they weren't worth your time?"

I was stumped, and the quiet, measured way he was speaking unnerved me. "I . . . I don't," I stammered. "It's just that she's a secretary and her friends are bound to be just like her and what would I have to talk with them about?"

"Do you realize what a nasty, horrible thing that is to say about someone? That you think you're better than they are because of your job, or where you live or anything like that?"

"She's the one who thinks she's better, telling everyone else what to wear and when to RSVP and making reminder calls so that I wouldn't wear jeans," I lamely tried to defend myself.

"So what? So she's concerned and she wants her engagement party to be a certain way and she's worried that because she doesn't have a lot of money, some people won't respect her. It's the people like *you* that she's worried about. That you'll dismiss her for exactly the reasons you did."

"Just because she's pretending to be some kind of aristocrat, with that weird fake accent? I mean, why wouldn't I dismiss her?"

"It's useless, Charlotte. Don't you see?"

"See what? See that she's a phony? See that I just wasted an entire evening of my life, of our lives, standing in a corner being ignored?"

"No, not that at all." He ran his hands through his hair, looking completely frustrated.

"Charlotte," he said, gently. "You're jealous."

"Jealous?" I spat back. "Of what? Of her beautiful home? Of her cool, hipster friends? Of that stunning engagement ring? Yeah, I wish I had all of those things, but I guess I'm just not good enough." I laughed, but it came out more like a cough.

"No, Charlotte, that's not it. You're jealous of the fact that even though you don't think Melanie is half as good as you are, or nearly as smart, and is a little pudgy, someone still loves her. Someone wants to marry her. That's what's got you so angry you can't even think straight."

"Right. I wish I were a fat, boring girl, marrying short, dull Jonathan."

"No, Charlotte, you don't wish that at all," he said, still in that even, level tone. "Girls like you don't understand that someone can be lovable even if they're not perfect, even if they don't have flat abs and perfect hair and a big career."

"Well, doesn't it make sense?" I asked. "Aren't those things all part of what makes someone attractive?"

"Yes, that's a *part* of it. But it's just a part. You don't think that someone like Melanie *deserves* to be loved, that she's *entitled* to it just like everyone else."

"Well, Dr. Phil, what will you talk about on next week's show?" I said in a desperate attempt to lighten things up.

"There is no next week's show, Charlotte. You just don't understand."

"Understand what?"

"How envious you are. How it's made you poisonous. Yes, Melanie's not as pretty as you are, and she's not as thin, and she's probably not as smart, but Jonathan loves her, and they're getting married." He put his face very close to mine, as if I were a small child being scolded. "Get over it. You've turned into an angry, bitter woman, and I don't even recognize you."

He was so right that it nearly knocked the wind out of me. I took a couple of limping steps toward a bench and sat down on it. Tim didn't follow me. I *was* jealous. Why didn't I have a ring? Why didn't anyone love me? And from the looks of Tim's back, striding away from me, I didn't even have a boyfriend. And what had Melanie ever done to me? Sure, she was a little pretentious and silly, but I didn't even really know her. She was the fiancée of someone who worked with the guy who was, at the present moment, dumping me.

And she was fat, and I was thin and she was getting married.

And she was dumb, and I was smart and she was getting married.

And she answered to someone like me, and I had eight people who answered to me, directly, and she was getting married.

And I wasn't.

And she had every right to pity me, but she was upstairs cuddling with her fiancé, and I was sitting on a bench, about to go home alone.

RACHEL PINE is the author of *The Twins of Tribeca* (Miramax Books, 2005). She is currently director of marketing and communications for Doubledown Media, LLC, the publisher of *Trader Monthly* and other magazines. She is also a contributor to the *Huffington Post*. She lives in New York City and Southampton.

Appendix

Reaching Across the Aisle

Jennifer Coburn recommends *The Outside World* by Tova Mirvis, a book about two Orthodox Jewish families whose members struggle to find their identity and place in the world, calling it, "A loving portrait of the warmth and imperfection of family, life and self."

Harley Jane Kozak recommends Alice Hoffman's *Turtle Moon*, calling it "one of those books that always takes me back to the time in my life when I first read it, the state of mind I was in and the man I was recovering from. I finished the book on a mountaintop in upstate New York, alone, in a sleeping bag, reading by battery-operated lamp, rediscovering the power of novels to heal, inspire and make all things right."

Ariella Papa recommends the short story "Bardon Bus" by Alice Munro, from the collection *The Moons of Jupiter*: "Like a lot of Munro's work, this story is about a real woman whose choices we don't always agree with, but through the words, we somehow get. Also it's got those stinging sad passages that just wow me. It rocks."

Cara Lockwood recommends *Girl Talk* by Julianna Baggott: "Her quirky humor and dead-on descriptions of family relationships make her a great read."

Kayla Perrin recommends *Waiting in Vain* by Jamaican-born Colin Channer. "This is Channer's first novel, one that received critical acclaim. He writes in lyrical poetic style that evokes all the senses. He is a natural-born storyteller, and in *Waiting in Vain*, he writes a breathtaking love story about two writers who meet by chance on the streets of Manhattan. It is as realistic as it is beautifully portrayed. Pick up this book! You won't be disappointed!"

Karen Siplin says, "*Liquor* by Poppy Z. Brite is a terrific novel about chefs and restaurants. The story follows Rickey and G-man, best friends and boyfriends, as they open a restaurant with a theme menu (every dish has alcohol in it) in their native New Orleans. Along the way Ms. Brite introduces the reader to several fascinating characters and we learn more about what it's like to work in the back of the house than we thought we ever wanted to."

Deanna Carlyle writes, "Anyone who enjoyed my story will probably also like Henry James' *The Europeans*, which is actually more about Americans than Europeans. A destitute French-German baroness arrives in nineteenth-century Boston to visit her American relatives. But in reality she's trying to land a rich husband in their circle. Delicious stuff! I love James' leisurely prose and his insights into cultural differences and human character. James shows time and again how the people we think of as weak or naïve may actually have a stronger moral fiber than the clever, power-mongering types they have to contend with."

Lauren Baratz-Logsted recommends *The Bitch Posse* by Martha O'Connor: "'You Have Now Entered a Chick-Lit-Free Zone,' one of the tart characters in this searing debut novel writes in her journal, and yet the novel itself is part of the chick story—the dark part. And we do all have our dark parts."

Heather Swain says, "I love anything by Kate Atkinson (*Case Histories, Not the End of the World, Emotionally Weird, Human Croquet, Behind the Scenes at the Museum*). She has that rare ability to form wonderfully weird aspects of life into compelling plots full of quirky characters so expertly drawn that they inhabit the reader's mind for years."

Caren Lissner recommends *At Home in the World*, the evocative memoir of dedicated writer Joyce Maynard, despite, as she says, "the unnecessary hype and criticism it got over the fact that Maynard details her relationship with J. D. Salinger in the work. The book is largely about a precocious and isolated female writer who struggles to find her place in the world."

Julie Kenner says, "Since my story has a ghostly element, I'm recommending *The Lovely Bones*, by Alice Sebold. A beautifully haunting story, my only caveat is to not read it as a new mommy. I read the book with tears streaming down my face, satisfied when I closed the pages that I'd had one heck of a good cry."

Karin Gillespie says, "One of the funniest books I have ever read is *The Accidental Tourist* by Anne Tyler, about a travel writer who hates to travel. Her humor is quiet and wise, my favorite kind."

Andrea Schicke Hirsch savored every unsettling moment of Sabina Murray's chillingly entertaining novel *A Carnivore's Inquiry*. The heroine, Katherine Shea, is Holly Golightly and Hannibal Lecter rolled into one charismatic young woman, who leaves a bloody trail in the wake of her madcap adventures: "Original, intelligent, a delicious read for a dark and stormy night."

Gena Showalter recommends *Where the Heart Is* by Billie Letts, a captivating, heartwarming book about an unlucky girl who finds herself pregnant, jobless and homeless, and secretly moves into Wal-Mart while trying to get her life on the right track.

Raelynn Hillhouse recommends *Reading Lolita in Tehran* by Azar Nafisi: "It's a fascinating glimpse behind the veil of a woman's life in the Islamic Republic of Iran, where women must cover themselves head to toe on the streets, then in the tenuous safety of their homes, they remove the chador and slap on makeup and jewelry in defiance of the fundamentalist regime. Even then they risk imprisonment if the morality squad raids their homes."

Stephanie Lehmann recommends *Household Words* by Joan Silber, which spans the '40s, '50s and '60s in New Jersey: "A woman's husband dies unexpectedly and she must raise her two daughters on her own, something she's not financially or emotionally equipped to do. I found this book moving and inspiring and funny in a wry, shrewd way."

Johanna Edwards says, "I strongly encourage you to pick up a copy of Jennifer Paddock's acclaimed debut *A Secret Word*. This novel-in-stories offers a glimpse into the lives of three high-school friends from Northwest Arkansas as they change and grow following graduation. Linked together by an unspeakable tragedy, the girls must find a way to move on and come into their own. The writing is beautiful and finely tuned and the storyline will both comfort you and break your heart."

Rachel Pine recommends Louise Erdrich's *Love Medicine*: "Erdrich's body of work is peopled by women who are wise, strong and often capable of magical cures for the body and soul. Men may be less than what they'd hoped, the government is unfair to the Chippewa Indians and nature deals hand after unfortunate hand of despair, yet Erdrich's marvelous, spiritual women survive. While almost any of her books would make an excellent choice, I recommend *Love Medicine* because it was her first novel, and just feels like the right place to start reading them all."

Jane Austen's *Pride and Prejudice* is one of the most beloved novels of our time, transcending the literary world to earn a spot on every woman's nightstand. Now, FLIRTING WITH PRIDE AND PREJUDICE takes a fresh and humorous look at Austen's classic tale of looking for Mr. Right, marrying rich and finding true love in the process.

Edited by JENNIFER CRUSIE, a *New York Times* bestselling author whose novels include *Fast Women, Faking It* and *Bet Me*. She is a frequent contributor to the BenBella Books Smart Pop series and editor of *Totally Charmed: Whitelighters, Demons and the Power of Three*.

~*visit*~
S M A R T P O P B O O K S . C O M

~Enter to win great prizes~

~Download free previews~

~Get the latest Smart Pop news~

~Receive offers for *exclusive*
Smart Pop specials~

SMART POP CULTURE
s m a r t p o p b o o k s . c o m